The RISING TIDE

Also by Patrick Easter

The Watermen
The River of Fire

Patrick Easter
The
RISING
TIDE

Quercus

First published in Great Britain in 2013 by

Quercus Editions Ltd
55 Baker Street
7th Floor, South Block
London W1U 8EW

A CIP catalogue record for this book is available
from the British Library

HB ISBN 978 1 78087 760 0
TPB ISBN 978 1 78087 761 7
EBOOK ISBN 978 1 78087 762 4

10 9 8 7 6 5 4 3 2 1

Printed and bound in Great Britain by Clays Ltd, St Ives plc

Typeset by Ellipsis Digital Ltd, Glasgow

In memory of my father, M.A.W.H.

CHAPTER 1

September 1799, the River Thames off Deptford Creek

Tom Pascoe sat in the stern sheets of the police galley and stared at the thick blanket of fog enveloping the River Thames, the usual noise and bustle of the port reduced to a dull rumble. He didn't see the shape in the water. It was doubtful he would have seen it even if the fog had not blanketed everything in its grey embrace, so slightly did the curved form protrude above the surface.

The force of the collision threw him forward.

'Floater on the larboard bow, sir,' said John Kemp, leaning over the gunwale from his position at mid-thwart and hauling a man's head clear of the water.

'Is he alive?' Tom pressed his fingers to his temple and tried to concentrate. It made no difference. His head was throbbing from the effects of a night spent drinking. He closed his eyes for a second, then tried to focus on the bedraggled shape slumped half in and half out of the galley. The hammering inside his head continued unabated.

'No, he's gone, sir,' said Kemp, examining the face with less than total interest. 'Ain't been dead long, though. I reckon less than an hour. Looks to have drowned. No, wait . . .'

Kemp pulled the body further into the galley. 'Belay that, sir. The cully's been shot.'

John Harriot, resident magistrate at the police office at 259, Wapping New Stairs, regarded the slouched figure in a chair on the opposite side of the desk, with a concerned frown. Tom Pascoe did not look well; his face was drawn and unshaven, his eyes bloodshot, his clothing dishevelled. It was not, Harriot had to admit, a sudden change in the man he had once regarded as his finest officer.

He sighed. It was easy to look back. With the benefit of hindsight, he could see the moment when Tom's destructive slide had begun. The drinking had begun soon after Peggy's death, the warning signs there for all to see. In the months since then, the magistrate had, more than once, been forced to consider his subordinate's dismissal from the marine police. What stopped him was a belief in Tom's ultimate ability to overcome his malaise.

'You were about to tell me about the body you found this morning in Greenwich Reach,' said the magistrate, getting to his feet and limping over to the sideboard, on which stood a silver coffee pot. 'I believe you said he'd been shot.'

'Yes.' Tom rubbed his eyes with the heels of his hands. 'Hadn't been in the water long. Probably less than an hour. Weren't your usual floater, though. Dress was too good for that. Looked to have been a gentleman.'

'Any idea who he was?' Harriot waved the coffee pot in Tom's direction and raised an enquiring eyebrow.

'Thank you, sir. I think I will.' Tom forced a weak smile and, with an effort, seemed to gather his thoughts. 'No. He had no papers on him and his pocket book had either been lost or taken.'

'A bit out of the way for a gentleman,' said Harriot. 'What d'you suppose he was doing down there?'

'I don't think he was killed there,' said Tom. 'There was a strong ebb tide which would have brought the body down from somewhere like Limehouse. We found a couple of folk who said they'd heard what sounded like pistol shots. But neither of them was sure.'

Harriot grunted. 'Where's the body now?'

'Deptford. The Navy's looking after it until we can get the inquest sorted. In the meantime I'll get some posters printed. Might help identify the man.'

'Good,' said Harriot. 'By the by, talking of the Navy, I had a lieutenant in here yesterday asking me to back an impress warrant. Seems they want to send out the press gangs along the waterfront. I think we can expect trouble over the next few weeks.'

'Aye,' said Tom. 'I've seen them. The fights have already started.'

'Where are they keeping the pressed men?'

'The Black Boy and Trumpet down by St Catherine's Stairs,' said Tom. 'Leastways, that's what I think, judging by all the bunting they've strung up over the door.'

'Keep an eye on things, will you,' said Harriot. 'And let me know how you get on with the body down in Deptford.'

'Very well, sir.' Tom gripped the side of his chair and climbed unsteadily to his feet, a line of perspiration visible across his forehead.

Harriot watched him head for the door, his sense of unease about his subordinate's condition deepening. There seemed to be nothing that the fellow would or could do to put himself onto the road to recovery. Perhaps nothing short of the capture of the man responsible for his condition would achieve that.

But there wasn't much chance of that. André Dubois was safely back in his native France and unlikely to want to return.

The fog of early morning had cleared by the time Tom left Harriot's office and descended the river stairs to the waiting patrol galley. He nodded at the crew and climbed into the stern sheets. For a moment or two, he sat looking about him, shielding his eyes against the reflected glare of the sun. It seemed as though the entire width of the tideway had disappeared under the press of brigs, snows, barges, skiffs and lug boats, the tall masts of the ships adorned with patches of white canvas brailed up like so much bunting. He suddenly wished himself back on the quarter-deck of his own command, surrounded by a vast expanse of blue water, the wind tugging at his coat tails, the salt-laden spume in his face.

'Cast off fore and aft. Let fall. Give way together.' Tom's orders came in rapid succession as the galley slipped its moorings and creamed away from the pontoon, the sweeps dipping and pulling in long, powerful strokes, the backs of the crew bending and straightening in perfect unison. Soon they were amongst the fussing tangle of lighters and wherries jostling for position at the legal quays in front of the Custom House.

'Where's we heading, sir? Somewhere special?' asked Sam Hart, seated at stroke oar.

'Limehouse.' Tom smiled for the first time in several days as he caught sight of the surprised expression on his friend's face. 'It's time to find out more about this morning's floater.'

CHAPTER 2

Sam Hart chose his moment with care. It didn't do to upset Tom these days. He glanced at the passing shoreline and then back at Tom seated in the stern sheets, a person he'd long regarded as his most particular friend. They had had their ups and downs, of course, but that was only to be expected, given the work they were required to perform and the circumstances under which it had often to be carried out. But this was different. Tom's behaviour had nothing to do with the stresses of their professional lives, or even those of personal differences.

'Begging your pardon, sir,' said Sam. 'But ain't we going the wrong way for Limehouse?'

He watched as Tom turned his head from side to side, as though waking from sleep. Then, without a word, he drew down on the larboard guy and brought the galley round to face the way they'd come. No one spoke for the rest of the journey. Sam kept his eyes focused on the tip of his oar, wondering if he had done right in publicly drawing attention to his friend's mistake. It wasn't the first time in recent months that Tom's judgement had failed him. So far, the consequences had not been serious and Sam had been able to cover for him, but for how much longer? He felt the galley swing towards the stairs at Ratcliff Cross.

'Way enough,' said Tom.

Sam glanced over his shoulder and waited for the soft grinding noise of the boat's keel touching the bottom. A moment later, they jolted to a halt, and Tom clambered over the gunwale into shallow water. He turned to look at Sam.

'Get yourself down to Limehouse Reach,' he said. 'I want every ship between St Anne's and Deptford Creek checked to see if anyone saw or heard anything that sounded like gunfire.'

'You want us to meet you back here, sir?' said Sam.

'No, I'm going to see an informant. I don't know how long I'll be.' Tom paused as though considering something. 'See me at the Devil's Tavern about six. I should be done by then.'

Sam opened his mouth to object – the tavern would only bring further temptation – but thought better of it. He'd deal with the consequences, later. Meanwhile, he had work to do.

Tom's anger flared as he noted the concerned frown on Sam's face. He thought of telling him to keep his opinions to himself, but changed his mind. He waded through the shallows of the gently rising bank, his boots sinking into the soft clay of the river bed. The headache that had been with him all day, the result of the previous night's drinking, was beginning to subside. He climbed to the top of the Ratcliff Stairs, stopped and looked back towards the Thames. Sam had taken his place in the stern of the galley and was already heading out amongst the maze of scuttling craft. He turned away and walked east along a highway thronged with the usual assortment of coopers, sail-makers, carpenters and sailors, all of them seemingly gripped by the need to shout at the tops of their voices.

He thought about the man he was going to see. He'd known

Jack Morrison for years. They'd been shipmates for a while and Tom recalled the other man's uncanny ability to gather information on any number of subjects. He was the one man who could nearly always be relied upon to know the ins and outs of every incident on board ship and while invariably discreet, would usually be prepared to indicate a favourable line of inquiry if he were asked. They'd lost touch when Morrison had retired from the Navy.

They'd met again quite by chance and Tom had, in the months that followed, often made use of his talent. Now he was hoping that Jack would again be able to help. He turned in through the door of the Red Lion on Narrow Street and looked round the almost deserted taproom. It was Jack's usual watering hole, but there was no sign of him. He nodded at the landlord.

'Seen Jack, have you?'

'Not for a day or so.'

Tom walked out, unsure of where to look next. He'd not considered the possibility that Jack would not be there with a pot of beer in his fist. It was the only place they ever met. Ahead of him, the street was blocked by a sizeable crowd, its attention focused on something in its midst. He approached and looked over the shoulders of those at the back. He could see two men. One of them was holding a chain attached to the neck of a scrawny-looking black bear. The creature was performing a series of forward rolls in time to the beat of a drum held by the second man. Tom pushed his way through the crowd and caught the eye of the man with the drum. He beckoned him over.

'Awight, Mr Pascoe? Ain't seen you for a while.'

'Morning, George. I'm looking for old Jack Morrison. Seen him around, have you?'

George pulled a face and shrugged his shoulders. 'He ain't in no trouble is he, Mr Pascoe? Wouldn't want that to happen.'

'No, just a chat, George, that's all.' Tom considered telling him more but decided it was none of his business.

'I ain't seen him for a while, Mr Pascoe, and that's the honest truth.'

Tom was conscious of the watching faces from the crowd. He drew the man to one side and spoke quietly. 'I need to find him, George.'

The man hesitated and looked back at the crowd.

'First turning on the left, your honour,' he said, a hand covering one side of his mouth. 'The house what's got caged birds in the window. Only don't tell him it were me that told yer.'

'I won't. Thankee, George.'

Tom continued along Narrow Street, the sun obscured by a dismal blanket of choking smoke rising from the dozen or so glue factories that stood on either side of the street. He put a handkerchief to his face. The stench was worse than he remembered. Passing a chandler's shop, its yard a jumble of coiled ropes, lengths of canvas, spars, rusting anchors, lengths of chains, and much else besides, he turned sharp left into an alley that led north, away from the Thames.

Here, a terrace of houses occupied one side of the street, their front doors facing a high wall that ran along the opposite kerb. There was an air of faded gentility about the place, a kind of quiet determination to remain aloof from the decay of the surrounding area; a mood that fitted well with what he knew of the man he'd come to see.

Tom stayed close to the wall as he walked past the line of houses, inspecting each in its turn. A minute later, he stopped in front of one of them. On a window sill, immediately to the left of the front door, stood a wire cage containing a pair of small birds, chirruping noisily.

He knocked at the front door. It was answered by a stout woman in her mid-fifties, her grey hair swept back off her face, accentuating her reddened cheeks and the folds of fat below her chin. She ran an appraising eye over him, her hands on her hips.

'Yes?' she said, her manner brusque.

'Is Jack in?'

'Who is it wants to know?'

'My name's Tom Pascoe. If Jack is—'

'Who is it, Ma?' a man's voice roared out from somewhere at the back of the house.

'A gentleman what calls himself Mr Pascoe, as wants to see you,' she bawled back, her stout frame still barring the way.

Jack Morrison was a solid, broad-shouldered man, over six feet in height, his face and hands pitted with innumerable scars, his hair a rough, untidy thatch of grey sitting atop his massive skull.

'Why if it ain't Captain Pascoe.' Jack's voice was loud at the best of times. 'Come in. Come in. Sit yourself down.' He pointed to the only chair in the room while he picked up an old wooden box, dusted it down and sat opposite his guest. 'It don't answer to stand on no ceremony with old Jack. How did you know where to find me, anygate?'

'Oh, just asked around,' said Tom. He turned to watch Jack's wife leave the room. 'You know how it is.'

The room was small. No more than about eight feet square, a flight of stairs occupying one corner. Below these stood an iron cage in which a ferret was slinking up and down, stopping every now and again to fix its small, pink eyes on the assembled company. On shelves around the walls were a number of stuffed birds, rabbits, a polecat and a large carp, each one in its own display cabinet. Next to one of these, on a small table, were the tools of what Tom assumed was Jack Morrison's trade of taxidermy – a pair of leather breeches, a quantity of knives and a bottle containing some sort of liquid. Against the back wall was the door through which Jack had come.

'Still busy, if I'm not mistook, Jack,' said Tom, nodding at the display cabinets.

'Right enough, Master Tom,' said the older man. 'But it ain't birds no more. Nor even rabbits or fish, neither. Ain't no money in that. It's mostly ratting these days. Folk pays me to catch 'em and then I sells the brutes to the sporting gentlemen.'

'Dangerous work, I'll be bound.'

'Aye, that's the truth of it,' said Jack, fingering one of the many scars about his face and neck. 'Them creatures can bite awful hard. But, the Lord help me, it don't happen too often, and I've still got all me fingers.'

'Rather you than me.' Tom smiled.

'So what brings you to see old Jack, Captain? If you don't mind me asking, like.'

'We found a floater in the tideway,' said Tom. 'Early this morning, it was. Bottom end of Limehouse Reach. He'd been shot.

I don't think he was from these parts but I need to find out who he is and why he died. Can you help me?'

'Why, bless you, sir,' said Jack, a sly smile crossing his lips. 'Why should old Jack know anything about a body in the river?'

'It's important, Jack,' said Tom, leaning forward and resting his forearms on his knees. 'The victim was a gentleman, judging from the way he was dressed.'

'And you don't know nothing about him?' The older man stroked the underside of his chin and stared at the ceiling. After a moment or two, he got to his feet, went over to the cage under the stairs and inserted his finger through the bars. The ferret, who had noticed the approach of his master, sniffed at the finger, discovered it was not food and moved away.

'See this little critter, Master Pascoe?' he said, without looking round. 'One of the finest ratters I ever did see. I puts him down a bolt hole and he runs, maybe a hundred, maybe two hundred yards, looking for them rats. But he always comes back to me when I call. You know what I'm saying, your honour? This 'ere ferret does his job, and then he comes home. He won't go to none other. It's the same with me, sir. I live and I let live and then I comes home. What other folks do ain't none of my business.'

'You and I know each other very well, Jack,' said Tom. 'You know I always play fair. All I'm trying to do at this moment is find out who this man was.'

There was a long pause while Jack seemed to weigh things up in his mind.

'There is something what I heard . . .' he said.

*

11

In the Parish of St George in the East, a mile or so north of the Thames, a phaeton drew up outside the Fox and Hounds, in Rosemary Lane. A tall, thin man got out and went into the premises. After some hesitation, he made his way along a row of booths, looking into each before stopping outside one and pushing open the door. Sir William Bolt was not in the best of moods. He looked down at the man sitting alone at a table, his head bent over a copy of *The Times*.

'They've found it, my lord,' he said.

'What!' Lord Camperdown looked up from his paper, half rising from his seat, a look of agitation on his face. 'How could they?'

Bolt shrugged and said nothing. He slid onto the bench opposite.

'But it's not possible. You told me it would sink.'

'It was found within the hour. Another hour and it would have disappeared, and no one would have seen it for weeks, perhaps never.'

'Who found it?' said Camperdown.

'A police boat.'

Camperdown wiped the palms of his hands on his breeches and stared at the table. 'What happens now?'

'I've spoken to some people. They tell me a man named Pascoe found the body.'

'Who's he?'

'A constable. The best there is. Or at least he used to be. I hear he's seldom sober these days. You've got to hope he stays that way. If he gets his claws into you, he could be a problem.'

'But you say he's a drunk.'

'Best you don't rely on that.' Bolt glanced at the steady stream of people moving back and forth across the entrance to the booth, the hum of their conversation rising and falling. 'There's more.'

'What?'

'I can't find his pocket book. It had a visiting card inside. I took it from the body but I must have dropped it.'

'Christ, you bloody fool.' Camperdown looked across at his companion, his mouth tightly drawn, his eyes narrowing. 'If this man Pascoe finds out what happened, he'll come looking for us and I've no intention of going down for this.'

'Have a care how you speak to me, sir.' Bolt rose to his feet, pointing an accusing finger. For a second or two, neither spoke.

'You need to stop him,' said Bolt.

'How, pray, am I supposed to do that?'

'Put him on a ship, why don't you?' said Bolt, getting to his feet and moving towards the door. 'That should save us a deal of trouble.'

CHAPTER 3

The sun was dropping towards the rooftops west of Shadwell, before Tom arrived at the Devil's Tavern. He knew he was taking a chance coming here. There were any number of eating houses within walking distance, where he'd be safe from the temptations of drink. He checked his pocket watch. Just after six. Too late to change the arrangements now. Besides, he was confident he could deal with his demons.

He opened the door and walked in, a gust of warm, fetid air filling his nostrils. He let the door close behind him and peered through the drifting tobacco smoke, hanging cloud-like below the yellow-streaked ceiling. Sam was standing by a window watching him, a look of mild concern on his face. Tom made his way over.

'Is this wise, sir?' Sam hesitated, gesturing towards a pot of ale on the next table. 'Would you not . . .'

'I'll be right, thankee, Sam.' Tom removed a handkerchief from his pocket and wiped the sweat from around his neck. He could feel the dryness in his mouth and a dull ache towards the back of his head. Saying no to a drink was going to be harder than he'd thought. 'How did you get on today?'

'We boarded every ship in Limehouse Reach, like you asked,' said Sam. 'Weren't that many, as it happens. Maybe twenty of 'em. Anygate, to cut a long story sideways, we got nowhere. No one saw nothing. We did find one or two what reckoned they might have heard something that could have been pistol shots but even they was unsure. What about you, sir? Did you have any luck with your snout?'

'Old Jack Morrison?' Tom smiled. 'He didn't say much. I thought he was going to turf me out with nothing to show for my morning's work.'

'But he did tell you something?'

'Yes, he did in the end,' said Tom. 'He told me that someone had found a pocket book on the Isle of Dogs, close to the river. It seems probable it belonged either to the dead man or to the person responsible for his death. Inside was a letter apparently addressed to the owner at the House of Commons, and a visiting card belonging to a Member of Parliament. Jack didn't have the pocket book with him and couldn't tell me the name on the letter, only that it was someone at Westminster.'

'What about the visiting card? Did he remember the name of it?'

'Yes, but that doesn't tell us who the dead man is.'

'So, what now, sir?'

'The serjeant-at-arms at the House of Commons, Sam. If the man in charge of good order and discipline in the place can't tell me anything, I don't know who can.'

It was mid-morning of the following day when Tom found himself walking along the path that ran up from the Thames, parallel to the Privy Gardens of the old Palace of Westminster, to Whitehall. At the top, he turned left, towards Parliament Street and the residence of the serjeant-at-arms.

The house at number forty-three lay close to the junction of Bridge Street. A narrow three-storey brick building, there was little to distinguish it from its neighbours apart from the pair of Doric columns below a moulded pediment that stood on either side of its black-painted front door. Tom knocked and, a moment later, was shown into a ground-floor room by a uniformed servant.

Left alone, he looked about him. The room was a large one, its twin casement windows, through which the daylight now streamed, looking out onto the street. Against the opposite wall was an ornate marble mantelpiece, above which hung a large oil painting of a man mounted on a horse. In front of this, and on either side of the mantel, were positioned a pair of high-backed, red-leather armchairs. Tom wandered over and gazed up at the oil. A sudden draught of cool air behind him made him turn. A man was entering the room.

'Good day to you, sir.' William Watson Esquire, serjeant-at-arms for the House of Commons, was slightly built and of medium height, his long, thin face and hooked nose giving him the appearance of being permanently ill at ease. He was dressed in a black coat and breeches, with a white silk stock at his neck, his attire merely adding to the impression of haughty disdain. 'It's a Seymour. Lucky to get it.'

'I'm sorry . . .' said Tom, nonplussed.

'The picture you were admiring, sir,' said Watson. 'It's by James Seymour.'

'Ah!'

'Now, sir, I believe you wished to see me? My servant tells me you are with the marine police institution at Wapping. Do sit down.' Watson eased himself into one of the armchairs and pointed to the one opposite.

'Indeed, sir.' Tom ran a hand over his unshaven chin, aware of his shabby appearance. 'I'm investigating the death of a man whose body was found yesterday morning, floating in the Thames near Deptford. He'd been shot.'

'Do I know him, sir?'

'There is a possibility that the gentleman had some connection with the House of Commons. A letter found near the scene of the murder was addressed to someone at the House of Commons. I regret we have no name,' said Tom. He thought of mentioning the visiting card that had also been in the notebook but decided against it. It would serve no purpose. Its owner would have given his card to any number of people. 'And I regret I don't know in what capacity.'

'And you are asking . . . what?' said Watson, spreading his arms.

'Whether you are you aware of any gentleman from this place who is missing?' said Tom.

'My dear sir,' said Watson, looking askance at his visitor. 'In addition to Members of the House of Commons and the House of Lords, there are any number of gentlemen who are employed in other capacities, such as my own. It is not unusual for Members of either House to be missing for weeks at a time while they return to their homes or their constituencies. Indeed, we have Members who seldom make *any* appearance at all in the House. Do we know what he looked like?'

'I have a description of him,' said Tom, handing over a sheet of paper.

Watson leaned forward in his chair and glanced at the paper. 'Very well, I shall make some inquiries and see what I can find out. I promise nothing, of course. I can scarce believe that any gentlemen from this house would venture to so godforsaken a place as you describe, but there it is. I will let you know the result of my inquiries as soon as I am able.'

A day or so later, a man slipped out of the door of a derelict hovel in Great Dover Street, in the Parish of Southwark, and headed across the River Thames. In his late twenties, he walked with an easy, loping stride that contrasted to the shuffling steps of the ragged multitude around him, suggesting a life far different to that of the average person he passed along the way. Yet a stranger seeing him for the first time might have detected an air of nervousness about him, the quick fearful movements of his eyes as he hurried over the slight rise in the surface of the bridge.

Reaching the north bank of the river, the man turned into Upper Thames Street, and dropped down the gentle slope thronged with a shifting mass of men, horses and carts, making its way into, or out of, the legal quays. He kept to the side of the road furthest from the river, his head down, his hands in his pockets as though anxious to avoid drawing attention to himself. Several times he flattened himself against the wall of a building as a laden cart scraped by.

Ebeneezer Samson had little knowledge of London or the ways of its inhabitants. During the short period that he had lived within its vast borders, he'd had scant opportunity to explore its intricate web of streets. Only in one small part of the metropolis

18

had he begun to feel at ease with himself and his surroundings. Only there did he feel moderately safe.

He passed the Tower of London and skirted round the small green that lay on the opposite side of the road. Once on the far side, he continued to his destination. Rosemary Lane lay to the east of the Tower and was a place where strangers might walk without arousing the least curiosity in their fellow humans. Yet it was not a place that it would be wise to take for granted. At times savage and pitiless, it could also offer sympathy and friendship. Thieves, prostitutes, pimps, sailors, watermen, artisans, bearded Jews in long black coats and vendors of all manner of goods, heaved, pushed and shuffled along its broad back. Here one might, on a Sunday morning, buy anything from sea shells to lumps of coal, from old clothes to sailcloth, from cooked foods to medicines.

It was a place Ebenezer had been to several times before, in the days since his escape. He knew it for its market stalls, its noise and sense of bustle where no one took notice of him, a beggar of alms. He sank to the ground, his back propped against the wall of a house and held out a hand, palm uppermost. With luck he'd garner a few pennies, enough to buy a slice of bread, some cheese and perhaps a pot of ale. He'd not eaten these two days past.

He must have dozed off. Something struck his outstretched leg and an angry voice swore. Ebenezer's eyes jerked open, and he shrank back against the wall, suddenly fearful. He peered up from under the brim of his hat. A man of about his own age was standing over him, his long, yellow hair hanging loose about a weather-beaten face. The faint outline of a vertical scar ran down from a point close to his right eye, almost to the corner of his mouth.

'What's your game, cully?' The man's speech was slurred. He was holding a bottle close to the side of his face, his thumb tracing the outline of the scar. 'Trying to trip me up, were you?'

Ebenezer's eyes widened. There was nothing to be gained by embroiling himself in an argument, quite apart from the fact that the fellow looked as though he could handle himself, drunk though he might be.

He glanced at the man's coat. It was blue with white lapels and a double row of brass buttons down the front. Though worn and grubby, there was no mistaking the uniform of an officer in the King's Navy. He'd seen the uniform before, on other men. It was another good reason for avoiding an argument. He'd had a bellyful of men in positions of authority. He started to get up. He'd find somewhere else to beg. A hand fell on his shoulder and held him in a powerful grip.

'Don't you be fretting on my account,' mumbled the man. Ebenezer watched in surprise as he slid down onto the roadway next to him. 'The name's Captain . . . No, belay that. Keep forgetting. I ain't a captain no more.'

He wagged a finger in the air as Ebenezer struggled to understand what was being said. 'It's Mister now. What was I saying? Never mind. Where's you from? Not from around here, I'll be bound.'

'No, not from here.' Ebenezer looked down at his hands, unwilling to meet the man's gaze. He was beginning to wish he'd never crossed the Thames. He felt suddenly exposed.

'Then where's you from?' The man eyed the bottle he still held in one hand, brought the neck close to his right eye and peered inside.

Ebenezer's mind raced. He'd never met anyone who'd heard of where he came from, still less anyone who'd been remotely interested in knowing.

'I—'

'There you are, your honour.'

Ebenezer jumped. A short, slim built man was standing in front of them. He felt the newcomer's eyes sweep over him before settling on the man next to him. 'Been looking for you the best part of the morning, sir. We're due afloat in an hour.'

'Never mind that, Sam. Stay and 'ave a drink. D'you know my friend here?' The man waved his bottle in Ebenezer's direction. 'Don't know his name m'self.'

'Come, Mr Pascoe, sir, we must go.' The newcomer bent forward and helped his friend to his feet. 'Got to get you cleaned up. It would never do for his honour Mr Harriot to see you like this.'

Ebenezer watched the two men disappear into the crowds. He breathed a sigh of relief. Now he could concentrate on his begging.

CHAPTER 4

It started to rain. Not the soft, warm rain of the Caribbean he was used to, but cold sheets of water that came out of a featureless grey sky. Ebenezer ducked his head and walked on, empty-handed after a long day of fruitless begging. The pangs of hunger were sharper now, as he recrossed the Thames and made his way down Borough High Street in the gathering dusk.

He'd often asked himself if running away from his master had been worth it. At least he'd been fed. Not much, it was true, but enough to keep him alive. All that changed on the day he left the house. From that moment he had become a fugitive in a land he'd not asked to come to, condemned to a state of perpetual hunger – and the constant fear of recapture. He dreaded that more than anything.

Looking back, he'd come willingly enough. He'd heard the men talking about the land where the *bakra* came from, and he'd often wondered what it must be like to live there. The men had said there was no such thing as slavery in England, although how they knew that, he couldn't say. Then, one day, the master had sent for him, given him a piece of paper on which to make his mark and told him he was to go to that far-off land he'd heard so much about.

The sudden squeal of coach wheels interrupted his thoughts.

It was too late for any of the stage coaches to be leaving London. He looked back. A chaise, similar to the one his master owned, was approaching. Ebenezer slid into a doorway, his heartbeat quickening. The chaise drew alongside him and he glimpsed the face of a young man at the carriage window, his head bent forward, as though reading a document or a book. It wasn't the master. The face was too young. Relieved, he expelled a lungful of air and watched the coach clatter its way to the bottom of the incline and disappear round the corner onto Great Dover Street.

He stepped out into the busy street and was about to continue on his way south when he heard the clopping sound of more horses approaching. Again, he scanned the street behind him. Less than twenty yards away he saw a rider, his tricorn hat pulled down over his eyes and a scarf hiding the lower part of his face. He'd seen men with their faces hidden before. It had always meant trouble. He pressed back into the recess of the doorway and waited. The horseman was leading a second, rider-less, horse and was looking straight ahead of him, as though viewing a distant object. Ebenezer's stomach tightened, his suspicions heightened. There was something threatening about the man, an aura of menace that seemed to surround him, his attention seemingly absorbed by the chaise.

Ebenezer wondered if there was a connection between the two. He waited for the stranger to pass, and disappear round the bend, unable to shake off a feeling of dread. He levered himself away from the doorway once more and continued down the street, his pace slower than before. He reached the corner of Great Dover Street. The road in front of him was almost deserted. On either side, the broad avenue was lined with hovels that seemed on the point of collapse, the frames of their windows and doors rotting, the paint long since peeled away.

In front of him, the box-like shape of the chaise he'd seen earlier emerged out of the gloom. Ebenezer slowed his pace still further, feeling the tension rise in his chest. The carriage was standing at an odd angle to the highway, its nearside door open. Close by, the rider who'd passed Ebenezer was standing facing the open door. He was holding a pistol, and was pointing it at the carriage. Ebenezer shrank back out of sight, suddenly afraid. He watched the passenger he'd seen a minute or two before stumble from the coach and be forced up into the saddle of one of the horses.

Ebenezer's gaze shifted to the line of darkened houses on either side of the road. There was no movement, no light, no face at any of the windows. If anyone had seen what was happening, there was no sign of it. He heard the sudden clatter of hooves and looked back towards the carriage. The two riders were leaving. Ebenezer waited. Whatever had happened, it was of no concern of his.

He had started to cross to the south side of the road when a sudden gust of wind caught the coach door and slammed it shut. The noise had sounded like the report of a gun. Ebenezer started and looked back. High up, on the driver's seat of the chaise, he saw the slumped outline of a body. He hesitated. The man seemed to be dead. But he might only be injured and in need of help. He looked away, every fibre of his being telling him to keep going, not to become involved.

Then he walked back. First he checked the inside of the cabin, putting his face to the window and peering into the gloom. It was empty. Then he looked up toward the driver's seat. The man was lying on his side, his face turned towards the heavens, one arm across his chest, the other hanging limp by his side. Ebenezer had seen death too often not to recognise its occurrence in a fellow being. But it didn't stop him calling out to the man; softly, as one might do to a sleeping child. There was no response. He'd not expected one, but it seemed the least he could do; a small courtesy.

He looked up and down the street. It was still deserted.

He didn't know why he chose to climb up beside the body, some vague notion of dignity, a wish to place it out of the sight of those who would eventually pass by. He didn't really think about it. He bent towards the inert frame and caught hold of the dead man's coat, noticing the livid marks about his neck.

Someone was shouting. It sounded close by. Other voices were joining in. Ebenezer turned. He could see half a dozen men running towards him. He released his grip on the dead driver and leapt to the ground, ducked his head and ran.

Sam Hart made his way down an alley off Clink Street, Southwark, a quarter of a mile upstream from London Bridge. There was a sharp stench of urine in the air that mingled with the odour of excrement and rotting fish. Sam wished he hadn't come. He'd only done so because Mordecai Phillips, one of his snouts, had asked to see him. The scrub had never been a particularly good informant, or even a very reliable one, but he was an informant, a nose, nevertheless. And Sam could never be certain that he would not, one day, produce some worthwhile piece of information.

The smells got worse as he picked his way deeper into the tunnel-like void that passed for a public road. From time to time, a light would shine from the shattered window of a long-derelict house or he would hear the screams of domestic conflict coming from behind thin walls.

He passed a group of ragged children playing amongst the rubbish, seemingly oblivious to the evening chill of early autumn. Beyond them, three or four men lounged against the wall of a building, their hands in their pockets, their unsmiling faces turned towards him. Sam tensed. Experience had told him what to expect. His fingers wrapped themselves round the hilt of his cutlass.

'Will it be Master Sam, now?'

The voice caught him by surprise. Sam looked at the man who'd spoken, a heavily built fellow of above average height, the furrows in his broad, pockmarked face engrained with coal dust. He seemed familiar; doubtless one of the hundreds of Irish coal-heavers that populated the wharfs on the south bank of the Thames. Sam drew closer. Now he remembered him. Shamus O'Connor, a petty villain who was lucky not to have been deported – or hanged – for his many transgressions, a man whose mood could change in the blink of an eye, particularly when he had been drinking. Sam had, on more than one occasion, needed to remind him of his good manners.

'All right, Shamus?' Sam nodded, warily.

'Never better, Master Sam.' There was a hint of mockery in O'Connor's voice. He grinned, exposing a row of black stumps. 'And yourself?'

'Well, thankee.' Sam moved on. He had no wish to prolong the exchange.

A minute later, he arrived at a windowless building, set back a little from its neighbours. At its centre stood a door whose rotting timbers seemed on the point of falling from the frame. Sam pushed it open and found himself in a smoke-filled room lit by, perhaps, a couple of dozen candles. He shivered in the cold, damp atmosphere of the place and waited for his eyes to adjust to the light.

About a score of men, women and children, some as young as three or four, sat at empty tables as though expecting the delivery of some food or drink or both, their soot-engrained, exhausted faces devoid of expression. The murmur of conversation dropped when he entered and faces turned towards him. Sam glanced round. In the far right-hand corner of the room, a blanket had been nailed over a doorway, acting as a curtain to another part of the building. There was no sign of Mordecai

He was about to turn away when the curtain was thrown aside and a short, slightly built man emerged, his hollow face heavily lined, his grey-streaked hair tied at the back of his neck with a soiled ribbon.

'Hello, Mordecai,' said Sam, catching the man by his elbow. Mordecai jumped, startled.

'As Abraham is our father in faith, Master Sam, you don't 'alf give a cully a fright.' Mordecai Phillips – opportunistic thief, fraudster and sometime snout, and Ashkenazi Jew – straightened up. 'And keep yer voice down, will yer? Don't want the whole bleedin' world knowing me business.'

'Sorry, but you asked to see me,' said Sam, looking round at the curious stares. 'Let's get out of here and go somewhere we can talk.'

Sam had not intended to come to the Blind Beggar, an old, three-storey inn close to St Saviour's Dock. It stood at the point where Clink Street ended and Church Street began, an ancient structure that should have toppled to the ground years ago. The last time he'd been here was with Tom, the memory of that day still vivid in his mind. He glanced in through the small side window, opened the door, and went in.

The place looked just the same; small, dark and grubby with tobacco-stained beams too low to allow a man to walk upright. Its once white-painted walls were now lined in black and brown smudges where countless shoulders had rubbed against them. Even the dirty-looking blanket used to divide the room into two was still in place. Sam was tempted to sweep it aside and see who was there, hidden from the rest of the customers.

He beckoned to Mordecai and led the way through the tightly packed drinkers to one of the benches set around three sides of the room.

'What did you want to see me about, Mordecai?' he asked, his voice more brusque than he had intended. He looked round for the pot-boy and ordered a couple of jugs of beer.

'Might be something, might be nothing, Master Sam.' Mordecai nodded knowingly, and looked round at the other drinkers. Then, dropping his voice to little more than a whisper, he said, 'I hears you's been putting the word out for anyone what might know of a body what's been found down Deptford way.'

'Aye, so I have,' said Sam, surprised that word of the finding should have reached Southwark. He looked up as the door to the tavern opened and several men came in, the group pushing its way through the crowd and seating themselves at a nearby table. Sam recognised one of them as Shamus O'Connor, the man he'd spoken to outside the lodging house in Clink Street. He was arguing about something, his voice growing louder and more aggressive by the minute. Sam tried to concentrate on what his snout was saying.

'The thing is, Master Sam,' said Mordecai, apparently oblivious to the darkening mood at the neighbouring table. 'I were at the Isle of Dogs t'other day. Before dawn it were. I sees a carriage come down Limehouse Hole and stop close to the path what leads by the river. Then out gets two gentlemen and they walk down the path. Seemed mighty strange for gentlemen to be there, especially at that hour. They didn't say nothing. Kept themselves to themselves. Well, it weren't none of me business, like, so I left them to it and . . .'

A loud, belligerent voice drowned his words. Sam turned to see who it was. Shamus O'Connor was staring at him from his place a few feet away. 'Will you be having nothing to say to old Shamus, Master Sam, you and that villain Pascoe? Too good for the likes of us, are you? There's folk I knows of what don't care for the pair of you, and that's a fact.'

Sam turned away, ignoring the insult. Mordecai was still talking.

'. . . it were about ten minutes later when I heard it. Course, I'd left by then, and were almost at Limekiln Dock. Two bangs. Sounded like pistol shots, but I couldn't be sure.'

A bench scraped on the wooden floor of the taproom. Sam

glanced up. Shamus was climbing unsteadily to his feet, his face florid with drink. Sam readied himself. There was no sense in not being prepared.

'What happened, exactly?' he asked, still looking at Mordecai while watching the Irishman out of the corner of one eye.

'I couldn't see. I were . . .'

But Sam had stopped listening. He sprang to his feet, ducking a swinging fist from Shamus. He waited a second while the momentum of the punch carried the man round, then kicked his feet from under him, sending him sprawling into the next bench. The uproar was immediate. Men and beer toppled to the floor, the immediate cause of little consequence to those involved. It was enough that they'd lost their drinks. Fists flew and oaths were uttered in a profusion of unbridled violence.

'Time we left, I think,' said Sam, finishing his beer and heading for the street door. 'You were telling me you heard some pistol shots.'

'What happened in there?' said Mordecai, ignoring Sam's question.

'It's not important,' said Sam. 'Tell me what you saw on the Isle of Dogs. Who was shooting?'

'Don't know, Master Sam.' Mordecai threw another anxious look behind him. The fighting had spilled out onto the street. 'I were too far away to see anything.'

Sam ballooned his cheeks and stared at the sky.

'But I did see them later.'

'Where?' Sam swung round and caught his snout by his arm.

'I were in Narrow Street. Saw them pass by. The same two I'd seen earlier.'

'Can you describe them?'

'Didn't take much notice of them, Master Sam. I know one were a big cully, but that were all.'

'But you said they both appeared to be gentlemen?'

'Aye, they were that all right. Young, too. Not more than about twenty-five, twenty-six.'

They walked in silence for a moment, listening to the fading sounds of the mêlée in the distance.

'Funny thing is,' mused Mordecai, 'it were only later I heard that a gentleman had been turned off.'

He turned to look at Sam, a troubled expression on his face. 'After the coach had gone by, I went back and had a look. I were curious, like. Wanted to see what the gentlemen had been doing. Thought they might have done the shooting, like. But there was nothing, Master Sam. No body, no nothing.'

'No, you wouldn't have found anything,' said Sam. 'I reckon the body were already floating in the tideway.'

CHAPTER 5

Tom Pascoe stood outside the door to the resident magistrate's room on the first floor of the Wapping police office and brushed the worst of the filth from his uniform coat and breeches. He wondered if Harriot had heard about the incident in Rosemary Lane this morning when Sam had found him, the worse for drink, talking to a negro. His head hadn't fully cleared and he wasn't at all sure Harriot wouldn't immediately know he'd been drinking – again. He pushed the thought to the back of his mind. He could handle his drink without Harriot's, or anyone else's, help. He glanced at his pocket watch. Still no word from the serjeant-at-arms on who might be willing to help identify the body in the river. He knocked on the magistrate's door and went in.

'I've had a note from the Southwark magistrate,' said Harriot, limping back to his desk with a cup of coffee in his hand. 'Seems that earlier this evening a coach was stopped at gunpoint in Great Dover Street, about half a mile beyond the Marshalsea. The driver was killed and his passenger abducted. My colleague has asked for our help in investigating the matter. I told him we'd do what we could.'

'Bit off our beat, sir,' said Tom, relieved to be talking about something other than his drinking habits. If the magistrate had noticed the state of his dress, he gave no sign of it.

'Yes, it is.' The deep lines on Harriot's face were accentuated by the lamplight on the desk beside him. 'I'm doing it as a favour. He was desperate for help.'

'Do we know the identity of the passenger? Why he was abducted?'

'No. The local constables have apparently made a few inquiries but with no success. I'm told they've left everything as they found it.'

'And you want me to deal with the investigation?' said Tom.

'Aye, Mr Pascoe, I do,' said Harriot, eyeing his subordinate with a doubtful stare. 'Think you can handle it?'

Still smarting from Harriot's implied criticism, Tom hurried down the river stairs to the waiting police galley. He crossed the pontoon and stepped aboard. There was a space where Sam should have been sitting. For a brief moment he wondered where he was, and then remembered his friend had been due to meet an informant.

'All correct, your honour,' boomed John Kemp.

'Thankee,' said Tom, looking at the rock-like presence seated in front of him. Along with Sam, Kemp had been a member of his crew since the first day of the new police, in July of last year. An ox of a man, he had served in the Navy until, aged thirty-five, he'd been discharged. In search of employment, he'd travelled up to London from Portsmouth and made his way to Wapping where he'd joined the newly formed marine police. Allocated to Tom Pascoe's crew, his size and strength had marked him out for his present position at mid-thwart where, alone of the three rowers, he was expected to handle two oars.

Tom settled himself onto the arms' chest, checked the state of the tide and glanced up and down the reach. He breathed deeply, taking in the familiar aroma of the river as a hundred or so ships' lanterns flashed and winked at him across the black, undulating sheen of the tideway.

He knew Harriot had been right to have his doubts about his ability to function. He had hardly covered himself in glory in these past few months; most of it a blur of memory – the constant and overpowering desire for a drink filling his every waking moment. There had been times when he'd found himself at dawn in some rat-infested alley, unable to remember where he was or how he'd got there. Then there were the flashes of unreasonable anger. He'd seen the pain in Sam's eyes and in those moments of lucidity had recognised what he had become. Yet in spite of this, he was unable or unwilling to act, afraid of abandoning the one thing that shielded him from the mental anguish of Peggy's death.

The galley slipped its moorings and swept round on a course for London Bridge, the tideway quiet at this time of the night, just the occasional skiff returning a master to his vessel, or a late-arriving passenger joining his ship.

'Something happened, your honour?' said Kemp, leaning back on his oars.

'What?' Tom snapped out of his reverie. 'Yes, a job we need to look at, in Southwark. Shouldn't take us long.'

The crew fell silent, concentrating on the dip and pull of their sweeps, the creak and thump of the leather sleeve against the thole pins, soporific in its regularity. A little short of London Bridge, Tom began to track across to the south bank, threading his way through the barge roads and ships' tiers, to Tooley Stairs.

'Stay with the galley, Higgins. We shouldn't be long,' he said, addressing the newest member of his crew. 'You, Kemp, bear along with the lantern, will you?'

'Sir?'

'Yes, Higgins, what is it?' said Tom.

'Begging your pardon, sir, you dropped this.' Jim Higgins held up a crumpled drawing of a young woman, her black hair peeping out from below a mob cap. 'Did you draw this, sir? It's beautiful.'

'Aye, it's mine.' Tom felt his cheeks redden. He leaned back into the boat and snatched at the paper, stuffing it hurriedly into his coat pocket. It was a sketch he'd made of Peggy. He'd forgotten he had it. 'Thankee.'

He led the way along the path leading to Tooley Street. Two minutes later, he and Kemp emerged into Borough High Street where they pushed their way through the throng, past a succession of coaching inns. A few yards beyond the grim walls of the Marshalsea Prison, they turned left into the comparative quiet of Great Dover Street with its broad acres and ramshackle dwellings.

Tom heard, rather than saw, the large group of people, a deep rumble of their voices drifting towards him through the night. It was another minute or so before he was able to see them and make out the shape of a carriage around which they had gathered.

'What happened?' said Tom, introducing himself to a solitary watchman whom he'd seen standing a little to one side of the onlookers. The man was clearly bored and anxious to be on his way. He shrugged and nodded in the direction of the driver's seat, high up on the coach. Tom turned and looked. The body was slumped on the bench, its head tipped backwards, exposing the throat, its legs splayed wide.

'How long has he been there?' Tom asked. 'Never mind. Fetch the hand ambulance. And be quick about it.'

The watchman looked as though he'd been slapped. He knuckled his forehead and began to shamble away.

'What about the passengers?'

'Didn't see no passengers.' The man stopped and looked back. 'Only the driver. I were told to stand 'ere till you came. No one's said nothing about no hand ambulance or no passengers.'

Tom ignored him and approached the carriage. There was a coat of arms that he didn't recognise painted on the door panel. He glanced inside the cabin and then swung himself up onto the driver's seat where he crouched down beside the cadaver. It was too dark to see properly.

'Bear along with the lantern, Kemp,' he said.

'One lamp coming up, sir.'

Tom took the light and held it close to the driver's contorted face, the wax-like skin a bluish-purple. He noticed a colourless welt around the man's neck and bent forward for a closer look. His heart missed a beat. He'd seen those marks before: the odd indentations in the bruising, as though a knotted cord had been used to choke out the man's life. The sight reawakened memories of someone else who'd worn those same marks about her slender, lifeless neck.

He pushed the thought from his mind. It wasn't possible that the man responsible for Peggy's death had returned. He tried to concentrate; looked for the watchman. He was still there.

'How long ago did this happen?'

'Don't rightly know,' mumbled the old man. 'I been here two, maybe three hours since. Reckon it must've been a while afore that.'

'Around dusk,' said Tom, consulting his pocket watch. He looked over at the crowd, silent now, listening to what was being said. 'Anyone see anything?'

There was no reply. People began to peel away.

Tom watched them go. He wasn't surprised. The fear of becoming involved was usually enough to override people's curiosity.

'Begging your pardon, your honour.' The voice came from close to Tom's boot. He looked down to see a man peering up at him. 'Ain't none of me business, like, but I see a cully – a nigger, he were – up on the bench where you is now. He ran off when he saw us coming. Couldn't see his face, like, but he were a big cove.'

'Where did he go?'

'Down yon alley,' said the man, pointing to a narrow pathway not far from where they were.

'More than three hours ago.' Tom leaned over the edge of the coach for a better view. There was little to be gained by a search now. 'Seen him before, have you?'

'Wouldn't know one nigger from another.' The man looked around at what was left of the onlookers, as though seeking confirmation. A few nodded their heads. 'There's a heap of them in one of them houses a little ways down the road. Reckon the cully could be there.'

'Show me,' said Tom, jumping to the roadway and catching the man by his arm. 'Kemp, stay here until I get back and get that charlie to arrange for the body to be taken away to the nearest dead house. He'll know where it is. It's his beat.'

Tom didn't wait for an answer. He strode off, still holding on to his new guide. A minute or so later, the man slowed and pointed to a two-storey terraced house, its windows in darkness. It looked identical to its neighbours.

'This the house?' said Tom.

'Aye.'

'What d'you know about this man, this negro you saw by the coach?'

'Nothing.' The man began to pull away from Tom's grip. 'I told you, I wouldn't know one blackamoor from another.'

'Wait here,' said Tom. He lifted the lantern above his head and pushed open the door. Stepping across the threshold, he entered what appeared to be an empty room, the air warm and thick with the sour smell of unwashed bodies. He dropped the lantern closer to the floor which now heaved and writhed as though alive. He bent down. Every inch of the floor was occupied by sleeping forms, and all, so far as he could tell, were black – men, women and children – some covered with strips of carpet or canvas, others with a coat, and some with nothing more than the clothes they wore. Tom moved carefully through the room, bending every so often to examine a face before moving on, aware that he had only the flimsiest of descriptions to help him find the man he sought.

He came to a second room, this one smaller than the first. It, too, was crammed with people, the sickly odour of their bodies stifling in its intensity. The task of finding the man from the coach seemed overwhelming. He was about to give up when he saw a flight of stairs in the far corner. He hesitated. There seemed little point in going on with the search. He turned towards the front door, stopped and then headed for the stairs. He'd come this far. He might as well finish what he'd started. He climbed to the first floor, which was as crowded as the one below, and turned to go back down. He would speak to the witness again; get a fuller description.

Then he saw the gap.

It was wide enough for a single person to lie down. He stepped across, squatted down and laid the flat of his hand on the layer of straw. It was still warm, as though someone had only recently left the space. He straightened, held up the lantern, and looked round the room. There were no other spaces. He'd have been surprised if there had been. A place to sleep was always in demand.

Emerging from the house, Tom looked around for the witness who'd led him to the house. There was no sign of him. He wasn't unduly concerned. He doubted the man could have told him much more than he'd already done.

He started to walk back to the coach and its grim load.

Ebenezer Samson stood at the corner of the alley and watched the big man with the corn-coloured hair come out of the house that he'd come to regard as his home, and turn towards the coach. The darkness made it impossible to see the man's face but that didn't matter. Whoever he was, he had the bearing of someone used to authority. And that, in Ebenezer's experience, was a good enough reason for avoiding him. It reminded him of the *bakra* who'd controlled his every moment.

He felt himself back on the island of Barbados, on the plantation, a mile or two south-east of Speightstown, where each day was the same as the one before. It wasn't his island. He didn't belong there. But it was where he had lived and worked, six days out of seven, sunrise to sunset, for the past ten years.

He covered his face with his hands. He could feel the heat of the noonday sun on his back, could see the sugar cane, as thick as a man's wrist, standing eight to ten feet tall, spreading away in every direction, his view of the world confined to its surrounding presence. He was swinging a razor-sharp cleaver, aiming it low, catching the cane as it fell, and placing it on the ground behind him for the women to collect.

Chop. Catch. Lay. Chop, catch, lay. The routine never varied. Only when the sun went down was there any relief. Then he and the others would look out for the sandbox tree that grew amongst the plantation huts where they lived, and the tree – all that was visible above the lofty canes – would guide them home.

He did not see him arrive. Heard only the angry bark of his master's voice. In his mind's eye, Ebenezer saw the tall, white-clad figure astride his bay horse, a coiled whip in his hand, his face shaded by the broad brim of his leghorn. He felt a trickle of sweat run down his back. The master was looking at him, pointing to something Ebenezer couldn't see. Now he was shouting, his face reddening, twisted in rage.

Ebenezer couldn't understand the words. He stared at the ground, removing his cabbage-tree hat from his head. To look up was to invite retribution, would be seen as a challenge to the master's authority. Too late, he heard the crack of the whip, felt its lick across his shoulders, its slithering tongue encircling his neck. He choked on the scream rising in his throat, struggled for the breath that wouldn't come. He fell to his knees. Another stinging blow. Ebenezer arched backwards, his hands clutching his stomach where the hungry tip of the leather thong had eaten into his flesh.

He turned to face his tormentor, his head bowed. Nearby, the women were gathering the lengths of cane and stacking them vertically in the horse-drawn cart. There was no pause in their work. No one looked at him.

The master was pointing again. Ebenezer followed the direction of his arm and realised the error of his ways. One of the canes had been cut too high. It was a waste. It should not have happened.

The man in the white suit and the leghorn rode on.

Ebenezer heard a shout, and realised he'd been dreaming. He stared at the yellow-haired figure walking back towards the coach in Great Dover Street. His master, the one from whose house he'd run, had walked in the same way. A man with right on his side. He watched as the man reached the coach and bent forward to look at something, the light from the lantern he carried falling on his face as he did so. Ebenezer stiffened as he recognised the drunk who'd sat beside him on Rosemary Lane, the drunk who now appeared to be searching for him.

He should never have become involved with the coach and its dead driver. It had been of no concern to him. He wiped his hands down the side of his breeches. Perhaps he shouldn't have run. Perhaps he should have waited and explained himself. But he hadn't. Eventually tiredness had forced him back to the house he called home, the place he shared with another thirty or so others.

The decision had nearly cost him his freedom. Only the noise of the crowd had saved him. He'd got up and gone to the window, in time to see the man with the corn-coloured hair approaching the house. He knew what would happen if he was caught. He'd seen it happen to others, witnessed the flogging they'd received and the bloody pulp that had once been the skin on their backs.

Ebenezer rubbed his eyes, suddenly tired. But he knew that sleep was impossible; not here and not now. He peered round the corner in the direction of the chaise. The tall man in the blue and white coat was leaving, the crowd was drifting away. Ebenezer waited a while longer. Then he, too, moved off. Where he was going, he had no idea. His thoughts drifted back to the coach and the horseman he'd first seen near the junction with Borough High Street.

Details came to him. He remembered the rider with the two horses who'd seemed to be following the coach. He'd not seemed comfortable astride his mount, as though he was unused to riding. He remembered, too, the way the man had worn his scarf round the lower part of his face, his tricorn pulled down over his ears as though anxious not to be recognised. He'd watched him duck as he passed a lantern hanging from the doorway of a tavern, turning his face from its faint glow. The light had shone instead on the scarf.

There had been nothing remarkable about it except, perhaps, its colour – the deep violet of the indigo plant. Ebenezer knew the colour well, had often been set to work cutting down the plant stems and taking them to the large, wooden, piss-filled vats at the back of the plantation house near Speightstown, where the women would tread them underfoot, to release the dye.

It was not a colour he'd easily forget.

CHAPTER 6

Tom did not sleep well, his slumbers interrupted by the recurring memory of what he'd seen on the neck of the dead coach driver. The livid welts had been all too familiar and he'd felt his own throat constrict as he considered the possibility that he might already know the identity of the killer. He'd pushed the thought away at the time, unable to accept the possibility that Peggy's killer was again in England and had again killed. Yet the notion kept returning to him, forcing him to consider the evidence of his eyes.

He rose early, washed and changed out of the damp clothes he'd worn the previous day. In spite of his restless night, he felt better than he had done in several weeks. There was no sign of the debilitating headache that had dogged his waking hours for so long, nor the foul taste in his mouth with which each day had seemed to begin. He slipped into a clean, if somewhat battered, uniform coat, and headed for the stall in St Catherine's Street for a breakfast of fried egg and bacon, and a mug of hot coffee.

An hour later, he was standing on the police pontoon at Wapping, gazing out over Lower Pool, shrouded in grey mist. He shivered and pulled his old Navy greatcoat about him.

'There wasn't much to go on,' he said, turning to look at Sam, standing next to him. 'The coach was empty. No sign of the passenger. Black fellow seen in the vicinity. Coach driver had been strangled—'

He stopped suddenly, his gaze fixed on the barge roads downstream of the police office.

'What was you going to say, sir?' asked Sam.

'What? Oh, nothing,' said Tom, remembering the indentations around the dead coach driver's neck. He started to walk up to the river stairs to the office, paused and looked back at Sam.

'I collect that you went to see an informant yesterday,' he said. 'Did he have anything interesting to say?'

'Not sure,' said Sam. 'Told me he'd been on the Isle of Dogs a few days since. Might have seen something in connection with the floater we found in Greenwich Reach.'

'Oh aye. Did he see how it got there?' said Tom, a hopeful note in his voice.

'No, but he did hear the sound of shooting.'

'Pity.' Tom turned and walked up the steps.

'He did see some cullies, later though.'

Tom spun round. 'Speak up, man.'

'A few minutes after the shooting he saw two young gentlemen in a chaise travelling along Limehouse Hole. He'd seen them arrive in the area a little earlier.'

'What did they look like?'

'He didn't take that much notice of them, sir, except to say they looked like gentlemen.'

'He must have seen something about them worth mentioning,' said Tom, exasperated. 'You said "young". How young were they?'

'Late twenties. No more. Now I think on it, he told me one of them were a big cully.'

Tom stored the information away. The descriptions fitted any number of people but that didn't mean they might not, one day, be useful. He took out a plug of tobacco from his coat pocket and bit off a chunk, feeling the sharp, bitter taste spread throughout his mouth.

'Mr Pascoe?' The duty waterside officer was standing at the door of the police office. 'There's a message for you, sir. A gentleman what said if you was at leisure, the serjeant-at-arms has some information for you.'

'Thankee. Please inform the messenger I'll be there directly.' Tom waited for the man to disappear before turning to face Sam. 'I may be a little while. See what else you can find about those two gentlemen your snout told you about. Somebody must know them.'

With that, he hurried out onto Wapping Street, turning west towards Parliament and the home of the serjeant-at-arms.

Almost directly opposite the police office at Wapping is a seldom used alley that runs along the side of the Pichard & Co. brew house before joining a lane at the back of the premises. Close to its junction with Wapping Street, two men were lounging against a wall, their heads turned towards the police office as though expecting someone. A short while before they had watched Tom Pascoe arrive at the office and walk down the passageway towards the river stairs. They already knew that if things went to plan, Pascoe would re-emerge in the next few minutes and begin his journey to Westminster for a meeting with the serjeant-at-arms at an address in Parliament Street. The purpose of that meeting was of no interest to them. Pascoe was not to get there.

Shamus O'Connor shifted his considerable bulk away from the wall and thought of his meeting with the gentleman who'd approached him before dawn with an offer of work. It had been a simple proposition, and the reward more than generous. He was to deliver Pascoe to a boat that would be waiting for him at the bottom of St Catherine's Stairs. O'Connor had hesitated. He had little appetite for confronting a man of Pascoe's reputation. Yet neither did he wish to pass up the opportunity of earning a tidy sum of cash for a few minutes' work. He'd finally agreed to the job although his nervousness had not improved when he'd told a friend what he was about to do.

Sure he's as fair a man as you'll ever meet, but b'Jesus, don't be messing with him, the friend had said. *I've seen as many as four or five bully boys as has tried to flog him, and regretted the day they was born.*

There was no going back now. He'd been paid half the agreed amount with the rest to follow when the job was done. The gentleman had been careful to remind Shamus of the consequences of any failure on his part to fulfil the contract. Shamus glanced at his companion. He'd worked with the cully before. There shouldn't be any difficulty.

He looked across the street. Pascoe was descending the steps and was turning towards Hermitage Dock. A moment later Shamus and his companion dropped in behind him.

Tom walked quickly. He knew better than to hope for a chaise anywhere round Wapping. He'd pick one up when he reached Tower Hill and be in Parliament Street within the hour. At the corner of Burr Street he paused. He'd not shaved this morning.

He thought he might just have time to return to his room and scrape away the night's growth.

'Mr Pascoe?' There was no mistaking the threatening edge to the man's voice. And it was close behind him.

Tom looked round and saw two men, both of them big, broad-shouldered hulks he'd not seen before. His eyes flicked down to the men's hands. One was holding a spliced rope's end and was swinging it gently from side to side. The other carried a short stave.

'That's the end of my shave', thought Tom, running a hand over the stubble on his chin. Then, aloud, he said, 'What can I do for you?'

'A gentleman friend of mine wants to see you.' There was the same hint of menace in the man's voice. 'You want to come quietly – or what?'

The man grinned, exposing a row of black stumps that was all that was left of his teeth. He took a step nearer, the intricately spliced rope's end now firmly gripped in one hand. Suddenly, he swung it at Tom, the tip catching the side of his jaw with savage force. Tom swayed onto his back foot and then came forward, his fist sinking it into the man's stomach. The fellow doubled up, his head falling forward as Tom brought his knee up, connecting it with the man's chin. There was a sound of breaking teeth. Blood poured from the man's mouth, running down his chin and onto his chest as he fell to the ground.

The second man was rushing at him, his stave held aloft. Tom watched the bludgeon begin its downward trajectory, warded it away with his left forearm, his right hand pulling the man towards him. Again, Tom stepped aside, the man's momentum carrying him past. Then he kicked his feet from under him.

It was over in seconds. Tom drew his cutlass but the man was already on his feet and running. He glanced down at his companion who was struggling to get up. Tom placed a boot on the man's neck. He wanted answers but knew they'd have to wait. The second man was still in the area, and might have friends. If they came looking for him, Tom would have his hands full. He pulled the man to his feet and pushed him down Burr Street, into St Catherine's.

'It weren't nothing personal, mister,' said the man, spitting out a mixture of blood and broken stumps of teeth.

'You should have thought of that earlier.' Tom was searching the street for any sign of a rescue attempt. He need not have worried. Within a few minutes they had arrived back at the police office.

'You can start by telling me what this is about,' he said, as soon as the two of them were alone. 'And it had better be good.'

'Sure, we was told to do it.'

'That much is bloody obvious. You knew my name,' snapped Tom. 'So who told you to come after me?'

Silence.

'You can please yourself, cock,' growled Tom. 'You can talk to me or I'll see to it you go to the Old Bailey with every chance of a Newgate Dance at the end of it.'

'Sweet Jesus, I never seen him before, your honour, and that's the honest truth. He gave us two guineas apiece and said there'd be more when you was brought to him.'

'Did he say why he wanted me?'

'Only that he were going to put you on the first ship out of port. He didn't seem to like you none.'

'What's he look like?'

Another period of silence.

'I'm waiting, mister.' Tom prodded the man's chest with his cutlass blade.

'He were a big cully. About twenty-five. A gentleman, with fancy clothes.'

'Anything else?'

'There'll not be anything else to say.'

'Who's your friend? The one who was with you when you tried to take me?'

'Jim. That's all I know.'

'And yours?'

'Shamus O'Connor, your honour. Will I be going now?'

'You must be bloody joking, Shamus, my old cock,' said Tom. 'You're going in front of the beak. And with any luck, you'll be going to the Bailey.'

'But . . .'

'But what? You think you can come after me and get away with it, you best think again. Maybe if you remember the name of the cully who paid you, I might think differently,' said Tom, walking out of the cell and slamming the door behind him.

'My dear fellow.' William Watson, the parliamentary serjeant-at-arms, gazed at Tom's swollen jaw. 'Are you quite well?'

'Quite well, sir,' said Tom, feeling the side of his mouth where the rope's end had connected. 'A slight altercation. No more.'

'Do sit down, sir.' Watson pointed to an empty chair by the fireplace and resumed his own seat. 'If you're quite sure, I shall proceed.'

'Please, go on,' said Tom.

'As I promised,' said Watson. 'I've made a few inquiries of my colleagues and of such Members of the House as I've been able to find. It seems there are two Members whose absence has been a cause for concern. The first is Sir Henry Thwaite-Thomas, the Member for Gatton, in Surrey. He hasn't been seen for some days, in circumstances which have led to anxiety about his safety. The other is Mr John Dean, the Member for Appleby in Westmoreland. He's not been seen recently either, but from the description you gave me, the body appears to be that of Sir Henry.'

'What, pray, were the circumstances of his disappearance?'

'I was never told.' Watson leaned forward and raked the fire with an iron poker. 'It was merely suggested to me that his absence, while of some concern, was not a matter of any great surprise. I got the impression that something had been troubling him in the days before he disappeared.'

'And this information came from . . . who, exactly?'

'This is unfortunate, sir.' Watson spread his hands. 'I was told upon the understanding of confidentiality.'

'While I understand your difficulty, sir, I must know all there is to know about Sir Henry if I'm to discover who killed him.' Tom felt the onset of a headache. He made a mental note to get a drink inside him as soon as the meeting with Watson was over. 'Perhaps you could speak again to your informant. In the meantime I take it there'll be no difficulty in you identifying the body? After that, the post-mortem can proceed.'

'Very well. I will do what I can,' sighed Watson, a look of resignation in his eyes.

CHAPTER 7

Tom took his leave of the master of the West Indiaman lying in the Custom House tier, climbed over the rail, and descended to the police galley lying alongside. He still had another five ships to visit. It was the least enjoyable part of his duties, the well-nigh constant round of inspections of the thirty or so West India ships in port at any one time whose captains had paid for his attendance. But it had to be done. He stepped into the galley and sat down.

It had been two days since his meeting with Watson, and he had, this morning, received the three items of information he'd been waiting for. The post-mortem examination at the naval dockyard at Deptford confirmed what he already knew: that the body in the river had died from a single gunshot wound to the side of the neck. More importantly, the body had been formally identified as that of Sir Henry Thwaite-Thomas, the Member of Parliament for Gatton. At the same time, Watson had provided Tom with the name of someone prepared to talk to him about Sir Henry.

The galley slipped away from the side of the West Indiaman and headed out into the central channel on their way back to Wapping. A brig was on their starboard quarter, clubbing down on the ebb tide. He waited for her to pass, her main t'gallant filling in the light breeze, a ripple of white water tumbling away from her bows and coursing down her hull. He watched her for a minute or two, his jaw still aching from the fight in Burr Street.

'Why d'you think them bully boys came after you, sir?' said Sam, seeming to read Tom's mind.

'O'Connor and his friend? Not sure, but I fancy they had a berth all ready for me aboard some brig. If they'd succeeded, I don't suppose I'd ever have been heard of again.'

'But who?'

'If I knew that, Sam, I'd have had him banged up at Newgate so fast his feet would have burned.'

'Could be someone connected with Sir Henry's death.'

'Aye, I think you're right.'

Tom was used to being threatened. It went with the job. And while he had not expected Shamus O'Connor to volunteer any information about who had sent him, he'd been surprised by the degree of resistance to his questions. Even the threat of the Old Bailey and the hangman's noose had failed to convince him to talk. It suggested that whoever had hired him had possessed sufficient wealth and influence to ensure O'Connor's silence. He brought the police galley up into the tide and prepared to fetch alongside the police pontoon.

'Someone waiting to see you, Mr Pascoe, sir,' said the waterside officer, taking the galley's bowline and making her fast.

'Very well, Gibbs. Where is he?'

'The main hall, sir.'

Tom motioned to Sam to follow him, and started up the stairs. Halfway along the passageway he turned in through the main door of the police office and entered the hall. A motley collection of men and women stood in small groups, some talking amongst themselves, others staring vacantly into space or wandering to and fro, their faces set in varying states of anxiety as they waited for their cases to be called before the duty magistrate. This morning that meant Dr Colquhoun.

Standing to one side of the crowd, Tom noticed a ruddy-cheeked, middle-aged gentleman, his style of dress suggesting he came from out of town.

'Mr Pascoe?' The man raised a jet-black eyebrow and held out his hand.

'How, sir, may I be of service?' said Tom, walking over to him.

'My name, sir, is John Butterworth. I am trying to trace a friend of mine who's missing. I have reason to believe you may know where I might find him.'

'And who, sir, might that be?' said Tom.

'Sir Henry Thwaite-Thomas. He is a Member of Parliament. I've just come from the House of Commons where I saw an official who told me you would probably be able to assist me.'

'Come with me, sir. We can talk in private.' Tom led the way up the main staircase. At the first floor he turned down a narrow corridor, past a number of doors, before entering a room overlooking Wapping Street. The place was bare but for a large wooden table and a few chairs, presently heaped with damp clothing. More garments hung from nails in the wall or were suspended from a rope strung across the room. Some old shoes lay discarded in one corner.

'I apologise for all this,' said Tom, waving at the clothing. 'We must patrol in all weathers and space for drying is limited. But you were saying you were looking for your friend, Sir Henry Thwaite-Thomas?'

'Yes. We were to dine at my club the day before yesterday but he failed to arrive. No one appears to have seen him for several days.'

'Where, may I ask, do you know Sir Henry from?'

'He and I are neighbours. We both have homes in Rye, on the Sussex coast. We've known each other for a number of years.'

'When was the last time you actually saw him?'

'About two weeks ago.'

'May I ask where?'

'At Sir Henry's home in Rye. Is . . .' Butterworth faltered. 'Has something happened to him?'

'I regret it extremely, sir, but I have to tell you that your friend is dead,' said Tom.

Butterworth's eyes widened in shock. For a moment or two he said nothing.

'How did he die?' he managed, at last.

'He was shot. We know no more than that,' said Tom. 'We found his body in the Thames near Deptford Creek. Do you know what he might have been doing in that part of London?'

Butterworth shook his head and leaned forward, covering his face with his hands. 'I did wonder . . .' His voice trailed away.

'Anything you can tell us about your friend would be most helpful.'

'I . . .' John Butterworth glanced at Sam before turning his attention back to Tom. 'I knew something was troubling him.'

He hesitated and again glanced at Sam.

'It would, sir, be helpful to me were you to ask this Jew to leave the room.'

'This Jew,' said Tom, suppressing a surge of anger, 'is a

waterman constable attached to the marine police. Moreover, he is my particular friend. He will not be leaving the room, sir.'

'I meant no offence, sir.' Butterworth coloured and swallowed hard. When he had composed himself, he said, 'Something happened to my friend a few days before he disappeared which I would not wish to become known outside this room. I was merely seeking to ensure the confidentiality of what I wanted to say.'

'I will do what I can,' said Tom. 'You said something had been troubling him. What did you mean by that?'

Butterworth nodded and looked towards the door as if expecting some interruption.

'Sir Henry usually lived at his club in London, where he could more easily conduct his business as an MP. But, on those occasions when he was at home in Rye, he would occasionally meet with local gentlemen in the area, including myself. The talk would generally be about issues of local interest as well as the broader political scene. They were pleasant evenings spent in the company of friends. But all this changed about four or five weeks prior to his disappearance. Our group was joined by a small number of men from London, most of whom were strangers to me. I gave little thought to it. It was, after all, entirely a matter for Sir Henry who he chose to entertain in his own home. But, about a week before he disappeared, he held one of his periodic meetings, after which his demeanour changed, and he appeared withdrawn and ill at ease. I confess his altered appearance concerned me and I tried to ask him what it was that was troubling him. He laughed it off and I chose not to pursue the matter.'

'But you think it was something said or done at this meeting that was the cause of his apparent change of mood?'

'I think it's possible,' said Butterworth.

'Was that the last meeting he held?'

'Yes.'

'You said that most of those attending these meetings were unknown to you. Were there any you did know?'

'Yes. Lord Camperdown was present at several of the meetings, as was Sir William Bolt.'

'Camperdown, you say?' said Tom, raising an eyebrow.

'You know him, sir?'

'Only by repute,' said Tom. 'We were in the Navy at about the same time, though never shipmates.'

'Then you'll know he's not a man to cross,' said Butterworth.

Tom avoided the invitation to comment. He'd heard the stories of the man known throughout the Navy as the Mad Baron. It was said that he had once thrashed a man in a London street who, some years previously, had been his captain and who'd ordered the young Camperdown flogged. The captain had, reasonably enough, complained and for a while Camperdown faced the threat of an appearance at the Old Bailey on a charge of assault. For reasons that were never made clear, the expected trial did not materialise. Nor, it appeared, did his lordship learn from his mistake. A year or so later, while on station off the island of Barbados, he became embroiled in a row with a fellow officer over the question of seniority. The argument quickly spiralled out of control and only ended with the mortal shooting of the other man. Once again, Camperdown escaped censure, much to the chagrin of their lordships of the Admiralty.

'Does he live in Rye?' asked Tom.

'No,' said Butterworth. 'The family seat is in Surrey, and he has a house in London.'

'Rye seems a long way to travel for a meeting.'

'The meetings weren't the only reason for his attendance,' said Butterworth. 'Sir Henry owed his seat in Parliament to Camperdown's late father. On the death of the father, his son continued to have regular contact with the MP. There are those who have suggested he might, in addition, have an interest in the beautiful Lady Annabel Stapleton.'

'And she is?'

'Sir Henry's sister,' said Butterworth. 'She lived with her brother. Had done so since her husband was killed in the war, three or four years ago. There are rumours that Camperdown has long shown an interest in her.'

'What about the other fellow? Sir William Bolt? What can you tell me about him?'

'I've never had much to do with him. Seems to spend most of his time in London.'

Tom got up from his chair and moved to the window where he stood gazing down onto a crowded Wapping Street, the bobbing heads of the mob, a sea of movement. A tall, narrow-shouldered gentleman caught his attention. He was standing in the alley that ran down beside the brewery on the opposite side of the street. He was looking up at the police office, his gaze moving from window to window. For a fleeting moment, their eyes met. Then the man turned and hurried away, down the alley. Soon, he was lost to sight.

'Would Lord Camperdown have been present at the last meeting?' said Tom, still staring at the place where the stranger had stood.

'I wasn't there, but his lordship was certainly a frequent visitor to the house, so I imagine he might have been.'

'And Sir William Bolt?'

'Possibly.'

Tom rubbed his chin with the back of his hand, his thoughts already elsewhere. 'Is there anyone else who might know who was present?'

'Only Lady Annabel.'

CHAPTER 8

André Dubois entered the first-floor room of the Dog and Duck inn on Tooley Street, locked the door and looked across to where the young man was sitting on a chair. He was bound hand and foot, a cloth covering his mouth. Dubois walked over and checked the bindings. He was glad to be back and out of public view. The inn was barely a mile and a half from where he'd stopped the coach and taken the young man captive. He fingered the silk scarf draped about his neck and pondered the possibility of having been followed. He doubted it but one could never be sure. It hadn't helped matters when the ostler to whom he'd returned the horses had begun asking questions about where he was staying. He shook his head and turned his attention back to the boy.

There was a sudden knock at the door. Dubois turned and gaped.

'Master Smith? You in there, sir?'

Dubois recognised the landlord's voice. He'd almost forgotten he'd told the fellow his name was Smith. There was another loud knock.

'It's a word I want with you, Master Smith.' The man didn't sound as if he meant to give up. 'I know you're in there.'

'A moment, Master Landlord, if you please,' said Dubois, in English. He thought quickly. It might just be possible to move captive and chair to another position where he'd not be seen from the door. He brushed the prospect aside. It would take too long and make too much noise. It would be equally absurd to release the young man and hope he didn't say anything to rouse the landlord's suspicions. He stalled for time.

'What d'you want? I was asleep.'

'It's begging your pardon, sir,' said the landlord. 'The pot-boy told me he saw you come in, not five minutes since. He thought he heard a noise in the room while you were out. Is everything all right, sir?'

'Yes, yes,' said Dubois. 'A chair must have fallen over. There is nothing amiss in here.'

'Very well, sir,' said the landlord. 'If you say so. I'll not trouble you again, sir.'

Dubois waited for a few moments, listening to the departing footsteps. He was not easily frightened but there had been something in the landlord's tone that had warned him to be careful.

He turned away from the door. The young man was staring at him, his eyes wide with fright. Dubois held his gaze, knowing what needed to be done. He suspected the lad knew, too. He moved across to the window and looked down onto the street and along to the junction with Mill Lane. The crowd still streamed back and forth along the highway. He had been hoping for an easier, less public outing for what he had in mind. He bit his lip and ran his fingers through his close-cropped hair. The outing would have to wait.

He looked again at the young man. He could not afford to let him go, not now that he'd seen him and would be able to identify him. He slipped a hand into his coat pocket, feeling for the length of cord that was always there. His fingers curled about the thread and drew it out, hidden now in the palm of his hand.

A mewing noise came from behind the young man's gag. Dubois saw his eyes widen still further and fix themselves on his closed fist. The mewing grew louder, a muffled scream of despair, the man's head shaking from side to side in a futile appeal for his life.

Dubois was aware of his growing sense of disgust. When the time came for a man to die, he should accept it silently and die with his dignity, his honour, intact. He walked over to the chair and stood behind the young man's head. Then he dropped the cord around his neck.

He knew what he was doing. He had, from his earliest days on the streets of Marseille, observed the simple truth that in order to survive one needed just two qualities – the will to strike first and the ability to do so. He knew there had been few within his peer group prepared to argue with him. Even if they had had a mind to do so, his strength and speed, coupled with the protection he enjoyed with the local police, were enough to stop all but the foolhardy from confronting him. By his eighteenth birthday he had added murder to his list of wrongdoings, escaping the consequences through the enforced silence of the dozen or so witnesses to the killing.

Dubois had thought himself safe from judicial interference until the abrupt transfer of his police handler, Pierre Moreau, a *commissaire de police* of the ninth *arrondissement*, to Paris. Stripped of his police protection Dubois was immediately conscripted into the French Army and posted, with his regiment, the *32e demi-brigade d'Infanterie de Ligne*, to Italy.

Within months, high in the Alps during one of the coldest winters anyone could remember, Dubois was engaged in fighting that was both fierce and brutal, often at close quarters, in conditions where the knife proved as effective as the bullet. He smiled. He'd seldom been as happy as he had been during that winter when, a knife or a garrotte in his hand, he'd been sent behind the enemy's lines to wreak such havoc as his fertile mind could devise. And there he might have remained – or died – had it not been for a call to report to the minister of police in Paris to work alongside Moreau, his old handler, on an assignment in London.

It was his ill fortune that the planned operation had involved crossing the path of Tom Pascoe, a man he'd first met some years previously in a naval action off the south coast of France. For while the first encounter had left Dubois with an abiding hatred of the Englishman, another had sealed their enmity for ever.

The mewing noise brought him back to the present. The young man's body thrashed about in his chair, his head bent forward, his chin pressed against his chest in a seeming attempt to cheat the garrotte. He was too late. Dubois jerked back on the cord, tightening the noose, one knee against the back of the chair. The young man's face turned a bluish-purple and his eyes began to bulge, a faint gurgling sound coming from his throat.

Dubois didn't release his grip until he felt the body go limp. He unwound the length of knotted string from the dead man's neck and returned it to his pocket. Without a backward glance, he walked to the bed and lay down to rest for a while. When the street outside was quieter, he would take the body and dump it in the Thames.

*

It was some time later when Dubois roused himself, rolled off the bed and walked over to the window. Mill Lane, the road leading down to the river, was no more than twenty or thirty yards away. The crowds of early evening had largely gone, but the street was still not entirely deserted. Somehow he was going to have to carry the body to the junction, and beyond, without being seen. If he was caught there was no doubt he'd hang. He brushed away a drop of sweat with the palm of his hand and turned back into the room. He'd left the body in the chair, still bound, the man's lifeless chin resting on his chest. He crossed the room, gripped a handful of hair and lifted the head. He couldn't have been more than twenty-five – the same age as himself.

Dubois was conscious of a fleeting sense of regret. He'd not wished to end the fellow's life. Yet as soon as he had taken him from the coach, there was no going back. Even when he'd discovered his mistake and found that his captive was not the man he had expected, he could not have avoided killing him. He let go of the man's head, remembering the only other time he had felt remorse at the taking of a life. The victim had been a nurse at a hospital in this same town. She had not deserved to die either.

He glanced out at the night sky. It would soon be dawn. He drew his knife and cut through the cord binding the body. Then he laid the corpse onto a blanket he'd taken from his bed and rolled it until it was fully covered, tying off each end with a length of hemp. He hefted the body onto one shoulder and went to the door. The house was silent. He waited for a second or two and then crept down the stairs into the deserted taproom. The front door creaked open, the sound exaggerated by the stillness of the night. He could hear the thump of his own heartbeat. He stood still, his ears straining for the least sound. There was none.

He stole into the street. In the distance, he could hear the parish watch calling his rounds. Dubois tried to gauge how far away the man was. He looked east, towards Bermondsey Street. He reckoned he had two, perhaps three minutes, before the fellow appeared. He wondered if he'd make it to the corner of Mill Lane. The weight on his shoulder was slowing him down.

He shifted the body to his other shoulder and scurried across Tooley Street, his breath coming in short, shallow bursts. He heard a sudden shout. It had come from somewhere close by. Dubois felt the blood drain from his face, and his stomach somersaulted. He staggered into the recess of an adjacent doorway and waited, his eyes searching the street. There was another shout, this one followed by a woman screaming. It sounded as if she'd been struck. A couple appeared through the gloom, arguing. Dubois waited for them to pass, listening to the gradually receding sound of their voices. The wait had cost him time he could ill afford.

He checked up and down Tooley Street. It was clear. He had stepped away from the doorway when he heard a light scraping noise. It had come from the direction of Mill Lane, about fifteen yards away. A gust of wind disturbed some litter, sending it spiralling into the night. But that wasn't what he'd heard. Something *had* moved. He'd not imagined it. He debated whether to wait or go on. The nightwatchman was getting closer, probably no more than a street away. He couldn't stay where he was, and he hadn't time to return to his room.

Adjusting the weight on his shoulder, Dubois staggered to the junction, stopped and peered round the corner. A black void faced him. He hesitated, remembered the movement he'd heard. Another shout. The parish watch was now no more than fifty yards behind him. Dubois turned the corner and hurried into the lane, the tall buildings on either side closing in on him, the smell of the Thames in his nostrils.

CHAPTER 9

At an address at Portman Square, close to the western extremity of London, Sir William Bolt gazed at the dying embers in the grate, a half-empty decanter of whisky standing on the small mahogany table at his side.

'What happened?' Sir William turned to face his guest, his face flushed with the effects of the night's drinking.

'About what?' Lord Camperdown looked up sharply.

'Pascoe. I thought he was supposed to be on a ship bound for Virginia.'

'So he was.' Lord Camperdown swilled the whisky round in his glass and held it up to the light. 'Didn't quite go according to plan. Seems the fellow is going to be more of a problem than I'd imagined.'

'I think you're right,' said Bolt. 'Didn't you tell me one of the men you sent along was caught?'

'Yes, but—'

'Does the fellow know you at all?'

'No.'

'So he can't identify you?'

'No.'

'Well, that's something,' said Bolt, sipping his drink. 'What d'you propose to do now? About Pascoe, I mean.'

'I was thinking of the Navy,' said Camperdown, downing the last of his whisky. 'I've still got some friends who owe me a favour.'

Ebenezer smelt the river before he saw it, an aroma of wet wood and rope, of fish and tar. He could hear the slap of the tide and the bump and squeak of the lighters rubbing against one another in the roads. He was tired. He'd not been home since the night the young man had been abducted in Great Dover Street. It was obvious who was going to be blamed for it. And the murder of the coach driver. Ebenezer trembled as he remembered seeing the man with the corn-coloured hair who'd been searching for him. He'd been walking ever since, sleeping where he could.

He was now in a narrow lane, bounded on either side by the tall, black shapes of buildings. Over his head the night sky was a little greyer than it had been an hour before, the stars a little dimmer. He could see the river and the lights of the ships. Once he'd reached the bank, he'd look for London Bridge. Then he'd know where he was, and – when he thought it safe – be able to find his way home again.

A few yards on, the lane widened into a broad, open space, the buildings on his left replaced by what looked like hundreds of barrels, randomly stacked, reaching as far as he could see. Not more than thirty yards away, a fire was burning in a brazier. Around it, he could see the dim shapes of five or six men, talking quietly amongst themselves, their hands held out towards the warming flames. Ebenezer ducked back out of sight and moved on, his eye never leaving them.

Soon, he'd reached the river's edge, and was looking out over the dark, flowing water, at the ships lying silent at their moorings.

To his left were several huts, each one perched on stilts, about fifteen feet from the ground. He knew what they were. He'd seen treadmills before, on the waterfront in Bridgetown, in Barbados. In the other direction, some steps led down into the waters of the Thames. Beyond them, far away to the east, a thin streak of grey was visible in the velvet sky.

He heard the faint crunch of footsteps approaching from further up Mill Lane. Slipping behind the nearest stack of barrels, he crouched down and waited, his pulse racing. The footsteps were slow and heavy. Abruptly, they stopped. A minute of silence went by. Then two. Ebenezer could still hear the men round the fire, the low growl of their voices in the cold, dawn air. They'd not appeared to have heard the stranger. Ebenezer peered round the side of his barrel. A man stood not five feet from him. Over one shoulder was what appeared to be a roll of something; a carpet, or perhaps a blanket. The man was breathing heavily, his face turned towards the nightwatchmen.

Ebenezer eased back out of sight. A moment later there was a thud as something bumped into the stack of barrels behind which he crouched. The top one rocked, looked as though it was about to fall and then settled. Ebenezer expelled a lungful of air and watched the man pass by, his features masked by a scarf of sorts, a tricorn hat pulled down over his eyes. It was, he realised, the same man he'd first seen riding a horse in Borough High Street, the man he'd later seen by the stationary coach on the Dover road with a pistol in his hand. He was certain of it. The man's walk, his stature, even the clothes he wore and the scarf about his face, pointed to the fact.

The roll of blanket on the man's shoulder flopped open, the

twine that had bound it probably loosened by its collision with the barrel. Ebenezer stifled a gasp. Even in the half light of the pre-dawn, he could see the outline of two feet protruding. He watched, horrified. He knew what was about to happen, had seen it done many times on the ship that had taken him across the ocean to a life of slavery. But then, the bodies of the men, women and children thrown into the ocean by the *bakra* had still been alive.

Ebenezer felt a sickening twist in his stomach as the memory of that voyage returned, the screams of those about to die, the shouted obscenities of their executioners, the tearing away of babies from their mothers, before each was thrown to the waves.

He stayed where he was, not daring to move. The man was out of sight now, down by the river stairs. Then he heard a splash and the sound of returning footsteps. When, finally, he looked from behind the barrel, the man had gone. And so had the body. The streak of grey in the sky was wider now, and splashes of pink lit up the underside of the clouds above Limehouse.

Ebenezer's eyes swept over the wharf, searching for the man who'd been carrying the body. There was still no sign of him. A few feet away he saw a strip of material, the colour of indigo, lying on the ground. He was sure it hadn't been there a few moments before. He leaned out from behind the barrel. Couldn't quite reach it. He tried again, supporting his weight with his free hand, when he heard the tap of a boot on the cobblestones. He stumbled back behind the barrel. A moment later, a figure had stooped and picked up the scarf.

Ebenezer could hear men shouting, their voices coming from near the buildings that lined the back of the wharf. He looked in that direction. It was the watchmen he'd seen gathered round a brazier. They were standing now, and pointing in his direction. A wave of fear passed through him. He jumped to his feet and was about to run when he saw the man with the indigo scarf racing up Mill Lane, towards Tooley Street. It was him the watchmen had seen. Now they were chasing him. Were too slow. Eventually, Ebenezer knew, they'd give up and come looking to see what he'd been up to. It was time to go.

He scuttled to the edge of the wharf and jumped down onto the foreshore, the mud, still wet from the falling tide, clinging to his feet, slowing him down. He had no idea where he was going, only that he might, at any moment, be seen and caught. He felt giddy with fear. He didn't believe what others had told him about there being no slaves in England. He'd heard of men who'd run from their masters in this country and been caught. Free or not, they had still been packed off to the islands, flogged and sold back into slavery.

The thought brought back memories he'd hoped he'd buried for ever – the moment of his capture at the hands of a neighbouring tribe in his native Sierra Leone, the endless march to the coast, the living hell of the sea journey that had taken him, and the others, to the Caribbean, his life on the plantation. Many times in the years that followed, the nightmares had woken him, screaming in the night.

The sea crossing had been the worst. The Middle Passage, the crew had called it. Six weeks to cross the ocean. Six weeks in which he'd been kept below deck, tightly packed and shackled to the man next to him, forced to perform his bodily functions, to eat and to sleep where he lay. There had been three or four hundred of them, in a space for a quarter of that number. He tried to think of something else.

He reached London Bridge, turned right, and ran across it to the north bank. To the east, plumes of thick, black smoke belched into the grey sky, signalling the start of another working day. He wanted to stop and rest. But not here, not on the Bridge where he might still be discovered. Besides, there was no room, each of the recesses over the buttresses filled with sleeping bodies.

He glanced over the parapet. The Custom House quays were already alive with the rumble of the treadmills and the shouts and hurry of porters. He ran on, to the church of St Magnus the Martyr where he turned towards Billingsgate fish market. Exhausted, he stopped and looked back, searching amongst the porters and cart drivers that were there for signs of pursuit.

Soon he was lost, the streets and alleyways a maze of the unknown. He rounded a corner and glimpsed the Thames through a gap in the houses. A little further on, he came to an old stone building festooned with coloured bunting, to one side of which he could see a narrow passage. It was deserted. He thought he'd be safe enough here, at least for the time being. He lay down on the damp ground and closed his eyes. An image of a yellow-haired man dressed in a filthy blue coat with white lapels and a double column of brass buttons down the front flitted across his mind. Then the image faded.

He slept.

At the front of the building, the sign of the Black Boy and Trumpet creaked as it swung back and forward over the front door and the bunting fluttered in the cool breeze of dawn.

CHAPTER 10

John Butterworth was startled by the knock at the front door of his home in Church Square, Rye. He looked at the carriage clock on the side table. It was a little late for callers. He got up and went to the window overlooking the narrow cobbled street with the walled churchyard of St Mary the Virgin on its far side. It was still daylight, the rays of the evening sun casting a warm glow on the serried ranks of tombstones. A coach stood outside his front door. For a brief moment, Butterworth wondered how it could have arrived without him hearing it. A tall, thinly built man stood with his back to the house, his face turned towards the solid walls of the ancient church.

The sight of the man sent a shiver of fear running down Butterworth's spine. Sir William Bolt lived a mile or two outside the town, on the Winchelsea road, but he knew him principally as a friend of Lord Camperdown. He'd always been wary of both men. There was another knock at the front door, louder this time. He heard one of the maids moving about, the sound of her footsteps crossing the floor above and descending the stairs. He thought of stopping her. Nothing good would come from answering the door. He hurried to intercept her but was too late. She was already at the door. He watched it begin to swing open before retreating into his room.

'Begging your pardon, sir, but there's a gentleman what's presenting his card, sir.' The maid seemed ill at ease, her mob cap askew as if she had put it on in a hurry. She held out a silver tray on which Butterworth could see an embossed visiting card. 'He says if you is at leisure, sir, he would be pleased if you would receive him.'

'Did he say what he wanted me for?' said Butterworth, picking up the card from the tray and glancing at it.

'No, sir.'

'Very well. Ask him to wait for me in the library, will you, Mary?'

'Good evening, Sir William,' said Butterworth, entering the library a minute or so later. 'This is, sir, indeed an unexpected pleasure. How may I be of service?'

His visitor sat sprawled on one of the chairs close to the fireplace, his back to the door through which Butterworth had entered. He didn't get up.

'What was your business at the Wapping police office?' said Bolt, ignoring the niceties of convention. 'What did you have to say to them?'

'Really, sir . . .' said Butterworth, momentarily taken aback by the bluntness of the question. He recovered quickly. It would do no good to make an unnecessary enemy. He wondered how Sir William had come to hear of his meeting with Pascoe, and whether it was worth denying the accusation. 'I wanted news of Sir Henry. I had not seen him for some time and was concerned for his safety.'

'Ah, yes, Sir Henry. You were friends, of course. How silly of me.' Bolt turned in his chair and regarded his host with a sarcastic stare. 'What did you tell them?'

'It is late, sir. What is the purpose of these questions? Can they not wait for some other time?'

'What did you tell them?' Butterworth was forced to lean closer to catch the words.

'Nothing. I wanted to know about Sir Henry.'

'And what did they tell you?'

'That he was dead. No more than that.'

'Did you talk about anything else while you were there?'

'They asked me what I knew of Lord Camperdown.' Butterworth wiped the palms of his hands together. 'He knew Sir Henry held his seat from his lordship's father and he asked me about that.'

'And what, sir, did you say?'

'I merely confirmed what he already knew.'

'What about the meetings at Sir Henry's house?' said Bolt. 'Did they ask about those?'

Butterworth swallowed, unwilling to admit to te truth. 'I told them I knew nothing. I was never present and Sir Henry did not confide in me.'

'Good. I do hope, for your sake, sir, that you're telling me the truth. You would not wish me to have to return.'

He uncoiled himself from his seat and walked to the door.

'One more thing.' Bolt glanced back into the room. 'Lady Annabel Stapleton . . .'

'What of her?'

'She . . .' Bolt hesitated, and then opened the door. 'It's nothing. I should not have spoken. Say nothing of this visit to anyone.'

The next moment he had gone, leaving Butterworth staring at the door.

*

Nathaniel Morgan was in a grumbling mood. He had enough on his plate without adding to it and he didn't mind who knew it. It wasn't as if there was no one else to deal with the inquiry. But it was always the same. Every time someone went missing, who should they call upon but the Bow Street Runners. He tutted as he crossed Borough High Street and turned down Union Street. He'd been told to follow up a chance remark about an incident in Great Dover Street, Southwark.

'The magistrate, sir? Who shall I say wishes to see him?' The constable behind the desk of the Southwark police office eyed Nathaniel suspiciously.

'Just tell him it's Nathaniel Morgan of the Bow Street office.'

Five minutes later, Nathaniel was being ushered into the magistrate's private room on the first floor, where Mr Charles Stockhill waved him to a seat.

'How can I help you Mr – ah – Morgan?' said the magistrate, looking tired.

'Thank you for seeing me, sir. I shall get straight to the point. Fact is, I've been asked to find a gentleman what's gone missing. Not just any gentleman you understand, sir, but a Member of Parliament what hasn't been seen for a few days.'

'I take it, Mr Morgan, you are referring to Sir Henry Thwaite-Thomas,' said Stockhill. 'He is thought to have drowned off the Rotherhithe Marsh a few days since.'

'No, sir,' said Nathaniel. 'That weren't the name of the gentleman what I've been asked to find. The name I have is Mr John Dean, Member of Parliament for . . . dear me, I appear to have forgotten his seat. No matter. He were apparently on his way home. The journey would have taken him over the Bridge and through Southwark.'

Stockhill's face suddenly cleared. 'Yes, yes, I know who you mean now. Another Member of Parliament you say? Dear me, this is most distressing.' He shook his head in what Nathaniel took to be a sympathetic sort of way. 'Doubtless the case you are referring to is the one involving the murder of a coach driver and the disappearance of his passenger. We had no means of identifying the driver. As for his passenger, well, we just assumed he had a passenger, although he was never seen. The case is presently in the hands of my colleague, Mr Harriot, at the Wapping police office. Perhaps, sir, you should direct your inquiries there.'

Tom sat by the window of the Devil's Tavern on Wapping Wall, and stared at the blurred images of the other drinkers reflected in the glass. It was almost midnight. He'd been drinking Courage for several hours. The headache with which most days seemed to begin had at last subsided, although whether as a result of the ale or the passage of time, he wasn't sure.

He looked down at the half-finished drawing on the table before him, the paper damp with spilt beer. He studied it with a kind of idle curiosity. He'd found the scrap of paper in his pocket – it was a charcoal drawing of a group of men in a tavern – this tavern – with tankards in their hands. One of them was in the act of drinking; the others seemed to be talking amongst themselves. Tom picked it up. He knew the sketch was his. He just couldn't remember doing it.

He put it down, his gaze travelling round the taproom, taking in the low beams, the swirls of yellow tobacco smoke, the crowd of drinkers. There was something comforting about the din of shouted conversation, and the way it melded with the clatter of plates and drinking mugs. He enjoyed the escape it afforded him from the demands of his daily life and the constant guilt that he felt over Peggy's death.

He reached into his coat pocket and withdrew a flask, tipping a liberal quantity of whisky into the pot of ale in front of him. He knew most of the men in the room; had been responsible for their appearance before the magistrate at some time or another in the past. Even those he'd not had previous dealings with knew of him. He sensed the tension in the room, a reaction to his presence. He'd grown used to it.

He looked up as the front door of the tavern crashed open. A dozen men raced in, heavy staves in their hands and pistols stuck in their trouser belts. Behind them came a boy of around fourteen, dressed in the blue and white of a midshipman in the King's Navy.

'Stand fast.' The boy's high-pitched squeal rose above the sudden hush in the bar. He got no further, his voice drowned out as fists flew, men cursed and benches and tables collapsed under the weight of falling bodies.

'The press,' muttered Tom, climbing groggily to his feet, aware of the need to make himself scarce. He might have felt more secure if he'd remembered to put his protection in his pocket, but he hadn't. And, anyway, he knew it couldn't always be relied on to save people from the attentions of His Majesty's Impress Service.

He stumbled, lost his footing and fell against someone. The man turned and aimed a punch. Tom swayed out of the way, and ducked as a second swipe came towards him. His fuddled brain wasn't working as fast as he would have liked. This should not be happening.

He held up the index finger of his right hand and wagged it at the man. The fellow kept moving. It was difficult to see him clearly. Tom rubbed his eyes and tried again. It was no better, the danger of his situation gradually becoming apparent to his drink-sodden brain.

'I's Captain Pascoe . . .' The excitement of the last two or three minutes had done nothing to sober him.

The man's eyes widened a fraction and the next moment Tom felt an arm encircling his neck, pressing him to the nearest post. 'Speak when you're spoken to, mister.' The tone did not invite argument.

Tom thought he saw a creeping doubt in the man's eyes as he appeared to notice Tom's battered uniform coat and the dark blue patch on the left shoulder where once had hung the single epaulette of a master and commander in the Royal Navy. He opened his mouth as if about to say something, but changed his mind as a shrill shout from the midshipman brought proceedings to a close.

'Ahoy, the *Ajax*. Pay away, my lads. On the double.'

Tom felt himself being pushed out onto the street, sobering fast as he tried to think of some way out of his predicament. He caught sight of the midshipman staring at him, a wide grin on his pink face. Without any evidence to support his claim for exemption, he knew his chances of avoiding a spell on the lower deck of one of His Majesty's ships were slim. He looked at the crowd, their curious eyes turned towards him and the three or four men taken with him as they moved west along Wapping Wall and into Wapping Street. Tom felt his hopes rising. Ahead of them was the police office. Someone was bound to see him and order his release.

But it wasn't to be. The office came and went, followed by the bridge at Hermitage Dock and then the corner of Burr Street, around which lay his rooms. A few minutes after that they arrived at the tavern, its outside walls festooned with bunting. A sign at the door announced it as the rendezvous for those who had a mind – voluntarily or not – to join the King's Navy.

The Black Boy and Trumpet, at St Catherine's Stairs, Wapping, was in a dilapidated state of repair even by the prevailing standards of that sorry part of London. Here and there, broken window panes were stuffed with scraps of faded cloth, and a rusty chain, that had once been attached to a bell, hung uselessly beside the door. Nor was the inside any better. A yellowish, sticky brown substance covered the uneven walls, and a cloud of evil-smelling tobacco smoke rose from the pipes of half a dozen elderly men, their eyes following the newcomers as they walked past and climbed a flight of stairs to the upper floor.

Here, the midshipman stopped in front of a door and knocked. A moment later it was opened and Tom and the others were ushered into a sparsely furnished room at the centre of which stood a table scattered with papers, inkpots, some pens and a sand box. Seated behind the table was a rotund figure dressed in the uniform of a naval lieutenant, scribbling furiously.

'Four prime seamen as has volunteered for His Majesty's service, sir,' piped the young midshipman. He nodded in Tom's direction. 'Including that beauty.'

'Volunteered, Mr Stevens?' The lieutenant did not look up from what he was doing.

'If you please, sir, in a manner of speaking.'

'Very well,' sighed the lieutenant. 'Carry on.'

'Lieutenant,' barked Tom.

The lieutenant leapt from his chair and looked expectantly towards the door before he realised who'd spoken. He eyed Tom with scarcely concealed venom, before appearing to register the blue and white uniform coat Tom was wearing. The venom was replaced with a sneering half smile.

'What is it?'

'I am, sir, a river surveyor with the marine police institution,' said Tom, trying not to slur his words. He put out a hand and gripped the edge of the desk to steady himself. 'I demand, sir, to be released.'

'Perhaps.' The lieutenant's eyes swept over the dishevelled state of Tom's dress. 'You would be good enough to show me the relevant documents in proof of what you say. After that, I should be pleased to order your release.'

Tom reached for the tipstaff containing his warrant of authority, and for his letter of protection from impressment. Then he remembered he'd already tried, to find them a short while before, without success. He let his hands drop to his side. The lieutenant's smile broadened slightly and he jerked his head in the direction of a second, heavily bolted door that Tom hadn't previously noticed. A sailor stepped forward, drew back the bolts and, in a moment, Tom and the others found them- selves being pushed through to an adjoining room. He heard the door slam shut behind him.

The room was dark, the only window being shuttered and, Tom guessed, barred from the outside. It took a moment or two for him to become accustomed to the gloom and the sour reek of unwashed bodies. Only then did he see that there were several men already there.

'Will it be Captain Pascoe, sir?' Tom peered through the darkness at a face that was vaguely familiar. 'It's me, sir, Mathew Stemp. We was shipmates on the *Minot*.'

'Why, Stemp, yes, I remember you,' said Tom, doing his best to recall any detail, however small, of the man's existence.

'Begging your pardon, sir, but you ain't been taken by the press, has you?'

'It looks that way, Stemp,' said Tom, wishing the fellow would go away and leave him to think.

'That ain't right, sir. Ain't you told 'em who you are, sir? It's different with the rest of us.'

'And you?' said Tom. 'What were you doing in London? Last I heard, the *Minot* was lying at Portsmouth.'

Stemp hesitated. 'Aye, so she is, sir, but it were like this . . .'

'You deserted,' said Tom. He looked round at the others. 'What about the rest of you? You deserters, too?'

The men shuffled their feet and avoided his gaze. Then he caught sight of a man sitting alone in the far corner of the room.

'You, sir.' Tom walked over. 'What's your name?'

'Me, master?' The man's head remained bowed, his eyes turned to the floor. 'They call me Ebenezer.'

'What are you saying? Ebenezer isn't your real name?'

'No, master. It is the name my master give me.'

'You're a slave?'

'Yes.' Ebenezer looked up for the first time and met Tom's

stare, a hint of defiance in his voice. 'But no more. I run from the master. No slaves in England, master.'

Tom tried to clear his head. There was something about the negro that was familiar. He was clearly frightened but it seemed as though his fear was of Tom himself, rather than the fact of his captivity. 'How long have you been in this room?'

'Since this morning. I were sleeping outside when the *bakra* catch me.'

Tom had heard the term for the white man before. He looked round at the others. 'Any of you men been here longer than a day?'

A series of muttered replies suggested no one had been in the room longer than a few hours. Tom went to the window and peered through a crack in the shutters. It was unlikely the press would wait much longer before taking them all to the naval tender anchored off Deptford Creek. If they succeeded in getting them that far, there would be little hope of escape. He looked back into the room. The men were watching him, expecting him to say something.

'You all know the Articles of War,' he said. 'You all know what's likely to happen when the Navy gets you back on board. You don't need me to remind you.'

There was absolute silence. The men's faces were ashen.

'It doesn't have to be like that, though,' Tom went on. 'I've no intention of serving before the mast again. Not this way. I'll be damned if I'm going to let the Navy take me.'

'That's easy enough for you, sir, on account of you being an officer an' all,' said Stemp. 'There ain't nothing the rest of us can do.'

'Together we can do something,' said Tom. 'But I need to know who's with me, who I can count on to help escape from this. Are you all with me?'

No one answered, their heads turned away, avoiding his questioning gaze. It was as though they had already resigned themselves to their fate. Without their help, his own chances of escape were hopeless.

CHAPTER 11

At the Wapping police office, Sam Hart wiped his mouth with his sleeve and stared at the floor of the magistrate's office. He wasn't used to talking to Mr Harriot, usually leaving such things to Tom. But this time there was no avoiding it.

'I ain't seen Master Pascoe since we finished the late-turn patrol yesterday,' he said. 'He told me he were going for a drink at the Devil's, along the way. I were there just now and the land-lord told me the press came in around midnight. He reckons they took Mr Pascoe. Said the midshipman in charge seemed to know he were there, your honour.'

'If you're right,' said Harriot, 'they will have taken him to one of several rendezvous houses. Fortunately, there aren't too many of them within a mile of here. Only the City of Rotterdam along the way and the Black Boy and Trumpet by St Catherine's Stairs. I reckon the Black Boy's got to be the favourite.'

'With respect, sir, it don't seem to matter, none, which rendezvous he's at,' said Sam. 'If the Navy has got him, there ain't nothing no one can do.'

'Whether we can do anything or not largely depends on the wording of the warrant, and the actions of the press gang,' said the magistrate. 'Didn't you tell me there was a fight when Mr Pascoe was taken? You said, I think, that Mr Pascoe was struck?'

'Aye, sir, that's what the landlord told me.'

'And he also told you the gang was under the command of a midshipman?'

'Aye, that he did,' said Sam, wondering where the questions were leading.

'I had a young officer in here the other day,' said Harriot, his voice quiet, as though thinking aloud. 'Dashed if I remember his name but it don't signify. The fellow asked me to back an impress warrant. I'm as certain as I can be that the rank of the officer named on the warrant was a lieutenant . . .'

Harriot's voice faded and he stared at his desk as if trying to remember some detail. 'If that's the case, we might have something . . .'

'Sir?' said Sam.

'I'm sorry, Hart. I'm not making any sense, am I? Warrants can only be executed by the officer named on them. I'm quite sure the warrant presented to me for endorsement had the name of a lieutenant on it. But you tell me that it was executed by a midshipman. If so, it was not valid, and since violence was apparently used to capture Mr Pascoe, those involved are liable to arrest and prosecution for assault.'

Harriot drummed his fingers on his desk and looked up at Sam. 'I want every available man in the constables' waiting room, on the double.'

Tom woke to the sound of a metallic scraping. For a second or two he couldn't remember where he was. He rolled over onto his side and looked about him. The dawn's half-light was seeping through the cracks in the window shutters.

Slowly the memory of what had happened returned to him. He heard the rattling of bolts being drawn back and, propping himself up on one elbow, looked towards the door.

'Six bells, middle watch, me beauties. Show a leg there.' The door flew open to admit a short, barrel-chested man with a pockmarked face and a caste in his left eye. He was carrying a rope's end in one hand that he twirled as he walked.

'Rise and shine. Victuals if you's quick. Bugger all, if you ain't. We's on our way in fifteen minutes.'

Tom glanced through a crack in the window shutter. Six bells in the middle watch – three o'clock in the morning. The Navy was clearly anxious to get them to the tender before too many people were awake. The smaller the audience, the less chance of trouble.

He had hoped they'd wait for a few more pressed men before taking them to the tender. It would have improved his, and the other men's, chances of escaping – always supposing the men changed their minds and decided to help him. As it was, it would be difficult.

Some words dropped into his consciousness, something somebody had said to him.

'. . . *That ain't right, sir. Ain't you told 'em who you are, sir?'* It was his former shipmate, Stemp, who had been speaking. Tom dismissed the comments. They had merely been the flattering remarks of a former shipmate and of no relevance now.

The words refused to go, creeping back to the forefront of his mind, an obvious comment for a seaman from the lower deck to make. King's officers were not pressed. If that were the case, why had he been taken? True, he'd been drunk. It was also true he presented every appearance of being a seafaring man – ideal fodder for the press. And to make matters worse, he'd been unable to produce any evidence of his status, or even a letter of protection.

He looked down at the shabby state of his uniform coat and smiled in spite of himself. He hardly presented a passable impression of an officer. Still, it was as though the press had been looking for him. He recalled what Shamus O'Connor, one of the two men who had attacked him in Burr Street, had said about being paid to capture him and put him on board a ship in the Pool of London. Had the same thing happened again? Had the Navy been suborned to the point where they would actively seek an officer and ship him before the mast? Perhaps not the Navy, but a junior officer, a midshipman with barely a penny to his name? Tom recalled the satisfied smirk on the midshipman's face outside the Devil's Tavern, on Wapping Wall. It was more than possible that he'd been paid to press Tom. But by whom?

'On yer feet.' The man with the rope's end had re-entered the room.

It was raining hard when Tom and the others reached the front door of the Black Boy and Trumpet and were herded down St Catherine's Stairs, into a waiting cutter. Apart from the pressed men, Tom counted ten seamen – six members of the press gang and a further four crew. Fourteen sailors to look after nine pressed men. He might, thought Tom, have stood a chance of escaping if they had been willing to join him. They filed silently into the waiting cutter.

'Cast off fore and aft,' barked a voice at the stern. 'Drop all. Give way together.'

Tom felt the familiar surge as the cutter moved away from the stairs. For a long moment he stared down the reach, towards Wapping, his view obscured by the curtain of drifting rain. It seemed to him they were alone on the tideway amongst the sleeping hulks of the ships. It was too early for the port to be awake. Perhaps in an hour or so, but not now. He glanced at the men sitting in the bottom boards around him. He knew he could not rely on them for help if the opportunity for escape presented itself.

Tom wasn't entirely surprised. They were seamen, with little in common with landsmen. Their speech, their dress, their lives, even their rolling gait, marked them out as sailors, wholly at odds with the mores and practices of those ashore. If they chose to desert, their lives would be spent looking over their shoulders, in fear of the pursuing press, and facing a life of poverty and isolation. He'd warned them of the penalty for those caught deserting. The Articles of War left little to the imagination but it hadn't moved them.

He caught sight of the negro. His was a different position. He was not yet in the Navy. Were he to escape there could be no repercussions. And yet . . . Somehow Tom doubted the man would have the will to become involved in a fight. Years of violent suppression would have seen to that.

Hermitage Dock loomed into view. Further downstream, on the Rotherhithe shore, he was able to make out the white spire of St Mary's Church. It stood directly opposite the police office. His hopes rose. Perhaps, this time, he'd be seen. Perhaps the waterside galley would put out to investigate. Perhaps . . . Tom's shoulders slumped. There was little about the cutter to raise anyone's suspicion. He closed his eyes, his fingers searching the pockets of his uniform coat for his whisky flask. It wasn't there.

The front door of the Black Boy and Trumpet had never been strong; not since an especially rowdy group of coal-heavers had seen fit to settle their differences there, one Saturday night, a year or two back. It was certainly no match for the massive shoulder of Waterman Constable John Kemp, who now stepped through the shattered remains of the door, closely followed by Sam Hart and a dozen other constables.

Harriot's briefing to Sam, John Kemp and the others, thirty minutes earlier, had left nothing to chance. Tom Pascoe was to be found and returned to the police office without delay. If, as was likely, he was found in the custody of His Majesty's Impress Service, he was to be released on his authority as a magistrate. He had signed and issued search warrants allowing any constable attached to the Wapping police office to enter and search, by force if necessary, the two rendezvous houses most likely to be keeping Tom.

The Black Boy and Trumpet was the first of the two houses to be entered.

'This way, Kemp,' said Sam, waving in the direction of the stairs with the heavy stick he was carrying. It wasn't part of his normal equipment but then he wasn't on normal duties, either. 'The rest of you, search the downstairs.'

He and Kemp raced up the steps just as a door at the top swung open and a man in the uniform of a lieutenant in the Royal Navy appeared, rubbing sleep from his eyes. Kemp didn't stop.

Scooping the man up with one arm he carried him back into the room and dumped him on a chair, just as two other seamen in the room reached for their staves.

'Police!' shouted Sam, stepping past the lieutenant, his fists balled and ready to strike. 'Sit down, and there won't be any trouble.'

The men looked from Sam to Kemp to the lieutenant and back again. The officer was shaking his head.

'What's the meaning of this?' he said. 'I demand an explanation. You may depend upon it that you'll hear more of this.'

'We are here under the authority of a magistrate's warrant and have reason to believe you've taken a man in breach of the protection offered to him under the law,' said Sam.

'What are you talking about?' said the lieutenant. 'No pressed man has produced a protection to me.'

Sam swallowed. If the experience of Tom's drinking over the past few months was anything to go by, it was doubtful his friend would have remembered to carry his tipstaff, still less have with him his certification of protection from the press. 'You don't recall Captain Thomas Pascoe? To be sure he wears the King's uniform.'

'No, I—' The lieutenant stopped in mid sentence and his jaw dropped open. 'That is, I may have seen—'

Sam grabbed the man by his collar and pulled him to his feet. 'Where is he, damn you?'

'They left about a quarter of an hour ago. The cutter was at St Catherine's Stairs. I knew nothing . . .'

Sam and Kemp were already running down the stairs and out through the front door. At the river stairs, there was no trace of the Navy cutter. Running back along the narrow alley, they turned towards the police office. Behind him, Sam could hear the other constables following.

Reaching the police pontoon, the men tumbled into a couple of galleys. Sam looked out over the water. He could see little in the half-light of early morning.

CHAPTER 12

Harriot glanced at his pocket watch. Nearly four in the morning. He picked up the court list from his desk and ran his eye over the names of the defendants and the charges they faced. It was unusually long. The expected cases of drunkenness, breaches of the peace and petty larceny had been added to by several committals that were bound to take more time than he could afford. Especially now, when his mind was on Tom's disappearance. He'd given the strictest instructions that he was to be informed the moment there was any news of his missing river surveyor. He looked up as someone knocked. A waterside constable stepped in.

'Begging your pardon, your worship.' The officer knuckled his forehead. 'There's two gentlemen what wishes to see you.'

'At this hour? Who are they? What do they want?' said the magistrate, irritated at the disruption to his morning.

'A Mr Watson, sir. Says he's the serjeant-at-arms at the 'Ouse of Commons, sir. He's with a Mr Nathaniel Morgan what says he's from Bow Street, sir. Didn't say nothing about what they wanted. Shall I send them up, sir?'

'Good morning, gentlemen. How can I be of service?' Harriot rose from his chair and went to greet his visitors.

'I understand, sir,' said William Watson, declining, with a

shake of his head, the magistrate's offer of a coffee, 'that your officers are investigating an incident across the river, in which a coach driver was murdered and his passenger abducted.'

'Yes,' said Harriot. 'We were asked to help by my Southwark colleague, and were happy to do so.'

'And your officers are also investigating the circumstances surrounding the death of Sir Henry Thwaite-Thomas, Member of Parliament for the seat of Gatton.'

'Aye,' said Harriot, frowning. 'Pray, where is this leading, sir?'

'I will, sir, explain in a moment,' said Watson. 'May I know what progress you are making in these inquiries?'

'The inquiry is in the hands of Mr Pascoe, one of my river surveyors. He has identified a number of potential witnesses in relation to the death of Sir Henry and will be interviewing them in due course. The second inquiry is in its earliest stages and there is nothing of consequence to report. Why, sir, the interest?'

'We now believe that the person abducted from the coach in Southwark is also a Member of Parliament.'

'And you suspect that the two cases might be connected?' asked Harriot, raising an eyebrow.

'There ain't no evidence of that, sir,' said Nathaniel Morgan. 'Leastways, not as I'm aware of.'

'But there is a reason, nevertheless, for your visit?'

'Yes, sir, there is,' said the serjeant-at-arms. 'The disappearance of this MP, coupled with the apparent murder of another, is a matter of considerable concern to the Administration. I am instructed to discover all available information concerning the investigation and report my findings to the secretary of state for the Home Department.'

Harriot sat back in his chair and inserted his thumbs into the pockets of his waistcoat, his thoughts straying to the present whereabouts of the river surveyor in charge of investigating both cases.

'I regret Mr Pascoe is currently deployed elsewhere,' he said. 'As soon as he becomes available, I shall instruct him to attend upon you.'

The weather had worsened. The sky over the Isle of Dogs was now a dark mass of cloud in a grey sky, a strong south-westerly wind driving the torrential rain into the faces of the men in the Navy cutter. On either side of them, what appeared to be an endless tier of shipping strained at anchors and mooring lines as the howling wind whipped the tideway into a carpet of white and grey.

Tom peered towards the Rotherhithe shore, at the bleak outlines of half a dozen manufactories, their tall chimneys jutting into the swirling clouds, asleep like much of the rest of the port, the silence disturbed by the occasional snap and bellow of loose canvas, flapping against the yards of ships. At the water's edge barges were drawn up on the hard awaiting the attention of the boat builders or the scrap yard. A few more rode at their mooring lines.

A sudden blink of light flashed close under one of the barges. Tom stared at it. It had looked like a signal lamp. He turned his head in the other direction, across to the Isle of Dogs, its flat acres stretching down the length of Limehouse Reach. An answering light flashed twice from behind the solid outline of a lighter. Tom's pulse quickened. Another ten minutes and the Navy cutter would be amongst the King's fleet, off Deptford Creek. Then it would be too late to think of rescue. He risked a small turn of his head to his right, to where he'd seen the first light. A dark shape, like that of a rowing boat, had emerged from the gloom of the shoreline. It was travelling at speed. Frothing white water tumbled away on either side of its bows, streaking down the length of its hull. If it held its present course, it would intersect with them in less than a minute.

From the Isle of Dogs, a long, thin object had detached itself from a ship's hull and was moving south, parallel to them. He could see the splashes of its sweeps entering the water. He thought he recognised the sleek lines of a rowing galley. It turned towards them, its bows lifting slightly as it accelerated, white, broiling water thrown high and wide.

On the Navy cutter, the seamen continued with their murmured conversations. Tom glanced at the man on the tiller and the young midshipman next to him. They, too, were talking and appeared to have seen nothing. Three hundred yards ahead he could see the bend in the river as it swept round into Greenwich Reach. Three hundred yards to their journey's end. The dark mass of Observatory Hill rose into the night above the village of Greenwich.

A sudden startled cry from the stern of the cutter made him jump. It was the midshipman. He was pointing over the starboard beam, his eyes widening in panic. Tom followed his gaze. The galley he'd seen approaching from the Rotherhithe shore was now less than thirty yards away and closing fast.

'This is the police. In the name of the King, heave to.' Tom recognised Sam's voice booming across the silent river.

He heard the rasp of steel as the sailors drew their knives and cutlasses and prepared to fight.

'Ahoy the cutter.' It was Sam again. 'I say again, heave to. This is the police.'

'Stand clear, sir,' shouted the midshipman. 'We are on the King's business and have men lawfully taken for duty in His Majesty's Navy.'

Tom looked at the seamen and his fellow captives in the cutter, their eyes focused on the approaching galleys. Ten, perhaps twenty seconds separated them from a collision. If he failed to act, men would die. He leapt to his feet and barged into the nearest seaman, toppling him into the river. Before anyone could react, a second man had been shoved overboard. He looked up to see a musket being levelled at his head. Shoving the barrel to one side, he smashed his fist into the gunman's mouth and watched him drop to the bottom boards, blood spurting from his mouth and nose.

'Behind you, master.' Tom ducked to one side and felt the rush of wind as something passed close to his head. He turned to see one of the seamen dropping to his knees, a cutlass still gripped in one hand. Behind him, the big negro was wiping his fist on a filth-stained jerkin.

'He done nearly take your head clean off, master,' said Ebenezer.

'Thankee . . . Watch out,' yelled Tom, as another seamen swung a heavy stick at the negro's head. The warning was too late. The cudgel caught him a glancing blow on the back of the skull and he fell forward. Tom lunged at the attacking seaman, aiming a punch to his jaw just as the splintering crash of a collision sent everyone sprawling. Another moment and the second of the two police galleys had sheared alongside, the pistols of its crew levelled at the still struggling seamen.

'Mighty glad to see you, Sam,' said Tom, as his friend stepped into the cutter.

'Happy to have been of assistance, sir,' said a grinning Sam. 'Ain't enjoyed meself so much in months.'

'You, sir.' A high-pitched voice interrupted them. Tom looked up to see the midshipman pointing at Sam. 'You, sir, and the rest of your motley friends are to consider yourselves under arrest. I demand—'

He stopped short, silenced by a withering stare from Tom.

'I think, sir,' said Tom, leaning towards the boy, 'the less you say on the subject, the better. Let me see your warrant of authority to press.'

'Damn your impudence, sir. You've no right—'

'Your warrant, sir,' repeated Tom, holding out his hand.

The boy pulled the heavily creased document from his pocket and handed it over. Tom quickly scanned it.

'This warrant authorises a lieutenant to perform the duties of impressment on land or sea. Forgive me, but from your uniform you do not appear to have reached that exalted rank.'

'What's that to you, you insolent fellow?' The midshipman was looking decidedly uncertain of his ground.

'I suggest you study the law in relation to impressment with a deal more care than appears apparent. Perhaps you would prefer to discuss the matter before a magistrate?'

There was no reply.

The sound of a groan made Tom look down. Ebenezer had sat up and was prodding his skull where he'd been struck. Tom squatted down and examined the wound. It didn't appear too serious. He helped the negro onto one of the thwarts.

'None of you,' he said, looking at the other pressed men, 'is yet in the lawful custody of His Majesty's Navy. If any of you so choose, you may leave with me and be taken ashore.'

No one moved. No one spoke. There was, instead, a look of resignation in their eyes. Whatever the future paths of their lives, it was inextricably bound up with the Navy. They would not leave now.

'What about you, Stemp?' said Tom, turning to his former shipmate. 'You coming with me or taking your chances with the Navy?'

'If it's all the same to you, sir, I'll stay. Never did know what to do with meself ashore.'

Tom nodded. He followed Sam and Ebenezer into one of the waiting police galleys. In less than a minute they were heading up the reach towards Limehouse, and a still distant Wapping police office.

'Them swabs deserved a flogging for what they done to you, your honour,' said an indignant Sam, after a minute or so of silence.

'They were only doing their job, Sam. The pity is that the nation wants the Navy's protection but doesn't want to do anything to help. I've seen it from both ends. Pressing men ain't pretty but there's no other way of getting the men we need to fight the country's wars.'

'Strange that the lads we just left didn't want to come with us.'

PATRICK EASTER

'It's not so strange,' said Tom. 'You're to consider they are all prime seamen and know of no other life. They deserted, it's true, but they would have gone back of their own accord in a month or two. Living amongst people who don't know you or understand you is a powerful reason to go back amongst your shipmates.'

'If you say so, sir,' said Sam, sounding unconvinced.

'What's more to the point,' said Tom, 'is why the press should have come into the Devil's Tavern in the first place.'

'I thought that was how the press operated, sir.'

'Yes, it is,' said Tom. 'But in this case, I think they were specifically looking for me. Why risk pressing an officer unless you've got a good reason to? I caught that imp of a midshipman staring at me and grinning like some overstuffed cat. He'd found the person he'd been looking for, and no mistake.'

'What are you going to do about it, sir?'

'About the Navy? Nothing,' said Tom. 'I'm more interested in who set it up in the first place. It was probably the same villain as set Shamus O'Connor and his friend on to me. That's the cully I want.'

'What about your friend, sir?' said Sam, jutting his head in Ebenezer's direction. 'What shall we do with him?'

'Friend? I've never seen the fellow before yesterday.'

Sam coloured and looked down in embarrassment. 'Don't you remember, sir? He were in Rosemary Lane. You was with him. On the pavement, like.'

'Was I?' said Tom. 'Come to think of it, I did reckon he looked a mite familiar. I must have had a skinful of ale that day, Sam, and no mistake.'

'There's something else, sir,' said Sam, dropping his voice to

100

just above a whisper. 'The nigger what were seen close to the coach in Great Dover Street?'

'What of it?'

'This cully fits the description. It's the fellow what you said you went looking for in that house.'

'I do believe you've the right of it,' said Tom, studying the seated figure of Ebenezer in the prow of the galley. 'We'll talk to him when we get back to Wapping.'

CHAPTER 13

André Dubois made his way across London Bridge towards the City, turning right as he reached the north bank. A minute or so later, he arrived at the Custom House quay and approached a broad flight of stairs leading to the water's edge, where half a dozen wherrymen stood waiting for business.

'Westminster, if you please,' said Dubois, approaching a bald, leather-faced man with a brass ring in his left ear.

'Awight, cock. Thomas Henry Wilkins at your service. Whereabouts in Westminster you after, then?'

Dubois was momentarily confused by the question. Although he'd been to London before, he couldn't claim to be familiar with it and, as far as he was concerned, his directions to the waterman should have been enough to get him where he wanted to go. A mild sense of panic swept through him as he realised he would have to give away more information than he was comfortable with.

He tried again.

'The nearest landing stage to your Parliament.'

'That'll be Palace Yard Stairs, me old cock. Get you there in no time.'

Dubois climbed into the stern of the boat and sat down as the waterman pushed the skiff out into the tide and eased his way through the heavy press of vessels. Dubois didn't like crowded spaces and he especially didn't like small boats in crowded spaces. He'd always worked on the principle that one should have an escape route available. But here, hemmed in on all sides by drifting lighters, yawls, luggers and a whole fleet of smaller boats, there was no escape. If anything happened, he'd have to trust the man with the oars.

'Always the same, this time of the year, cock,' said the waterman, appearing to read Dubois's mind. 'Bit clearer on the south side. Soon as we get there, we'll be on our way, don't you fret.'

Dubois was conscious of a growing sense of apprehension as the skiff approached Hays Wharf and the stairs from which he'd dumped the body of the young man a little while before. He knew enough about dead bodies to know that this one might not yet have sunk.

He saw an object floating in the water, less than thirty yards away. It was impossible to see what it was at this distance, its appearance no more than a rounded hump just breaking the surface of the river. It was caught up by a mooring line, and surrounded by a jumble of other rubbish. Dubois stared at it as they drew closer. He still couldn't be sure it was what he thought it was. He glanced at the waterman. The man had his back to it and hadn't yet seen the half submerged dome. He was too busy navigating the skiff past a brig presently dropping down through the Pool. Dubois turned back to the hump. It had gone, apparently swept away by the tide.

He stared at the spot where it had been and then at the surrounding water. Whoever or whatever it was that he'd seen was no longer in sight. He began to wonder if he'd been worrying unnecessarily; if he'd mistaken a floating log for a man's body. It was an easy assumption to make. Bodies always floated face down with only the curve of their backs breaking the surface in the same way as length of timber. The rest of a human's body – head, arms and legs – would hang down out of sight. Dubois's fast-beating pulse began to slow. The Thames was full of flotsam.

As if in confirmation, a barrel floated past, a tangle of rope and netting and canvas attached to it. Then he noticed a rowing galley, close to the Southwark shore, about a hundred yards south of Hays Wharf. It was travelling very much faster than he would have expected. His heartbeat quickened. He raised a hand and shielded his eyes against the sun. He didn't like the look of it at all. He heard the sharp bark of an order and the galley seemed to leap forward.

'*Mon Dieu*,' he whispered. 'It's Pascoe.'

Tom slowed the police galley and dropped astern a brig making its way downriver. He looked towards London Bridge. It always surprised him there were not more collisions, given the number of vessels on the water. One sculler in particular appeared in a great hurry. He watched for a moment. There was a passenger in the stern, his hat pulled down over his eyes, his shoulders hunched. No doubt the fellow was late for something. Tom grunted and turned away, steering the galley towards the Middlesex bank, before heading down to the police pontoon.

He wasn't looking forward to the next half-hour. The interview with Harriot was bound to be an uncomfortable one. The magistrate was certain to know that his drinking had been a major contributory factor in his capture by the press. Tom could blame no one but himself for what had happened.

'Ah, Mr Pascoe. Come in, come in,' said Harriot, putting down his pen and looking at him over the rim of his spectacles. 'You had us all worried. But I'm pleased to see you're quite well and with us again.'

'Thankee, sir,' said Tom, cautiously.

'There are, however, a number of matters of concern that I need to talk to you about.' Harriot paused and brought the tips of his fingers together. 'I understand that you were caught by the press in the Devil's Tavern, the worse for drink.'

Tom opened his mouth to speak but was silenced by the magistrate's raised hand.

'I regret, Mr Pascoe,' said Harriot, 'that this is not the first occasion on which you've let yourself down in this fashion. I'm well aware of the immediate cause of your drinking and have every sympathy for your loss. But I cannot allow the situation to continue to the detriment of your duties. You therefore face a choice. Your drinking must stop immediately, or I shall have no alternative but to dismiss you from this organisation.'

It was no more than Tom had expected. There was only one decision he could sensibly make. What troubled him was whether he had the mental strength to stick with the decision to stop. He had to try.

'It'll not happen again, sir.'

'I very much hope not, Mr Pascoe. I don't want to lose you.'

A moment of awkward silence ensued. Then Harriot said, 'I've had a visit from Mr Watson . . .'

'The serjeant-at-arms at the Commons?'

'That's the man. He was with a fellow whom I believe you know. Mr Nathanial Morgan of the Bow Street Runners. It appears that the passenger abducted from the coach in Great Dover Street may have been a Member of Parliament and Mr Watson said he would like a further meeting with you to talk about it.'

'I'd be happy to. I think we may have found a witness who was in the vicinity shortly after the murder. Sam Hart is with him now.'

'Excellent!' Harriot glanced down at his desk and picked up a sheet of paper. 'That ties in nicely with some information I've just received. It seems that a nightwatchman employed on Hays Wharf saw what appeared to be the body of a man being thrown into the Thames.'

'Was he able to describe the suspect?'

'Up to a point. The fellow claims to have seen the suspect earlier in the evening. He told one of the Southwark constables that the person he saw throwing the body into the Thames is the same man he saw in Great Dover Street at about the time the coach was stopped.'

'As I recollect, sir, the only person seen there was a negro,' said Tom. 'Is the witness claiming the person he saw carrying a body was black?'

'Yes, it appears so. I have the details here,' said Harriot, handing over the sheet of paper. 'Apparently, the witness was on his way to work when he saw the stationary coach by the side of the road. He says there was a negro man crouched over the body of the dead driver, but he ran off when the witness and several other men arrived on the scene. Shortly before dawn he saw what he claims was the same man carrying a body down to the Thames. When challenged, the man made off.'

Tom looked at the paper in his hand and read the few jotted notes in Harriot's spidery writing. He walked over to the fireplace and stood looking down into the flames, a puzzled frown creasing his brow. The description fitted Ebenezer, yet something was not quite right.

'He saw this man by the river stairs?'

'That's what he said to the constable.'

'And he was carrying the body?'

'Apparently so.'

'The same man he earlier saw with the dead driver?'

'Yes.'

'But that's the fellow I was telling you about. He's in the cells talking to Sam Hart.'

'What! Here?' said Harriot.

'Yes, he'd been pressed by the same gang as got me. He decided to take his chances with me rather than the Navy.'

'Has he admitted anything?'

'No, but then I don't expect him to. If the witness saw my man standing over the dead driver, when do you suppose he would have had the opportunity to abduct the missing passenger? And even if it is claimed he did so earlier, why would he return to the scene and risk detection?'

'He may have left some incriminating evidence behind and returned to retrieve it,' said Harriot.

'It's possible, sir, but hardly likely. He would've had to find somewhere to hide his prisoner and return to the coach before anyone noticed the body of the driver.'

'Yes, I take your point, Mr Pascoe, but the fellow is again seen dumping a body in the Thames.'

'I doubt the witness was able to see everything he claims to have done,' said Tom. 'According to those I spoke to in Great Dover Street, a negro was seen on the coach but it was dark at the time and he would have been viewed at a distance. Almost certainly from too far away to be able to make a positive identification. The same witness then claims to have seen the same negro on Hays Wharf. That, again, was during the hours of darkness and I doubt he could be certain it was the same man as he'd seen on the coach. He may have seen *someone* carrying something. But whether he would be able to recognise that person again is less clear.'

'You don't believe he was there at all?'

'I didn't say that, sir. I think he might well have been present at both locations but I doubt he's guilty of murder. The evidence doesn't support it. Not yet anyway.'

'Best you see the witness, Mr Pascoe. Talk to him. The light may have been better than you suppose and he may have seen more than you give him credit for.' Harriot paused. Then, 'Why d'you think the negro ran, if he had nothing to hide?'

'For two reasons,' said Tom. 'In the first place he's a negro, the butt of the same taunts and beatings to which all of his race are subjected in this country. In the second place he's a runaway slave and would, doubtless, have considered himself at risk of capture and return to his owner.'

'Yes, I suppose you could be right. So what now?'

'I think the negro might still have something of interest to say to us. And since it looks as though I shall be busy at the Palace of

Westminster, I'll arrange for Sam Hart to see the witness, and then speak to our negro friend.'

'Very well,' said Harriot, sucking on his pipe, his hands laced behind his neck. 'By the by, what's happening about Sir Henry's case?'

'I travel to Rye tomorrow morning,' said Tom. 'Sir Henry has a sister who lived with him and I'm hoping she may be able to help. She may be able to give me the names of the men Sir Henry met in the days and weeks before his death. Someone in that group will know something worth knowing.'

CHAPTER 14

Tom woke several times that night and found himself thinking about Ebenezer. It didn't seem possible he was guilty of murder. The marks he had seen about the coach driver's neck suggested another man's involvement. The pattern of bruising pointed to the use of a knotted cord, and he knew of only one man who used that method.

If he was right – and he was sure he was – it meant that not only was André Dubois back in the country, but that he was up to his old tricks. Tom stared at the ceiling. Thoughts of Dubois always brought back painful memories of what had happened to Peggy. Was he back in England? It didn't seem possible. Why would he come back? He'd been fortunate to escape last time and would not do so again; not if Tom had any say in the matter.

He drifted off to sleep. For how long, he didn't know. Suddenly his eyes snapped open, thoughts of Dubois coursing through his head as if they had never stopped. If the Frenchman was back, there had to be a good reason. The man was a soldier, subject to military discipline; the decision to come would not have been his own. And if he'd been sent, then for what reason, exactly? Tom's eyelids drooped. He would think about it in the morning.

Daylight was streaming in through the window of his room

by the time Tom awoke again. He threw back the blanket and got up. He was due to catch the coach to Rye in a little over an hour. He wasn't looking forward to it, especially his meeting with the Lady Annabel. He'd always found it difficult to relax in female company, remaining stiff and largely tongue-tied in their company. Even with Peggy, he had initially found conversation difficult.

The diligence from London approached the George Hotel in Rye with a loud blare of its horn and clattered to a halt amidst a great deal of shouting and hallooing. Tom waited for his fellow passengers to alight before climbing, stiff-limbed, down the steps onto the town's main street. He looked up at the handsome stone frontage of the hotel and pushed his way through the small army of porters and ostlers to the front entrance.

'Welcome, sir, to the George,' said a jolly-looking man, standing in the hotel portico.

'Thankee, Master Landlord.' Tom had seen him as soon as the coach came to a halt and had noticed the searching gaze with which he'd appraised each of the passengers. It had seemed more than professional interest in a guest, almost as though he was expecting the arrival of someone specific. Tom dismissed the thought as the overactive imagination of a cynical mind – part of the price of being a policeman. 'I shall need a bed for a night or two.'

'Very good, sir. A bed you shall have,' said the landlord, gesturing to one of the porters to bring Tom's bag. Then he led the way along a short, narrow passage, through the taproom, and up a flight of stairs. Reaching a door on the second floor, he flung it open and ushered Tom inside. 'I trust this room will be to your liking. We changed the sheets only last week, sir, and the bugs ain't too bad, neither. Here on business, are we?'

Tom was again conscious of a feeling that the man was not all he seemed. The question was, in itself, innocent enough, the sort of casual enquiry that any landlord might make. And yet . . .

'Just visiting,' he said.

He waited for the man to leave. Alone at last, he took out his pocket watch. Nearly seven o'clock. He would have to leave his visit to the Lady Annabel until the morning. He crossed to the window. The diligence had gone. And with it, the welcoming crowd, its place taken by a few boys playing outside the school that stood opposite.

He thought of John Butterworth. There was just time to call on him before darkness made the journey difficult. After asking for directions, he climbed the short incline behind the hotel. At the top, he skirted a low perimeter wall surrounding the church of St Mary the Virgin, into a narrow, cobbled street, bounded on one side by a terrace of houses. The man he'd come to see lived in the fourth building along.

'Mr Butterworth ain't at home, sir,' said a uniformed maid, in answer to Tom's enquiry.

'Thank you, miss,' said Tom, walking past her towards the room he'd seen her emerge from, 'I have but little time to spare.'

'What the devil . . .?' Butterworth's face paled and he started to his feet as Tom entered.

'I beg pardon, sir,' said Tom. 'But time is short and I have a few questions that I need answers to.'

'I cannot see you, sir. It's . . . it's impossible,' stuttered Butter-worth.

'Has something happened?' Tom shot him a curious look.

Butterworth didn't answer. He bit his lip and twisted his fingers in upon themselves. Once or twice he opened his mouth as though to speak, and then changed his mind.

'Is there something you know about the death of Sir Henry you've not told me?'

Butterworth turned away and stared out of the window, his face hidden from Tom's view. The moment passed, and when he again looked at his visitor, he had regained much of his compo-sure.

'The fact is I'm anxious that no scandal should visit itself on our small community,' he said. 'I know no more about the death of my particular friend than I've already told you.'

Tom recognised the resolve in the other man's eyes. A point had been reached, a decision made. There was little to be gained from continuing to question him. He decided to leave things as they were. He would come back to them another time.

Shortly before ten the following morning Tom stood at the end of the high street overlooking the flatlands of Romney Marsh, several hundred feet below him. In the distance, he could make out a flock of seagulls following in the wake of a lug boat gliding through the silver thread of the River Rother, to the sea. Behind him, where the high street ended and a lane leading down to the marsh began, was a large, whitewashed house, the home of the Lady Annabel.

He had meant to delay his visit to the sister of the late Sir

Henry until later in the morning, and would have done so but for his concerns about what Butterworth may have omitted to tell him the previous evening. Tom approached the front door.

'Can I help you, sir?' A maid was squinting up at him.

He was ushered into a large, airy room on the first floor, its windows looking out over the East Cliff to the marshes beyond. At the far end of the room, a woman rose to greet him.

'I understand, sir, that you wish to see me.' Lady Annabel smiled and waved Tom to a chair.

'Indeed, madam.' Tom bowed, wishing he'd dressed with greater care. Years of exposure to the elements had taken its toll on the old uniform coat and breeches he was wearing. And what the weather had failed to achieve, the muck and grime of the Thames had certainly made up for. He would, he thought, take the first opportunity to buy himself some new clothes. He ran a self-conscious hand over his three-day stubble and sat down opposite her. She looked to be about twenty-five years old, her slim figure sheathed in a cream-coloured satin dress, her auburn hair worn high on the back of her head and held in place by ribbons of the deepest pink.

'How can I be of assistance to you, sir?' She smiled again, her eyebrows arching, her head held slightly to one side. 'My maid tells me you are from the marine police in London.'

'It is about your brother.' Tom paused, unsure of how to continue. He'd assumed she was already aware of Sir Henry's death, although on what basis, he didn't know. 'May I assume, Lady Annabel, you are aware of what has happened?'

'To my brother?' she said. 'Yes, I was told he had died in a shooting accident.'

'It's my job to find out what happened. I'm hoping you will be able to help me.'

'I don't see how I can be of any assistance, Mr Pascoe. I wasn't present when he died.'

'I'm interested in anything you can tell me about your brother's movements in the weeks before his death; where he went, who he met, whether or not anything seemed to be troubling him.'

'My brother was not the sort of man to show his feelings, Mr Pascoe.' Lady Annabel paused, as though considering a point. 'There was, however, one occasion when he seemed ill at ease. I would say almost nervous. I spoke to him about it but he assured me that nothing was amiss.'

'When was that?'

'It was about a week before he died.' Lady Annabel sat on the edge of her chair, her hands resting in her lap, her head still turned to a portrait hanging over the mantel – a portrait of a young man of about her own age. Tom thought he could see a family resemblance and wondered if it might be Sir Henry. 'A number of gentlemen were at the house. A few of them I knew but most I did not. They often gathered here to talk about politics, and whatever else was of interest to them. It was not the sort of gathering to which I, as a woman, would have been made welcome, so I left them to it and retired to my room for the night. At some point I was awakened by the sound of raised voices, but when these subsided after a minute or so, I returned to my slumbers.'

'Did you ever discover the cause of the disturbance?'

'No. By the following morning I had forgotten the matter, but when, later, my brother came down to breakfast, he appeared unwell, and I asked him what ailed him.'

She stopped and again looked at the mantel picture, a thoughtful look in her eyes as if recalling the incident. Tom waited for her to continue.

'He told me it was nothing but a slight fever and, doubtless, it would pass in a day or two. That morning he left for London. When he returned home some days later, he was in a state of considerable distress. Again he would not tell me the cause. It was only later that I heard someone within the Palace of Westminster had warned him that his life was threatened, although why, I still don't know. My brother remained here for the night and returned to London in the morning. That was the last time I saw him.'

'Did you discover the name of the person who threatened your brother?'

'Alas, I did not.'

'D'you remember the names of the men who came to the house on the night of the disturbance?'

'Several,' said the Lady Annabel, reeling off a few names.

'You mention Lord Camperdown and Sir William Bolt. How well do you know them?' asked Tom, writing down the names she'd given him.

'I occasionally see Sir William and his wife at social gatherings although I cannot claim to know him well. Lord Camperdown ...' Lady Annabel paused and Tom thought he saw her face soften at the mention of the baron's name. Then her face cleared and she went on, 'Lord Camperdown was a frequent visitor to this house. He and my brother had been friends when they were younger, but were now in what I believe is called a business relationship. I had . . .' she hesitated, 'little to do with him in recent years although he was always very civil towards me.'

'Were there any disagreements between Lord Camperdown and your brother?'

'None of which I'm aware. At least none in recent times.'

'Or with any of the others at that meeting?'

'No. Why do you ask?'

'You have already mentioned that you heard raised voices on that occasion. The following morning your brother looked unwell. When you next saw him later that same week, you tell me he'd been informed of a threat to his life. I think it at least possible the two incidents are connected.'

'My answer, sir, is the same,' said Lady Annabel. 'I'm not aware of any recent disagreement between my late brother and Lord Camperdown or any of the other men who were here that night.'

'But it remains the case that there was some sort of altercation at that last meeting which might have affected your brother,' said Tom.

'Yes, I suppose you're right,' she said.

Tom looked at her, sure she was holding something back, something she had initially wanted to say but had, for whatever reason, chosen not to.

'No, sir,' she said, at last. 'There is nothing.'

Tom stood to take his leave, disappointed that the interview had not produced more information. But it had, at least, confirmed Lord Camperdown's presence at that last meeting – a meeting during which voices had been raised, and which had left its mark on Sir Henry.

'If there's anything else that occurs to you, my lady, you know where I can be found. May I take it that you will be here if I need to speak to you again?'

'I'm not sure,' she said. 'I have rooms in London, and may choose to spend a few days there. I shall keep you informed.'

Tom stepped out into the morning sunshine and crossed the lane to the cliff face from where he glanced back at the house. The door was closed and there was little sign that he had ever been there. He felt an odd sense of disappointment, as though an opportunity had somehow been missed. A mental image of the Lady Annabel flitted briefly across his mind. He shook his head. He wasn't ready. Not yet. The image faded.

He covered his eyes with the palm of one hand and felt the physical pain of Peggy's loss flood through him once more. Yet again, he found himself going over every action he had taken, every missed chance afforded him to protect her. It played through his consciousness like a bad dream. He should have known, or at least guessed, what was about to happen. She had suffered once before because of him. His hand fell away from his eyes and dropped to his side. For a minute or two he stood watching the seagulls, envying their carefree existence.

He glanced to his left, suddenly aware that he was being watched. He caught a glimpse of a green coat disappearing round the corner of a house forty yards further down the lane. It was a coat he'd seen somewhere before. He let it go. It probably wasn't important.

He walked back to the George. At first light tomorrow he would catch the coach back to London, and begin the task of seeing the men known to have been present at Sir Henry's last meeting. The names Lord Camperdown and Sir William Bolt had cropped up most frequently. Both men were known to have addresses in London.

He looked round at the sound of footsteps clacking on the hotel's wooden floorboards. It was the landlord. Tom watched him come in through the front door and turn left, into the taproom. He was, Tom noticed, wearing a green coat, similar to the one he'd seen a few yards down from the home of Lady Annabel Stapleton.

CHAPTER 15

Sam Hart was standing at the cell door of the Wapping police office, looking out through the iron grille onto the enclosed yard. Two days had passed since Tom's departure for Rye, two days in which Sam had searched, unsuccessfully, for the nightwatchman who'd claimed to have seen a black man disposing of a body in the Thames. He wasn't entirely surprised. Nightwatchmen rarely remained in the job more than a week or so. Long enough to earn the price of a drink or three and then they'd go. With luck the scrub would be back in due course – when the need for fresh funds concentrated his mind.

'What were you doing in Great Dover Street,' he said, turning to face the man in the cell behind him, 'the night you saw the coach?'

'I go to my bed,' said Ebenezer.

'Is that where your master lives? In Great Dover Street?'

'No. He live on other side of river. Since I run away from my master, I sleep here with the other niggers.'

'What's his name?'

'Master. That what we niggers call him. But sometimes I hear him called Master Alexander. That's all I know.'

'Why did you run?' asked Sam, scribbling the name on a scrap of paper.

'Master not a good man. Ebenezer no want more beating.'

'Was that the only reason?'

'Yes, master. We say, only a dog returns to his vomit.'

'Tell me again about the horseman you saw close to the coach. You say he had a cloth covering his face.'

'Yes, master,' said Ebenezer. 'It were the colour of the indigo. I know, I see indigo every day on the plantation, when the women is making the dye.'

'And then you saw this same man pointing a gun at the passenger in the coach?'

'Yes, master.'

'Did you see his face?'

'Yes, master. The cloth round his face, it fell and I saw his face.'

'What happened after that?'

'I see the man get out from the coach. He were told to get onto the horse. The man with the gun, he get on another horse and they ride away.'

'If you had nothing to do with the killing of the driver or the taking of the passenger, why did you run away?'

'Some *bakra* men came.'

'What?'

'White men, master.'

'And?'

'Make no sense to wait and see what the white man want. On the plantation, we say "If the blackbird fly with the pigeon, he get shot." I no want to be shot.'

'Later that night,' said Sam, 'you saw the same man carrying what looked like a body, down by the Thames.'

'Yes, master.'

'It were dark. How do you know it were the same man?'

'The cloth round his face. It dropped to the ground. I saw the colour. It were indigo. Same as before.'

'Did you see his face on that occasion?'

'I see the cloth. That's all.'

'What about when the cloth fell to the ground? Didn't you see his face then?'

'No, master. When I saw him, the cloth, it were covering his face. After he'd gone to the river, I see the cloth.'

Sam leaned against the cell door and looked thoughtfully at Ebenezer. Despite the thick crust of cynicism with which he had surrounded himself, he wanted to believe the man's story. Yet, if he was being honest with himself, the reason had less to do with a dispassionate consideration of the evidence than a deep-seated feeling that, despite every appearance to the contrary, the negro was telling the truth. There was also the question of the marks round the coach driver's neck that Tom had said pointed to someone else being responsible for the murder and, probably, the abduction as well.

But there was another reason, more indistinct, less well formed in his mind. He understood, only too well, what it was to be the object of scorn, to be dismissed as an irrelevance, to have one's worth as a human reduced to that of an animal. Ebenezer was a slave. Whatever the law of England might say on the subject, in reality he was a chattel, a thing to be bought and sold at will. It would have been an easy matter to dismiss what he had said. Perhaps for that reason, Sam had chosen to give his words greater weight than he might otherwise have done.

His thoughts moved on to the scarf Ebenezer had said was

covering the face of the horseman. Indigo, he'd called it. Sam had heard of it, of course. In the days when he'd worked for Jonas Levi, selling rags and old clothes, the colour had been common enough amongst the sailors returning from China, India or the Caribbean. But he'd not seen it away from the port – except in the clothes of the rich. A bluish-purple was how he would describe it.

He looked back at the negro. There was nothing further the cully could tell him and nothing to be gained by keeping him locked up. Even if there had been, it wouldn't take long to find him again. He held the cell door open.

'You're free to go,' he said. 'If I need you again, I'll come calling.'

Sam watched the big man shamble out through the door, a bewildered look on his black face. He thought again of the indigo scarf. He might mention it to Tom when he next saw him. Then again, perhaps not. It was probably of no interest.

A mile or two west of Rye, on the Winchelsea road, a horseman drew up outside a large house set well back from the public road. The rider was a portly man, ill at ease in the saddle and clearly relieved to be leaving it. He slithered off the animal's back and hit the ground with more force than was good for him.

'I'll take her for you now, sir.' A groom had appeared and was grasping the reins. 'The master expecting you, is he, sir?'

The landlord of the George ignored him. He was not expected. Not that it made any difference. The man he had come to see would want to hear what he had to say. He knocked on the heavy oak door and waited. From deep inside the building he could hear the tap, tap, tapping of approaching footsteps and, a short while later, he was shown into a sparsely furnished, high-ceilinged room, and asked to wait. A minute later the door swung open.

'Good morning, Master Hickish.' The tall, thin frame of Sir William Bolt entered the room. 'What can I do for you?'

'Good day, sir,' said Hickish. 'I'm sorry to disturb you, but you asked to be kept informed. It's as you suspected, sir. The cully what you told me about, arrived yesterday.'

'Pascoe?'

'That's the gentleman, sir. He went to see Master Butterworth last night. Then, this mornin' he ups and goes to the other house what you mentioned.'

'Where is he now?'

'Back at the George, sir. He returns to London tomorrow.'

'Thank you, Hickish,' said the stooped gentleman. 'I'll deal with it from here. Someone will see you out.'

The landlord did not look back as he walked to the stable block and retrieved his mount. He had been handsomely rewarded for his time. What people did with his information was none of his business.

Less than an hour after his release from the Wapping police office, Ebenezer was on the Ratcliff Highway, in search of food. He was still shaking from the experience of the last two days and had no wish to repeat it. He turned at the sound of a man singing a ballad. The singer was black, like himself. Ebenezer stopped and listened, his eyes straying to the small group that had also stopped to listen.

One man, in particular, drew his attention. He didn't need more than a fleeting glimpse to be sure of who he was. The swagger, the heavy stick he carried, the colour of his hair. It was all the confirmation he needed. Ebenezer slipped down an alley and watched his master, Alexander Thorngood, turn his head in his direction.

He had always considered it likely he would be caught. The master would accept no explanations or excuses if he ever got hold of him. As like as not, after the customary beating, he'd be put on the first ship back to Barbados, and the nightmare would begin again.

Not that he'd ever ceased to be a slave. Even after he had come to London. There had been a time when he had thought it a possibility, when his master had gone so far as to promise that he would be paid as a servant once he was in England. The money had never materialised, of course, and Ebenezer had not had the courage to remind him of his promise. He suspected it would have been a waste of time anyway. He'd met other niggers since he'd run and they'd confirmed what he'd already suspected. The word of a servant would never be accepted over that of his master; more so if the servant was black.

His master's gaze swept the crowd, as though he knew that Ebenezer was there, eliminating each one in turn until they reached the spot where he stood, unable to move. It was as if lead weights had been attached to his feet and nailed to the roadway.

Alexander Thorngood walked towards him, his gait unhurried, a contemptuous sneer on his upper lip. Ebenezer knew that look. It was the same one he'd worn on a previous occasion;

an occasion Ebenezer would never forget.

It had been a day like any other on the plantation, a sprawling estate on the hills above Speightstown, overlooking the distant Caribbean Sea. Ebenezer and the other men had risen before dawn and walked to the cane fields. Throughout the day they had toiled, swinging their machetes with practised ease, striking the thick cane close to its base and tossing it behind him ready for the women to load onto the carts.

When evening fell, Ebenezer walked back with the last of the carts, heading for the mill where he would help the women with the unloading. Speed was essential. The cane had to be crushed within an hour of being cut if it was not to be spoiled. He'd known something was wrong. Had known it from the moment the mill had come into view and he'd seen the tear-stained faces of the people gathered in a little knot by the loading door. Standing a little apart were the master and another *bakra*, their faces devoid of expression. They had all watched his approach in utter silence.

It was the other *bakra* who'd been the first to speak. There had been no pity in his voice as he informed him of his wife's death. She'd been crushed between the wooden rollers and her muti-lated body laid out in the back of a cart with the body of a second woman.

Blind with grief, it had been several hours before Ebenezer had been able to take in the detail of what had happened. The two women had been punished – for what, he was never to discover – and chained by their ankles to one another before being told to feed the canes through the revolving timbers.

The rollers often jammed. Sometimes as often as three times a day. Then someone would have to free them by pushing the canes through. It was a routine task, the work of a few seconds. It seemed that the other woman had leaned forward and grasped the thick bunch of canes, ready to pull them free, when the big stones suddenly turned, catching the woman's fingers, then her arm.

There was no escape, no time to summon help. It would have been too late anyway. The chain linking the two women was too short for there to have been any hope for Ebenezer's wife. She, too, had been dragged through the crushing rollers after her friend.

And that was it. Her life passed without further comment. In the weeks that followed, Ebenezer had learned of a collection being organised by several of the plantation owners. The money was for the master. Compensation for the loss of two of his slave women.

'Did you think you could run from me, nigger?' Alexander Thorngood, the Second Baron Camperdown, swung his heavy briar at Ebenezer's head. 'Did you think I'd not find you? I knew where to come. People tell me what I need to know.'

The blow sent Ebenezer tumbling to the ground. He climbed unsteadily to his feet, his fingers splayed, nursing the cut to his head, his eyes turned to the roadway. Slowly, he balled his fists, his anger rising. There had been a time when it would have been unthinkable for him to question the actions of the *bakra*. But that was then. Since he had arrived in England, his attitude had begun to change. He felt less inclined to take the beatings that had been his daily fare on the island. For a moment he considered taking Camperdown's stick and breaking it over his master's head. It would not be difficult. Strong and fit though his master was, Ebenezer was faster, stronger and fitter. Long hours in the cane fields had seen to that. He glanced down the street. It was crowded with white men. Too many to fight if they turned on him.

'Go in front,' said Camperdown. 'You run and I'll cut you down like the dog you are.'

Ebenezer stooped and did what he was told.

CHAPTER 16

On the Ratcliff Highway, Mordecai Phillips, sometime police informant, stopped what he was doing and watched the altercation between the gentleman and the negro. The gentleman he knew by name and by repute, a violent man it was best not to cross. The negro he had never seen before. Not that that mattered. What mattered to Mordecai was the possibility of earning a few pennies. And he had the feeling that his old friend Sam Hart might be interested in what he was seeing – and paying for it.

The two men were moving off, the blackamoor in front and the gentleman close behind. Mordecai fell in at a discreet distance behind them. At the junction of Fox's Lane, the pair turned right and headed down the slope towards the river. The lane was deserted save for a group of small children playing barefoot amongst the rotting waste. Mordecai waited a minute or two, watching the two men weave between the children, the negro being prodded in the back as if he were no more than an animal being driven to market. He started after them, keeping close to the soot-blackened walls of the buildings. Twice, the gentleman turned to look over his shoulder, as though aware of Mordecai's presence, but seemed not to see him.

He could smell the river now, that special odour of damp wood and rotting fish carried along on the south-westerly breeze. In his mind's eye, Mordecai could already see the tall masts of the ships moored along the length of the Pool. It was the world he had inhabited for as long as he could remember. From boyhood he'd gone from ship to ship offering old clothes and rags and general trinkets for sale. It was dangerous work, mind. The sailors seldom missed an opportunity to have some sport at his expense, knock him about a bit, pull his beard, steal his wares if they could. But for all that, it was a living. He knew the name of every ship in the port, where she came from and where she was bound.

Mordecai slowed as the men reached the junction with Lower Shadwell, and waited until he saw them turn down the passage leading to Pelican Stairs. Quickly, he made his way over. The men were standing at the top of the river stairs, looking out over the reach. A short while later, he saw a skiff fetch alongside and the negro was pushed in, followed by his lordship.

Mordecai watched the skiff pull away from the steps and then made his way down the path, to the water's edge. The wherry had already been swallowed up amidst the host of small boats darting from one ship to the next. He wasn't unduly concerned. He knew the waterman. If he needed to know where the pair had gone, he had only to ask.

He strolled back up the passageway and turned towards Wapping.

It was time he saw Master Sam.

André Dubois lay on his bed at the Dog and Duck inn, on Tooley Street, his eyes closed. He thought about moving to another inn, perhaps one a little further back from the Thames. One that was more discreet, less likely to attract attention to itself. But then again, he was comfortable here. More to the point, in spite of the large number of people who resorted here, no one had yet questioned the presence of a Frenchman – an enemy alien – in their midst, or sought to ask why he chose to spend an inordinate amount of time locked up in his room.

It was exactly how he liked it.

He thought about his sighting of Pascoe and wondered if the river surveyor had seen him. The speed with which the police galley had been closing with him seemed to suggest that he had. But then, to his relief, the galley had swung across the Thames and disappeared. It wasn't that he was afraid of Pascoe. Nor was he afraid of death – the inevitable sequel to capture. No one who had spent the number of years he had, treading the fine line between life and death, could really be afraid of the prospect of his own demise. He had come to accept the possibility of an early death as a consequence of the life he led. No, what concerned him was the possibility of his arrest before he had completed the task he'd been sent to perform.

The body of the man he'd killed was a problem. He had to consider the possibility that it was still afloat. He'd imagined the body would sink, only later to wash up on the foreshore when all trace of the manner of his death had rotted away. He'd seen it happen before, in the harbour at Marseille, when he was young. But there was nothing certain about it. If it was still afloat, what then? If Pascoe were to find it and pull it from the river, he would see the marks on the neck of the body, and would guess who was responsible. Dubois knew he was going to have to deal with the man.

It wouldn't be easy. But the pleasure he'd derive from Pascoe's death would more than make up for the difficulties he might encounter. He knew the street where Pascoe lived, had been given the information by his English contact who had seemed as anxious as he was to see an end of the man.

He thought again of the body. The young man had talked a great deal before he died; had probably thought it would buy him his life. It never failed. Leave them with hope until the end. That way, they talked. But he'd felt sorry for the man. It wasn't he who was supposed to die. He'd simply been in the wrong place at the wrong time, a victim of circumstance.

Dubois rolled off the bed and walked to the window. Below him, Tooley Street was packed, the noise of the mob a subdued roar in the outer reaches of his mind. With an effort, he put his immediate concerns to one side. He had been sent to England for a single purpose; a purpose he'd yet to perform. How he did it was a matter of little concern to those under whose direction he worked. But perform it he must. Or face the consequences.

Pulling on his coat, he headed out into the street and hailed a cab.

Dubois stood in the shadow of a building in St James's Street, and looked through the gloom of late evening at the stone building opposite. His patience was growing thin. He'd been here for several hours and still there was no sign of the man he was waiting for. According to the information he'd been given, the fellow should have arrived some time ago.

He heard the approaching clatter of horses' hooves and the grinding noise of coach wheels on the cobbled surface. Dubois leaned forward and peered round the corner. A curricle had appeared. It clattered down the hill towards him and stopped in front of the stone building. Moments later, a gentleman got out and walked the short distance in through the door of the building.

'So the information was correct,' breathed Dubois.

At exactly half past eight in the evening, the diligence from Rye pulled into Bellsavage Yard on Ludgate Hill. Tom rubbed the back of his neck and clambered out onto a rain-soaked fore-court, the prospect of a three-mile walk to Wapping still before him. He thought about stopping for a drink, just until it had stopped raining. He'd only have one and be back on the road in minutes. He wetted his lips, could almost taste the ale. He fought the temptation, remembering his promise to Harriot, and forced himself to walk on.

Drenched by the steady downpour, he turned into Ludgate Hill and squelched his way past the Tower of London before turning right towards the Thames.

'Welcome back, sir,' said Sam Hart as Tom pushed open the door and walked into the spacious, stone-flagged entrance hall of the Wapping police office an hour later. Tom scowled and climbed up the stairs to the constables' waiting room, his progress marked by a trail of puddles. Sam followed at a safe distance.

'Bloody rain,' said Tom, stripping off his outer garments and throwing them onto a chair. He looked round at his friend. 'What are you grinning about?'

'Nothing, sir.' The corners of Sam's mouth twitched and rose still further. 'Why don't I fetch you a jug of hot coffee while you hang them slops of yours in front of the fire?'

Ten minutes later, with clouds of steam rising from the various items of his clothing draped in front of the coal fire, Tom nursed a mug of strong black coffee and listened to Sam's account of what had been happening in his absence.

'. . . and you was right about that scrub. The one what reckoned he saw our nigger friend carrying a roll of cloth towards the river. He couldn't 'ave done. It were too dark to see what a man looked like. I were down there last night to see for meself.'

'I thought not,' said Tom. 'Did you discover anything else?'

'No.'

The pair lapsed into silence for a moment.

'Except for the neckcloth,' said Sam staring moodily into the fire.

'What neckcloth?'

'The nigger we had in the cells, sir. He told me the cully he saw following the coach was the same one he saw down by the fore-shore. He were wearing a neckcloth over his face.'

'How does that help us?' snapped Tom. 'I'd hardly expect anyone bent on villainy to do anything else.'

'It were the colour, sir,' said Sam. 'Ain't too many folk in these parts can afford a neckcloth dyed with indigo. The nigger saw the scrub what were carrying the body drop his scarf. It were then that he recognised it from before.'

'Ebenezer,' said Tom.

'Begging your pardon, sir?'

'I said, "Ebenezer". That's his name. Is he still in the cells?'

'No, sir, he ain't. There weren't no reason to keep him.'

'Find him, will you?' said Tom. 'We're not exactly overloaded with witnesses in this case.'

Sam looked at the floor and said nothing.

'What's the problem?'

'He were captured and taken aboard a brig in the Lower Pool. Leastways, we think it were him. One of me snouts saw him with Lord Camperdown.'

'Christ, Sam, if Ebenezer saw everything you say he did, we need him. Speak to your snout and find out the name of the ship. We may not have long before she sails.'

'Very good sir, I'll . . .' They both looked up as the door to the room opened and Bill Thompson, one of the other river surveyors, walked in.

'Sorry to interrupt you, Tom,' said Thompson. 'But I thought you might like to see a floater I've just brought in. I think it's the fellow you've been looking for.'

CHAPTER 17

John Harriot leaned back in his chair at the Rainbow Coffee House on Fleet Street, and waved away a cloud of tobacco smoke.

'You're sure it's the MP?' said the magistrate.

Tom nodded. 'Watson came straight down and identified him.'

'Have you any idea who might be responsible? And why?' Harriot sounded tired. He rubbed his face with both hands.

'Not sure,' said Tom, recalling the sight of John Dean's battered body laid out on the police pontoon. It was obvious it had been struck several times. But that wasn't unusual. Bodies were often hit by passing ships, or rolled beneath moored lighters by the force of the tide. Even those who had avoided contact with ships or barges would be found with the skin torn from forehead, nose and chin. The tips of their limbs, too, where they had scraped along the bottom of the tideway would often be damaged or broken. It was the reason he didn't immediately see the telltale marks.

Kneeling beside the body, Tom had been on the point of getting to his feet when he'd noticed the ugly weals encircling the neck. They would once have been a deep reddish-blue. Now they were almost white against the ivory grey of the skin, the marks interjected by deeper bruises caused by the knots in the garrotte that had been used to kill him. He'd been sure, then, of the identity of the killer.

'But you have an idea?' said Harriot, stabbing at a sliver of beef and forking it onto his plate.

'Yes, I have an idea, but I'd like to wait a day or two before giving you a name.'

The two of them lapsed into silence as they tucked into their meal. It was Harriot who spoke first.

'Do I remember hearing that someone has got your witness? The black fellow?'

'It seems likely,' said Tom. 'A man, believed to be Lord Camperdown, was seen by an informant apparently abducting a negro. The description is hazy and, quite frankly, could apply to any one of the ten thousand or so negroes in London.'

'Hmm.' The magistrate sounded distinctly doubtful. 'Why would Camperdown be interested in a negro? Or is there a suggestion his lordship might be involved in your case?'

'I've no evidence yet that links Camperdown to either of the deaths I'm looking at. But then I don't think that's what lies behind this incident,' said Tom, glancing out onto a sunlit Cornhill. 'Assuming that the negro is Ebenezer, he was brought to this country as a slave and subsequently ran from his master. And while we don't know the name of that master, we do know he is thought to be a peer of the realm.'

'And you think Camperdown might be that peer?'

Tom shrugged. 'I think it's probable.'

'There must be a risk of this negro being placed on a ship and taken back to the West Indies,' said Harriot, sipping his coffee.

'I'm afraid he already has been,' said Tom. 'Or to be precise, we think he has already put this negro onto a ship. We're making inquiries to find out the name of the vessel. Fortunately, nothing has left the port in the last two days.'

'Even if you find him,' said Harriot, 'you might find it impossible to get him back.'

'Why so? I didn't think you could lawfully seize a man and put him on a ship without the authority of the court. I thought all that nonsense had stopped years ago.'

'Yes, you're partially right. There was a judgement, some years ago. Many thought it ended slavery. Unfortunately, the judgement related only to the forcible removal of citizens and residents of these islands.'

'Then where, sir, is the problem?' asked Tom. 'Ebenezer Samson has been a resident here for some months.'

'I can only tell you what the law says,' said Harriot. 'Ever since that judgement, plantation owners have required any slave they intended to bring to England to sign a form of indenture. The effect of this is to bind the slave to his master in exactly the same way as for an apprentice.'

'Supposing Lord Camperdown had forgotten to do that. What then?'

'Then it would be possible to bring a complaint against him for unlawful imprisonment, or assault. But I'm afraid the chance of success would still be very small.'

'Why? Because Camperdown had forced an illiterate man to sign a form of indenture he didn't understand?' said Tom, an angry flush rising to his cheeks.

Harriot held up the palms of his hands. 'You must understand the practicalities of the case. In the first instance, yes, it is more than likely that Lord Camperdown has obtained an indenture from this man, Ebenezer. But even if he has, by some miracle, forgotten to do so, consider the position of the magistrate who has to hear the case. It would place him in a difficult position.'

'How's that?'

'The police offices here and at Shadwell are dependent for their existence on the contributions of the merchants whose ships use the port. Any judgement that precluded these merchants from moving their slaves wheresoever they wished would not be welcomed and would almost certainly result in the withdrawal of their financial support.'

'In spite of the fact that their property would no longer be protected?' said Tom.

'We must all live in the practical world,' said Harriot. 'They would simply revert to the old system of paying old men to keep watch over their cargoes.'

'So we allow Camperdown to return Ebenezer to slavery and, in the process, lose a witness to murder?'

'We may have to.' Harriot's eyes took on a hard glare as he glanced at Tom. 'If no one brings a complaint, the fellow will remain in Camperdown's custody and be taken back to the West Indies, whatever we think of the situation.'

It was the silence that caught Tom's attention. The usual hubbub that accompanied each day was inexplicably stilled. He had, in the last few minutes, returned from his lunch with Harriot and was sitting in the constable's waiting room, writing up his notebook. He got up and strolled over to the window overlooking Wapping Street. A knot of people were gathered round a black lacquered chaise, drawn by two of the most beautiful greys he'd seen in a long time. A uniformed coachman stood motionless by the open door. The passenger had left and, it seemed, was on his way to the police office. Tom wondered who it was. Coaches, of whatever size or description, were a rarity in these parts, and those that stopped outside the police office even rarer. He caught sight of his coat, lying where he had dropped it, and picked it up. He studied it for a moment. Sooner or later he was going to have to purchase a replacement, but not yet. He smiled to himself. He'd been putting off the decision for months, reluctant to let go of his link with the past.

There was a knock on the door and one of the petty constables from the judicial department poked his head into the room. 'Begging your pardon, sir, there's a lady to see you in the front hall.'

'A lady?' said Tom, his eyes widening in surprise. 'Did she give a name?'

'No, sir.'

Tom slipped into his coat, and followed the man down the stairs. At the bottom, he stopped suddenly. 'Why, Lady Annabel . . .' He paused while he recovered from his surprise. Then, 'I believe you asked to see me.'

'Indeed I did, sir.' Lady Annabel looked round at the dozen or so men and women who were waiting for their cases to be called. 'Is there somewhere we may speak in private? It is a matter of some delicacy.'

Tom hesitated, unable to think of anywhere suitable.

'Please don't concern yourself,' said Lady Annabel. 'I'm quite used to discomfort. They tell me it is good for one's soul.'

Tom led the way back up the stairs and in through one of a number of doors on his right of the corridor. Like the rest of the building, the room was sparsely furnished with a single table and a few chairs.

'The committee room,' said Tom by way of explanation. 'We shan't be disturbed.' He drew back one of the chairs and waited for her to sit down. 'Now, how may I be of assistance?'

'I scarce know where to begin, sir,' said Lady Annabel. She gazed round the room as though seeking inspiration. 'You will doubtless recall your visit to my house and your questions regarding the state of mind of my late brother in the days before he died.'

'Yes, I remember,' said Tom, acutely aware of his visitor's presence. He had felt the same when he'd first seen her at her home in Rye. He tried to dismiss the vague sense of excitement he felt and the guilt that rose from deep within him. Peggy had been gone less than six months. It was too early to be drawn to someone else.

Annabel looked down at her hands resting on the table. Then drawing a deep breath, she went on. 'Yesterday afternoon, I received a visit from a gentleman who lives not far from me. I enquired of him the nature of his business and, after offering his condolences on the loss of my brother, he said he had information about him which might be of some interest to me.'

Tom waited for her to continue. After a short pause, she said, 'I was, as you may imagine, intrigued. I bade him continue. He began by warning me that I should treat with care what he was about to tell me since there were those who might have a great deal to lose were the information to become generally known. He told me that he had often attended the meetings that my brother held at our house and had been present at the last one

141

before my brother's death. He said the purpose of the meetings had been to enable men of standing in the community to discuss matters of interest to our country. Specifically, to talk about the future of the slave trade.'

'What, exactly, did he mean by that? Did he say?'

'Not in so many words,' said Lady Annabel. 'But you are to consider that all the men at those meetings, including my late brother, owned slaves of their own. I took it, therefore, to mean that they talked about the ways and means by which the abolitionists could be defeated.'

'How did they intend to achieve this end?'

'I don't know. He did not elaborate. But whatever it was, it seems my brother was rash enough to oppose the suggestion, and made his feelings clear. An argument ensued – you will recall I mentioned hearing the sound of raised voices. My visitor told me that he, too, had been opposed to the proposed course of action, but had been too afraid to speak out. My brother, it seems, said no more that night, and the argument was apparently forgotten. It was only later, when my visitor heard of the threat to my brother, and of his later death, that he remembered what had been said, and decided to see me.'

Tom nodded. He had thought along much the same lines himself. 'May I, my lady, ask the name of your gentleman caller?'

'Why, yes, of course. It was Sir William Bolt.'

'And did Sir William inform you of the identity of the men who advocated violence?'

'No, I regret he did not, but he left me with the impression that all those at the meeting, with the exception of himself and my brother, were of the same bent.' Lady Annabel stopped and raised an eyebrow. 'You seem, sir, surprised.'

'Forgive me, m'lady,' said Tom. 'It seems a little odd that Sir William, who is, I understand, a particular friend of Lord Camperdown, should have chosen an opposite path.'

'They were friends. That is true,' said Lady Annabel. 'But I believe there was a falling out over something. I don't know the details. It might be why he chose to oppose his lordship and, later, speak with me.'

Tom looked across the table at his visitor. There was something she wasn't telling him. He could sense it. There was a hesitation in her voice, a note of apprehension that bordered on fear.

'Lady Annabel . . .' It was Tom's turn to hesitate. 'The last time we spoke, you . . . That is, I, thought you were about to tell me something. That feeling is again with me. Is there anything else you would like to tell me about this, or any other matter?'

She gave him a startled look before turning quickly away.

'Perhaps, one day,' she said, her words almost drowned by the din of the crowds in Wapping Street.

CHAPTER 18

The note had been delivered to Tom's rooms in Burr Street, the night before. It had been from the Right Honourable William Wilberforce suggesting a meeting at Brooks's, in St James's Street, the following morning. He again read the note, folded it and placed it in his coat pocket before crossing to the police galley moored at the edge of the Wapping pontoon.

He had, in honour of the occasion, managed to wash off the worst of the accumulated filth of the previous day, and shave the unsightly three-day stubble covering most of his face. From somewhere, he'd located a tolerably clean pair of stockings and a less than evil-smelling uniform coat that he'd discovered at the bottom of his old sea chest.

'Good morning, sir.' Tom glanced up. Sam was looking approvingly at him. 'Where to this morning?'

'Westminster,' said Tom. 'I've a note from Mr Wilberforce. He wants to see me about Sir Henry.'

A stiff, south-westerly breeze caught the splashes of the oars, sending a fine spume sweeping over the galley as it nosed its way out into the centre of the channel and headed west with the flood tide. Soon they were amongst the press of vessels standing off the legal quays, the shouts of the watermen deafening in its confusing din. Ahead of them Tom could see the menacing downward sweep of the water racing through the narrow arches of London Bridge, sucking them onwards. The next moment they were through.

It was a pleasant run from there, the morning sun reflecting off the dome of St Paul's and lending an air of faded elegance to the cluster of rooftops gathered at its base, thin columns of smoke drifting up from their squat chimney pots. Soon, Wren's masterpiece had fallen astern, its place taken by the distant sight of Blackfriars Bridge.

Tom thought of his meeting with Lady Annabel the previous day. He could not pretend he'd not been absurdly pleased to see her, much as he might have wished it otherwise. The trace of a smile crossed his lips at the memory. He pushed it to one side and tried to concentrate on what she had told him about the visit she'd received from Sir William Bolt.

He wondered what Bolt had hoped to gain by telling her of the argument between her brother and Camperdown. There seemed little point to it except to increase the suspicion that Camperdown was, in some way, involved in Sir Henry's death. But why would Bolt choose to raise the matter? As a result of the alleged falling out between himself and Camperdown? It did not seem plausible. But if not that, then what?

Tom let it go. Bolt remained on the list of people he had yet to see. He would use the opportunity to raise his concerns during the course of the interview. And Bolt might also be able to cast some light on the nature of the threat made to Sir Henry, a few days afterwards, at the Palace of Westminster.

Temple Gardens came and went, the leafy boughs of the plane trees drooping over the water's edge, partially obscuring the view of the ancient buildings of the Inns of Court. A minute or two later a soft breeze brought the scent of sawn timber from the yards at Christchurch on the south bank of the Thames. It all seemed far removed from the noise and urgency of the Port.

From Savoy, the river curved away to the south and it was another twenty minutes before they could see Westminster Bridge and the abbey just behind it. Further south, through the bridge arches, Tom was just able to make out the trees of Vauxhall Gardens. He could never see the place without thinking of Peggy. He'd not been back there since her death, although he'd often thought of doing so, his mind recalling the halcyon summer when they'd often strolled along the Grand Walk with its avenue of trees and its magnificent pavilions. More than once they had visited the great rotunda where they had listened to the orchestra playing the music of Handel, Mozart, Rossetti, Haydn, and others.

He looked away hurriedly, and blinked.

'Whitehall Stairs hard on our starboard bow, I reckon, sir.' Sam's voice brought him back into the present. He looked over to his right, to the Privy Gardens, and what was left of the palace from which a king had once walked to his execution.

'Thankee, Sam.' Tom brought the galley round into the tide and steered towards the stairs. 'Way enough. Toss oars.'

The galley slid to a halt and was made fast to the mooring poles close to the bottom step.

'Wait here for me, Sam,' said Tom. 'I shouldn't be too long.'

The walk to Brooks's for Tom's meeting with Wilberforce did not take as long as he thought it might, and he had reached the corner of St James's Street and Pall Mall with almost a quarter of an hour to spare. He slowed his pace and strolled up the shallow incline, towards Piccadilly. The gentlemen's club to which he was going was about halfway up, on the left. He stopped to let a phaeton out of St James's Place and watched it turn down the hill. Then something caught his eye. He looked back up the street with that odd sense of purpose that occasionally prompts people to satisfy an idle curiosity. A drayman's cart was approaching down the slope. On the opposite side of the street a couple sauntered up towards Piccadilly. Tom was about to give up when he saw him.

The man was leaning against the wall of a house in Little Ryder Street, his face turned towards the front entrance of Brooks's, as though waiting for someone to appear. There was, Tom thought, something familiar about him that he couldn't quite fathom. Then the stranger turned in his direction and their eyes met.

There was no mistaking Dubois.

Dubois saw him immediately. His heart was pounding as he levered himself away from the wall, turned and sprinted down Little Ryder Street. Capture was out of the question. He had a job to do. He turned into Bury Street and raced to the next corner, sweat pouring down his face. Ahead of him, on the left, was the entrance of a court. He darted in and ran to the end, a terrace of houses barring his further progress. A horse and cart stood against the eastern side of the court, the animal munching from a nosebag, sacks of what appeared to be coal in the back. Of the driver there was no sign.

Dubois thought quickly. It would take him around thirty seconds to reach the cart. Another twenty – possibly thirty – to hide, always supposing he could find the space. He wasn't sure he could make it in time. He looked at the mouth of the court. He could hear the sound of running feet getting closer. On the other side of the court, a door slammed shut. Dubois started, his heartbeat soaring, his mouth dry with fear. He twisted his head, searching for an alternative hiding place, somewhere closer than the cart. He had to find somewhere, anywhere. His hand fumbled for the hilt of his knife, his breathing seeming to scorch the back of his throat.

He could no longer think rationally, a feeling close to panic overtaking him. If he couldn't hide, he'd fight. And if he had to die, he'd take Pascoe with him.

All the way to hell.

Tom stood in Great Ryder Street and looked down the length of a court, bordered on three sides by large, stone-built houses, each painted a brilliant white. The place was deserted, save for a horse and cart standing idle about halfway down on the right. He glanced at it, wondering where the driver was. Then his eyes moved away, examining each of the houses in turn, looking for any evidence that one of them might recently have been entered. He looked back at the cart. It was loaded with what appeared to be sacks of coal. He took a step towards it, just as the blackened face of the coal merchant appeared from the side entrance of a nearby house and got into the driving seat. Tom walked towards him as the cart turned to leave the court and waved the driver to a halt. The fellow might have seen Dubois.

From the opposite side of the street there was a sudden commotion. The side door of one of the houses flew open. A woman was shrieking at someone. The figure of a man, partially hidden by the door, came into view, a flash of indigo at his neck.

Tom ran towards the house, drawing his sea service pistol from his coat pocket. He reached the door of the house and pushed the startled woman out of the way. The man was still there, the bright indigo scarf thrown carelessly around his neck. Tom brought his gun up, pointed it, and ordered the man out from the corner into which he'd retreated.

It wasn't Dubois.

Apologising, Tom backed out of the house, and looked up and down the court. The horse and cart had gone. He thought for a moment. The cart had represented the only realistic hiding place for Dubois. He had to be there, buried amongst the sacks of coal. Tom cursed his own stupidity and ran to the corner of Great Ryder Street. It was deserted. The coal merchant could have turned left or right and taken any one of the turnings off. Tom took a gamble and sprinted to the corner of Duke Street. He saw the tailgate of a cart disappearing into Mason's Yard. He sprinted to the entrance. A young boy was getting down from the driver's seat, the back of the cart empty. The boy – he can't have been more than about fifteen – looked at Tom's sudden appearance at the entrance to the yard and his eyes widened with concern.

Tom waved and turned away. He wouldn't find the cart now and even if, by some chance, he was to do so, Dubois would have gone. He shook his head in frustration. Suddenly, he remembered his appointment with Wilberforce. He checked his pocket watch and hurriedly retraced his steps to St James's Street.

CHAPTER 19

'Mr Wilberforce, sir? Is he expecting you?' The porter in the lobby looked Tom up and down, hesitating for a moment before showing him to the Stranger's Room. 'I will inform the gentleman you are here, sir.'

A few minutes later, Tom heard the sound of approaching footsteps in the hall outside. A short, slim, ill-looking man of about forty came in and walked towards him, his hand held out in greeting.

'Mr Pascoe? My name is William Wilberforce. Thank you for coming to see me. Shall we find somewhere more private to talk? The Great Subscription Room, I think.'

Wilberforce led the way up a flight of steps and into a large, rectangular room with a double-vaulted ceiling, furnished with a number of sofas and circular gaming tables. The room was empty apart from a small group of members who were sitting at one of the tables at the far end, playing cards.

'Now,' said Wilberforce, lowering himself onto a comfortable-looking sofa. 'Watson, the serjeant-at-arms, tells me that you have been given the task of investigating the death of poor Sir Henry Thwaite-Thomas.'

'Yes,' said Tom. 'And that of Mr John Dean.'

'So, I'm told,' said Wilberforce, a troubled look in his eyes. After a moment's silence, he continued, 'How much do you know of these two men?'

'Very little. Beyond the fact that both were Members of Parliament.'

'Yes,' said Wilberforce. 'The fact that both men were Members of the House is the cause of some concern within the Administration and I have, in consequence, been asked by the minister to render you such assistance as I am able.' He smiled briefly. 'Now, how to begin. Sir Henry was elected for the seat of Gatton, in the county of Surrey, about seven years ago—'

'Although his home was quite some distance away, in Sussex,' said Tom, interrupting.

'Quite,' said Wilberforce, giving Tom an odd glance. 'Sir Henry had no need to live within his constituency since he had no constituents to speak of. To put it bluntly, Mr Pascoe, Gatton is what is commonly known as a rotten borough; that is, a parliamentary seat within the effective gift of one man. The House has made a number of attempts to reform the system but without success. There's simply too much influence at work.'

'You say the seat was a gift?'

'Yes.'

'I understand it was given to him by Lord Camperdown's father. Is it possible that his lordship would have expected some favour in return?'

'It's possible.' Wilberforce paused and gave Tom a questioning glance. 'D'you know Lord Camperdown?'

'I've not met him,' said Tom. 'But his name is familiar. What sort of favour would he have expected?'

'Oh, I don't know,' said Wilberforce. 'Perhaps the ability to influence the political process. Something like that.'

'And if, for any reason, Sir Henry were to fail to keep to his side of the bargain?' said Tom.

'Your guess is as good as mine.' said Wilberforce. 'I imagine his patron would not be best pleased.'

'I see.' Tom thought for a moment. 'Were there any difficulties of that nature between Sir Henry and the present Lord Camper-down?'

'None that I'm aware of.'

'What of his politics? Did he have any enemies?'

'I can't tell you a great deal on that score, I'm afraid. He was, by profession, a merchant, trading in sugar, and that's where his chief interest seemed to lie. His time within the House of Commons was not remarkable. Indeed, I would go so far as to say his only value to the Administration was in his vote.'

'Was it important? His vote, I mean.'

'You will appreciate, Mr Pascoe, that everything the Administration wishes to do depends upon the support of the House. In that sense the votes of individual members, over whom the minister has no authority, are often crucial to the minister's plans.'

Wilberforce paused to draw breath.

'There are,' he went on, 'several bills presently waiting to come before the House for which there is insufficient support. Amongst these is a Bill for the abolition of the slave trade. Are you, sir, at all familiar with the trade?'

'I know of its existence,' said Tom, reluctant to go into the details of his own exposure to slaving. He remembered the occasion as clearly as though it were yesterday.

He'd been standing on the quarterdeck of the King's sloop of war, *Minot*, watching a dirty smudge of grey canvas on the southern horizon grow larger. He'd known she was a slaver even before he'd forced her to heave to, with a shot across her bows. The stench, across a quarter mile of ocean, had been enough to tell him that.

He grimaced. He should have sent his first lieutenant to inspect her. It would have been better that way. Instead, he went himself, the groans and cries of those confined below decks apparent even before he climbed the companion ladder to the brig's upper deck.

The master was reluctant about the prospect of a search and it had taken the point of a gun to allow Tom into the hellhole below deck where the human cargo lay chained. He remembered reeling back as the hatch cover was removed. It was dark, the scuttles closed. No fresh air could reach the confined spaces. He descended the ladder, hardly able to breathe. Someone – he'd not seen who – had lifted a lamp, the dull glow shining on a wooden gutter running with human waste. There was barely room to walk, the narrow passage hemmed in on either side by broad shelves on which men lay, naked, each one shackled to his neighbour, unable to move, unable to raise his head more than a few inches to the shelf above him.

He couldn't stay, the odious stench was too great. He turned for the ladder and climbed to the upper deck. He fought down the urge to throw the master to the sharks, his revulsion added to by his own shame. He was powerless to act. No law had been broken.

Tom looked up. He realised Wilberforce was still talking. He

PATRICK EASTER

struggled to listen, his other self still aboard the slaver on the Middle Passage, his pulse beating faster than usual, the urge for a drink sapping his strength.

'A vile and inhuman practice, I hope you will agree, sir,' said the older man, tapping the arm of his chair with his index finger. 'But one which is proving astonishingly difficult to banish into history.'

'Why d'you suppose it is so?' asked Tom, his mind still on the subject of drink.

'It's really quite simple, Mr Pascoe. Abolition of the slave trade would mean ruin for a great many of the wealthiest men in the country. Their income is largely dependent not only on the production of sugar which is, itself, dependant on slave labour, but on the highly lucrative trade in slaves from Africa. I said . . . Forgive me, Mr Pascoe, I am quite forgetting my manners. May I offer you some refreshment?'

'A tea, thank you.'

Wilberforce waved over a waiter and placed the order.

'Now, where was I? Ah, yes. I said to you a short while ago that Sir Henry was a sugar merchant. In fact he was also the owner of a sugar plantation on the island of Barbados and is believed to have been involved in conveying and selling slaves from west Africa. As such, he would, had he lived, have been ruined by abolition.'

'He owned and traded in slaves?' said Tom, surprised. 'Then, with respect, sir, his vote on this particular issue would not have been in any doubt, would it?'

'In normal circumstances, sir, I would agree with you,' said Wilberforce. 'But these are not normal circumstances. The minister has long been determined to press for abolition, but has been thwarted at every turn. In July, a bill to limit the trade in slaves is due to come before the House. In order to ensure its safe passage, Mr Pitt has been willing to reward those who are prepared to support him. Among those rewarded was Sir Henry.'

'Are you saying that Sir Henry voted against his own interests?' said Tom. 'What was the promised reward?'

'A peerage,' said Wilberforce.

'But he never received it?'

'No. He died before it could be bestowed.'

Tom whistled under his breath. 'How would his vote have been viewed by other traders, men with a great deal to lose by the passage of this bill?'

'They were extremely angry,' said Wilberforce.

'Enough to want to kill him?'

'Many of us in the abolitionist movement have had our lives threatened.'

Tom stared at the politician in silence for a moment. If the offer of a peerage had persuaded Sir Henry to vote against the interests of his former friends and colleagues in the slave trade, it was small wonder that he should have had his life threatened.

'What of John Dean? Was he, too, involved in the slave trade?'

'No, he was not,' said Wilberforce. 'He entered Parliament three years ago as the Member for Appleby. He was considered a bright young man with a promising career to look forward to. Most of his work would have been concerned with his constituency, although I do know that Mr Pitt had been making increasing use of his help.'

'Do we know what Mr Dean was doing in Southwark on the

night he was killed?' said Tom, sitting back in his chair as the waiter arrived with the tea tray.

'I assume he was going home. When he was in London, he would take rooms at a tavern in the village of Brixton, a few miles south of here. The route through Southwark was the most direct for him.'

Tom picked up his cup and swallowed a mouthful of tea, wishing it was something stronger. 'Why d'you suppose he was killed?'

'I really have no idea, unless he just happened to fall prey to some footpads.'

'I don't think so. A witness saw a man on horseback following the coach down Borough High Street and into Great Dover Street. By the time the witness reached Great Dover Street, the coachman was dead and Mr Dean was being forced from the coach at gunpoint. A common thief would not run the risk of abducting a passenger like that. He'd be more interested in the valuables he could find. And if he needed to kill, he'd do it then and there, as happened to the driver.'

'Then why d'you think he was killed?' asked Wilberforce.

Tom put his cup down on the table and ran a hand over the top of his scalp. 'I believe Mr Dean was deliberately sought out and forced into captivity. What is less clear is why, and why there was a delay in murdering him. I'm inclined to think that his killer wanted some information from him, or perhaps money, in exchange for his freedom.'

'Mr Dean was not a wealthy man, sir,' said Wilberforce. 'If a ransom was the killer's motive, he should have selected his victim with greater care.'

'What about information? We are at war. Could he not, as a Member of Parliament, have been carrying information of interest to the enemy?'

Wilberforce laughed. 'You have a high opinion of the worth of a Member of Parliament, sir. Why, he . . .'

'Yes?' said Tom.

'A thought has occurred to me, Mr Pascoe. You say Mr Dean was forced from his coach. Do you have a description of the coachman or the coach itself?'

Tom told him what he knew. When he'd finished speaking, Wilberforce said, 'Mr Dean did not, as far as I know, possess a chaise, but your description strongly suggests that it was the minister's carriage that was stopped.'

'That means,' said Tom, 'that whoever abducted Mr Dean may have mistaken him for Mr Pitt.'

'Quite.'

'Why would the minister permit Mr Dean the use of his carriage?' said Tom. 'Surely he would require it for himself.'

'Normally, he would,' agreed Wilberforce. 'But a week ago he was taken ill and confined to bed at his home. He is not, I regret to say, in the best of health. Nevertheless, news of his condition is not generally known outside the Palace of Westminster.'

'It still doesn't explain why his coach should have been in the possession of Mr Dean.'

'It's possible that he was conveying the minister's papers to him at his home. Mr Pitt has often asked for this to be done in the past. Indeed, I've performed the task myself on several occasions.'

'But the coach was found in Southwark. Is that where the minister resides?'

'No, his home is a little to the south of Bromley, in Kent,' said Wilberforce. 'The route would have taken Dean over London Bridge and down Borough High Street.'

'Are you aware of any specific reason why anyone would wish to kidnap the minister?'

'You are to consider, sir,' said Wilberforce, 'that many of the decisions made by politicians are likely to prove odious to the people. Mr Pitt, though generally well thought of, is not immune to such feeling of loathing amongst some.'

'So he stands at risk?'

Wilberforce didn't answer immediately. He picked up the teapot from the tray, his hand shaking as he refilled their two cups. When he next spoke, his voice was grave.

'For some considerable time now, I and my colleagues in the abolitionist movement have faced a number of threats designed to prevent, or at least delay, the abolition of the slave trade. A fortnight ago, intelligence was received from Royalist sources in France to the effect that there had been a meeting in Paris between Monsieur Jean-Pierre Duval, the Minister of Police, and some unknown Englishmen. We understand the purpose of the meeting was to explore ways in which mutual assistance could be rendered. Specifically, the French were to be provided with information useful to their war effort. In return, some form of operation was to be mounted against a public figure in this country concerned with the abolitionist movement.'

'Like Mr Pitt?'

'Our informant was unable to say who the target might be. All we have been able to deduce is that the enemy will, in all probability, wish to send an agent to this country to carry out the operation. For aught we know, the agent is already here. It now seems likely it is the minister whose life is threatened.'

'Is the minister currently at home?'

'Yes, at Holwood House, in Keston.'

'And well guarded?'

'No, there has never been the need but from what you seem to be saying, that has now changed.'

'I think it would be wise.'

CHAPTER 20

André Dubois stood by a gate leading into the Privy Gardens, and cast a casual glance down the length of Downing Street. It was the fourth time he'd been here. He knew he was taking a risk, but there was little alternative. The briefing he'd received from the aide to Monsieur Jean-Pierre Duval, the *ministre de la police* in Paris, had confidently suggested he would find his intended target in Downing Street or in the vicinity of the English Parliament building. 'He has,' the aide had told him, 'a house elsewhere and is known to visit his club from time to time but you won't need to search for him there.'

A carriage rolled down Whitehall. On the other side of the street, a man and a woman strolled past the mouth of Downing Street. The man glanced at him. Dubois sank further back into the shadows and waited for them to turn the corner into King Street before resuming his watch. Another carriage was travelling south down Whitehall. It slowed as it reached the entrance to Horse Guards Parade, and stopped. A moment later, the door of the carriage opened and Tom Pascoe got out, waved at someone inside the carriage, and began walking in his direction.

Dubois ducked through the gate into the Privy Gardens and reached for his knife. He waited, listening for the sound of approaching footsteps before peeping out. Pascoe had crossed

160

Whitehall and was now less than fifty yards away, by the Banqueting House. Dubois slid back out of sight, waited and then chanced another look. Pascoe had disappeared.

It took him a second or two to remember the passage leading to the Thames. It was no more than five feet wide, bounded on one side by the Banqueting House and on the other by a terrace of houses. A pair of arched gates, halfway down, gave access to the Privy Gardens. He could see them from where he stood. If he was quick, he'd reach the gates before Pascoe. He glanced round, checking he was alone. Then he sprinted down the path leading to the archway and eased open one of the doors. He could see Pascoe approaching, less than fifteen yards away.

Dubois drew his knife, his pulse quickening. He had looked forward to this moment for five long years, since the day Pascoe had stolen his ship from under him, shamed him in front of his crew, and taken him as a prisoner of war. He wiped a line of perspiration from his face and realised he was shaking. He tried to control it, holding his breath and tensing his body. It made no difference.

Pascoe's head was bent forward as if in thought. He would be opposite the gate in less than three seconds. Dubois tightened his grip on the hilt of his knife. He knew he had only one chance. Speed was vital. The smallest mistake and it would not be Pascoe that died. He stretched out a hand, his fingers gripping the edge of the gate. It was time.

Then he heard a voice.

He stumbled back, releasing his hold on the gate.

*

'All correct, sir.' Tom was directly opposite a double gate when he heard Sam's voice. He looked up to see his friend standing at the bottom of Whitehall Passage, close to the river stairs. Behind him he could see the rest of the crew sitting in the police galley.

'There you are, Sam. Come, we've not a moment to lose. It seems my friend Dubois has murder on his mind. His intended victim is going to be asked if he wants to return to London, or stay put in—'

Tom stopped. He'd heard a faint click coming from the double gate. He turned to look. One of the doors appeared to be ajar. He took a step towards it.

'Something wrong?' said Sam, walking towards him.

A casement window in one of the houses banged shut and a woman's face appeared, staring out at Tom through the glass before disappearing from view. Tom relaxed.

'No, nothing,' he said. 'I'm getting jumpy in my old age. Thought I heard one of those gates moving. Seems I was mistaken.'

He continued to stare at the gates, a lingering doubt in his mind. Had he imagined it? If it *had* moved, why had it not opened further? He stretched out a hand to push it open.

'Tide's falling, sir.' Sam's voice interrupted his thoughts. 'We'll soon be stuck fast on the hard.'

'I'm coming,' said Tom.

Dubois listened to the departing footsteps, his sense of frustration at the missed opportunity tempered by the realisation that Pascoe not only knew of his presence in the country but of the plot which had sent him here. He had always been aware of the possibility that the information would come out eventually. But he'd not bargained on it coming out so quickly.

He put his ear to the gate. He could still hear Pascoe's voice, down on the river, the words faint now, the sound mingling with the clump and splash of oars dropping between the thole pins, and entering the water. The police galley was leaving.

He leaned his back against the gate and sank to his haunches, his hands clasped over his ears. No, he wasn't surprised that Pascoe knew. The Englishman was no fool. Killing a man in the minister's coach had been bound to cause a reaction. And yet . . . Dubois paused, lifting his head and letting his fingers run down the side of his face – he might still have got away with it. His mistake, if he could call it that, was being seen by Pascoe. Not once, but twice, in recent days.

He wasn't sure which part of his failed mission he resented more – the one he'd been sent over to do, or his desire to end Pascoe's life. He remained squatting by the gate, deep in thought. Then he remembered something which, in the shock of near capture, he'd almost forgotten. It was something Pascoe had said. He searched his memory. Slowly, the words returned to him. *He's going to be asked if he wants to return to London, or stay put* . . . Pascoe had said.

But as far as he knew, the man he was after was in London, and had been all along. The words he'd overheard seemed to suggest that this was not the case, that his target was presently elsewhere but might return. But when? And to what address?

Dubois cursed the stupidity of the briefing he'd been given in Paris. It was typical of the arrogance of those who sat behind desks and who knew nothing of operational matters. He walked slowly towards the Whitehall gate, unsure of what to do next.

Then his face cleared. There *was* someone who might know the answers to his questions.

Ebenezer had not slept properly since his imprisonment on the Thames. A pair of iron shackles were attached to his ankles, preventing any real movement. The metal had torn at his skin, reducing the flesh to a bloody and swollen pulp. He could sit and, if he chose, stand, but that was all. The chain was too short for anything else.

He lay back and closed his eyes, thinking over the course of the last few weeks. If truth be told he had never felt entirely free in England, even after he'd run from the master's house and found shelter in a derelict house, south of the river. Freedom, he'd discovered, had its drawbacks. Quite apart from the hunger and discomfort, there had been the constant fear of detection.

In a sense his capture, when it came, had been a relief. At least he knew what to expect: the beating, the transportation back to Barbados, and the short journey to the marketplace on the Bridgetown waterfront, there to be sold back into slavery.

He could hear raised voices on the deck above his head. Doubt-less it was the crew making ready to sail. Then he heard the clatter of the hatch cover being removed and saw the daylight streaming in. He blinked and shielded his eyes against the unaccustomed glare as a pair of feet appeared over the hatch coaming and began to descend the companion ladder. A second person, then a third, followed. Ebenezer sat up, his stomach twisting in fear. He'd been beaten on his first day of captivity. Now he was to be beaten again. He shuffled back as far as the chains would allow him, his heart thumping.

'Ebenezer?' The voice was vaguely familiar. He looked up, but the light dazzled him. He nodded, not daring to speak.

The man turned to someone standing next to him. 'Take those shackles off and look lively, d'you hear?'

Ebenezer's eyes widened. He felt the weight of the metal fall away and saw the man who'd spoken bend down towards him. He recognised the corn-yellow hair held at the nape with a black ribbon, the blue coat with white lapels and the brass buttons.

'I see that you remember me, Ebenezer. Come, it's time to go. You can thank these two gentlemen from the Abolition Society.'

He had to be helped up the ladder, his joints stiff from the long hours of enforced inactivity, his mind in turmoil. He couldn't pretend that he knew what was happening or what lay ahead. Nor could he ask. If his years on Barbados had taught him anything, it was not to ask questions. Yet he couldn't help noticing that the man with the yellow hair held a gun in his hand.

They reached the deck. Men crowded round him, seemingly intent on preventing him from leaving.

'In the King's name,' barked the man with the yellow hair, raising his pistol. 'Stand aside.'

'You'll be hearing more of this, Pascoe.' It was the ship's captain shaking his fist, his face reddened with rage. Another minute and Ebenezer was at the ship's rail, being helped over the side, onto the ladder. Below, he could see a boat with more men in it. The man with the yellow hair, the one the captain had called Pascoe, seemed to know them. Slowly he climbed down the narrow strips of timber nailed to the side of the ship and was helped into the boat. He looked up and saw Pascoe and the abolitionists climbing down.

He still could not quite believe he was off the ship.

Ebenezer felt a deal better. His chafed ankles had been encased in rolls of bandages and he'd eaten a hot meal. He lifted his head off the cot and looked at the cell door as a rattle of keys warned him that someone was coming in. The door swung open and he recognised the men who'd rescued him from the ship, including the one he'd heard called Pascoe.

'Feeling better?' Pascoe didn't wait for an answer, instead waving a hand at the two men with him. 'You've already met these two gentlemen. They want to ask you a few questions.'

'Good afternoon, Mr Samson,' said one of the men. 'My name is Thomas Clarkson. I belong to the Society for the Abolition of the Slave Trade. This is my colleague, Mr Granville Sharp. We believe we might be able to help you.'

'Thank you, master.' Ebenezer had rolled off his cot as soon as the door of his room had opened. He stood with his head bowed, his eyes fixed on the floor.

'The person who abducted you,' said Sharp, 'may be guilty of assault and false imprisonment. We intend to lay information before a magistrate as the first step towards a trial. If we can prove the assault at court and he is found guilty there is a reasonable prospect of the magistrate ordering your immediate release. There have been several cases in the last few years where this has happened and we see no reason why your case should be any different.'

Ebenezer listened politely. He wanted to believe them but was not convinced. No white man had ever, in his experience, been taken to court for assaulting a nigger, never mind being imprisoned for it. Meanwhile, his master would still be searching for him.

CHAPTER 21

Tom closed the door of the constables' waiting room on the first floor of the police office and strolled down the stairs to the main hall. In spite of the cautionary note struck by Harriot when he'd told him what the abolitionists had had in mind, a day or so earlier, he was a deal more optimistic about the future. The prospect of Ebenezer appearing as a witness in any trial for the murders of John Dean and his coach driver was now a great deal better than it had been. Getting this far was, by any standards, a major step forward.

A low murmur of voices drifted up the stairs from the hall. He could see a group of people sitting on benches, awaiting their appearance before the magistrate. He recognised most of them, the same faces who came here, day in and day out, for offences too trivial to warrant imprisonment. More voices seeped through the closed door of the court, bursting into life each time the door opened, the sound mixing with that of the people still in the hall.

'Sir.' Tom looked over the banisters. It was Sam. He waited for his friend to join him.

'Trouble?'

Sam shook his head. 'Had a visitor asking for you. Wouldn't give his name. When I told him as how you was with Mr Harriot and couldn't be disturbed, he asked me to give you this letter.'

'Thankee, Sam,' said Tom taking the proffered note and opening it. 'That's odd.'

'What is, sir?'

'Not here,' said Tom. He checked his pocket watch before stuffing the letter into his coat pocket and walked towards the main door. 'I'll tell you when we get to the galley. Fetch the rest of the crew and tell them we're going afloat immediately.'

'They's just starting on their victuals—'

'Don't argue, Sam,' snapped Tom. 'Bear along there, on the double. We ain't got all day.'

A few minutes later, the police galley had cast off from the pontoon and was running upriver through the noise and confusion of the Upper Pool.

'This anything to do with that note I gave you, sir?' said Sam.

'Yes. It seems Sir William Bolt might have something to tell us about his friend Camperdown,' said Tom, 'I want to see him before he has a chance to change his mind.'

'What about your meeting with the secretary of state, sir? You ain't forgotten have you, your honour?'

Tom hadn't forgotten. Wilberforce had been in touch with the news that he'd informed Lord Portland, the secretary of state for the Home Department, of their concerns surrounding the minister's safety. Portland had immediately demanded a meeting for this evening. Tom wasn't looking forward to it. He would have preferred to spend the night drinking at the Devil's Tavern.

'It'll be close, but we should make it,' he said.

Reaching Whitehall stairs, the two of them strolled up

through St James's Park to Crockford's, the club in St James's Street where Bolt had asked to meet them. Announcing themselves, they were taken through to the Strangers' Room, and asked to wait.

'Mr Pascoe, I believe,' said a thin, elegantly dressed man of about thirty, who now entered the room. 'William Bolt. Delighted to meet you at last.'

'This is my colleague, Mr Hart,' said Tom. 'How can we help?'

'If you'd care to follow me,' said Bolt. 'I've arranged for the use of a private room where we might speak without interruption.'

The three of them walked along a corridor to the rear of the building and entered a large, richly decorated room, its twin sash windows hung with heavy damask drapes.

'Please sit down,' said Bolt, waving at a circular table around which were grouped a number of chairs. Tom guessed the room was used for gaming of one sort or another. He waited for Sir William to begin.

'It's my understanding, Mr Pascoe, that you have been appointed to investigate the death of Sir Henry Thwaite-Thomas, a neighbour and friend of mine from Rye. I believe that I may have some information which may assist you in that regard.'

'Please go on, Sir William.'

'You are aware, I think, of the identities of a number of gentlemen, including myself, who attended a meeting at the home of Sir Henry a few days before his death. My inquiries also indicate that you are aware of . . . how shall I put it . . . a disagreement which arose amongst ourselves, during the course of that night.'

Tom nodded, but said nothing. He waited for Bolt to continue.

'All of us present that night had an interest in slavery and were, as you might expect, opposed to the cause of abolition.'

Bolt stopped and looked from Tom to Sam and back again as though expecting some reaction. When none came, he went on, 'We wanted to influence the debate and persuade Parliament to vote against abolition. So far we have been successful but I fear the mood of the country is changing. It seems the majority now favour the end of slavery.'

'And that realisation led to a disagreement amongst you?' asked Tom.

'In a manner of speaking, yes,' said Bolt. He got up from his chair and stood looking out through the window at the late afternoon sky. Finally, he turned and looked at them, his face grave.

'I used the word "influence". Unfortunately there were those amongst us whose notion of influence was at variance to my own. Sir Henry objected in forthright terms to the proposals being put forward, and the argument which ensued was a heated one. Eventually things quietened down, and I thought the matter was at an end, but I was wrong.

'The following morning, I met with Lord Camperdown and he told me he was going to France where he hoped to meet with the governing *Directoire*.'

'Did he go?' asked Tom, taking a slug of tobacco from his pocket and sliding it into his mouth.

'Yes,' said Bolt with a shake of his head. 'He told me about it on his return. It seems he made his way to Paris where his presence was discovered and he was arrested. How he escaped the guillotine I don't know, but he was released.'

Tom had heard nothing of Camperdown's past to suggest he was sympathetic to the French cause, and still less that he might – despite his violent nature – entertain a murderous attack on the King's first minister. Yet if he had not offered his French captors something of value, it was difficult to imagine how he might have escaped from their custody. 'Is it possible Lord Camperdown might have struck a bargain with the French? Promised them something in return for his freedom?'

Bolt looked uncomfortable. He leaned his back against the window frame and eyed Tom from below a thick pair of eyebrows.

'Yes, I suppose it's possible,' he said, his tone wary.

'You mentioned there was a disagreement at the last meeting at the home of Sir Henry,' said Tom. 'What did you mean when you said you were wrong in thinking the argument had blown over?'

'It did not end that night,' said Bolt. 'The disagreement was principally between Sir Henry and Lord Camperdown. Unfortunately, his lordship does not easily forget an insult and there is no doubt he regarded Sir Henry's outburst as an insult that required satisfaction. He had obviously brooded over the matter while in France and, on his return, he sought Sir Henry at Westminster and called him out.'

'For disagreeing with him?'

'I'm afraid Sir Henry let his temper get the better of him and threatened to expose Camperdown's journey to France.'

'Knowing it would lead to a trial, and a likely death sentence for his lordship?'

'I don't know that he'd thought through the implications of his threat but the result was fairly predictable.'

'Are you telling me Sir Henry died in a duel with Camperdown?'

'I don't know. I wasn't there. All I will tell you is that there was a disagreement between the two of them and his lordship subsequently demanded satisfaction.'

'Why are you telling me all this, Sir William?' Tom kept his tone neutral. 'I understood you to be a particular friend of his lordship.'

'Your reputation precedes you, Mr Pascoe,' said Bolt, the ghost of a smile on his thin face. 'I knew that, sooner or later, you would learn of the argument at Sir Henry's home. I was anxious that you should be made aware of what actually happened.'

'I see,' said Tom. 'Yet you've chosen not to tell me anything about the duel.'

'For the reason I have already given,' said Bolt, his voice betraying his nervousness.

'That you were not there? Unfortunately, sir, there is an eyewitness who can place you at the scene of Sir Henry's death.'

'Really, this is preposterous. I . . .'

Tom knew a lie when he heard it. He had taken a risk and won. If Bolt had continued to deny any involvement in Sir Henry's death, there was not much Tom could have done about it. The alleged eyewitness to Bolt's presence had, itself, been a lie. But, in any case, he doubted the courts would wish to pursue a charge of murder in these circumstances, particularly given the fact that Pitt, the King's first minister, had himself engaged in a duel two years previously, and nothing had been said about the matter. Yet it did no harm to shake Bolt up a little, make him more pliable and ready to talk.

'I trust I don't need to remind you,' said Tom, 'that aiding in the commission of a crime is a serious matter, particularly where that crime is murder.'

'I may have accompanied Camperdown,' said Bolt, dabbing at his brow with a large silk handkerchief. 'But I was not involved in anything that happened that morning.'

Tom let it rest. He'd already decided to see Camperdown and ask him for his version of what had transpired. And while he was at it, he'd see what his lordship had to say about his visit to France. He was beginning to wonder if there was a connection between that and Dubois's presence in England.

'Does, sir, the name André Dubois mean anything to you?'

'No. Should it?'

'I don't know. I simply ask the question.'

'I regret I cannot help you,' said Bolt.

CHAPTER 22

Dubois left his room in Tooley Street and made his way through the evening crowds, west towards London Bridge. The little he'd overheard of Tom Pascoe's conversation in the Privy Gardens had initially confused him. Without information of the present whereabouts of the man he sought, he was bound to fail in his mission. And with his presence in this country now known, there was a limit to how long he could remain.

He reached London Bridge and turned to cross the Thames, the lights of several hundred ships' lanterns stretching away in a fiery thread that reached the bend of the river at the head of Limehouse Reach and the Isle of Dogs. He hurried across, ignoring the sleeping bodies propped against the parapets, huddled together as much for safety as for warmth. He wanted nothing so much as to be done with this assignment and be gone from this place. His thoughts wandered to the snow-capped peaks of northern Italy and the biting cold of the battlefields around Loano. The terrible privations of those months were at least made bearable by the presence of his comrades. Here, he was alone. Every decision was his to make, his to live – or die – by.

At the northern end of London Bridge, Dubois continued on straight, up the slope of Fish Street, past the Monument, and into Gracechurch Street, uncertain of precisely where he was going. He'd only been to the man's home once before, and that on the night of his arrival in London. He paused at the junction with Fenchurch Street, looking for anything that might seem familiar. He wiped the palms of his hands against his breeches and felt a cold sweat break out along his forehead. He was a stranger in a strange town, and more than that, an enemy alien. He wondered if he was taking too big a risk, but knew he had no alternative.

A coach drove past and turned into a deserted Lombard Street. He caught a fleeting glimpse of the driver. His heart leapt. He recognised the fellow, the peculiar shape of his head, the large, hooked nose, the broad red collar of his Richardson coat. The last time he'd seen the man was on a Kentish beach on the night of his arrival from France. The two of them had ridden through the night to a back street in Southwark where a coach – this coach – had been waiting to carry him the rest of the way.

The house outside which the man now stopped was small and run-down. The only sign of life from within was a single light shining from one of the ground-floor windows. He watched the driver step down before turning to speak to a young man who had been on the seat with him.

'All right, George, take it away. Make sure the horses are rubbed down and fed. When you're done, come home. Your ma will have something ready for you to eat.'

Dubois waited until the man was alone and then approached him.

'A moment of your time, my friend,' said Dubois, in English.

The man spun round and levelled a pistol at the Frenchman's chest. 'Stay where you are, cully, and state your business.'

'A word, that is all,' said Dubois, raising his hands. 'We have met before, you and I.'

'Oh, aye? Come a little closer where I can see you. Not too quick, mind.'

Dubois took a pace closer.

'Now I see you,' said the driver, peering at him. 'You's the cove what I brought up to London from the coast. What you doing hereabouts? Thought the master told you to stay away.'

'I need to see him,' said Dubois, wishing he'd had the foresight to bring his own pistol. At least it would have evened the odds.

'Cor love us, cock. What makes you think he'd want to see you?'

'It is important. I must see him.'

The man looked over his shoulder as though to ensure they'd not been seen or overheard. Then he jerked his head at the front door. 'Best you come in. As soon as my boy comes back, I'll send word to the master. See what he says.'

It was well after midnight by the time the boy had returned from his errand. The master had agreed to the meeting, insisting only that Dubois be blindfolded for the journey. After some hesitation Dubois had reluctantly agreed to the condition and waited while a length of material was found and tied about his eyes.

Moments later they were on their way, the coach creaking from side to side as corners were negotiated and potholes avoided. Finally it came to a halt and Dubois felt it rock slightly as the driver got down and came round to the door. He felt an uncharacteristic wave of self-doubt as a hand caught hold of his elbow and helped him down the step. The briefing in Paris had been quite clear on the subject of his contact in England. He would be met at the coast and conveyed to London where he would be introduced to the contact. It was, he had been told, imperative that he make no attempt to meet him after the initial briefing. To do so would jeopardise his cover and risk future operations.

But he had to see the man. The information he'd been given about his target was wrong and, without additional intelligence, the operation was bound to fail. Dubois heard voices. He imagined them to be servants. The cloth about his eyes moved slightly and he could see the open door of a house in front of him. He turned his head. Behind him was a square of trees and shrubs, similar to those he'd seen in the wealthy parts of Marseille. He'd already made a mental note of the route they had taken to get here and was confident he could retrace his steps if it were necessary. The view of the square was the final link in the chain. The next moment someone was guiding him into the house. He'd know, soon enough, whether or not he was welcome.

CHAPTER 23

Tom stood at the bottom of the police stairs and watched a lighter making its way upriver on the tide, its freeboard no more than about six inches, the ragged figure of its lighterman crouched over his sweep oar as he eased his heavy charge through the Lower Pool. Another half-dozen were following on behind. Soon they would all arrive off the Custom House quay and be required to wait at one of the barge roads, perhaps as long as three or four weeks, before their turn came to berth alongside and be relieved of such of their cargo as had not been plundered.

'Did your meeting with the secretary of state produce anything of interest?' said Harriot.

'About the threat to the minister?' Tom shrugged, recalling the details of his visit to Portland's office in Whitehall. It had been a fractious affair, Portland on the one side and Wilberforce on the other, each arguing for different things. In the end Portland had been forced to accept that the decision about whether Mr Pitt returned to London or not would have to wait until Wilberforce had seen him.

'Portland wanted the minister back in London?'

'Yes. He thought it would be easier to protect him if he was in Downing Street.'

'And Wilberforce wanted him to stay put at Holwood House, I suppose?'

'Yes.'

'What d'you think?'

'From what I'm told, the estate is quite isolated but could be protected if a sufficient force of men were deployed. He is a sick man and moving him would likely make things worse. On the other hand, it would be easier to ensure his safety were he to return to Downing Street. The problem is the journey. The safest route would be by river from Woolwich but there would still be danger.'

'From Dubois?' said Harriot.

'Yes. I think assassinating the minister is what he's been sent to do.'

'And you don't know where he is.'

'No, I think he's being sheltered by someone.'

'Any idea who?'

'Possibly Camperdown. We've been watching his London house for some days now, so far without success.'

'Have you spoken to anyone at the Foreign Office about any of this?'

'No, I haven't.'

'Then perhaps you should,' said Harriot. 'I'll let you have a letter of introduction to the under-secretary of state. He's fairly new in post but I've no doubt he'll be able to let you have a few facts that might be useful. His name is Hookham Frere. Nice chap. You'll like him.'

Harriot paused for a moment as though a new thought had struck him. 'Lord Camperdown . . .'

Tom waited.

'Didn't you tell me he was involved with that negro slave? What was his name?'

'Ebenezer Samson? Yes, he was Camperdown's slave.'

'I've received word from Mr George Storey, my colleague at the Shadwell police office. He tells me there's to be a hearing tomorrow morning at the Court of King's Bench. The abolitionists intend making an application for a writ of *Habeas Corpus* in the case of the negro.'

'Yes, I knew the case was pending. What are his chances?'

'Difficult to say. Storey is no fool and if he couldn't make up his mind on the issue, I'm not sure I'd want to try and second-guess the Lord Chief Justice.'

'If he loses the case and gets sent back to the West Indies, it'll mean the end of the murder case against Dubois,' said Tom. 'Ebenezer is our only real witness.'

'We won't need him at all if you don't find Dubois,' said the magistrate.

'I do realise that, sir,' said Tom, a little more testily than he'd intended. 'I'll find him.'

André Dubois contemplated the shaft of mote-filled sunlight lancing through the first-floor window of the inn on Tooley Street. His meeting the evening before had gone tolerably well, in spite of the initial hostility displayed by his host. But then he'd hardly expected to be made welcome. He knew his visit had risked not only his own life, but that of his host, as well.

Not that that had made any difference. Twice, in the space of the first thirty seconds of the door being opened, Dubois had found himself reaching for his knife, intent on dealing with what he had perceived to be a slight.

He walked over to his bed and sat down. He realised he knew nothing about his English contact, beyond what he'd been told by the aide to the *ministre de la police*. And that had been little enough. Just that he was an aristocrat sympathetic to the cause of the Revolution. Nothing more. No name, no address and no background information. The initial anger with which the meeting began had gradually dissipated as each got the measure of the other. They'd spoken for perhaps fifteen or twenty minutes.

'As far as I am aware, your man is still in London,' the contact had told him. 'If he's not at his usual address, then he's probably with friends in the country.' The information had not helped much. There had been no details of the friends with whom the target might be staying, except a passing reference to a Holwood House, in Kent.

Dubois climbed to his feet, walked to the window. It could be a day or two before he found out where his target was, a day or two he could ill afford, especially when his contact had confirmed what he already suspected: that a witness had seen him disposing of a body in the Thames. He wondered who it could have been. Probably the nigger he'd spotted running away. Or perhaps one of the nightwatchmen. He would deal with them later. He put the problem to the back of his mind and tried to concentrate on the operation.

The reference to Holwood House hadn't sounded particularly hopeful. Yet it was the only lead he had. He'd begin his search there – hire himself a horse and ride out to Kent. He turned away from the window and walked to the door. He was feeling better already.

CHAPTER 24

Mr John Hookham Frere, under-secretary of state at the Foreign Office, removed a pair of spectacles from his beak-like nose and proceeded, with the utmost vigour, to polish the lens. Completing the task, he placed them on the bridge of his nose and squinted at his visitor.

'I'm still not entirely clear Mr . . . ah . . . Pascoe, what help I can be to you. My learned friend, Mr John Harriot, whose letter of introduction I have here, is silent on the matter. He says only that you are a senior officer in the new marine police establishment and would welcome any information I may give you. What, exactly, is it you're after?'

'We think an enemy agent has arrived in London with a view to assassinating a senior figure within the Administration.'

'And you think the Foreign Office can help?'

'I very much hope so,' said Tom. 'Your office is, I understand, aware of a meeting that took place a week or two ago, in Paris, between an unknown Englishman and the French minister of police. I believe the possibility of a mutually advantageous operation was discussed.'

'Go on,' said Hookham Frere, cocking an eyebrow.

'I've been given a name which may be that of the Englishman concerned.'

'And that is?'

'Alexander Thorngood, the Second Baron Camperdown.'

Hookham Frere pursed his lips and leaned back in his chair as he regarded his visitor. 'You are well informed, sir. We'd heard the same information, but for reasons I'll not trouble you with, it was decided that, beyond speaking to Lord Camperdown, nothing was to be done that might result in embarrassment to the minister or his Administration.'

'Yet it remains the case,' said Tom, 'that Lord Camperdown travelled to France and met the minister of police. I think that meeting resulted in the arrival of the agent I've mentioned.'

Hookham Frere steepled his fingers and breathed in deeply. 'This is a delicate subject. What I'm about to tell you comes from a number of trusted sources whose identities I am not at liberty to divulge. Suffice it to say that I'm satisfied as to its veracity. What I say to you, therefore, must be treated with the utmost confidence.'

He leaned back in his chair and looked up at the ceiling before continuing. 'Lord Camperdown has long been a thorn in the side of the Administration. His exploits would, in another man, have resulted in appearances before the courts and would have ended in his execution for treason. We know he crossed the Channel into France, and on his return to England we spent some time questioning him. He stated his sole intention in going there was the murder of General Bonaparte. At the time we were unable to prove anything to the contrary and he was released.'

'But now?' said Tom.

'I'm simply saying that as matters stand, there's no evidence to suggest he's responsible for the agent's presence.' Hookham

Frere stopped suddenly. 'May I ask how you came to know of his meeting in Paris?'

'A friend of his told me,' said Tom.

'A friend?' The under-secretary's eyebrows shot up. 'And who might that have been?'

Tom hesitated. He wasn't at all sure he liked giving away his sources without receiving anything in return. 'Someone his lordship thought he could trust.'

Hookham Frere smiled. 'Let me guess. Sir William Bolt.'

Tom inclined his head, his nod barely perceptible.

'It would be surprising, would it not, if we didn't interest ourselves in those who keep company with his lordship. Sir William has become a firm favourite of ours in the last year or so. What surprises me is that he should have spoken to you in such candid terms about his friend. But, in truth, it was only a question of time before two such volatile characters fell out.'

'What, sir, can you tell me about him?'

'He's a complicated cove, that's for sure,' said Hookham Frere, pulling a buff file towards him and opening it. 'He, like Camperdown, is capable of great brutality, but manages to hide this under a veneer of charm and respectability. The two of them are boyhood friends, although there was a long period when they lost touch with one another. At fifteen, Camperdown – or plain Master Alexander Thorngood as he was then – was sent away to sea, while Bolt managed to buy himself a commission in the Seventeenth Light Dragoons. Within a few years he had been sent with the regiment to Jamaica. There, I understand, he quickly saw action in what became known as the Second Maroon War.

'We think it was during this period that Bolt was first

introduced to the slave trade and saw the vast profits that could be made. On the regiment's return to England, in 1797, he resigned his commission and again met up with Thorngood who had, by this time, succeeded his father's title to become the Second Baron Camperdown. If anything, Bolt's behaviour had become even more extreme in the intervening years, and stories circulated which painted a picture of a young man out of control who thought little of meting out savage punishments to all who were considered to have crossed him.

'We know he's been involved in the slave trade since he left the army. He's now up to his neck in the business and often travels to the Bight of Biafra where he'll purchase two or three hundred men, women and children for conveyance to the West Indies. Of all Lord Camperdown's friends, Bolt would certainly have the most to lose were the trade to be abolished.'

'Odd.'

'What is?'

'Are you aware of the death of Sir Henry Thwaite-Thomas, the MP for Gatton?'

'I could hardly have failed to be aware,' said Hookham Frere. 'Was Bolt involved?'

'He may have been,' said Tom. 'But that's not why I mention it. He told me he was present at a meeting at Sir Henry's house shortly before Sir Henry's death. During the evening there was an argument about the use of violence as a means to an end. Sir Henry was opposed to it and made his feelings known. Bolt told me he had sided with Sir Henry, albeit without actually joining in. At the time, I had no reason to doubt the truth of what he was telling me, but now . . .'

'Did he say against whom the violence was intended?'

'He did not,' said Tom. 'But I think it is safe to assume it was the abolitionists in general and Mr Pitt in particular.'

'And you're wondering why a man normally given to violence, who has much to lose if slavery were to be abolished, should choose to tell you that he was opposed to violence, even in the defence of his own interests.'

'Precisely.'

'Perhaps he didn't want to be accused of complicity in Sir Henry's death.'

'Unfortunately for him, he's gone too far to avoid that,' said Tom.

'And in the meantime,' said Hookham Frere, 'you have still to find an enemy agent who may be planning to use some sort of violence towards a member of the abolitionist movement whose identity is yet unknown. Not, I think, the easiest of tasks, sir.'

CHAPTER 25

Tom woke to the sound of rain drumming against his bedroom window. He leaned over and picked up his discarded coat from its usual place on the floor. From one of the pockets he drew out his watch. Five o'clock. He sighed and let his head fall back on his pillow. He didn't feel at all well. His joints ached, his mouth felt dry and he could feel the start of yet another headache.

He reached for a half-empty bottle of gin under his bed. A little drink and he'd feel better. He struggled up onto one elbow and brought the glass close to his lips, savouring the tantalising thought of what lay inside. He knew what he was doing, knew he had to stop before it was too late; before it ended his life. But that could wait for another day. Right now he needed a drink – to go with the others he'd had last night.

An image of Peggy filled his mind, her smile that had lit up his life, her hands outstretched towards him, beckoning him to her. He leaned towards her, his hands trembling as they reached for hers. Then, as quickly as it had come, the image faded.

Tom stared at the foot of his bed, willing the image to return. Slowly, he looked down at the bottle in his hand, his tongue running over his parched lips. He pushed back the blankets and swung his legs out, shivering in the cold air of the early dawn. Carefully, he put the bottle down and reached for his breeches, still damp from his last tour afloat. Then he padded across to the wash basin in the corner of the room and poured in some cold water from the pitcher. He splashed some onto his face, dried himself and walked to the window. It was still dark, the scudding black clouds scarcely visible through the gloom, the rain still beating against the glass. The headache was getting worse. Returning to his bed, he drew on a pair of soiled stockings, and hunted round for his shoes.

A sheet of paper was poking out of his coat pocket, on the floor. He bent down and picked it up. It was the pencil drawing of Peggy that his crewman, Higgins, had seen in the bottom of the police galley and returned to him. Tom smoothed it out, laid it on his bed, staring at it. He'd drawn it soon after they had met, standing outside the Rotunda at Vauxhall Gardens. He'd managed to catch her smile and the light in her eyes, her head tilted to one side, her hands behind her back. The picture had lain, long forgotten by his fuddled mind until the moment Higgins had retrieved it from where it had fallen.

He walked across to his old sea chest and rummaged through it until he found what he was looking for. The vellum pages of his battered, linen-covered sketchbook were bound together with string. Carefully, he opened it. Every page was filled with drawings in charcoal or graphite. Most of them recorded shipboard life. A few more contained scenes of far-off places, of islands and ports to which his travels had taken him. And near the back were the pictures of the woman he had loved. For a long time he looked at them. Then he closed the book and returned it to its place at the bottom of the sea chest.

He finished dressing, his thoughts returning to his meeting

with Hookham Frere and the extent of the Administration's interest in Camperdown. Again he wondered why his lordship had crossed the Channel and what had been discussed during his meeting with the *ministre de la police* in Paris. Camperdown's own explanation to the Foreign Office was contradicted by intelligence received from French Royalist sources. It was clear from the efforts made by the French to find and detain him that they had feared his motives. Why, then, had they released him? It made no sense – unless he had offered them something in return for his life.

Tom mulled the matter over in his mind. He had already floated the idea that the price of his freedom from the French was the introduction of an agent to London. Certainly his contacts would be invaluable for hiding someone like André Dubois.

He put the thought to the back of his mind. He had more immediate problems to deal with. Yesterday evening he'd gone straight from his meeting at the Foreign Office to see Lord Portland.

'I have just received word from Mr Wilberforce who has returned from his visit to Mr Pitt,' Portland had said. 'I'm delighted to say that the minister has agreed to return to London. Mr Wilberforce, together with a troop of cavalry, will accompany him for the first part of his journey overland to Deptford. Once there, the minister will transfer to a Navy cutter and complete his journey along the Thames. I think this is by far the safest option for him.'

Tom's heart had sunk. A journey along the Thames meant close protection would not be possible. His crew would never keep up with the greater speed of a sailing vessel. He'd have to choose the area of greatest risk from attack and hope he was right. Even then, the task would be difficult. He didn't care for the idea of trying to escort the minister through the crowded waters of the Upper and

Lower Pool. And to add to their difficulties, the crew of the cutter would have to ensure their arrival at London Bridge before the tide turned and made it impossible to get through the arches.

He shrugged on his heavy uniform coat and headed for the door. The decision about Pitt had been made. Nothing he could say would alter that. If Dubois attacked, Tom wanted to be ready for him.

'There you are, Sam. Is there any of that stuff left?' said Tom, walking into the constables' waiting room and catching sight of the coffee pot.

'One coffee coming up, sir,' said Sam, pouring the scalding, dark brown liquid into a mug and handing it to his friend. 'You look as though you could do with it.'

'Where are the others?' said Tom, ignoring the comment.

Sam shrugged. 'Be along any minute, I shouldn't wonder. They wouldn't want to miss this job. You heard about the nigger?'

'Ebenezer? No. What's happened?'

'He's been sent back to his master. The King's Bench threw out the application.'

'For *Habeas Corpus*? I don't believe it,' said Tom. 'Did they give a reason?'

'I only knows what the Shadwell beak were telling Mr Harriot. They was talking in the hall, after you left last night. Seems that while the judge accepted Ebenezer couldn't read nor write, he reckoned that since he'd put his mark on the form of indenture, there was nothing the Court could do for him.'

'Did anyone tell the judge what would happen to him? That he would certainly be sold back into slavery?'

'Aye, he were told right enough. It didn't make no difference though. Judge reckoned his stay in England only suspended his slavery, and didn't end it. Said it weren't no concern of his what the law was in Barbados. If they allowed slavery, that were their affair. He were only concerned with the law of England.'

'Ye gods, was ever justice served in Westminster Hall?' said Tom, throwing up his hands. 'Do you know where Ebenezer is now?'

'I did hear he were going to be taken—'.

Sam was interrupted by the door opening.

'We'll speak about this later,' said Tom, turning to greet the arrival of the remaining members of his crew.

'As you already know,' he said, as soon as the newcomers had helped themselves to coffee, 'we've received information regarding an attempt on the life of a senior public figure. We think that person is the minister, Mr Pitt, and that the attempt will be made this morning as he travels between his home in Kent and Downing Street in Westminster. We have no information about where the attack is likely to take place but he will be escorted by a troop of cavalry over the land section, so it's unlikely to be there. That leaves us with the journey on the river and a short walk at the Whitehall end. Normally, we would stay with him throughout the journey, but in this case we'll not be able to. The minister is being conveyed in a sailing cutter whose greater speed means we'll be unable to keep up. Instead, we are going to have to wait for him at the place where the danger is at its greatest. I think that place is the Upper Pool, where the river is at its busiest and where there are a number of river stairs from which the attacker can select his escape. I've asked our other two boats to cover the Lower Pool and Limehouse Reach. God help us if we've got it wrong.'

Dubois could see a smudge of grey in the eastern sky, visible through the trees, as he turned off the Westerham road and guided his horse up through the woods, towards the summit of Holwood Hill, a mile or so east of the village of Keston. He could see the isolated house ahead of him, overlooking an escarpment of the North Downs, its white-painted walls washed clean by the rain. He drew in the horse's reins and stopped, aware the place was probably guarded. He dropped back, tied his horse to the branch of a tree, and climbed through the ancient stand of beech, oak and elm, rivulets of rain cascading from the rim of his hat, onto the shoulders of his cape.

A hundred yards from the house, he stopped and wiped his eyes as he squatted onto his haunches and peered through the dawn light at the two-storey building in front of him. Its smallness surprised him. He'd expected something much larger, more in keeping with the status of the British minister. Twenty or thirty yards east of the property, he could make out some more buildings – probably stables and accommodation for the staff. From the west, a rough track meandered up the hill from the Westerham road, past the front door, and on towards the stables.

Dubois turned his attention back to the house. A light flared in one of the upstairs rooms and a shadow passed across the window. A moment later, a second light appeared in another room. He heard the rumble of wheels and the stamp of horses' hooves and, a moment later, a black lacquered carriage swayed into view round the corner of the main house and came to a halt outside the front door. Behind it was a troop of cavalry, their harnesses jingling as they rode.

Dubois sank further out of sight and waited. The door of the house opened and some men came out, carrying chests which they loaded onto the roof of the coach. Another minute ticked by and the door again opened, light from inside the house flooding the drive. Two men came out, one ahead of the other. The second man was bent almost double and appeared to be in some pain as he hobbled forward. Reaching the coach, they both climbed in.

Dubois gave a silent whistle of excitement. He had recognised both men. There was no mistaking Wilberforce or the Right Honourable William Pitt, the King's first minister.

Dubois ran back to where he'd left his horse. Making sure that he remained out of sight, he waited for the coach and its escort to pass by along the road. Then he followed.

CHAPTER 26

Columns of sulphur-laden smoke rose from the chimney stacks lining the Shadwell foreshore and spread over the early morning sky as the police galley approached the King and Queen Stairs, on the Rotherhithe shore.

'Way enough. Toss oars.' The forward movement of the sleek, clinker-built craft slowed to a halt as it came alongside the mooring poles at the foot of the stairs.

'Boat your oars.' Tom shrugged off the two tiller guys that had been looped over his shoulders, his fingers cold and stiff from the continuous grip of the ropes. 'Make fast fore and aft.'

From a crane house on the wharf, high above his head, he could hear men singing a sea shanty, keeping time with the stamp of their feet and the click of the pawls in the tread-mill where they toiled. He cocked his head and listened, the haunting sound transporting him back to his days at sea when, each evening, he would watch the ship's people gather at the forepeak to sing and dance to the hornpipe and the fiddle.

He turned away and looked down through the jumble of shipping in the Lower Pool. He'd already made several sweeps of the reach, passing up and down through the chaos and noise of the port, his eyes scouring every shape and shadow for any trace of Dubois. He'd seen nothing; no sudden turn of the head, no frantic dip and pull of oars, no stifled gasp of recognition. Of course, he couldn't be certain he'd not missed him. The rain made it difficult to see anything and the scrub had a lifetime's experience of avoiding detection.

Tom had tried to put himself into the Frenchman's mind. He had to assume that Dubois knew the minister's route and had made plans on exactly when and where to strike. He would probably remain ashore, out of sight, yet be capable of seeing the approach of the minister's craft. Only at that point would he come out onto the river. And that meant proximity to one of the many river stairs. But which one?

Tom glanced over the side of the galley. The tide had turned, gradually gaining in strength as it moved upriver towards London Bridge, the slopping, gurgling sound growing louder as the water swept round the mooring poles at the base of the river stairs.

He heard a sudden cry from the other side of the river. Men were running along the upper deck of a brigantine, leaning over the rail, looking at something in the water. He tried to hear what they were shouting, their voices carried away on the wind.

'. . . overboard. He . . . quick . . . drown.'

'D'you hear there?' Tom picked up the tiller guys and looped them over his shoulders, his eyes fixed on the brigantine. 'Cast off fore and aft. Give way together. Smartly, my lads.'

The big galley surged into the tide, flecks of spume blowing over her bows and drenching the crew as it picked up speed, the long sweeps dipping into the tideway with barely a splash, the thole pins squealing in protest at each pull. Tom knew he didn't have long. A man falling into the Thames when the tide was at its strongest had little hope of avoiding death, even if he could swim – which was unlikely.

'Cutter rounding the point, abaft Limekiln Dock, sir,' shouted Sam. 'Looks to be the one what's carrying the minister.'

'Thankee, Sam.' A knot of anxiety formed in Tom's gullet. He glanced over his shoulder and saw a gaff-rigged cutter bearing round into the Lower Pool. He would just have time to find the missing person. He turned back, judged the moment and brought the galley up into the tide, close to where the body had fallen. 'Easy all. I wouldn't want to miss the cully.'

'Cutter closing fast astern, sir,' said Sam. 'Maybe four hundred yards.'

'Very well,' said Tom, the knot in his stomach becoming tighter as he searched the rain-pitted surface of the Thames. 'There he is. Twenty yards up on the larboard bow.'

'Sir?'

'Aye, Sam, what is it?

'There's a wherry approaching the cutter from the north bank, sir. Two cullies aboard.'

Tom looked back at the ship from which the man had fallen, now far astern. A boat was being lowered but it would never reach him in time. He looked round. No one else had joined the search. If he didn't pick the man up, he'd drown. He looked down the river, could see the minister's cutter and the wherry approaching it. For another second he hesitated.

'Very well. Keep me informed. We'll pick this lad up and then attend to the minister. You ready, Kemp?'

'The wherry's closing fast, your honour,' said Sam, panic in his voice.

Tom risked a backward glance and the blood drained from his face.

Ebenezer Samson heard the metallic scrape of a key being inserted into the lock of his cell door. A moment later the gaoler was beckoning him out. Ebenezer shuffled forward, the leg irons chafing painfully against his ankles.

'Stand over here, sooty chops.' The turnkey pulled him over to a low block and picked up a hammer. 'Put your foot here. I got other bleedin' things to do besides attending to the likes of you.' A couple of expert blows from the heavy implement and Ebenezer's shackles fell to the floor.

'Where am I going, master?' said Ebenezer, dredging up the courage to speak.

'You go where you're told to go. That's where.' The turnkey gave a toothless grin and jerked a thumb towards two men he'd not previously noticed. 'You go with these gentlemen. There's someone what wants to see you, like.'

Ebenezer felt a cold shiver running down his spine. He guessed the men had been sent by his master. A few minutes later, the three of them had left the prison, his guards walking directly behind him as they turned out of Old Bailey and into Ludgate Street. Soon they'd ascended the slope to St Paul's and were amongst a throng of people browsing the bookstalls. Books were everywhere, stacked on tables, on the backs of carts, under awnings and on chairs. He stared at the scene, his attention absorbed. He didn't see the man in front of him until after he had collided with him.

The man's expression turned from surprise to fury as he

looked round and saw who had bumped into him. He launched himself at Ebenezer, throwing him back against his guards. In a moment all four of them were sprawled in the dirt, dragging others with them in an untidy heap of tangled arms and legs.

Ebenezer was the first to recover. He scrambled to his feet and found himself being pushed aside by people trying to avoid the crush. In a moment he'd lost sight of the two guards. He moved forward, pushing his way back towards them but found his way blocked. He looked around. No one was paying him any attention.

He backed away. If his guards saw him now, they'd think he'd brought about the whole incident to aid his escape and give him the flogging he didn't deserve. Another quick glance at the sprawled bodies and he was running.

He'd reached the south bank of the Thames before he slowed to a walk. He passed an open door. Warm air wafted out and enveloped him. He stopped. The door led through to a large rectangular hall crowded with men. They were wearing white shawls draped over their shoulders and small black skullcaps on their heads. Ebenezer was aware of an elderly man standing to one side of the door, watching him, his bony features almost entirely hidden behind a long grey beard. Ebenezer dropped his gaze and began to walk away.

'*Shalom aleichem.*' Ebenezer jumped at the sound of the man's voice. He stopped and looked back. 'Come inside, rest and warm yourself.'

Ebenezer stood still, unsure of what to do. He was tired and hungry. The shock of the last twenty-four hours had drained him of his strength and confidence. Those who'd promised to help him had deserted him. The man was still watching him, smiling. He decided he would take a chance. Things could hardly get worse. He had nowhere to rest and no means of feeding himself. He walked slowly back. The elderly man stood aside and waved him in. 'Welcome,' he said, waving Ebenezer to a chair. 'I'll fetch someone.'

People were singing, the rise and fall of their voices soothing. It was nothing like the music of home but, he thought, beautiful nevertheless. He remembered the Joan and Johnny dances under the tropical sky. He could almost hear the screech of the fiddle and the whooshing beat of the calabash with which each dance was accompanied. He must have dozed. Someone was shaking him.

'My name is Joshua Van Oven.' The speaker, a man in his mid-thirties, was clean-shaven and with a receding hairline. 'My friend tells me you have run from your master.'

'Yes, master.' Ebenezer looked nervously from one to the other of the two men, unsure of how they had come by the information. Perhaps the elderly man had simply guessed the truth. He looked at the door of the hall. It was still open. If he needed to run, he could do so. He looked up at Van Oven. There was a gentleness there he'd not seen in a long time, a compassion he could almost feel. He felt his fear slipping away. 'The master beat me, so I run. I . . .'

The men listened in silence as Ebenezer poured out his story. When he'd finished, Van Oven said, 'I know of a man who might be able to help. Sir William Bolt has a certain amount of influence in these matters.'

CHAPTER 27

Tom stared at the two vessels. There was no doubt they were on a collision course. The cutter carrying the minister up through the Lower Pool of the Port of London was heeled over in the moderate south-easterly breeze, her mainsail boom skimming the surface of the river. She was passing Shadwell Dock and keeping to the centre of the channel, well clear of the tiers of shipping on either side of her. A rowing skiff was heading for her from the Shadwell side of the river.

He glanced down at the bedraggled figure, half in and half out of the river. It was going to take another thirty or forty seconds before the crew had him out and settled in the bottom boards. 'Bear along there, Kemp. We need to be going pretty damn quick.'

'Aye, sir. Be ready in a flash,' said Kemp giving the man a final heave over the gunwale.

Tom was no longer listening, his gaze fixed on the two boats less than a quarter of a mile down the reach. They were too far away for him to see anyone's face.

'Give way together. Handsomely, handsomely.' The galley swept round and raced downstream through the crowded waters of the port. Tom peered over the heaving shoulders of his three-man crew. He might just be in time.

Someone was shouting. He looked to his left. Some lighters were drifting across his path, less than twenty yards away. The lighterman on the nearest vessel was waving him away. Tom cursed and hauled down on the starboard guy. The galley creamed round, skimming close under the bows of the leading barge. Tom searched the water ahead. The gap between the cutter and the wherry was closing faster than he'd thought.

'Give way together.'

They weren't going to make it. The man in the stern was still hunched into his coat, his hat low over his eyes, seemingly oblivious to his surroundings. Tom looked at the crew of the minister's cutter. They, too, appeared unperturbed. A doubt seeped into his mind. He stared hard at the man in the stern of the skiff as it altered course and slipped astern of the cutter. It wasn't Dubois.

A mixture of relief and disappointment sweeping over him, Tom wondered what had gone wrong. He'd been sure the attack would take place at this point on the Thames. Here were the greatest number of escape routes available to Dubois and here the press of ships, lighters and other vessels would provide him with cover to aid his escape. Further up, towards the Bridge, the crush of river traffic might have worked against him.

Tom had a feeling he was missing something. He tried to gather his thoughts, trawling through his memory, searching for the clue that he knew had to be there. The argument about the slave trade at the home of Sir Henry Thwaite-Thomas had, almost certainly, been the catalyst from which all the rest had flowed. It was probably at that meeting that the decision had been taken for Camperdown to travel to France and enlist the help of the French. It was probably Camperdown who had arranged for Dubois to be sent over to this country. Sir William Bolt had hinted as much. The target was to be the abolitionists.

Yet Bolt had not named the intended victim. Nor had he indicated how the action was to be carried out. It was only when he had spoken of Camperdown's crossing to France – later confirmed by Hookham Frere, at the Foreign Office – that Tom had considered the possibility of a French agent in London. His mind had immediately gone back to the marks he'd seen on the neck of the coach driver in Great Dover Street and his suspicion that Dubois might have returned to England.

The attack on the coach, initially regarded as an unfortunate and regrettable incident, had only begun to assume greater importance when the connection between it and Mr Pitt became evident. The prospect of an attempt on the life of the minister had suddenly loomed large.

Yet, what if that were not so? What if Dubois had been sent to assassinate someone other than Mr Pitt? The attack on the minister's coach had first introduced the idea that Pitt might be the intended target. And once that idea had taken root, it had been difficult to dislodge it. Something Wilberforce had said dropped into the outer reaches of Tom's mind. *Many of us in the abolitionist movement have had our lives threatened.* It took a heartbeat for the significance of the remark to sink in. The target for Dubois's attack had always been Wilberforce, not Pitt. Wilberforce, more than anyone else, personified the abolitionist movement. It was he who Dubois had been after when he stopped and abducted John Dean in the mistaken belief that Wilberforce was on board, as he had been on several previous occasions. It was Wilberforce who had travelled to meet the minister and accompany him part of the way back to London and who, even now, was travelling to Blackheath without an escort.

'Is everything all right, sir?' Sam Hart's voice seemed a long way off.

'I hope so, Sam,' said Tom, grim faced. 'But I won't be sure until we get to Deptford. D'you hear there? Give way together. And look smart about it. We ain't got a minute to lose.'

'Deptford, sir? What about the minister?' protested Sam. 'I thought we were supposed to be looking after him.'

'Not any more,' said Tom. 'It's Mr Wilberforce I'm concerned for. I reckon that's who Dubois is after. I wondered what the villain was doing outside Brooks's when I went to see Mr Wilberforce the other day. Now I know.'

Dubois remained below the archway of the King's Head at Deptford. He'd been there for nearly an hour, ever since the coach carrying Pitt and Wilberforce had turned into the approach road leading to the perimeter wall of the naval dockyard, forty or fifty yards away.

The squeal of the metal gates warned him they were opening. He eased his mount forward a pace or two and peered down the street. A coach was emerging; the same one he'd followed from Keston. He watched as it turned right and headed down Victualling Office Row, towards him. He smiled as he noted the absence of the cavalry escort and recognised the sole occupant of the coach. Then he dropped in behind it and followed. Opposite the Victualling Office, the coach turned towards the Lower Deptford Road, a route that would take it to Blackheath and beyond.

Dubois was one of many on the road this morning. Some, like

him, were on horseback, others – the majority – were on foot. No one would take the least notice of another rider.

'If you please, sir.' Sam Hart leaned back on his oar and looked at Tom. 'We ain't going to make it to Deptford in time to be of any use.'

'What d'you suggest?' said Tom, irritated by his friend's comment. 'We've got to get there somehow.'

'We could go by road, your honour. There's a man I knows of in Prince's Street, across the water, there,' said Sam, pointing with his chin, at the Rotherhithe shore. 'His name is Elijah. He's in the rag trade, same I was once. He's got a couple of nags what he might let us have for a shilling or two. Then we could take the Deptford Road, across the marsh, and be at the dock gates in no time.'

'How far to Prince's Street?'

'It's a little ways upriver from St Mary's Church. Easiest way would be to fetch alongside Prince's Stairs. After that, it's no more than a Sabbath Walk.'

Tom swung the galley hard over, narrowly missing a wherry coming the other way, ignoring the resultant torrent of abuse.

'D'you hear there? Belay all,' said Tom, a minute or so later as the galley cruised to a halt at the bottom of Prince's Stairs. He opened the arms' chest and took out a pair of sea service pistols, a couple of gunpowder pouches and some ammunition. Stepping ashore onto the granite steps, he gestured to Sam to follow him before turning to Kemp. 'Take the galley back to Wapping, Kemp. Tell Mr Harriot that Hart and I have gone to Deptford, and why.'

CHAPTER 28

The two horses were not the swiftest of beasts. They were more used to hauling the cart of a petty chapman at a sedate walk than the slightly more adventurous pace now required of them. Nevertheless, Tom and Sam covered the distance between Rotherhithe and Deptford in tolerable time and had soon reached Lower Deptford Road, on the outskirts of the town.

'Where to now, sir? The dockyard?' Sam reined his horse to a walk. 'I ain't been here since I were a lad with me father, trading in rags and the like. We never went near the dockyard on account they wouldn't let us Jews in.'

Tom navigated his way past a line of carts heading for the victualling area. Two hundred yards away, a black coach had emerged from a side road, and was travelling away from them. Fifty yards behind it, and travelling in the same direction, was a horseman. Tom stared at the rider. The man was too far away to be recognised but he appeared to be wearing a scarf, the colour of indigo. A moment later the rider had disappeared round a bend in the road.

Tom searched for a way through the crowds. The convoy of victualling carts was still abreast of them, their wheels churning up the mud of the road surface. A gap opened and Tom spurred his way through. He looked behind him and saw that Sam was still with him. God, the horses were slow. He reached the bend in the road round which the rider had passed. The coach and its following horseman had increased their lead and were about to round another bend.

Ten minutes later they reached a crossroads. There was no sign of the coach or the horseman. To the right lay New Cross, and the road to Peckham. To the left the road rose steeply towards Blackheath. Tom wiped his eyes with the back of his hand and stared through the sheeting rain.

'Where do we go now, sir?' Sam had twisted in the saddle and was waiting for Tom to come up beside him. 'They can't have got up that hill without us seeing them. I reckon they must have gone down there towards Peckham and New Cross.'

'I don't think they've taken the Peckham road,' said Tom. 'It's more likely he'd head towards Blackheath. Mr Wilberforce mentioned he had a friend who lived a few miles the other side of the village. If he's got this far, then that's where he'll be going.'

'But he couldn't have got up the hill in time. The rain's turned everything to mud.'

'No, but he might have stopped to rest the horses over there.' Tom pointed to a ramshackle wattle and daub building at the side of the road. The words *Spread Eagle* were painted in large black letters across its front wall. A timber archway on the left side of the main door gave access to what appeared to be a stable yard at the rear. Tom prodded the flanks of his mount, approached the inn and stopped in front of the arch. He bent down in the saddle and searched the ground.

'There,' he said, pointing to some deep wheel marks leading through the arch. 'They're inside.'

He drew his pistol and dismounted.

'You go in through the front door. I'll take the back. Give me a couple of minutes to check the yard and then go in. Ready?'

Sam nodded, his face grave. 'Have a care, sir. If Dubois is in there, he won't hesitate none afore he shoots you.'

'The villain won't get the chance, Sam.' Tom turned away and walked quickly down the passage, hugging the side wall of the inn. In spite of his outward show of confidence, he knew Sam was right. Dubois would not hesitate to shoot – or garrotte – him, if he got the chance.

He stopped at the corner of the building. The yard was about sixty feet wide and ninety deep. Along one side of it was the stable block, a low, stone building set with a number of doors. At right angles to this was a sort of lean-to structure, its front and sides open to the elements, its roof made of tightly woven thickets of straw.

An empty coach stood in the middle of the yard, its shafts resting on the earthen surface. Tom glanced at the coat of arms on the door. It was the same one he'd seen that night in Southwark, its lifeless driver slumped on his seat, his passenger missing.

He swung round at the sound of a muttered voice. A horse was tethered under the cover of the lean-to, steam rising from its flanks. Behind it, the head of a young boy was bobbing up and down as he went about the task of rubbing down the animal. Tom's gaze shifted back to the stone building. All but one of the doors was closed and bolted. The last stood ajar. Tom caught sight of a shadow moving across the entrance. He cocked his pistol and crept over to the boy, the steady drumbeat of rain hitting the mud surface.

'Christ, mister . . .' The boy jumped back in fright, his eyes fixed on the muzzle of the gun. Tom put a finger to his lips, and pointed to the open door.

The boy turned and looked. 'It's George, your honour. The ostler.'

'Anyone with him?'

'Only the coach driver, sir. He came in with his master about ten minutes since.'

'No one else?'

'No, your honour,' said the boy, beginning to shake.

'Where did the gentleman go? The one who arrived in that coach?'

'Inside, to have a bite to eat and a drink, I wouldn't wonder.'

'Wait here. I'm going to talk to the ostler. You say his name is George?'

'Aye.'

Tom turned away, wondering if he could trust the boy to keep silent. He considered taking him with him but decided against it. It might prove more trouble than it was worth. He delved into his coat pocket and drew out his tipstaff, its gold crown gleaming in the dull light of a September afternoon. Reaching the door, he pushed it with his foot. It creaked as it swung open. Inside were two men, one of whom was now reaching for a blunderbuss that lay on a small table in a corner of the room.

'Drop it,' barked Tom, levelling his pistol.

The man backed away, a look of relief on his face as he spotted the tipstaff in Tom's hand.

'Expecting someone, were you?' said Tom, lowering the hammer on his gun.

'Who's asking, mister?' It was the second man who spoke, a large, barrel-chested fellow, the sleeves of his blouse rolled to the elbow.

'This is all you need to know,' said Tom, holding up his tipstaff. He turned back to the first man. 'You the driver of that coach out there?'

The man nodded.

'The cully who's been following you – where is he?' said Tom, brusquely.

'What cully is that, mister?'

'Never mind,' said Tom, deciding the driver was probably telling the truth. 'Mr Wilberforce? Inside, is he?'

'Aye, he—'

Tom was already heading for the back door of the inn.

Dubois slipped back behind a clump of trees on the side of the Blackheath road. He'd recognised the two men who'd passed in front of him, and stopped outside the Spread Eagle. He wondered if their presence was a coincidence and then dismissed the idea. He knew Pascoe operated on the river, and the Spread Eagle was some distance from that. If Pascoe was here, then it was because he knew something. He wondered if someone had talked. There were only two people who knew the purpose of his visit to London – the man who'd met him on the English coast and brought him up to London, and one other. His English contact knew every aspect of the operation. It was his contact who had mentioned Holwood House and it was because of that information that he, Dubois, had been able to follow Monsieur Wilberforce to this location.

Dubois stared at the ground. It was inconceivable that the contact was the source of this betrayal, and yet . . . Dubois was nothing if not cynical. His survival on the streets of Marseille and, later, on the battlefields of northern Italy owed much to his refusal to accept things at face value. He questioned every motive, saw the dirt on the underside of every stone. He'd been duped, been sent on a fool's errand by a perfidious Englishman, to be killed by Pascoe. There had never been any intention of harming Wilberforce. That much was now clear. There was no other explanation for Pascoe's presence.

His anger mounted. Someone would suffer. Slowly, the rage left him, replaced with something akin to the exhilaration that often came to him in moments of extreme peril. He had always wanted to be rid of Pascoe, to avenge himself of the hurt he'd suffered at the hands of the Englishman. Now the opportunity presented itself. He could finish Pascoe and complete his mission.

He looked again at the lopsided inn with its arch leading through to the stable yard at the rear. He'd seen the coach carrying Wilberforce go through that arch. And it had yet to come out. He'd originally intended to wait until it had reached a quiet stretch of road before attacking it. He doubted that would now be possible. Not if Pascoe and his friend decided to stay with the coach, as seemed likely.

Leaving his horse tied to a tree, Dubois crept to the edge of the wood. He had the advantage of surprise but would still need to act with speed if he was to have any chance of success. There were, after all, three of them – four, if one included the driver. There was no sign of life that he could see, either in the inn or that part of the yard that was visible. He sprinted across the road and stopped at the yard entrance, listening for the least sound.

He heard nothing save the harsh patter of rain on the roadway.

He drew his pistol, eased back the hammer and moved closer. Then he stopped. Someone was talking. It was a voice he knew.

CHAPTER 29

Tom left the ostler and coach driver and walked across the yard to the back door of the inn. Inside, he immediately found himself in a small vestibule, the walls yellow with age, the air pungent with the smell of damp. Some faded posters had been nailed to one wall, offering rewards for help in tracing fugitives of one hue or another. To his left, a corridor disappeared into the semi-darkness, a flight of stairs leading to the first floor just visible. In front of him stood a ledge-and-brace door. He lifted the iron latch and eased it open a fraction. It gave onto a large, oak-beamed room at the far end of which was a latticed window overlooking the road. He could see Wilberforce sitting in a high-backed chair in front of an inglenook fireplace. Opposite him was Sam. They were alone.

'Why, there you are, sir,' said Sam, jumping to his feet as Tom entered. 'I were beginning to think about coming to find you.'

'No sign of Dubois?' Tom looked questioningly at his friend.

'None, sir.'

Tom turned his attention to Wilberforce. 'I think, sir, you are in some danger . . .'

'So I understand, Mr Pascoe. I regret I am becoming quite accustomed to the threat of violence. It's the price I pay for doing what I do. Would you, and your colleague, care to join me in a little repast? You must be cold and rather hungry, I fancy.'

'Perhaps another time,' said Tom, striding to the window. A movement amongst the trees on the other side of the road had caught his attention. His eyes swept in amongst the leafless boughs. Another movement. It was a horse. He searched for its owner. Couldn't see him. His pulse quickened. If he wasn't by his horse, then likely he was somewhere close to the inn.

'I think, sir, it would be wise to leave now.' Tom turned from the window and walked back to the fireside. 'Sam, pray be good enough to cut along to the ostler and ask him and the coach driver to step this way.'

He waited for Sam to leave the room.

'I'd be most obliged to you, sir, were you to move further away from the window. Behind this pillar would be fine,' said Tom, pointing to a stout oak post in the centre of the room.

'This is probably not the moment to ask,' said Wilberforce, getting up from his seat and striding to the oak pillar, 'but I confess I'm somewhat intrigued. Even by the standards of violent opposition I have become used to, this seems a little excessive. Pray, tell me, who is it that's trying to kill me?'

'You will recall telling me of a meeting between an unknown Englishman and the minister of police in Paris, where in return for information, the French would provide assistance to conduct an operation against a public figure in this country?'

'Yes, I well remember our conversation. What of it?'

'We both thought the public figure was the minister. It now appears that you are the target.'

'But why? I'm not in office. Why would the French send an agent to kill me?'

'The Englishman concerned is involved in the slave trade and has a great deal to lose by abolition. I think he provided the enemy with intelligence of use to them and they, in return, have undertaken to have you disposed of.'

'Do you know who this Englishman is?'

'Lord Camperdown's name has been mentioned.'

'But you don't think it's him?'

'I don't know,' said Tom. 'Camperdown certainly travelled to France. He told several of his friends that he'd done so, including Lady Annabel Stapleton, the sister of the late Sir Henry. His willingness to speak on the subject is suggestive of a man unconcerned about the consequences of what he has done. I hardly think this would be the behaviour of a man engaged in a capital offence.'

'What now?' asked Wilberforce.

'As soon as my colleague returns with your driver and the ostler, we'll get you back on the coach and escort you to London,' said Tom, glancing longingly at the barrels of beer behind the bar. He pressed his fingertips to his temples and concentrated on what he was saying.

'You are pale,' said Wilberforce, a concerned look in his eyes. 'Do you suffer from the fatigue? Perhaps we should rest a while.'

'Pray, don't trouble yourself on my account, sir,' said Tom, as the door opened and Sam came in with the coach driver and ostler. 'A little headache. Nothing more. I regret we have no time to waste. We must get you to safety before nightfall.'

From close by, Dubois heard a door bang shut. Someone had just gone in through the back entrance of the inn. He inched his way to the rear of the building and peeped round the corner, into the yard.

A boy was backing a horse between the shafts of the coach, talking to the animal as he did so. Dubois toyed with the idea of removing him from the scene. The fewer people he had to deal with when the time came, the better. The boy moved away, across the yard to the stable block. Dubois hesitated. Following the boy would expose himself to the risk of being seen from the inn.

He stayed where he was, slipping the pistol he'd been carrying into his coat pocket, his fingers searching instead for his knife. It wasn't his weapon of choice. That belonged to the grubby, discoloured cord, knotted at regular intervals along its length, and frayed at the ends. But the knife had its uses. It was just as quiet as the garrotte, yet much quicker. Sometimes speed was needed to end a man's life, to put an end to the choking sounds that were an inevitable part of using the garrotte. He had a feeling that speed and silence might be needed this morning.

He heard the door opening. Pascoe was coming out. The ostler was with him. There was no sign of Wilberforce. The two men stopped and looked round, then walked to the coach and opened the passenger door. Dubois considered risking a shot at his nemesis. Mentally, he weighed up the chances of killing him with a single shot. They weren't good. Not from this distance. He needed to get closer.

He remembered the second rider who'd been with Pascoe. They'd split up and entered the inn from opposite sides. Was that what they were planning for him? An attack from two sides? He turned and dropped to one knee, expecting to see someone creeping up on him. There was no one in sight but the thought unnerved him. He climbed to his feet, sweat trickling down his face. He wiped it away; a short, aggressive movement, embarrassed by the manifestation of his fear.

The men were still by the coach. If he was quick, they'd both be dead before they knew he was there. He hesitated and swallowed hard. His hands were clammy, his mouth dry, his feet like leaden weights.

He put the knife back in his pocket and drew a pistol, one of a pair he was carrying. He needed to be closer. Pascoe had stepped onto the footplate and was checking the inside of the carriage. For the next few seconds he would be blind to what was going on around him. Dubois moved out from behind the wall. He could hear the two men talking, their voices low. He checked the back door of the inn. It was closed. He found himself wondering where the others were – Hart and Wilberforce and the driver. They should have been out, getting Wilberforce into the coach.

If they came now he'd never make it back to the passageway before someone took a shot at him. He gave another quick, furtive glance in the direction of the inn door. It was still closed. He wanted to turn and run. The thought both shocked and appalled him. He'd never before backed away from a fight; had always revelled in the danger.

Ten yards to go. One more step and he'd be close enough for a shot. The noise would alert the others but he had little alternative. He curled his index finger round the trigger and squinted down the length of the gun barrel.

He felt the toe of his boot connecting with something solid and heard the soft scraping noise of something rubbing against the rough surface of the brickwork. He glanced down and saw the length of wood topple to the ground. The noise, when it landed, was not great.

But Pascoe had heard it.

Dubois saw him turning, his head twisted over his shoulder, the long barrel of his sea service pistol swinging up into the firing position. The Frenchman brought up the muzzle of his own weapon. There was no time to aim.

He squeezed the trigger.

The roar of the exploding gunpowder reverberated round the stable yard, Dubois's view reduced to a cloud of acrid smoke rising from the muzzle of his firearm. Then he saw a movement to his right. The door of the inn was opening. Sam Hart stood in the doorway, looking in his direction.

Dubois turned and sprinted down the passage to the road beyond, his ears still ringing from the sound of his own gun. Behind him, someone was shouting. He yanked his second pistol from his pocket, praying he'd remembered to load it. At the mouth of the passage he swung right, out of Hart's line of fire.

Breathing hard, he reached the trees on the other side of the road, stopped and turned. A moment later, he saw Hart arrive at the arch and look left and right along the road before seeming to sweep through the trees. Dubois thought about shooting him but changed his mind. He'd never hit him from this distance. He watched as Hart turned on his heel and ran back out of sight, to the stable yard. He thought of Pascoe, wondered if his shot had found its mark. He could hardly go back and check. Nor, now that he'd time to think about it, had he seen Wilberforce.

'*Mon Dieu*, what a mess,' he muttered, reloading his pistol and checking the second one. He looked back at the inn. Someone was moving about in the front room. The reflection of light on the glass made it difficult to see who it was. Dubois changed his position. The view was no better. He tried again, and waited for whoever it was to move. Then he saw him.

It was Wilberforce. And he was alone.

Tom looked down at the tear in the sleeve of his old uniform coat where the bullet had penetrated the cloth. Blood was seeping from a wound and forming an increasingly large, dark and sticky patch. Soon it would begin to hurt, but for the moment he was conscious only of a dull ache to the upper part of his left arm, close to the shoulder.

It should never have happened, and would not have done so had he not spent the greater portion of last night in one of the taverns off Wapping Street. He clenched his fists. The effect, quite apart from a feeling of drink-induced nausea, had been to slow his reactions to the point where he might easily have been killed. He looked down and saw the ostler who'd been with him by the coach door. The man was lying motionless, face down in a puddle of rainwater. Tom stooped and turned him onto his back, the effort sending a spasm of pain up into his shoulder. The man's eyes were open, staring fixedly into the heavens. Tom cradled the man's head, feeling the warm wetness of blood at the back of the skull where the bullet had entered. He turned to see Sam run back into the yard, a dejected expression on his friend's face.

'Got clean away, sir. I reckon he's in them woods t'other side of the highway. Don't suppose we'll see him again.' He looked at the prone figure of the ostler, as if noticing him for the first time, and muttered, 'Poor beggar.'

'You could be right,' said Tom, his thoughts still on the gunman. 'But I doubt it. He'll want to finish what he's started.'

'You think we should go after him, sir?'

'Without a doubt, Sam, but we can't leave Mr Wilberforce unprotected. Not with that villain on the loose. We'll have to get him back to Deptford and put him under the protection of the Navy. After that . . .' Tom shrugged. 'After that, well . . . with any luck the scrub will follow us and try his luck again. This time we'll be ready for him.'

'What d'you want done about this poor fellow, sir?'

'I regret it extremely, Sam, but we're going to have to leave him to the landlord. We ain't got the time to do anything else. It'll be dark in a few hours and . . . Christ, I'd forgotten Mr Wilberforce. He's alone with the driver.'

CHAPTER 30

Joshua Van Oven walked past the Mile End Hospital for Jews, and turned in towards a small brick house, standing in its own grounds. Glancing quickly up and down the street, he pushed open the low gate and hurried up the stone-flagged path to the front door.

'How is the patient?' he asked, as soon as the door had been opened.

'Well enough, seeing what he's gone through,' said a plump, grey-haired woman. She turned and led the way down a short corridor before entering a room on the left.

Van Oven followed her in. The room was simply furnished with a bed and a chair, its single window overlooking a pleasant garden laid out with apple and cherry trees. Ebenezer was sitting hunched in the chair, his eyes closed. He started as Van Oven entered.

'I regret the news is not good,' said Van Oven, resting a hand on the negro's shoulder. 'It is as you thought. The court has ordered your return to your master even though he will, almost certainly, compel your return to slavery in the West Indies.'

'I go, master. No trouble,' said Ebenezer, getting to his feet and supporting himself against the back of his chair.

'Stay here for a day or two,' said Van Oven. 'Think about what you would like to do. I can arrange for your passage to Holland where I have friends and where you would be safe from your master.'

'No, master, Ebenezer leave now.'

'Let me see the man of whom I spoke. He may be able to help. Come to the synagogue at Bevis Marks the day after tomorrow and I will have an answer for you.'

The big negro walked unsteadily to the door, leaving it open as he passed through. Van Oven watched him go. There was no more he could do for him. He wondered how long he'd last before he was seen and taken up.

Ebenezer Samson walked down Whitechapel Road towards Shoreditch. He wasn't sure he could take much more of life. The strain of the last few weeks had been immeasurably greater than anything he'd had to bear during his years of captivity in Barbados. The harsh realities of slavery seemed preferable to the unknown horrors that now lurked around every corner. Sooner or later, his master would catch up with him. Then would follow the beatings and the long sea journey back to Bridgetown.

He passed through Shoreditch and along Fenchurch Street, the houses becoming taller, cleaner and more substantial as he moved further west, the people better dressed. After another half an hour, he arrived at a broad thoroughfare where a seemingly endless column of coaches rattled along in either direction and finely dressed men and women strolled arm in arm as though without a care in the world.

He nearly didn't see the curricle that passed by on the other side of the road. There had been nothing special about it. No reason why he should have paid it any attention – except for the face staring out at him.

He knew him only as Sir William, a *bakra* who owned one of the larger plantations on Barbados, a mile or so outside Hole-town in the parish of St James. The man would often come to the master's house and the two of them would ride out to the cane fields and watch the cutting of the sugar crop. It was Sir William who had been with his master when Ebenezer had learned of his wife's death. He had never forgotten the look of indifference on the man's face, his reputation for brutality well known.

Ebenezer struggled to breathe as their eyes met. He turned and ran back along Fenchurch Street. He passed a coffee house down the side of which ran a narrow passage into which he now turned. From somewhere behind him came the sound of shouting. He ran faster, not knowing where it was taking him. The shouting faded away. He stopped and gazed about him. He was lost.

A gust of wind blew up from the south-west, carrying with it the smell of the river. It was his only point of reference. He broke into another run, passing the church of St Dunstan's in the East, its spire reminding him of the church in Speightstown where he'd prayed since becoming a Christian, a few years since. He would have liked to go in but thought better of it. His master's friend would still be looking for him.

A single mast poked into view above the rooftops, others followed. He rounded a corner into a broad street, overheard someone calling it Lower Thames Street. Relief flooded over him. He knew his way from here. He slowed to a walk and began to relax, his immediate problem receding. He had time to consider his next move. Van Oven's words came back to him: *I know of a man who might be able to help.* He wondered what manner of person could help where the abolitionists had failed. But then perhaps Van Oven knew someone important, someone who could save him. He'd mentioned a name but, for the life of him, Ebenezer couldn't remember what it was. It probably meant nothing. He been let down so often in the past.

He walked on, up the slope to the church of St Magnus the Martyr, and left onto London Bridge. He had until the day after tomorrow to make up his mind. Meanwhile, he had to find somewhere safe to stay. It had, he thought, been foolish of him to refuse the Jew's offer of a temporary shelter.

Dubois could still see Wilberforce in the front room of the inn. He checked the side passage leading to the stable yard and the front door. There was no one else in sight. The rain had stopped but the morning light bouncing off the window glass was making it even harder to see inside the room. He was fairly sure Wilberforce was still alone, but he wanted a degree of certainty before he made his move.

He slumped against the massive trunk of a beech, contemplating the risk. Best he didn't think about it too much. Otherwise, he'd never go through with it. In his youth, he'd seldom given any thought to the likely consequences of the fights he'd been involved in. Questions of life or death had seemed far removed from the arena of his own experience. And, by extension, fear had always remained at arm's length, somehow divorced from the activity in which he was engaged. Even war had had a knack of inuring him from the paralysing fear that now inhabited his soul. He had possessed an ability to translate that fear into a rage not far short of madness and, in the process, exorcising the natural instinct for survival.

But this? This was different. He rubbed the palms of his hands together and licked the dryness from his lips. Wilberforce was moving away from the window. He had to act. He took out one of the two pistols, ducked and sprinted parallel to the road for about twenty yards before crossing over. Pausing to regain his breath, he crept back up, past the arched passage, to the window. Peeping in, he could see Wilberforce pacing up and down the room, his fingers entwined in upon themselves in small, nervous movements, his head turning frequently towards the door at the far end of the parlour as though expecting someone.

Dubois looked up and down the road. To his right it climbed steeply to Blackheath, a scattering of perhaps four or five houses bordering the highway. In the opposite direction, meadows occupied most of the land to the outskirts of New Cross, some distance away. His only threat would come from within the Spread Eagle.

He lifted his loaded pistol and again peered through the window. A shadow moved, close to the fireplace. Dubois fell back out of sight, waited a moment, and then chanced another look. The light from the fire fell on a face he hadn't seen before. He stared at it, his heart pounding. He *had* seen it before. It was the coach driver. It would be surprising were the scrub not armed.

Dubois settled his back against the wall. He was sweating, the cold droplets running down his neck and inside his blouse. He clamped his teeth together. Perhaps he should wait for another opportunity. He craned his neck for another look. The door at the far end of the room was opening. He jerked out of sight, the vein at his temple pulsing. Pascoe and Hart were in the room, both men looking towards the window as though they had guessed he was there. Dubois felt his stomach somersault. They could not have seen him. Of that he was sure. And yet . . . If they came to the window, they'd discover him. He flattened himself against the wall, forcing himself to remain still. He had no choice. If he ran they'd hear him. At least this way he had a chance.

He could hear the murmur of voices from inside the room. A door creaked on its hinges as it opened and closed. Then there was silence. Dubois risked a last glance. The room was empty.

A relieved Tom ushered Wilberforce through to the ante-room of the Spread Eagle, close to the back door. He thought he'd seen a movement by the parlour window as he and Sam had entered, a fleeting change of light, over so quickly as to raise a doubt in his mind as to its existence. He might, in other circumstances, have gone over and checked that his imagination had not played tricks on his mind. But the risk of doing so now was too great. His responsibility was the safety of the man Dubois had come to kill.

'Bear along there, Sam,' he said, nursing his injured arm. 'Have a look round the yard and see there's no one waiting for us. Dubois's still in the area. I think I saw him, or at least his shadow. I'll ride in the carriage with Mr Wilberforce. You follow on horseback.' He glanced at the driver and said, 'Go with him. I want you ready to leave on the instant. Landlord . . .' Tom turned to the ashen-faced man standing in the doorway. 'What guns do you have? I need them. Now.'

He watched the man scuttle off and return a minute later with an ancient-looking fowling piece and some ammunition. 'It's all I've got, your honour.'

'Thankee, I'll see it's returned to you,' said Tom, taking the weapon. He removed his own pistol from his coat pockets and checked it was loaded before handing it to Wilberforce. 'You may need this, sir.'

Three minutes later, Tom's horse hitched to the back of the coach, he and Wilberforce were edging their way out of the courtyard, the harsh squeal of the coach wheels echoing in the confines of the passageway. At the entrance they stopped and waited while Sam checked that the road was clear.

'Take that window,' said Tom, glancing at Wilberforce. 'If you see anything, let me know and then get out of the way. There ain't no point in both of us getting shot at.'

'All clear.' Tom looked out and saw Sam waving from the middle of the road.

'All right, driver, when you're ready.' Tom heard the crack of the horse whip and felt the coach jerk as it began to move out into the Blackheath road, past an abandoned cart, the shriek of the iron-clad wheels jarring in its ferocity. A commotion in the roadway. Sam was shouting. The horses had reared up, snorting in fear. Someone was running, the footsteps getting closer.

A loud explosion. It had sounded close. Then a cry of pain and splinters of wood flying past the open carriage window. Another sharp crack of a pistol, similar to the first one, this time further away.

Tom levelled the fowling piece, propping the barrel on the window ledge. He pushed Wilberforce to the floor and peered out. Sam had jumped from the saddle and was running towards the woods on the other side of the road, his cutlass drawn.

'You all right, sir?' Tom removed his boot from Wilberforce's back and helped him up. 'I want you back in the tavern. Have the landlord take you upstairs to a secure room. Lock the door and stay there till I come for you.'

Tom leapt to the ground and helped Wilberforce from the coach. Then he waited for him to turn the corner at the back of the inn before looking to see where Sam had gone. A groan made him glance up. He'd forgotten the driver. The man was holding his leg, blood seeping out between his fingers. He'd been shot. Tom hesitated, looking at the thick clump of trees into which Sam had disappeared and then back at the driver. The man didn't look to be badly hurt. He would be able to reverse the coach into the yard.

Nursing his injured arm, Tom crossed the road as fast as he could and reached the edge of the woods where he stopped and listened. He could hear nothing but the occasional tweet of a bird and the rustle of bare branches swaying in the light wind. A yard or two to his right, where he'd last seen Sam, he saw that the undergrowth had been disturbed, the long wet grass lying on its side as if trodden underfoot. He thought for a moment. If he followed, he risked Dubois doubling back to the inn. He had to stay and protect Wilberforce. He looked across at the coach. The driver had already begun to back it into the yard, out of harm's way. Tom crouched down onto his haunches, below an oak. From here he had a clear view of the inn and its approaches while, at the same time, remaining out of sight.

A faint rustle in the woods behind warned him that someone was approaching. He raised the fowling piece and pointed it in the direction of the sound. He knew that when the time came he'd have less than a second to decide to shoot or not. The rustling stopped and then began again. Whoever it was, was less than ten yards away. Tom slowed his breathing and nestled the butt of the gun into his shoulder. The stranger was going to pass within a yard or two.

Sir William Bolt was surprised to see his visitor. He'd not met Joshua Van Oven more than a handful of times over the last two or three years, and then only to talk about matters of concern to the Jewish community. He clicked his tongue, irritated by the intrusion on his morning. He had inherited from his late father a number of properties in the Aldgate and Whitechapel areas, most of which were now occupied by Jews. Without doubt, Van Oven's current visit would concern one of these.

'Good day to you,' said Sir William, forcing a smile. 'This is, indeed, a pleasure. It's been far too long since we last met.'

'The pleasure is mutual.' Van Oven bowed and followed Sir William into the library.

'Now, sir, to what do I owe the pleasure of this visit?'

'A man has come to me for help,' said Van Oven. 'I said I would speak to you on his behalf in the hope that you might feel able to assist. He's a slave. Some weeks ago he escaped from his master, here in London, but was subsequently found and returned to his previous occupation.'

'I really don't see how—'

'Allow me to continue,' said Van Oven, holding up the palm of his hand. 'Following his recapture, the man's friends sought a writ of *Habeas Corpus* to prevent his removal from this country, back to a condition of slavery in the West Indies. Alas, the application was rejected by the Lord Chief Justice, and the man is ordered to return to his master with all that that entails.'

'I still don't see how I can help,' said Sir William, looking distractedly round the room.

'The man's owner is Lord Camperdown . . .'

'Good God, sir. If it is who I think it is, I know the wretched fellow. Saw him in Gracechurch Street, only this morning. I thought you said he'd been returned to his lordship.'

'No,' said Van Oven, 'I told you the court had ordered the man to be returned to his master. He was handed over to his lordship's servants but managed to give them the slip. That's when he came to the synagogue and saw me.'

'And what, pray, is it you want of me?'

'I'd like you to speak to his lordship; persuade him not to send this man back to the West Indies where he will surely die.'

Sir William looked thoughtfully at his visitor for a moment or two.

'I'd need to see the fellow first. Get the measure of him. See exactly what he wants.'

'I'll speak to him,' said Van Oven, a small frown creasing his forehead. 'I'm sure something can be arranged.'

Tom pulled back the hammer, closed one eye and aimed the gun at the spot where he expected the stranger to appear, his left elbow resting on his knee. He winced as a bolt of pain passed through his arm and he struggled to hold the barrel steady. His finger tightened on the trigger, squeezing it gently, judging the pressure exactly. A few feet away a tree branch moved and a hand appeared, quickly followed by a face that appeared to be staring at the inn.

'You're fortunate I didn't blow your head off, Sam,' said Tom, recognising his friend. He lowered the gun. 'Where's Dubois?'

'Lost him. I saw him hiding over there.' Sam nodded at the old cart they'd seen when they'd first arrived. 'Leastways, I think it was him.'

'Is that when the shooting started?'

'Aye, it was. Anygate, I lost him . . .'

'He's in the yard, Sam. He's got to be,' said Tom hurrying back towards the entrance.

'Dubois?'

'Yes. It's the only thing that makes sense. He wouldn't leave without finishing what he came to do. When the shooting started, he must have seen me take Mr Wilberforce back inside.'

'But how would he have got past us without being seen?'

'Over the wall at the back of the stable yard. He must have gone round in a circle and approached from behind. Get over there, will you? I'll catch up with you as soon as I can. I can't run with this bloody arm.'

The body of the ostler had been removed and the yard was deserted, a dark pool of blood on the cobbled surface the only sign of what had happened a few minutes before. For a brief moment Tom stared at the ground. The man was dead because of him, because his reactions had not been as fast as they should have been. His drinking had slowed him down. He clenched his teeth, a sense of remorse overtaking him. He shook his head. This was no time for soul searching. He looked over to the stables. They, too, seemed deserted. He caught Sam's eye, put a finger to his lips and jabbed in the direction of the ostler's room. Sam nodded and slipped away round the edge of the yard. Tom watched him go in and reappear a minute later shaking his head.

'Check that pistol of yours,' whispered Tom when Sam had rejoined him. 'We're going in.'

Silently, he pushed the door with the toe of his boot. He could see the door to the taproom facing him and, to its left, the opening to the corridor leading to the stairs. He listened for any sign of life. There was nothing. It was as though the whole place was empty. Slowly, he crept forward and put his ear to the taproom door. Still nothing. Pulling the door towards him, he pushed down on the iron thumb plate. It snapped open with a sharp crack that sent his heart racing. Tom raised his gun as the door swung open.

A pair of terrified eyes stared back at him from the far end of the room. The stable lad was standing by the oak pillar, next to the body of the ostler. Tom looked round. Seated in a chair by the fire was the coach driver.

'Where's the landlord?'

'He's upstairs, your honour. The scrub what's looking for Mr Wilberforce forced him to go.'

From downstairs Dubois heard the sharp crack of a door latch opening. He motioned to the landlord to be quiet and crept to the head of the stairs. He stood listening for a moment, could hear the indistinct murmur of voices. He knew at once who they belonged to. He turned to face the landlord.

'Where is Monsieur Wilberforce?'

'In that room.' The landlord pointed to a door further down the corridor. At that moment, the voices from downstairs suddenly got louder, as though the door of the taproom had been opened.

'Show me, quickly.' Dubois tensed and felt his throat constrict. He caught hold of the landlord and pulled him along.

'This is the one.'

From below there was the crash of what sounded like a second door being thrown open and then the thud of running feet coming along the downstairs corridor. Dubois glanced at the stairs and then at the door in front of him. A single kick would open it. If he was quick he would have time to shoot Wilberforce and be away before Pascoe reached him. He glanced down the corridor, away from the stairs. He'd already worked out his escape route. Had studied the inn from the woods across the road.

He braced himself and kicked at the door. It shuddered but held firm. He aimed a second blow and felt something hot pass close to the left side of his face. It was followed by the roar of the pistol shot, splinters of wood peppering his face. He reeled back, temporarily blinded by the muzzle flash, his ears ringing. Dazed, he turned and ran down the corridor. He turned into an empty bedroom, opened a window and jumped out. He had reached the woods before he dared to stop and look back.

Tom reached the top of the stairs and almost collided with the landlord. The man was standing trance-like, staring vacantly at the wall of the corridor.

'What happened?' Tom's eyes swept over the scene. 'Where's the scrub who was with you?'

'He's gone,' mumbled the landlord. 'Ran off when he heard you coming.'

'Is Mr Wilberforce all right?'

'Is that you, Mr Pascoe?' Wilberforce's voice drifted through the wreckage of the door and a key scraped in the lock. A moment later, he appeared in the doorway.

Tom pushed past him and went to the window. A shadow moved amongst the trees. He couldn't be certain but he thought it had looked remarkably like Dubois. For a brief second he thought about going after him until a jolt of pain reminded him of the injury to his arm. Reluctantly, he turned to face Wilberforce.

'Come, sir, we must get you to safety before dark. The man who attacked you is still in the area and I believe may strike again.'

CHAPTER 31

Tom strolled up Oxford Street and stopped outside an imposing, double-fronted house of Portland stone. Two days had passed since his return from New Cross and he had thought of little else but what had happened. Dubois would not give up. Tom was quite sure about that. True, the journey from the Spread Eagle had been uneventful and there had been no sightings of the man. Of course, it was quite possible that he'd been injured when he tried to kick down Wilberforce's door, and been shot at for his pains. If so, that would explain why he'd not again attacked the coach.

Whatever the reason, Tom had not wanted to risk escorting Wilberforce all the way back to Westminster and he had, instead, taken him to the Royal Dockyard at Deptford where he'd requested that the Navy convey him the rest of the way. It had taken all his powers of persuasion for the port commissioner to agree to the proposal and a deal more talk before the captain of a first-rater could be found to provide the escort. Still, he'd been able to fill the time with a visit to the port surgeon who'd cleaned and bandaged his arm.

Tom looked up at the house. The message from the Lady Annabel, asking him to call on her on a matter of some delicacy, had come as something of a surprise.

A footman answered the door and took Tom's greatcoat and hat before showing him up a broad flight of steps to a large room into which the afternoon light was now streaming. A display of roses stood on a polished mahogany table.

'Why, Mr Pascoe.' Lady Annabel held out her hand and walked towards her visitor. 'Thank you for coming to see me. Please, do sit down. May I offer you some tea? Coffee, perhaps?'

'That's most kind of you, my lady, but nothing, thank you.' Tom waited for Lady Annabel to be seated before perching on one of the other chairs. He felt absurdly self-conscious, had washed, shaved and changed into his best breeches and grey coat, and now wished he hadn't made it all so obvious. The coat might be his best, but he still felt shabby in the presence of such obvious wealth and breeding.

'You must be wondering why I asked you to call.' Lady Annabel sat with her hands in her lap, her eyes fixed on his. 'Doubtless you will recall the last time we met? You asked if there was anything else I wanted to tell you concerning Sir William. I told you there was not.'

She paused and looked away, a hint of anxiety in her eyes. 'Well, there *was* something that I should have told you. I chose not to mention it because, at the time, it appeared of no great consequence. It was only in the light of what I subsequently learned that I felt I should have spoken more freely.'

Again, she stopped, turning her gaze towards him before looking away at the fire in the grate. Tom shifted awkwardly, his fingers laced and resting on his knees.

'Not long after my brother died, Sir William came to see me at my home in Rye. I think I may have mentioned it to you. Anygate, during the course of the conversation he told me – in connection with what, I cannot now remember – that Lord Camperdown had crossed to France and had met a representative of the Republic. It amused him that his lordship had, on his return to this country, faced the ire of the Administration and the threat of a capital trial, when he, himself, had escaped detection. I asked him what he meant and he told me that he had also been to France, crossing the Channel about two weeks after Lord Camperdown.'

'Sir William crossed the Channel?' asked Tom. 'Forgive my interruption, my lady, but has he told anyone else about this?'

'I really have no idea. You will have to ask him.'

'Do go on.' Tom gave an apologetic wave of his hand.

'I enquired of Sir William as to the purpose of his journey, but he merely smiled and declined to speak further on the subject. Yesterday evening, I was returning from the home of a friend in Portman Square when I happened to notice a foreign-looking gentleman leaving Sir William's house. The strange thing is that it was the second time that day I had seen strangers leaving the house.'

'What did this foreign gentleman look like?'

'Why . . .' Lady Annabel paused and appeared to gather her thoughts. 'He was of less than medium height but broad in the shoulder, about twenty-five years of age, his hair cut short, his complexion somewhat swarthy.'

'And you say he was leaving Sir William's house yesterday evening?'

'Indeed,' said Lady Annabel. 'Do you know the man?'

'I believe I do, madam,' he said, sinking back into his chair. 'If I'm right, his name is André Dubois.'

Sam Hart was waiting for Tom in the passage outside the police office when, later that afternoon, his friend returned from his visit to the Lady Annabel.

'Why, Sam, you look as if you've seen a ghost. I trust all is well.'

'It's Ebenezer, sir. He's gone.'

'What d'you mean, gone?'

'He were captured and taken aboard a West India brig yesterday morning. Sailed with the noon tide.'

'How d'you know all this?' said Tom, shocked.

'I sees Master Van Oven at the synagogue in Duke's Place. He told me he'd met Ebenezer and had been trying to help him. A meeting was arranged with someone who he thought could help. But when Ebenezer and Van Oven arrive at the cully's house, there were some bully boys waiting for them. They took hold of Ebenezer and said they had a right to do it on account the court said so. There weren't nothing Master Van Oven could do.'

'Did he say whose house they went to?'

'Aye, he did. A cully what's called Sir William something.'

'Sir William Bolt? This doesn't make sense,' said Tom.

'What don't, sir?'

'Ebenezer is Camperdown's slave, not Sir William's. Why would he go to the trouble of recapturing a runaway slave for a man he's apparently fallen out with? I would have expected him to do the exact opposite, unless . . .'

'Unless what?'

'Sir William crossed to France about two weeks after Camperdown,' said Tom. 'So far, no one knows anything about it and he's not said why he went.'

'Still don't explain why he's involving himself with the black cully,' said Sam.

'No, it doesn't, does it,' admitted Tom, lapsing into silence.

There appeared no reason for Bolt to become involved in what amounted to no more than a minor domestic matter of no apparent interest to him. In other circumstances it might have been possible to argue that Bolt had been acting out of a feeling of loyalty and friendship towards Camperdown but, given their supposed falling out, that seemed unlikely. Why, then, had he acted? They had both chosen to visit France but whereas his lordship's connections to those in high office had ensured he would not be prosecuted, the same would not necessarily apply to Bolt. He would have felt exposed and anxious to remedy the situation, perhaps by recapturing Camperdown's runaway slave. Tom sighed. The argument was a weak one. There had to be another reason why Bolt should have become involved.

He led the way through the main door of the police office and crossed the hall, through a scattering of people awaiting their turn in court, the smell of their unwashed presence seeping into every part of the building. Beyond the courtroom door he could hear Harriot's deep, booming voice. 'Fined five shillings, seven days to pay. Next case.' The routine seldom varied, nor the identity of those appearing before him. Tom grimaced and headed on up the stairs to the first floor, with Sam close behind. He walked along a short corridor and entered the constables' waiting room.

'Sir William Bolt.'

'I beg pardon, your honour,' said a startled-looking Sam.

'I'm still trying to work out Sir William's interest in our witness,' said Tom, seating himself on the corner of the only table in the room. 'We know that Ebenezer saw Dubois disposing of a body in the Thames. We believe that body to have been the MP, John Dean, who had been travelling in the minister's coach and was probably mistaken for Mr Wilberforce. We also now know that Dubois is, in some way, connected with Bolt. The Frenchman was seen coming out of Bolt's house a day or two since.'

'You think, sir, that if Bolt is giving the orders, then he has an interest in making sure Dubois is not arrested for murder?' said Sam.

'That would be part of the reason. I think he also wanted Dubois free until he had finished the job he came here to do. Without Ebenezer . . .' Tom shrugged and didn't finish the sentence.

'What about Lord Camperdown, your honour? Where does that leave him? He went over to the Frogs, too.'

'I'm not sure about him. I'm not even sure about Bolt. I was just thinking aloud.' Tom rubbed his chin and stared at the empty wall opposite. What Sam said was true. Both men were known to have crossed to France – a capital offence in time of war. Neither would have undertaken such a journey without careful thought and a strong motivating influence. In the case of Camperdown, he had, when questioned, denied any suggestion that his actions had been treasonable. He had, nevertheless, been unable to explain why the enemy should have released him. He claimed – at least to his own countrymen – that his purpose in going to France had been to seek out and kill General Bonaparte. This version of events was called into question by intelligence from

French Royalist sources, indicating his willingness to bring an agent across the Channel.

Then there was Sir William. His interest to the Foreign Office was the result of his known friendship with Camperdown rather than any specific act on his part. His crossing to France had been unknown to the authorities in London and might have remained so but for his conversation with Lady Annabel. On its own that might have passed without further comment, buried in the welter of private conversation. What now made it interesting was that Dubois had been seen emerging from his house. But why? Why had Sir William gone to France in the first place and why was he involved with Dubois, if not to attempt the assassination of Wilberforce?

Tom eased himself off the table and began pacing up and down the room, his hands behind his back, his head bent forward. He remembered what Hookham Frere, the under-secretary of state at the Foreign Office had told him about Bolt. *Of all Lord Camperdown's friends, Bolt would certainly have the most to lose were the trade to be abolished.*

What would a man in his position be prepared to do to protect his interests? Kill? It was possible. And if so, would it not make sense to kill the person most responsible for attempting to bring about one's ruin? Better still if the killing were done by someone else, someone unconnected with the anti-abolitionist cause. Who, then, better than an enemy agent?

Tom's thoughts ran on, conscious that much of what he'd been thinking amounted to no more than conjecture, valueless as evidence in a court of law. Without tangible proof of Bolt's complicity in the attempted assassination of Wilberforce, or even his relationship with an enemy agent, he would simply deny everything. With Ebenezer gone, they'd struggle to get the case past the Grand Jury.

'So what now, sir?'

'Keep a watch on Sir William,' said Tom. 'As like as not, Dubois will make contact. And when he does, we'll have them both.'

CHAPTER 32

Lord Camperdown stared out of the window of his coach as it bounced slowly down the uneven surface of a farm track, a mile or two east of the village of Bromley-by-Bow in the county of Essex. He was deep in thought. After a moment or two he looked across at his companion, seated opposite.

'You say Pascoe has talked to John Butterworth again?'

'So I believe.' Nathaniel Morgan flicked away a particle of dust that had appeared on his clean breeches. 'One of my snouts saw him arrive in Rye, and followed him to the house.'

Camperdown nodded and resumed his gaze through the window. A noisy crush of humanity stretched away behind them. He leaned forward and poked his head out. A hundred yards ahead was what looked like a farmhouse and, beyond it, a collection of tents and stalls. In front of these wandered any number of Punch and Judy men, dwarfs, quack doctors, soothsayers and divers others, each one shouting encouragement to the thickening crowd.

He shifted his gaze to an area behind the farmhouse where a group of people had formed a circle on a strip of coarse grass. He watched them for a few moments, more joining their number with each passing minute.

'I think you also said that Pascoe had been to see the Lady Annabel?'

'That's what I'm told, your lordship,' said Nathaniel. The Bow Street Runner shifted uncomfortably in his seat.

'Any word on what they might have spoken about?'

'I regret not.'

A pause, then, 'Who's fighting this afternoon?'

'Jack Bartholomew. He's against Jem Belcher. They drew last time but I think Jack'll take him this time round.'

The coach reached the farmhouse and pulled into the yard. Camperdown stepped down and walked towards the informal ring, bowing at the few acquaintances he passed on the way. The mass of bodies parted as he and Nathaniel walked to the front where some chairs had been made ready.

A minute or so later, the crowd erupted into a roar of approval as the huge shape of Jack Bartholomew, the reigning champion of all England, walked into the ring, saw Camperdown, and strolled over. They stood talking for a minute or two before a second roar announced the arrival of Jem Belcher, with his seconds.

Camperdown eyed the young pretender with keen interest. A slim, good-looking young man of about eighteen, with an almost deferential air about him, he had none of the scars carried by his thirty-seven-year-old opponent. Jack Bartholomew should have no difficulty in overcoming the fellow.

'Best I were going, your lordship,' muttered Bartholomew as he was pulled away by his seconds.

'Aye, and God speed, Jack. There's a hundred guineas says you're the fancy.'

Camperdown took his seat next to Nathaniel and watched the

fighter stride back across the little green to his allotted place.

The noise from the crowd rose to a hellish din as the time-keeper signalled the start of the fight, and the two men closed with each other, the ground shuddering under the stamp of their feet. Soon, both men's faces were a bloody pulp, their lips and eyes swollen beyond recognition as round followed bloody round, the heavy blows falling in relentless succession, Belcher's speed matched by Bartholomew's skill, neither man giving an inch.

A sudden blow to Belcher's throat sent him crashing, unconscious, to the ground. The crowd fell silent. No one moved, least of all Jem Belcher.

'His neck's broke,' said a man close behind Camperdown. 'He'll not get up from that.'

'Reckon you've the right of that, Bill,' said another voice. 'Copped a nobber right in his throat, and no mistake.'

Ten seconds passed. Then twenty. Belcher's seconds ran to his side and knelt. Still no movement. Then a leg twitched. A moment later, it was an arm that moved. Slowly, Belcher raised his head, his eyes seeming to focus on the crowd with a look of bewilderment. With what seemed a supreme effort of will, he levered himself up onto his knees and then stood. He swayed slightly, looking about him. Another second or two and his head seemed to clear. He turned to face Bartholomew, his fists balled in front of him. The crowd was cheering wildly, bets were being laid and accepted. The whips of those employed to keep the ring free of onlookers snaked and cracked above people's heads.

'This Pascoe fellow,' said Camperdown, leaning his head close to Nathaniel. 'You know him well?'

'Well enough, my lord,' said the Bow Street Runner. 'I sees him from time to time when one of us has a problem, like. We helps each other when we can.'

'And you were saying he asked about me?'

'Aye.' Nathaniel looked back over his shoulder at the crowd.

There was a pause, then, 'There's a hundred guineas for you, Master Morgan, should you care to tell me what I wish to know.'

Nathaniel nodded slowly, as if considering the offer.

'What is it you want to know, my lord?' he said, the words cautious and slow.

'Why was he asking about me?'

'He knows you and Sir William was involved in the death of Sir Henry Thwaite-Thomas. But he can't prove it 'cos no one's talking to him – yet.'

'What else?'

'There's talk of a Frenchman, an assassin, what's come to London. Tom Pascoe reckons you and Sir William are involved in that, as well. Someone high up in the government told him that you'd crossed to France. He thinks Sir William's been and all. The government suspect that the Frenchman is here because you asked for him to come. Tom reckons that as soon as he catches the Frog, he'll have the evidence to hang you and Sir William, my lord.'

'Anything else?'

'Now that you mention it, he asked me if I knew anything about a body what was found in the Thames; a Member of Parliament what had been throttled. I told him I'd heard a little but not much.'

'Then best you keep it that way, Master Nathaniel. I don't want that cully poking round my business. D'you hear?'

'Might be too late for that, my lord. He reckons he knows who did it. And if Tom reckons he knows who's responsible, then he does. My advice to you, sir, is to keep well out of his way. Once he sniffs trouble, he don't give up easy.'

Camperdown turned back to the fighting. For a while he seemed engrossed. Then, 'I think I'm going to have to deal with Pascoe,' he said.

'Be careful, my lord. It don't do to get on the wrong side of Tom Pascoe.'

A roar rose up from the mob. Camperdown turned to see Belcher attacking his opponent, raining down blows on the older man, now half blinded by the blood erupting from the cuts above his eyes. A bell clanged and the men were pulled apart.

Camperdown felt a touch on his arm. Nathaniel was staring at something behind him. 'Talk of the devil, my lord.'

'What am I looking for?' said Camperdown, scanning the crowd.

'Behind you, my lord, the fellow in the blue jerkin, next to that bruiser with the hat.'

'Why, it's Mendoza.' Camperdown's face lit up with pleasure. 'Now there's a fighter worth the name. Getting on a bit now, but still useful.'

'Next to him, my lord. The little fellow with the pigtail. See him?'

'Yes, I see him. Who is he?'

'His name's Samuel Hart. He's a waterman constable. Serves under Pascoe.'

'Confound the fellow,' said Camperdown, his eyes narrowing. 'Do you think he heard us?'

'Not sure, my lord. Might be watching the fight, or he might be watching us. Either way, it ain't good for us to be seen together.'

Camperdown glanced across to where Sam and Mendoza were still talking. Neither gave any indication of having seen him, still less of having heard anything remotely compromising. But Nathaniel was right. He couldn't take the risk of his conversation with him being overheard. He brooded on the problem. Several minutes went by. Then he saw a tall, thickset man standing a little way off. He beckoned him over. Whispered words were exchanged.

The man left and disappeared through the crowd.

Sam had known Mendoza since, as a boy growing up on the streets of Wapping, he'd learned to box under the older man's tutelage. Even when Mendoza had left to pursue his career as a prize fighter, he had maintained an interest in the welfare of the Yiddish boys he'd trained, often returning to enquire after their progress. And it had been he who had suggested to Sam that they should go and watch a long-awaited contest between the present champion, Bartholomew, and the young pretender, Belcher.

Sam had seen Camperdown's arrival. He'd noted it as of passing interest, in much the same way as he'd viewed the man who'd arrived with him. He would tell Tom when he saw him, but there was nothing particularly unusual about the sighting, especially since Lord Camperdown's interest in the sport of boxing was as well known as the wide circle of people with whom he mixed. All the same, he'd not expected to see Nathaniel in his lordship's company.

The fight reached the fifteenth round. The cuts above Bartholomew's eyes were still bleeding as he and Belcher left their corners and advanced towards one another for yet another two minutes of savage punishment. But it couldn't last. The younger man was too fast. What he lacked in strength, he more than made up for in agility, his stinging blows sapping the strength and will of the other man. Bartholomew was tiring. Forty seconds into the round, two powerful jabs to Bartholomew's face finally decided the matter. He toppled like some giant oak whose day has come. In a minute or two, his semi-conscious form would be removed and preparations made for the next contest to begin.

Sam turned to go. He was already late. Hurriedly making his apologies to Mendoza, he slipped through the crowd, stopping only to exchange a few words with old acquaintances he'd not seen in a while. A few minutes here or there would not make much difference to his journey back to Wapping.

It was a dry and unusually warm autumn day, puffs of white cloud scattered about the blue of the late-afternoon sky, the dappled sunlight playing in the dust of the path that ran round the side of the farmhouse to a wicker gate. He passed through and joined a rutted track, hemmed in on either side by a tangle of gorse and the occasional beech or hawthorn, whose boughs hung low over his head in a canopy of twisted wood.

Ahead of him, the deserted lane bent round to the left. The trees seemed closer together now, the road darker, somehow more sinister. The roar of the distant crowd was barely audible.

From behind him came the sudden rustle of branches. Even before he had begun to turn, his hand had dropped to the hilt of his knife. Three men were dropping through a gap in the

---

hedgerow, onto the track. Sam thought he'd seen them earlier, standing next to Camperdown.

He waited for them; had already caught sight of the glint of steel in their hands. Briefly, he wondered what they wanted. He wasn't carrying any money. He doubted that knowing the answer to his unspoken question would make any difference. But it would have been nice to know, anyway.

'Nothing personal, mate,' said the first, and largest, of the men. He was bent forward, almost crouching, his knife slicing the air in wide, sweeping motions. Sam waited for the blade to come in, slipped outside its arc and hit the man in the stomach, a single savage blow. The man doubled forward and sank to the ground, winded. Sam turned to face the other two. They were already running at him, screaming abuse. Funny, he thought, how some men felt the need to make a loud noise when attacking. Perhaps it helped them to overcome their own fear. It wasn't something that troubled Sam unduly.

He brought his own knife out into the open, the blade pointing directly at the leading man. He saw it, his eyes widening in surprise. He tried to stop, veering off to one side, tripping over his fallen comrade in the process. Sam paused and then lashed out as the man fell, the toe of his boot catching the fellow on the side of his face. There was an odd sound of snapping bone, and then silence. Too late, he turned to face the third man. He felt a stinging blow to the back of his head and then – nothing.

'Sam? Wake up, boy. D'you hear me, already?' Sam groaned, put his hand to the back of his head and opened his eyes. A face was peering down at him. He tried to focus. The image was fuzzy, indistinct. 'It's me, Daniel. Wake up, I tell you. You can't sleep all day.'

'Daniel? Mendoza?' Sam's head felt as though it had been run over by a coach and four. 'What are you doing here?'

'We can't stop here, Sam,' said Mendoza. 'As soon as these cullies are missed, others will come looking for them. On yer feet now. We can talk as we go along.'

Sam felt himself being lifted to his feet and supported until he could find his balance. He looked down to see the three men who'd attacked him bound with strips of material that looked as if it might have been liberated from their clothing. More strips of cloth had been jammed into their mouths.

'What about them?' said Sam, as Mendoza dragged him away.

'Leave them,' snapped Mendoza, looking back along the track. 'We must go.'

They'd been walking ten minutes before Sam felt well enough to talk again. They had reached the end of the farm track and joined the lane running south to Ratcliff and the Thames. Still there was no one in sight and no sign that they were being pursued.

'I think we should be safe now,' said Mendoza.

'Safe?' said Sam, staring at him. 'From who, or what?'

'From your friend Lord Camperdown. He was sitting just in front of us.'

'Yes, I saw him. He was with Nathaniel Morgan, a Bow Street man,' said Sam. 'What of it?'

'I saw them looking back at you. They were frightened of something. It puzzled me, so after you left, I stood out of their sight, behind some other men, and waited. After a while, I saw Camperdown call over one of those bully boys what tried to kill you just now,' said Mendoza, jerking his head in the direction of the farm track they had just left. 'I couldn't hear what they were saying, but I followed them anyway and saw them hide. I reckoned, then, they meant to put you to bed with a shovel.'

Mendoza paused and looked quizzically at Sam. 'What's that rogue, Camperdown, to you, Sam? Why d'you suppose he wanted to turn you off?'

'Master Pascoe believes that Camperdown may have killed a man in a duel. But we ain't got no evidence to take him to court. He may be involved in other matters, too. But, again, we've no evidence. He might have thought I was there to spy on him, but who knows?'

'D'you want me to get a few of the lads together? Sort him out for you?'

'No,' said Sam, smiling, 'but thankee, anyway. We need him the way he is, for the time being. He might still give us the evidence we need to clear up a few things.'

'What about the runner?'

'Nathaniel? No, he and Master Pascoe is friends. There ain't no problem there.'

CHAPTER 33

With little prospect of finding Dubois in the immediate future, Tom seized the opportunity of paying a long overdue visit to an address on Conduit Street, not far from the junction with New Bond Street. He had, in his Navy days, been there many times, but he'd not been back for over a year; not, indeed, since he'd been deprived of his sea-going command and recommended for the post of river surveyor with the Thames marine police.

Turning into the old street, he saw the narrow bow-fronted house at number thirty-six that he remembered so well. Over the front door was a wooden sign with the words *Jonathan Meyer, Military Outfitters* painted in gold letters.

The door was ajar. He pushed it open and stepped inside. The room was exactly as he remembered it, the panelled walls lined with bolts of serge and hopsack, stacked one on top of the other, an oil lamp suspended from the ceiling, a faint smell of chalk and new wool. In the middle of the room was a large, rectangular table over which a dapper, grey-haired man was now stooped, a pair of scissors in his hand. He looked up as Tom came in.

'Why, Captain Pascoe. How very good it is to see you, sir.' The man bowed and approached Tom from behind the table. 'It's been too long, sir.'

'Likewise, Meyer, likewise.' Tom felt the other man's appraising glance pass over him, faintly disapproving. He wondered if he should explain but decided against it. It was none of his business. 'I need half a dozen shirts, some neckcloths, a couple of pairs of breeches and two coats. The ones I've got are past redemption. Oh, and I'd better take some stockings as well.'

'Very good, sir. We can certainly see to that for you. Have you anything particular in mind for your coat? Swallow-tail, perhaps? Or straight? And what about the cuffs, sir? Silk, shall we say? No? Very good, sir, no silk cuffs, then.'

Bolts were brought forth, examined and rejected as too dark, too light, too brown, or too grey until Tom settled on heavy serge of the deepest blue with a pair of breeches from the same bolt. His paper pattern was sent for and brought up from the basement, his vital measurements checked – chest, waist, seat.

'Sir's measurements have not changed,' purred Mr Meyer, scribbling furiously with a large, blunt pencil.

It didn't take long; an appointment secured for the first fitting, and a promise that his new garments would be ready for him in two and a half months. Taking his leave, Tom left the shop and walked to New Bond Street. He considered taking a cab to Savoy from where he could take a wherry to Wapping, but then again . . . He took out his watch. His next patrol was not for some hours yet.

At New Bond Street, he turned south towards Green Park, feeling better than he had done in months. He fumbled in his coat pocket for the letter he'd received earlier in the day and took it out. It was from his mother, one of several she wrote to him every year. She still lived in the village where she (and he) was born, in Bamburgh, on the north-east coast of England, not far from the border with Scotland.

Her letters always reminded him of his boyhood when he'd sometimes stand on the dunes and look out at sea for his father's fishing boat. At other times he'd walk across the mud flats, to Lindisfarne, following the wooden stakes that had long marked the route of the visiting pilgrims to the great abbey. There, amongst the ruins of the old priory, he'd sit on a rock and sketch the puffins or guillemots or the occasional osprey, before running back to the mainland as the tide swept in. He'd never shown the pictures he'd drawn to anyone but his mother. He didn't know why. It was instinctive, afraid of the reaction they might provoke.

He held the thin paper, picturing the woman who'd written it. He'd not seen her in over seventeen years, since he'd first gone to sea as an eleven-year-old. He reread the letter, his heart sinking as he did so. She'd written with the news that the half-brother he'd never met was coming to London to find work. She didn't actually ask him to take care of him but it was implicit, lurking between the lines. How he was expected to look after a nine-year-old, he couldn't imagine. Perhaps the boy would change his mind, do the sensible thing, and return home before he got too far.

Tom put the letter back in his pocket, crossed Piccadilly and turned west, past Devonshire House, to Green Park. It was not particularly busy. Mainly couples strolling in the autumn sunshine. He found an unoccupied bench at the side of the path and sat down. He knew that the cause of his concern about his young brother had more to do with his drinking than the question of how the two of them might get on. He had to face the problem, if not for his brother's sake, then for his own. Harriot had warned him of the consequences for his future, should he fail to deal with it.

But there was another reason.

The entry into his life of the Lady Annabel had brought home to him the extent to which his drinking had begun to affect not only his physical appearance but also his intellect. It was as if she had shone a light into his soul, exposing his every weakness.

He looked up at the passing couples. He had taken the first tentative step towards his journey back to health. He had ordered a fresh wardrobe and, in the last two days, had not touched the bottle. It was going to be hard but he was determined to win.

Sir William Bolt's London house on Portman Square lay at the western extreme of the capital, not far from Oxford Street. It was not of the grandest set, either in size or in appearance, but a desirable property nevertheless. And Tom was beginning to feel that he knew every block of stone used in its construction.

He stared through the fading light of late afternoon as a chaise rattled round two sides of the square and came to a halt outside one of the houses, its iron-clad wheels shrieking in complaint, its driver leaning back as he hauled on the reins. His thoughts drifted. The attack on Sam perplexed and worried him. Had it simply been an extreme reaction by Camperdown to Sam's presence at the prize fight? It seemed unlikely. Even the presence of Nathanial Morgan in his lordship's company could not adequately explain the attempt on his friend's life. There had to be some other explanation, something more than an extreme reaction of a man fearful of his own future. It raised still further the prospect of Camperdown's involvement in criminality, perhaps even his involvement with Dubois. Tom tutted to himself. The evidential trail on that was tenuous in the extreme.

Tom looked across the square at Sir William's house. It was directly opposite the vantage point he'd chosen for himself in the centre of the square. He could see servants moving about the house, lighting candelabra, carrying coal scuttles for the fires, tidying side tables. More lights were appearing in other houses, deepening the sense of the gathering gloom. At the north end of the square, close to the junction with Upper Berkeley Street, he could just make out Sam's slim figure, a tray loaded with buttons, beads and other assorted trinkets suspended from a strap round his neck.

'Buttons. Buttons for sale.' Sam's voice had assumed an almost feminine quality as he wandered up and down the north side of the square, advertising his wares.

During the three days the two of them had been watching, Sir William's routine had not varied; rising at about noon and travelling – according to one of his footmen whom Tom had befriended – to Garraway's, in Exchange Alley. He would remain there until about six, and then return home. Never earlier. On occasion, according to the same source, he might choose to spend the evening at Boodle's, but that was comparatively rare.

In answer to further questioning, and in consideration of a fistful of pennies, the man had confirmed the arrival, in the past few days, of several visitors he'd not previously seen, including a foreign-looking gentleman.

Tom was still smarting at the villainous cost of the information he'd purchased when he heard the rumble of a phaeton turning into the square from the direction of Oxford Street. Easing himself away from a plane tree, he watched its progress, as the driver drew back on the reins and brought the coach to a halt outside Sir William's house.

A moment later, he saw the tall, stooped shape of Sir William step down into the roadway and make his way to the front door. Tom checked his watch. It was just after six. Bolt was not normally this early. He looked in Sam's direction. He, too, had noted the arrival of the chaise.

Tom glanced over his shoulder and caught sight of a man moving along the southern perimeter of the square. It was hardly unusual and the hour was not late but something in the man's gait was familiar. The swing of his arms seemed exaggerated and he had the stride of a much taller man. The man passed out of the square and into Upper Seymour Street where he was lost to view. Tom let the matter go.

'Begging your pardon, sir.' Tom spun round to find Sam standing beside him. 'Yon cully . . .'

'What of him?' said Tom. But he knew the answer. 'Shit. It was Dubois, wasn't it?'

'Aye, I reckon it were,' said Sam, throwing off his tray of trinkets and running to the corner where the stranger had last been seen, Tom close behind.

The street was deserted.

'I reckon he's gone to ground, sir,' said Sam.

'See that path?' said Tom, pointing to the narrow mouth of an alley leading down behind the houses on the west side of the Portman Square. 'I reckon he went down there. It leads to the back of Sir William's house.'

'What now? You want me to get a warrant?' said Sam.

'No time for that, and anygate, I doubt you'd get one.'

'Why's that, sir?'

'You know why, Sam.'

'Because I'm a Jew?'

'Look, I don't like it any more than you do, but there ain't nothing I can do about it. Meanwhile, there's a villainous scrub in there that I want to get my hands on. You want to come with me?'

'Without a warrant?'

'Of course, without a warrant.'

Sir William Bolt picked up a copy of *The Times* and settled himself into his favourite chair in the library. Dinner was still a distant prospect, but anyway his appetite had gone. He put the paper down on his lap and stared at the fire. Camperdown had told him about what had happened at the prize fight. A knot formed in his stomach. It had been a stupid thing for his lordship to have done and would doubtless have consequences for all of them.

It had all begun with an argument that should never have been allowed to progress as far as it did.

There had been six of them gathered in the library of the house in Rye. He couldn't now remember the original purpose of the meetings; probably something to do with protecting the slave trade on which they all depended. Over time, that subject had come to dominate their conversations, and it was this which had attracted the Londoners amongst them – including Camperdown.

Sir William shrugged as he recalled first one and then another of the guests – all of them sugar merchants and plantation owners – arriving. As a fellow traveller he knew them all, of course. It would have been strange if he had not. But he had, nevertheless, felt an irrational resentment of their presence. Rye was his and Sir Henry's town. The meetings, social gatherings, really, had not been intended for people beyond the county boundaries.

It was, he supposed, this underlying resentment of the interlopers which had initially caused him to take Sir Henry's part in the argument with Lord Camperdown. Odd, really, particularly as he had never had much time for his neighbour, with his strident opposition to violence as a means of defeating the abolitionists. It could hardly be otherwise, especially since he had, himself, recently returned from a meeting with the *ministre de la police* in Paris where the subject of violence had been discussed in some detail.

The argument that evening in Rye had been bad tempered from the start. He remembered Sir Henry jumping to his feet, his face reddening, a finger pointed at Camperdown's face. *I'll be damned, sir, if I'll be quiet. What your lordship proposes is preposterous. I'll have nothing to do with it, sir. And if you persist in this madcap scheme, I shall have no alternative but to denounce you.*

Sir Henry had thrown down the glove. The challenge was unmistakable. There had been nothing anyone could do to alter that fact. Camperdown's face had whitened in fury, although there had been no other sign of his anger. For a moment, the room had gone quiet and Sir Henry had sat down, the redness leaving his face as quickly as it had come, as though he realised he'd gone too far. The threat of exposure had touched a raw nerve in all of them. It was as if each had seen the shadow of the noose falling across their eyes. There was little sympathy for Sir Henry's outburst.

Sir William had not been present when Camperdown demanded satisfaction of his host. He'd learned of it soon after, when Camperdown had approached him and asked him to become his second.

He passed a hand over his eyes, his thoughts dwelling on that fateful morning on the Isle of Dogs, east of London, where the two men had fought.

They had agreed on a signal. He remembered the metallic clicks as both men cocked their pistols and raised them to the firing position. He remembered seeing the bright flash in the pan of Camperdown's pistol and then, silence. He'd known at once what had happened. The main charge had failed to ignite.

It was at that moment he had made a decision he was later to regret.

He'd shot Sir Henry.

Had he needed to do it? He had thought so at the time. He knew that if he had failed to act, Camperdown would have died, and with his death would have gone the hopes of those opposed to abolition.

A knock on the library door made him jump. He turned to see his butler.

'I beg your pardon, sir, but there is a . . .' the man paused, searching for the right word, 'a foreign gentleman who wishes to know if you are at home. He refused his name, sir, and said it was a matter of the utmost urgency.'

'Damn the fellow's impertinence,' said Sir William. 'Send him on his way, Jenkins, there's a good fellow.'

There was a sudden commotion at the door and Dubois strode in.

'I regret this intrusion, *monsieur*, but the matter is urgent.'

'All right, Jenkins. I will see to this gentleman.' Sir William waited for the butler to leave, and turned to Dubois. 'What is the meaning of this intrusion, sir? I thought I had made it perfectly clear, the last time we spoke, you were not to come to this house again.'

'You will doubtless recall, *monsieur*, the terms of your agreement with my government,' said Dubois, a faint sneer crossing his face. 'Should I fail to return to France, the consequences would be grave.'

Before Sir William could reply, there was the sound of hammering at the front door. He stared at Dubois, as though expecting an explanation. Footsteps hurried across the floor of the hall.

'Were you followed?'

'*Mon Dieu*, I might—'

'Run,' said Bolt, jumping to his feet.

Dubois bounded to the nearest window and opened the sash, just as the library door burst open.

CHAPTER 34

Tom stepped into the library in time to see Dubois disappearing through the window. He ran across and peered out into the darkness. There was neither sight nor sound of him. He turned to face Bolt.

'What was Dubois doing here?' he said, jerking his head at the window.

'Really, sir, this will not do,' stammered Bolt. 'By what right do you come barging into my home? By Harry, I shall have you before the magistrate, sir. Why, I'll—'

He got no further. Tom stepped towards him, picked him up by the lapels of his coat and thrust him against the bookshelves. Bolt's eyes widened, his hands dropping to his sides.

'Don't trifle with me, or you'll answer for it before a judge and jury. What business did you have with Andre Dubois?'

'Who?' said Bolt, his face paling. 'I've not seen the fellow before.'

'You're lying, sir. That man has been seen leaving this house before tonight.'

'What of it?' said Bolt, appearing to regain some of his composure. 'Many people come to my house without my knowledge. I do not see them, and have nothing to do with them.'

'Except that the man who was in this room until a moment

ago is a French agent who is known to have arrived in the country shortly after your own return from France,' said Tom. 'Why, you look startled, Sir William. Did you imagine that your crossing to France had passed unnoticed?'

'How did you . . .?'

'How did I know you had been to France?' said Tom. 'In the same way that I know everything else about you; your plantation in Barbados, your ownership of slaves, your involvement in the slave trade itself. And that is the reason you crossed the Channel. You went to seek the help of the enemy in eliminating the chief architect of the abolitionist cause. Why the French? Because you did not want to be associated with a course of action that would cause outrage throughout this country.'

'This is preposterous,' said Bolt. 'You see a man jumping from my window and make the wild allegation that he is a French agent. What is the basis for your belief?'

'Other than his name, you mean?' said Tom. 'Dubois is a French soldier with the *Trente-deuxième demi-brigade d'Infanterie de Ligne*. You realise that consorting with the enemy is a treasonable act, and carries the appropriate penalty? Of course, should you decide to tell me what I need to know . . .'

Tom's voice trailed away and he watched Bolt struggle with his thoughts.

'What will happen if I told you everything I know?' said Bolt.

Tom exhaled a lungful of air. He wanted the fellow's cooperation but he needed to be careful. If he told him the truth – that he would, as like as not, hang – he'd not get the information he needed to convict Dubois. It was, he thought, time for some judicious lying.

'As things stand at present,' he said, 'there's no doubt you'd swing for treason. You not only introduced an enemy agent into this country, you also directed his efforts with the intention of murdering a prominent citizen of the realm. If you want me to save your life, you're going to have to tell me everything.'

'I won't hang?'

'I cannot entirely save you from the consequences of your actions but you'll escape with your life. Isn't that enough?' said Tom, wondering, for the first time, what had happened to Sam. He was supposed to have come into the house through the front door – let in by one of the servants – but had yet to appear. He supposed he'd seen Dubois jump from the window and given chase.

'Very well, I'll—'

The crack of a distant pistol shot drifted in through the open window. Tom strode over to the open window. He could see nothing beyond the dark shapes of the shrubs and trees in the centre of the square.

'Sam,' he shouted. There was no response. He called again. This time he heard a faint cry. He turned and ran to the library door, yanking it open. 'Wait here until I return. We'll talk further.'

Tom didn't wait for a reply. He pushed past a startled butler and made for the main door. A few people had already begun to gather in the square. Others were peering from their windows. He guessed they must also have heard the gunshot.

'Anyone see what happened?' he said. His question was met by the shaking of heads. He ran to the next house, where a man stood alone at an upstairs window, watching his approach.

'Are you looking for the man who jumped from Sir William's window?'

'I am,' said Tom. 'Did you see which way he went?'

'That way.' The man pointed to the north end of Portman Square. 'He was chased by a small fellow. Looked as if he was a sailor of sorts.'

'And the shooting? Did you see who did the shooting?'

'No,' said the man. 'By the time I heard the shot, the pair of them had gone out of the square, into Upper Berkley Street.'

Tom sprinted up the side of the square, turning left at the top. No pedestrians were about, only a coach or two. He ran to the corner of New Quebec Street and looked left, then right up Montague Street. What looked like a heap of clothing lay in the centre of the carriageway, about forty yards from the junction. He ran towards it and dropped to one knee beside the crumpled form of a man, his face covered by an arm thrown carelessly across his forehead.

'Sam?' he whispered.

Dubois's heart was pounding. His near capture had frightened him more than he liked to admit. He'd caught a glimpse of Pascoe coming through the library door of Sir William's home and knew he'd been recognised. He turned left at the top of Montague Street and slowed to a walk. He wasn't sure who he'd shot at, or even if he had hit the fellow. What he did know was that the man had been after him, the distance between them closing with each stride. He'd had no option but to fire.

He ducked into a doorway and looked back the way he'd come. No one appeared. He began to breathe a little easier. Either he'd killed the man, or he'd lost him. Either way he was safe – for the moment.

He caught the scent of freshly cut grass and looked up. A large, formal garden occupied the space between two lines of houses, opposite. There was another one, fifty yards or so further on. London, or at least this part of it, seemed to be full of them. He considered hiding amongst the shrubs, but decided he was still too close to Sir William's house. He'd be found. He walked on, looking over his shoulder at frequent intervals, but there was no sign of his pursuer.

None of the roads was familiar. Even if he could find his way back to the inn on Tooley Street where he'd spent the last few nights, he could no longer be sure that Pascoe wouldn't be waiting for him. He remembered the look of suspicion that the landlord had given him the night he had strangled the man from the coach. It was almost as though he had known about the captive in his room. By now the authorities would have published posters about the deaths of the driver and his passenger. And his own description would also be there.

He thought of the warehouse on Hays Wharf where he stayed the last time he was in London. On that occasion he'd been with Pierre Moreau, his old police handler, chafing at the restrictions the *commissaire de police* placed on his activities. But the old man had been right, as always. Moreau was dead now. Struck down by typhus.

A shout from across the street jerked him back to the present. He spun round, searching for its source. Two men were having an argument. Nothing to do with him. Dubois waited for his heart to slow down. It was getting late. He wondered if it would be safer going back to Hays Wharf rather than Tooley Street but knew it was a risk whichever place he chose. He reached a junction and turned south onto a broad avenue, a line of large houses occupying its western kerb.

It was busier here, a constant flow of coaches, chaises and cabri-olets chasing each other, the rumble of their wheels mingling with the clip of horses hooves and the angry shouts of the drivers. He felt safer, surrounded by noise and movement. It was a world he understood. But he was still lost. A name painted on the side of a house read Edgware Road. It meant nothing to him.

He wondered where Pascoe was.

Tom cradled his friend's head against his knee. He looked at Sam's face. His eyes were closed, his skin pale in the darkness. He laid the back of his hand on his forehead and felt cold sweat.

'Sam?'

There was no response. Tom bent down and put his ear close to his friend's immobile face. There was no sign of life. He leaned back on his haunches, a sense of loss threatening to overcome him, memories of times past crowding his mind. They'd been friends since the early days of the new police, an unlikely alliance between an immigrant Jew born and raised in Poland, and an Englishman possessed of a commission in the King's Navy. There had been no reason, other than the capricious hand of fate, for their worlds to meet, a series of events that had eventually led them both to the door of the Wapping police office in July of 1798.

They had endured much in those early months of the new organisation. The violence of the opposition they faced from men long used to plunder as a means of reward for their labours was matched by difficulties in their own lives that threatened their friendship and called into question whether trust could ever be said to truly exist between Jew and gentile. In the harsh environment of their lives, such considerations had often to be swept aside in the face of expediency and the common cause they espoused. But it could not eradicate it. The dismissive attitude of the wider society to Jews in general was a constant reminder to Sam of the low regard in which he felt himself to be regarded. Yet, despite all this, the bond of mutual respect and friendship had survived and grown stronger between the two.

Tom bent, gently lifting his friend and carrying him to the side of the road, where he laid him down. He saw a movement. So slight he thought he'd imagined it. He searched Sam's face and saw a faint tremor of his lips. He bent down, his face close to his friend's, and felt a breath of air against his cheek, a shallow wash so weak as to be almost indiscernible. He looked up at a small crowd that had gathered to watch.

'For all love, will someone find a carriage?' he said.

The events of the last half-hour had taken their toll on Dubois. The immediate danger of pursuit had passed and he felt his energy draining out of him. He was exhausted, his eyes drooping, his legs feeling as if they carried lead weights. He fought the desire for sleep and forced himself to keep walking. Pascoe had to be somewhere in the area and would be searching for him.

A chaise, one of several he'd seen in the past five minutes, appeared out of the darkness, moving fast down the Edgware Road towards him. He could see a single male passenger in the back, his face dimly lit by one of the coach lanterns. It was Pascoe. Dubois lurched back towards the safety of a doorway and watched the carriage draw opposite him. Pascoe was looking down at someone lying on the seat. He glanced up. Dubois was sure their eyes met, a look of venom in the other man's eyes. Then the coach was gone.

From somewhere he found the energy to run to the nearest junction and dart down a side alley. Ducking behind a cart, he drew his knife and waited for Pascoe to appear, his body tense, his eyes reaching into every shadow, his mouth dry with anticipation. The minutes ticked by. No sign of Pascoe. He couldn't understand it. It made no sense. Pascoe had seen him yet appeared to have ignored him. Why? He thought of the man he'd seen in the back of Pascoe's chaise. It had to be the man he'd shot, probably the man Pascoe worked with. That would explain why he'd not come looking for him. A smile of relief crossed his face. He climbed to his feet and headed back towards Edgware Road.

CHAPTER 35

Bolt stared at the dying flames in the grate. He'd not moved since Tom left. He doubted he would have been able, even if he had a mind to. He was struggling to make sense of what had happened. Portman Square was a long way from the Thames, and even further away from Wapping. It didn't seem possible that Pascoe had discovered his connection with the French agent Dubois. He paused as a thought occurred to him. He'd almost forgotten his difference of opinion with Camperdown and wondered if that had anything to do with his present difficulties. He knew, better than most, how sensitive Camperdown could be, how quick to take offence.

He dismissed the idea. It was too absurd. Camperdown would not have betrayed him to the authorities. Yet the suspicion returned to haunt him. He remembered that he, himself, had gone to Pascoe. If he was capable of doing that, why would Camperdown be any different? The niggling doubt grew in his mind. Dinner was served and consumed alone, without enthusiasm. He returned to the library. There had to be an answer to his present difficulties. His mind drifted to happier times.

He imagined himself back in the Caribbean, a time of his life when he had been most content. He closed his eyes, could almost feel the heat of the sun warming his back. He was riding his horse along Cattlewash Beach on the wild, east coast of Barbados, watching the cobbler birds swoop low over the huge Atlantic rollers that crashed ashore on the coral reef. It was a route he would often take early in the mornings, before the sun became too hot. Then he would turn away and head up into the hill country of deep gullies and streams and woodland, in an area that the early settlers had called Scotland. From the summit he could see for miles in every direction, to the plantations of his neighbours – to Bissex Hill and Mellowes to the south, to Cambridge behind him and to Turner's Hall in the west. His own land lay beyond Mellowes, hidden from view by the bulk of Mount Wilton, while far away, to the west, near Speightstown, was the Camperdown Plantation. They had been halcyon, carefree days, too quickly gone.

Bolt frowned as his mind reverted to his one-time friend. Theirs had always been an uneasy relationship. He wondered if it would have survived had it not been for the years of military service they had both undertaken. They had grown apart, their interests diverging, a gradual disintegration of the loose bonds that had bound them since boyhood, a scratching of the surface that had finally torn aside the fabric of their friendship. The duel in which Sir William had acted to save Camperdown's life had seen a brief reawakening of the relationship, but it had not, it seemed, lasted for long.

Bolt poured himself a drink from the table beside his chair and leaned back, rolling the glass between the palms of his hands. Whatever his present difficulties with Camperdown, he needed the fellow's help. He had no one else to turn to.

Draining his glass, he called for his phaeton.

*

The carriage with Tom Pascoe and the injured Sam Hart sped down Park Lane and turned right into Knightsbridge before passing through the turnpike and stopping outside the main door of St George's Hospital. Minutes later, Sam had been carried up the steps, through the front door and into the receiving room where he was now being examined by the duty physician.

'He is,' said the physician, wiping his hands on a piece of cloth and turning to look at Tom's anxious expression, 'an exceedingly fortunate man. The hurt is not serious. The bullet merely grazed the skull, causing the object to lose his senses. For sure he will have a sore head for a few days but I make no doubt he will fully recover. I'd like him to remain with us for the night, lest he catch the fever. After that, he should rest for a day or so. Does he have a room? Yes? Good. Now, if you will permit me, I will make the necessary arrangements, after which I must continue with my other duties.'

Tom stayed to see Sam taken by the porters to one of the wards, before making his way back to Wapping, a huge sense of relief spreading through him. He smiled at the thought of trying to persuade Sam to rest once he was out of hospital. Sam seldom rested for any reason at all, let alone for what he would regard as the minor inconvenience of a flesh wound.

It was nearly ten o'clock before Tom finally got back to the police office and realised that he'd not thought about a drink all day. Things were, he thought, getting better.

'Is Mr Harriot still about?' he asked as he passed the gaoler's room.

'Aye, he is, right enough. And he were looking for you, and all,' grinned the man.

Tom shook his head and made for the stairs. He could imagine Harriot fretting about his long absence from the office. He'd not told the resident magistrate about his intention to pay a visit to the home of Sir William. He'd not had the opportunity, not that that was likely to placate the old man.

'Mr Pascoe,' boomed Harriot. 'Just the man I was looking for. I was beginning to think you'd died and gone to heaven. I hear you've been looking for your suspect, Dubois, at the other end of London. Did you have any success?'

'Up to a point,' said Tom, suppressing the urge to ask the magistrate how he knew where he'd been. 'I had reason to believe that Dubois might be involved with Sir William Bolt. He was seen coming out of Sir William's house a day or so ago. We went there and waited to see what would happen. Eventually Dubois turned up and went in. We went in after him but were only in time to see him disappearing through a window.'

'I don't suppose you thought to get a warrant?'

'Not in those circumstances, no. As it was, he shot and injured Sam Hart.'

'Good God, man, is he hurt bad?'

'Fortunately, the injury is not serious. The hospital is keeping him for the night and expects to discharge him tomorrow. The physician has advised that he rests for a few days, after which he should be fully recovered.'

'I'm relieved to hear it, Mr Pascoe.'

'May I ask how you knew where I was?' asked Tom, his curiosity getting the better of him.

'Oh,' Harriot swept the air with a hand, 'I had a visit from Mr Van Oven. I gathered he'd already seen Hart and told him your negro witness had been taken by Sir William, so I guessed it was where you would be going. I sent a crew along to give you a hand but by the time they arrived, you'd gone, and so had Sir William.'

'Sir William has gone? Do we know where?'

'The servants were questioned, of course,' said Harriot. 'Seems he told the butler he'd be gone some time, and not to wait up for him.'

'And Dubois? Was there any sign of him?'

'No, I regret not. The men searched for him, but he'd gone also.'

'There are only a limited number of places he could be hiding,' said Tom. 'I'll take the rest of my crew and see what we can turn up.'

'Where are you thinking of?'

'Hays Wharf.'

CHAPTER 36

André Dubois knelt behind a stack of sugar barrels on Hays Wharf and looked towards the warehouses. Behind him, he could hear the black, oozing mass of the river, slapping against the hulls of the lighters, their mooring lines squealing under the strain. A crescent moon appeared from behind some clouds, its light reflected on the dark water like some silver dagger. He crouched deeper into his hiding place, watching the door of the warehouse where he had once taken refuge with his late colleague, Pierre Moreau. The nightwatchmen were standing almost directly in front of it.

He was nervous. There was no getting away from it. He was not so much concerned about the men. They were there every night; watchmen appointed to guard the hundreds of barrels of sugar and spices and tea that lay scattered on the quayside. No, the reason for his nervousness was that Pascoe knew he'd used this place before. It was a risk coming back. But if not here, then where was he to hide? He'd asked himself the question before. And he still had no answer.

A cold breeze sighed up the river, ruffling its surface and tugging at the hem of Dubois's coat. He drew the garment about him and shivered. There was a part of him that wanted to head for the coast and home, but he knew that wasn't an option. The *ministre de la police* had made it abundantly clear that a second botched mission would not be tolerated.

The clouds had largely drifted away, the black vault of the heavens splashed with a thousand tiny pinpricks of light. He glanced up, dazzled by its beauty. A movement on his left, near the corner of Mill Lane, caught his eye. He stared into the still blackness of the shadows thrown out by the buildings. He could see nothing. He glanced back at the group gathered round the brazier. Six of them. The same number he'd seen when he first arrived. If it was not one of the watchmen then who or what had caught his attention? His eyes drifted back to the corner of Mill Lane. Still no movement. It *must* have been a trick of light.

His eyes drooped. More than anything he wanted to sleep. From somewhere out on the river came the faint splash of an oar entering the water. He looked out over the reach; could see only the winking of the ships' lanterns high above the waterline and the faint glimmer of the moon reflected on the furled sails.

The men round the brazier were talking now, their voices low. He couldn't hear what they were saying; had no interest in knowing. He got to his feet, his mind made up. Sleeping in the warehouse was too dangerous. He would find somewhere else. A loose stone rattled on the cobbled surface of the wharf. Dubois's head spun round. The noise hadn't come from the watchmen. It had been too far to the left. His pulse quickened. Someone was there. He could sense it. He moved back, to the edge of the quay. If it was someone searching for him, he'd stand a better chance of escape close to the river. He glanced over the edge and then wished he hadn't. The swirling river was in full spate, racing past him. A little way off he could see some lighters moored end to end in the roads. He wasn't a good swimmer. He'd never been interested in learning, in spite of growing up close to the sea, preferring the rough and tumble of the back streets of his youth.

He looked back across the wharf; could see only the watchmen around their warming fire. Had he been mistaken about what he thought he'd heard and seen? It was possible. Even probable. Tiredness and the night could do that to a man. But, all the same, he thought it would be best if he went.

He stopped, aware of a sudden quiet. He shot a glance at the men round the brazier. They were no longer talking. They were looking in the direction of Mill Lane. A figure had emerged out of the gloom and was approaching them. Dubois slipped back behind some hogsheads and watched. The stranger was talking, pointing to the warehouse where Dubois had been heading. The men shook their heads. A moment later, one of them was pointing in his direction. Dubois felt his heartbeat surge.

He crawled closer to the edge of the quay and worked his way along, searching for a narrow alley he vaguely remembered from the last time he was here. If he could reach it without being seen, there was a good chance he'd get away. The stilts of a treadmill loomed out of the darkness. He sidestepped them and moved on. The group by the brazier hadn't moved. He felt a small surge of exhilaration. He was going to make it.

'Way enough.' Dubois jumped. The voice, not more than a whisper, had come from the river. It was too far away to be an immediate threat. He thought he had recognised it but couldn't be sure. He glanced back at the group by the warehouse. Two men were walking in his direction. The rest had fanned out across the wharf, their shapes caught in the light of the flickering flames.

278

They were all heading for the river. Dubois leapt to his feet and ran.

There were no lights to guide him. He had to hope there would be nothing in his path as he raced along the narrow strip that separated the edge of the quay from the treadmill housings. He should only have the heavy iron cleats, used to moor the lighters, to worry about. From behind came shouts and the stamp of running feet. He chanced a backward glance. It was a mistake. His foot stubbed against one of the cleats. He fought to save his balance, stumbled sideways and crashed over the edge into the fast ebbing tide. He came to the surface, gasping for air, his arms thrashing the water. Panic set in, his body stiffening. Again he sank below the surface, the force of the tide pushing him further and further from the shore. Again his head bobbed up. He was shouting now. He didn't want to die. Not like this. The water he'd swallowed was choking him.

His shoulder struck the hull of a lighter with sickening force, his body spinning down the vessel's length before being shot out at the other end. He felt the rough surface of a mooring line graze his face. He grasped the thick rope, first with one hand and then the other, the tide threatening to yank him free. He looked up at the deck of the lighter, high above his head. Getting onto the barge would be too difficult, even if he had the energy. He looked round. Another, much thinner, line was trailing from the stern of the lighter. He followed it with his eye and saw it was attached to a skiff, ten yards astern.

Dubois knew that rope was his only chance. But it was out of reach. He would have to let go of the mooring line and hope he could stay afloat long enough to reach the second line. If he succeeded he'd be able to follow it down to the skiff. If he failed, he would unquestionably drown.

He had no choice. He let go.

The tide caught him again, tossing him this way and that. He could hardly see or breathe. He kicked hard, determined to stay afloat, to stay alive. He reached up, his fingers clutching at the thin rope above his head. He sank, came up, and tried again. This time his fingers touched the line and wound round it. He got the other hand to it and pulled it towards him. He paused for a moment, catching his breath. Then, hand over hand, he inched his way to the skiff. He caught hold of its gunwale and hung on, relief sweeping over him as he dragged himself into the small craft. His strength gone, he lay down, closed his eyes and waited to regain his breath.

He felt a slight bump against the side of the skiff. He took no notice. The tideway was a crowded place. Besides he was exhausted.

'Get up, Dubois. You're coming with us,' barked a voice, close above his head.

Dubois's hand shot to the pocket where he kept his knife.

'One more movement like that will be your last.' Dubois slowly removed his hand from his pocket and opened his eyes. The barrel of a pistol was less than a foot away from his face, its hammer drawn back. He closed his eyes again.

'Why don't you shoot, *monsieur*?' he said. 'It is what you want.'

Tom Pascoe leaned closer to his prisoner. 'What I want is to see you hang. And hang you shall, my friend. Now, on your feet and lay along to the galley before I change my mind and shoot you anyway.'

*

Sir William Bolt brought the phaeton to a halt outside Camperdown's address on Baker Street, waited for one of the grooms to take the reins, and stepped down into the street, a distracted look in his eyes. He still wasn't sure he was doing the right or even the sensible thing in coming to see his lordship.

Handing over his visiting card, he was ushered into a ground-floor room and left alone. He knew the house well, had been here many times over the years, when it had been owned by Camperdown's father, the first baron, but he'd not visited since the old man's death. Now, as he waited for his host, he again thought about what it was that he intended to say. He wanted – needed – Camperdown's help if he was to have any hope of avoiding the accusation that he was involved with an enemy agent. He rubbed the palms of his hands together, feeling their dampness; conscious of a feeling of dread in the pit of his stomach as the consequences of his actions began to grow in his mind.

What possible explanation could he offer for Dubois's presence in his house? He'd all but agreed to tell Pascoe everything he knew in exchange for his life. He paused, remembering the sound of a gunshot in the street outside his house. Perhaps it wouldn't be necessary to say anything. Perhaps Dubois had escaped. His spirits soared and, just as quickly, plummeted. He had no idea who had been shot, or even if the ball had found its mark. If it had been Dubois on the receiving end, he might, even now, be in custody and telling Pascoe all he needed to know.

He wandered over to the fireplace and stared at the burning coals, his head resting on the mantel, his thoughts returning to Camperdown and their deteriorating relationship. *Was* he involved in this? Had he told Pascoe about that last meeting at the home of Sir Henry, when the question of French involvement in the assassination of Wilberforce had been discussed? It was inconceivable that Pascoe could have learned so much about the affair unless he'd spoken to someone who knew the details. Mentally, Bolt ran down the list of men who'd been there. He'd not quarrelled with any but Camperdown. And even in the case of his lordship, the ill will had largely vanished. Yet if not Camperdown, then who? Pascoe himself had been careful not to say from where the details had come.

Whatever the truth of the matter, he still needed Camperdown's help. He turned at the sound of a door opening behind him.

'My dear Bolt,' said Camperdown, in a flat tone of voice. 'I was not expecting to see you again so soon. Is all well?'

'Give you joy, my lord. I regret this intrusion but it is necessary, I find.'

'How so, pray?' Camperdown's eyes narrowed and he walked over to where a mahogany tantalus stood on a small table. 'Brandy?'

For a second or two Bolt didn't answer, his face turned to the fire. When he looked back, he said, 'It seems, my lord, we are undone. Someone has talked of our plans.'

'What?' Camperdown spun round and fixed Bolt with a cold stare. 'Speak plainly, man. What's happened?'

'The French agent brought over to assist us was discovered in my house by that fellow Pascoe. He managed to get away but Pascoe saw him; even called him by his name.'

'I'm sorry to find you so distressed,' said Camperdown. 'But I am at a loss to see what this has to do with me. I know nothing of this Frenchman you mention. Nor am I aware of the plans you allude to.'

Bolt's eyes widened in shock. 'Why, my lord, we talked about it on several occasions when we met at Rye, at the home of Sir Henry. Surely, you cannot have forgotten. We agreed that we should each cross to France and seek the assistance of the French in preventing the abolition of the slave trade. In return we were to provide them with information relating to our allies.'

'I have no idea what you're talking about,' said Camperdown. 'It's certainly well known that I went to France. The authorities have spoken to me about it and are satisfied with my replies. You, on the other hand, they do not yet know about, although it seems that may be about to change.'

'My lord, I killed a man to save your life. You must help me.'

'*Must*, sir?' Camperdown's voice had risen a fraction. 'You forget yourself, Sir William. Have a care what you say to me, sir, else there may be consequences.'

'Why, you scoundrel!' shouted Bolt. 'You're no better than a rogue and a vagabond!'

Camperdown took a couple of steps towards him, his face set hard, his eyes as cold as ice. 'You will hear from my assistant, sir. In the meantime, I bid you goodbye.'

CHAPTER 37

The despair Ebenezer felt was absolute. He had not a shred of hope for the future. Whatever reputation he had enjoyed as a trusted slave to his master – and it was little enough – was now to be taken from him. He was, once again, to be bought and sold like a cow or a sheep.

He was naked, lying on the orlop deck, iron chains threaded through the shackles attached to both ankles. It had been like this since he'd been brought on board the West India brig *Renewal* in the Lower Pool of the Port of London, two days before, eating, sleeping and defecating where he lay. In his lucid moments, he wondered how long he would survive.

From somewhere high above his head, he heard the scraping sound of a hatch being opened. Someone was entering the hold, the clumping noise of his boots on the rungs of the ladder getting louder as he descended. A pair of legs came into view. Then a face appeared. Ebenezer recognised the ship's mate.

'You still with us, cock?' The tone was not unfriendly. 'Thought I'd have a look at you. Make sure you were still alive. Got your victuals here, and all.'

The mate stepped off the ladder and came towards him, carrying a cloth bag and a mug of water in one hand. He handed them over and watched as Ebenezer hungrily took out from the bag a thick slice of bread and a lump of cheese.

'We sail at dawn,' said the mate. 'Soon as we're clear of land, we'll have you up on deck for a spell. Might even let you have some slops. Take away the worst of the chill, like.'

Ebenezer chewed on the bread and cheese, his head bent close to the deck. He wondered if anyone from the abolitionist movement was still looking for him. He thought it unlikely, but it didn't stop him thinking about it.

'Thankee, master,' he said. He'd have liked to ask if it was day or night, but he'd find out soon enough, when the crew were ordered on deck and the brig weighed anchor. Soon he was left alone again with his thoughts and his misery.

He must have fallen asleep. He woke to find someone shaking him by the shoulder. The chain passing through his shackles had been removed and he was able to move freely. He glanced forward. The chain had been thrown into a heap on the deck and was sliding slowly to starboard. The brig was under way. He must have slept through everything.

'Lay along there, nigger,' said a grime-stained face close to his own. 'Ain't got all bleeding day. Captain wants you all clean and tidy afore you get your wittles.'

Ebenezer levered himself into the sitting position and, by degrees, to his feet, his ankles chafed and bleeding from the rub of the shackles. Still naked, he followed the crewman to the companion ladder.

It was still dark when he stepped over the coaming and onto the upper deck of the *Renewal*, wincing as a sudden gust of cold wind caught him unawares.

'Stand yonder, nigger,' said the same crewman who'd brought

him up. He was pointing to the larboard scuppers.

Ebenezer shuffled over and waited for the dousing of cold water he knew was to come. He was used to it. It had been a regular feature of the Middle Crossing – the long weeks of the journey across the South Atlantic from Bance Island, off the coast of Sierra Leone, to Barbados – the daily hosing of the men who'd been kept in the cesspit of a hold for the previous twenty-four hours.

He stood quite still, looking out over the black marshland stretching away into the night, a seemingly endless prospect of reed and gorse. There was no sign of human life, save only a wind-mill here and there, the moonlight falling on their revolving sails. He looked up through the bows of the ship to where the river curved to the left. There, half a mile away, on the south bank, he could see the glimmer of ships' lanterns and, beyond them, the lights of a town that seemed to climb high above the river as if on a hillside. Woolwich, someone had said as he had come on deck. He looked behind him. The crew were busy about their tasks. For a moment, no one was watching him.

He didn't have time to think about the consequences of his actions. He knew only that an opportunity was in front of him that he could either seize or let slip.

The next second, he had vaulted the rail and was falling to the Thames.

The explosion of musket fire from the *Renewal* seemed a long way off, as Ebenezer came to the surface and struck out for the shoreline, lead shot peppering the surface of the water round him. He dived, confident he could stay below the surface long enough to take him out of the range of the muskets. He'd often before stayed under water for long periods while fishing in the Caribbean. But the Thames was not the tropics and the shock of the cold water was already beginning to affect him.

He stayed down for as long as he was able and then came up, his lungs on fire. A fresh volley of shots rang out, less accurate than the last time but still uncomfortably close. He dived again, the shore now only fifty yards away, and came up amongst the reeds lining the banks. He stumbled ashore and looked back at the *Renewal*, now far down the reach, a few men lining her larboard rail, muskets in hand. He didn't know much about ships but he knew it would be some time before they could think about pursuing him, what with the tide pushing them ever further away from him.

Ebenezer had never felt so cold in all his life, an easterly wind biting his naked flesh. He looked longingly at the lights of Woolwich where he might beg some food or at least a place to shelter and dry himself. But it was out of the question. As like as not the *Renewal* would put in there and a search party be sent to look for him. Yet without food or shelter, he knew he'd not survive long. He looked up into the sky, now a uniform grey. It looked like more rain.

It took Ebenezer nearly an hour to cross the marsh and reach a dirt track that appeared out of nowhere. Beyond it, and running parallel to it, was the Thames. He stopped and looked both ways. The road was deserted. Cautiously, he stepped onto the hard surface. A few hundred yards away to his right, just where the Thames swept round and began its journey south towards

Woolwich, he could see the dull outline of a number of tall ships lying at anchor. In the opposite direction were some lights of what appeared to be another small town. With little option but to carry on, he turned south and headed for the town.

'You won't get far like that, lad.' Ebenezer spun round. A grizzled old man had emerged from amongst the reeds on the foreshore of the river. Behind him was a skiff from which he must have climbed. 'On the run, are ye? Don't look so glum, boy. I seen a few niggers before, round these parts. They was all on the run. Mostly, though, they was still wearing their clothes. Eaten, have ye?'

Ebenezer shook his head.

'Then best you come with me. We ain't got much but you is welcome to share what we have. And we'll find ye some breeches, an' all.'

André Dubois sat on the wooden cot in his cell in the basement of the Wapping police office and contemplated the possibility of death. It all depended on how much Pascoe knew of his activities. The policeman didn't need to know it all; just a fraction of what he'd done would be enough to hang him in front of a jeering English mob. A knot formed in his gut. They did that in this country – subject a man to a slow and painful death. If it came to a choice, he thought he might prefer Madame Guillotine.

He forced himself to think logically. There was nothing he could do about being seen escaping through the window of Sir William Bolt's house. On its own, the incident might not have mattered too much and might be explained away as a simple burglary. Dubois shook his head. He doubted Sir William would have had the presence of mind to think of that. He was more likely to want to save himself by telling Pascoe everything the policeman wanted to know, including the plot to kill Wilber-force. It would be hard for him to convince the British of his innocence, particularly if Pascoe had seen him in the yard of the Spread Eagle, near Blackheath.

The handle of the cell door squealed on its hinges as it swung open. Pascoe stood in the entrance. He had to duck to get in. Dubois watched him shut the door and lean against it. He tried to read the other man's face but could not, the pale eyes giving nothing away.

'If you expect me to talk, *monsieur*, you are wasting your time.' Dubois sounded a great deal more confident than he felt.

'I'm not the least interest in what you have to say, Dubois. I have all the evidence I need to see you swing.'

'Then why, *monsieur*, are you here?'

'Merely to inform you of the charges that will be laid against you and what you can expect thereafter.'

'I'm not interested.'

'Nevertheless, you will be charged with two counts of murder. It would have been more, but since there is a limit to how many times we can hang a man, we've settled on two. Would you like to hear which ones?'

'No.'

'The murder of Mr John Dean, the man you abducted from his coach in Southwark, and the murder of the ostler at the Spread Eagle tavern, near Blackheath. I've little doubt you were aiming at me, but you missed and killed another fellow.'

'You can't prove anything, Pascoe. I am a prisoner of war and demand to be treated as one.'

'Unfortunately for you, Dubois, we have a witness who saw you abducting Mr Dean at gunpoint. The same witness later saw you disposing of his body into the Thames.'

'You're lying!' shouted Dubois.

'I understand you saw the witness yourself. A negro. Does that mean anything to you?'

Dubois's mouth gaped open. He said nothing.

'Then there's the second murder. The ostler near Blackheath. We know you were sent to this country to kill Mr Wilberforce. We also know that your contact in this country was Sir William Bolt. We have spoken to him and he has confirmed what I've just said. He, naturally enough, has no wish to hang and has therefore agreed to help us. Not that we really need him in this case because I saw you at the scene. But his evidence is useful as to your presence in this country.'

Dubois thought he detected the smallest of hesitations. Was the man lying? He tried to remember the exact sequence of events as he had crept up behind Pascoe and the ostler in the yard of the tavern. Certainly Pascoe had not seen him fire his pistol but he might have turned and seen him run from the yard.

'You would not, I am sure, wish me to lie in the witness box,' Pascoe went on. 'So I shall tell the court everything I saw. The shooting was also witnessed by Mr Wilberforce as well as my assistant, Waterman Constable Hart.'

Dubois felt suddenly cold, wishing Pascoe would go and leave him to his thoughts. If only half of what the man was saying was true, he was in serious trouble.

He'd know soon enough.

CHAPTER 38

The smell of fried bacon wafted across the street from the early breakfast house where Tom stood leaning against the wall of a house. He could see the belfry of the parish church of St Catherine's in the hazy half-light of the dawn. Behind him was the Thames, hidden from his immediate view by a row of decrepit houses.

'What will happen to Dubois now, your honour?' said Sam, his mouth full of the remains of a portion of bread and bacon. A mug of steaming hot tea stood on the ground between his feet.

'Difficult to say,' said Tom, picking a piece of gristle from his teeth and flicking it into the road. 'A lot depends on our finding Ebenezer and getting him into the witness box. At the moment, we've no idea where he is. For all we know he could be on a brig halfway to the West Indies. Our only other witness is Sir William, but on his own he's not enough to secure a conviction.'

'What about all the others the froggie has turned off, sir?'

'What others, Sam?' said Tom, a sudden hard edge to his voice. 'D'you mean Peggy? Or maybe the hat seller? What evidence do we have that would satisfy a court? He was never seen by anyone we've been able to find.'

'But we know he was following Mr Wilberforce. We saw him, didn't we?'

'What we saw was a horseman some way behind Mr Wilberforce's coach, who we *thought* was Dubois. But we never got close enough to be sure.'

'What about the time he shot at you and killed the ostler?'

'Did you see who pulled the trigger? Because I certainly didn't, in spite of what I told him. None of us actually saw the man responsible, either then, or subsequently,' said Tom, picking up his own mug of hot tea and nursing it in the palms of his hands. 'No, I regret it extremely, Sam, but without our negro friend, we don't have a case.'

'I thought we could hang enemy agents, sir,' said Sam. 'What's he doing in this country if it ain't to do some mischief?'

'He claims he was taken as a prisoner of war and was being brought to this country when he managed to escape.'

'And you believed him?' said Sam, incredulous.

'It don't much matter either way, Sam. Unless we come up with evidence that he's lying, he's entitled, under the prisoner exchange scheme, to be considered for release back to France. Mr Harriot has agreed to give us another two days to find Ebenezer. If we do find him, Dubois will be committed for trial. If not . . .'

'We ain't got no chance, sir. You said yourself, Ebenezer is likely halfway across the Atlantic.'

They munched in silence for a while, occupied by their own thoughts. It seemed inconceivable that Dubois might, in the end, be released as a prisoner of war.

'Begging your pardon, your honour?' Tom looked round,

surprised by the sound of John Kemp's voice. He'd not heard him approaching.

'Yes, Kemp. What is it?' said Tom, finishing the last of his tea.

'Mr Harriot presents his compliments, sir, and asks that you see him at your earliest convenience.'

'But we've only just . . .' Tom sighed. 'Very well, I shall be there directly.'

John Harriot looked tired, and older than his fifty-seven years, as though the strain of his responsibilities was beginning to have its effect. He leaned back in his chair as Tom walked in, tossed an ancient pair of spectacles onto his desk and laced his fingers behind his head.

'There's been a development with Sir William Bolt that you ought to be aware of,' he said. 'I've received word that he and Lord Camperdown are to duel. I know no more than that at the moment. The message came from Lady Annabel Stapleton who, I seem to remember, you've had some dealing with.'

'Did she come herself?' Tom was conscious of a burning sensation in his cheeks. He coughed and moved over to the fireplace.

'No, not that I'm aware,' said Harriot, oblivious to Tom's discomfort. He picked up a piece of paper from his desk and held it out. 'I was handed this about an hour ago. It might be an idea were you to see her and see what else she has to say on the matter.'

Tom glanced at the note. It was short and to the point. Camperdown had, it seemed, called to see Lady Annabel last night, in a state of some distress. In answer to her questions he had reluctantly informed her that he had, in the past hour, been visited at his home by Sir William Bolt. An argument had ensued between them, as a result of which he had felt compelled to challenge Sir William to a duel. He had, according to Lady Annabel, declined to answer her questions as to what the initial argument had been about and her attempts to dissuade him going through with the matter had been to no avail.

Tom finished reading and looked up.

'What, pray, d'you make of it?' asked the magistrate.

'I regret it extremely, but I have absolutely no idea. I can only assume it has something to do with Dubois. It's possible that both Sir William and Lord Camperdown knew of Dubois's presence in this country. If so, doubtless they are considering their future and this has led to the prospect of a little bloodletting between them. Do we know where they plan to meet?'

'No, but you don't need me to remind you that your case against Dubois now rests almost entirely on the evidence Sir William is in a position to give. He's not going to be a lot of good to us if he gets killed, so I suggest you find him as a matter of urgency.'

There was little sign of the approaching dawn and the air was damp and cool as the two men alighted from a curricle, close to Limehouse Hole Stairs. Together, they walked down the footpath alongside the river, dew covering the grass. To their right, a low mist shrouded the hundred or so ships lying in the reach.

Camperdown, his face unshaven and paler than usual, was accompanied by Lieutenant Hugh Graham of the Royal Navy. A short, stocky, confident man in his early twenties, Graham carried under his left arm a wooden case containing a pair of duelling pistols. Neither man had spoken in the last hour, the silence of the morning disturbed only by the swish of their boots in the long grass.

Camperdown had no illusions about what he could expect in the coming minutes. He knew of his opponent's reputation with both sword and pistol, knew the odds of his survival were slim. He wished there was some way he might avoid the coming trial but knew it wasn't possible. The previous evening, he had summoned his solicitor and made the necessary alterations to his will. Later, after he had taken supper, he'd gone to see the Lady Annabel and they had talked well into the night. At around two in the morning he had left her, and spent the remainder of the night walking the silent streets until it was time to meet Graham, his second.

He looked along the path. Sir William was waiting for them. He was standing under the shelter of a windmill, some thirty or forty yards to the left of the footpath. Beside him was a man of about thirty, his white silk stockings spattered with mud. Camperdown recognised him from the meetings at the home of the late Sir Henry, in Rye. He tried to recall the fellow's name. Bennett, he thought it was.

A few yards away from them was a short, hunchbacked man, dressed entirely in black, his long hair framing a morose face, the skin deeply pitted. Next to him was a small, folding table on which had been placed a number of knives, a small saw, two scalpels, a pair of forceps and various other implements of the surgeon's trade. The sight did nothing to steady Camperdown's nerves. He looked away hurriedly.

The man with the mud-spattered stockings approached them and, after a curt nod in Camperdown's direction, addressed himself to Lieutenant Graham.

'I act, sir, for Sir William Bolt. It is my duty to enquire if there is any prospect of finding an amicable resolution to this matter.'

'I am instructed,' said Graham, 'that there is no such prospect.'

'Very well, I suggest the normal rules should apply. Shall we agree on twelve paces, firing to commence when I drop my hand-kerchief, and to first blood?'

'Agreed,' said Graham. 'Nothing has changed since we spoke on the matter, yesterday evening.'

Camperdown glanced over to where Bolt stood staring at him. There was no expression on his face, either of hate or fear, or even sorrow at the inevitability of what was to happen. Behind him, the mist that had lain over the Thames had lifted and a dull grey light suffused the bleak scene. He shifted his weight from one leg to the other and tried to concentrate on what the seconds were doing. Both pistols had been removed from the velvet-lined wooden case that Lieutenant Graham had been carrying and were lying on a second table, close by. Bennett was loading them while Graham looked on. He was slow, careful and methodical. Camperdown wished he would hurry. He didn't think he could take much more of the waiting.

'When you are ready, gentlemen.' Camperdown started at the sound of Bennett's voice. 'You may choose your weapon.' He held out the case to which the loaded pistols had been returned. Bolt chose first and removed the weapon, eying it carefully before moving to position. In a moment he was joined by Camperdown and the two friends stood back to back, their pistols at their sides, pointing to the ground.

'I remind you, gentlemen' – Bennett was speaking again – 'there is to be no deloping. Aim straight and true, if you please.

The contest is to first blood. You may now take up your positions and, following my signal, fire at will.'

In the silence that followed, the metallic clicks of the pistols being cocked seemed very loud. Camperdown was the first to move, counting off his six paces before turning to face his opponent, slowly raising the barrel of his gun until it pointed at Bolt's chest.

Out of the corner of his eye he saw one of the seconds – which one he couldn't see – raise his arm, a white handkerchief held between his fingers.

'Fire!'

The sound of the man's voice felt as though someone had struck him in the ear. He didn't look to see if the cloth had been dropped. There was no time for that. He pulled the trigger, saw the flash of powder igniting and heard the boom of the main charge, the gun jumping in his hand. At the same moment, he felt a breath of wind pass by his left ear. Bolt's shot had missed. He stared through the clouds of gun smoke. His opponent was still standing. Then he saw him topple forward and crash to the ground.

The mist of early morning had lifted when, later that day, Tom stepped into the stern sheets of the waiting police galley and gazed along the Lower Pool towards Shadwell and Limehouse. The information was vague. A passing cooper had reported hearing the sounds of gunfire on the Isle of Dogs. A pedlar, who had been in the vicinity, was more specific. A duel had been fought, and the condition of one of those taking part was thought to be serious. There was little doubt in Tom's mind about who was involved.

He wondered where Camperdown and Bolt were at this moment; which one of them was hurt, or even dead.

He watched a dozen or so lighters making their way upriver to the legal quays, the shoulders of the lightermen hunched against a cold, east wind. He waited for them to pass and then took the galley out into the middle of the river. He wouldn't normally have chosen to row where the force of the opposing tide was strongest but for the moment the advantages of a clear channel outweighed its disadvantages. He expected there would be plenty of witnesses still there. They were likely to remain for some time, talking to one another, discussing what they'd seen or heard, where the injured man might have been taken, and who he was. 'Wait for me, here,' said Tom, after he'd fetched the galley alongside the mooring poles at Limehouse Hall Stairs. 'I'll be about an hour.'

He walked to the end of the passage and turned right along the river path onto the Isle of Dogs. The dew of early morning had gone, and in its place the grass looked clean and fresh.

It was the mill house he saw first, its rust-coloured sails a familiar enough sight, turning slowly in the light air, the timber arms in need of a fresh coat of paint. Then, almost immediately afterwards, he saw a group of perhaps half a dozen people standing in a circle a little to the north of the building. They seemed engrossed in something. Tom hurried towards them.

'In the King's name, stand aside, there.' Tom pushed his way through. A man was lying in the grass, his head held in the arms of a woman kneeling beside him. The man was unconscious, his face deathly pale. A bright crimson stain was visible in the middle of his chest.

'Sir William?' Tom dropped to one knee. 'Can you hear me?'

Bolt's eyes flickered and then opened for a second or two. 'Is that you, Pascoe? I wondered if it would be you who came.'

He lapsed into silence, licking his lips, his face drawn in pain.

'Is this Camperdown's doing?' said Tom, nodding at the crimson patch.

Bolt tried to smile. 'I'm done for, Pascoe. My spine's broken. Can feel it. What happens is between me and my Maker. As for Camperdown, I'll warrant you'll not see him again.'

Tom's gaze swivelled to the woman kneeling with him. 'What d'you know of this?'

'I didn't see nothing, your worship. Leastways, I didn't see the gentleman shot. Heard it, right enough, but by the time I got here, there were only the surgeon what was looking after him.'

'A surgeon? What happened to him?'

'Legged it, like the rest of them. I tried to pick the gentleman up. Take him to the accident hospital. But I couldn't move him. He were in too much pain. These other folk . . . Well . . . they came later.'

'Can you talk to me, Sir William? What happened here? Where is Lord Camperdown?'

'I've not long to go, Pascoe.' Bolt's breathing was shallow and laboured. 'Let me go in peace. Surely you understand I cannot speak of what happened. I may have nothing else, but allow me to keep my name and my honour.'

Tom knew enough of the *Code Duello* to realise that Bolt would not talk of what happened. Nor was this the moment to try. He gazed up at the ring of onlookers. He doubted they would have anything to add to what the woman had said. Those who might have seen something would know to keep out of the way for a day or two; not become involved.

'What of Dubois? We have spoken of this before. Was it you who brought him over to this country?'

Bolt licked his lips and coughed.

'Sir William?'

'I hear you. Yes, it was me but we needed to do something to stop the abolitionists else they would ruin us.'

Tom waited a moment.

'Where is Dubois now?'

'I've not seen him since the night you saw him in my house.'

Tom climbed to his feet and looked west towards London. 'Your honour?' Tom looked down. The woman still cradled Bolt's head in her lap. She was shaking her head. 'He's gone, God rest him.'

CHAPTER 39

It had been Harriot's suggestion that they talk over lunch. Tom was sitting opposite the magistrate in one of the upstairs booths, at Jerusalem's on Cornhill, a generous plate of cold meats accompanied by a pot of oysters and some slices of white buttered bread adorning the centre of the table.

'So, Sir William Bolt is dead, you say.' Harriot picked up his mug of Whitbread and drank a mouthful. 'Where does that leave us with the Dubois case?'

'We're still hoping to find our black witness.'

'You've got another day to find him,' said Harriot. 'After that . . . well, we've already talked about what will happen. I know it's not what you wanted to hear, but without some credible evidence I very much doubt he'll be sent for trial.'

The two men ate in silence for a minute or two as the din of murmured conversation went on around them.

'What of Camperdown?' said Harriot, breaking the silence. 'What's he got to say about the death of Sir William?'

'We've not been able to find him. I've had inquiries made at his usual haunts. It seems he might have gone into hiding. I think he'll try and leave the country, most likely for his plantation on Barbados.'

'Do you think he was responsible for Sir William's death?'

'It would seem the obvious choice,' said Tom. 'But I've not been able to find anyone willing to talk to me about it. Funnily enough, I think we'd have more of a chance of convicting him on the shooting of Sir Henry Thwaite-Thomas. Yet, even there, I have my doubts. The point of entry of the bullet is wrong. It's as if the shot came from the side, rather than the front.'

'I see,' said Harriot, examining a morsel of beef on the end of his fork. 'Wouldn't Sir Henry have been presenting his shoulder to his opponent? That would explain the bullet's point of entry, wouldn't it?'

'Wrong side,' said Tom. 'Sir Henry was left-handed. I would have expected the wound to be on the left, not the right.'

'So if Camperdown didn't fire the fatal shot, who did?'

'My guess is Sir William. He admitted being present at the duel and was known as an excellent shot. Moreover, as one of the seconds, he would have been armed in case something went wrong and he would have been close enough to ensure that he hit his target.'

'Really?' Harriot's fork stopped midway between his plate and his mouth. 'Why shoot in the first place? It was a duel, after all. Why not leave it to Camperdown?'

'I think that both he and Camperdown regarded Sir Henry as a threat to their campaign against the abolitionists. He would naturally have taken Camperdown's side. As to why he felt it necessary to shoot at all, I have no idea. I can only think that something must have gone seriously wrong.'

Harriot chewed on his food for a moment or two. 'None of this implicates Camperdown in Dubois's presence in England.'

'No, it doesn't, sir,' said Tom. 'At least, not directly. But the threat posed by Sir Henry to the plans to thwart the abolitionist cause was sufficiently serious to lead to his death. If they were prepared to go that far, I imagine they'd not hesitate in seeking French assistance for their cause.'

'And you're suggesting what, exactly?' said Harriot, spooning some oysters onto his plate.

'I think it was a joint enterprise entered into by both Camperdown and Bolt to ask for French assistance in the assassination of Mr Wilberforce. I think Camperdown's attempt to recruit French help failed because he was arrested before he could put his case to the *Directoire*. Once that happened, he could not be seen to be involved in any plot against his own country. He probably felt he was in enough trouble already.'

'So it was left to Sir William Bolt to cross the Channel and try again, as a result of which Dubois finds himself back in England?'

'Precisely, sir.'

'But did you not tell me Camperdown and Bolt did not get along together?'

'Both men had a great deal to lose by the abolition of the slave trade. I suspect it was this consideration rather than any feelings of friendship which ultimately drove them to contemplate treason.'

'Yes, you could have the right of it,' said Harriot, looking up at Tom. 'But with Sir William dead and Camperdown missing, it's all rather academic, wouldn't you say?'

'We still have Dubois,' said Tom.

'Ah, yes, Dubois. Yet you still need to produce your missing

303

witness at the committal proceedings at eight o'clock tomorrow evening,.'

By three o'clock the following afternoon, Tom was beginning to lose hope of finding Ebenezer. He, Sam and the rest of the crew had trawled through every tavern, inn, common lodging house and brothel between London Bridge and Limehouse in a vain search for news of either Ebenezer or Camperdown. Inquiries at the Camperdown family seat in Surrey had also been fruitless and Tom had been left with a sense of looming failure.

'It don't look like Lord Camperdown has left the country, your honour,' said Sam, when the crew had met for a bite to eat, earlier in the day. 'But Ebenezer is a different story. I saw Master Mendoza in the synagogue up at Duke's Place. He didn't want to say much but the word is Ebenezer got taken aboard the West India brig *Renewal*, what sailed at first light yesterday.'

Tom watched the flat, empty acres on either side of the river slip past, their arrival disturbing a heron fishing the shallow waters, close to the shoreline. The bird flapped its wings and, long legs trailing below it, climbed away into a leathern sky. Little else moved in this quiet stretch of water between Blackwall Point and the military town of Woolwich, at the southern end of Bugsby's Reach. Tom glanced down into the water. Another ten or fifteen minutes to low tide. After that, unless they turned and began their return journey, rowing would be hard work.

He peered over the shoulders of the crew. Three or four hundred yards ahead, he could see the naval supply base at King's Yard. In front of it, about half a dozen men-of-war lay at anchor, their gun-ports closed, their paintwork fresh, their yards perfectly square. Before the town itself, three more vessels – two brigs and a barquentine by the looks of them – stood off Ship Stairs, close to the military arsenal.

'We'll pass under the stern of the last of them brigs and come up on the land side,' said Tom, as they approached the merchant ships. A few minutes later he drew down on the larboard guy and let the galley swing round in the slack tide, the exposed mud-banks off the Woolwich shore, ominously close.

'Your honour,' said Sam. He was staring at the stern of the last ship in the tier.

'Aye, Sam, what is it?'

'It's the *Renewal*, sir.'

'By God, you've the right of it, Sam,' said Tom, altering course to bring the galley alongside. Leaping across the narrow strip of water separating the two craft, he ran up the companion ladder and onto the upper deck of the brig.

It helped that they knew each other, Tom and the master of the *Renewal*. They had both served with the West India Merchants and Traders for the three years prior to Tom joining the marine police and, as is the way with seafaring folk, had formed a lasting friendship. Yes, the negro named Ebenezer Samson had been brought aboard on the orders of the ship's owner, Sir William Bolt, for conveying to Barbados. No, he was no longer aboard, having made good his escape early yesterday morning, in Bugsby's Reach, and swimming to the west bank. The *Renewal* had, in consequence, been forced to put into Wool-wich and send out a search party which had only just returned, without finding him. The ship would now sail with the next ebb tide, in about seven hours.

'I reckon the nigger had help,' said the master of the *Renewal*. 'He couldn't have survived else, what with him not had his victuals. Nor his slops, neither. He were naked as nature intended, he were. What's to tell Sir William? That's the rub. Got to hope that by the time we get back here, he'll have forgotten all about it. But if he asks, I'll tell him the nigger died at sea.'

Tom nodded sympathetically. 'I don't think you'll have any problems with Sir William.' He paused and then, as if an afterthought, 'Lord Camperdown. Seen anything of him, have you?'

'Heard some talk around Wapping,' said the *Renewal*'s master. 'But I ain't seen him none. Folk reckon he's in some sort of bother but no one knew what, exactly. They say he's looking for a berth out of the country. Why d'you ask?'

'Just curious. The slave who escaped belonged to Camperdown, not Sir William.'

CHAPTER 40

'Ever ridden a horse, Higgins?' asked Tom, looking at the newest member of his crew. They were standing in the high street of Woolwich, close to the junction of the alley leading down to Ship Stairs, and the river.

'Can't say I have, your honour,' said a nervous-looking Jim Higgins as though anticipating where this conversation was leading. He'd joined Tom's crew straight from a lifetime at sea. 'Ain't too many where I just come from.'

'Then it's time you did,' said Tom with a grin. 'Cut along to the nearest stables – I believe there's one down Hog Lane – and ask them for a nag. I want you to search the marshes between Bugsby's and Blackwall reaches for our negro friend. If you find him, hang on to him. The rest of us will take the galley round into Blackwall Reach and we'll meet you at Greenwich. Is that clear?'

'Clear, aye, clear, sir,' said Higgins, touching his forehead and trotting off.

Forty minutes later, the police galley had rounded Blackwall Point and was cruising towards the Royal Hospital at Greenwich. Tom could already see the Royal Observatory nestling on its peak above the town.

'Way enough,' said Tom, catching sight of a skiff pulled up

onto the larboard foreshore, almost hidden amongst the reeds. He steered the galley onto the hard and waited for the keel to scrape onto the mud before climbing over the side. He waded over to the empty boat, a strong smell of fish confirming its everyday purpose. Its presence on the foreshore at this hour suggested its owner worked at night. He left it and walked inland. Ahead of him he could see what looked like a dirt road, running parallel to the river.

'Cut along to Greenwich,' he said, looking back at the crew. 'Find Higgins and see what he's got, if anything. I'll walk the rest of the way and see you all there.'

He turned onto the roadway and headed south. It was unlikely, he thought, that even if Ebenezer had chosen to hide from pursuers, he would choose to go north where he'd be trapped by the bend in the river. South led to Greenwich and the possibility of food and shelter. He thought of the boat. It clearly belonged to a fisherman, a fisherman, moreover, who was likely to have been returning home after a night's work at about dawn – the same time Ebenezer had jumped from the *Renewal*. It was entirely possible the two had met. If that were the case, it might be that Ebenezer had found his food and shelter quicker than he could have hoped for.

The hovel on the eastern fringe of the town was not hard to find. Built of stone, with a low pitched roof of slate, it was set down by the side of the track along which Tom was now walking. To the left of the ramshackle door stood a wooden frame on which some fishing nets had been hung out to dry. Next to it, and propped against the front wall of the building, were a couple of spare oars and an upended hogshead filled with water. The latter appeared to have been used for cleaning fish. Tom approached the door and knocked.

From the inside came the sound of heavy footsteps, and then the door opened a fraction to reveal a white-bearded man, his face deeply lined and weather-beaten, his white hair long and unkempt.

'Aye, lad, what is it I can do for you?' The voice was richer and deeper than Tom would have guessed.

'I'm looking for someone,' said Tom. 'A black fellow that was seen in these parts. Know anything about it, do you?'

'And who might you be, young fellow?'

'My name is Pascoe. I'm with the marine police at Wapping,' said Tom dragging out his tipstaff. 'If the man I'm looking for is with you, I'd like to talk to him.'

The old man cocked his head to one side and looked quizzically at Tom. Finally, he said, 'Come in, boy. Don't know why I should trust you any, but you look to be an honest man.'

He opened the door wide and waved his visitor inside.

It took a little while for Tom's eyes to become accustomed to the gloom and his nostrils to the powerful smell of fish. The room in which he now found himself was no more than about eight feet square. A small table and two chairs stood against one wall while what appeared to be a bed occupied an adjacent position. To the right of the door was a large fireplace on which had been placed an assortment of cooking utensils.

An elderly woman was sitting on one of the chairs, a knife in her hands, a pail of fish on the floor beside her. Tom watched as her hand plunged into the tub and withdrew a small fish which she placed on the table in front of her. In an instant, the blade had slit the creature from throat to vent. Another glimmer of steel and the fish's innards were cut loose, the head removed and the lot swept to one side. At the same time, the body of the fish was caught and thrown into a second tub of water he'd not previously seen. The woman's hand scooped up another fish and prepared to repeat her task.

A rustle distracted Tom's attention. He looked towards the sound and saw a man asleep on the bed. He walked over.

'Ebenezer? That you?' Tom shook the African's shoulder and waited for him to sit up. 'Yes, master, it's me, Ebenezer.' His voice was flat, defeated, as though all hope had died within him. Slowly, he rolled off the bed and stood by the table, glancing down at the old woman. She paused in what she was doing, looked up at him and laid a hand on his arm, the briefest of smiles crossing her face.

'I want to talk to you,' said Tom, noting the too-tight, ragged trousers the negro was wearing, and the sack that was draped over his massive shoulders, holes cut out for his head and arms to pass through. 'That's all.'

'What you want to talk to Ebenezer for, master?'

'I want you to tell me about the man you saw carrying a body, and throwing it into the river. I want you to tell me what he looked like, and if you would know him again.'

'I done speak to the other *bakra*, master.'

'Yes, you spoke to Master Sam, but I want to hear it again. You saw a man with a body which he threw into the river. Is that right?'

'Yes, master.'

'Did you see his face at any time?'

'Yes, master. I see it before, when I sees him by the carriage.'

'Tell me what he looked like.'

The questioning went on. Little by little, Ebenezer began to relax, to tell Tom the story of what he had seen that night, on Great Dover Street and then, later, down by the river on Hays Wharf. He was sure that the man he'd seen standing by the coach with a pistol in his hand was the same man he'd later seen carrying a body in a roll of carpet. He had, he said, on both occasions seen the man wearing an indigo scarf, a colour he'd not seen since arriving in England.

'But there's someone who said he saw you, a black man, carrying the body,' said Tom.

'I done carry nobody,' said Ebenezer, trembling.

The question of whether or not Tom believed what he was being told was one he would, had he been asked, have refused to answer. For him honesty and dishonesty were two sides of the same coin, often employed according to the situation in which a man might find himself. Where there was no cause to lie, most would tell the truth. But where the consequences of veracity spelt ruin or death, even an honest man might be tempted to lie. And Tom wasn't yet sure which side of the coin he was looking at.

He moved on. His priority now was to persuade Ebenezer that his best interest lay in giving evidence against Dubois. It was not going to be easy. The negro had little reason to trust those he'd come into contact with. He'd been let down too often for that. Yet if Tom failed, he'd lose Dubois.

'What happen to me when the master find me?'

Tom hesitated. It was a difficult question to answer. He knew he could take care of him during the course of the trial and the days leading up to it. But afterwards, when his usefulness as a witness was at an end? What then? He knew that whatever he said, the likelihood of Ebenezer evading a lifetime of slavery was slim.

'Let's take things one at a time,' said Tom, sidestepping the question. 'You can't stay here. You'll be discovered within the week. If you come with me, you'll be safe until after the trial. Then we can think about what to do.'

Ebenezer's eyes widened and he shook his head.

'I didn't want to say this to you, Ebenezer,' said Tom. 'But you have no choice. You are a suspect in a murder case. You were, as I've said to you, seen carrying the body of a man later found floating in the Thames. Until that matter is cleared up, I need you to come with me.'

The Honourable Alexander Thorngood, the Second Baron Camperdown, was in a state of considerable agitation as he walked up Whitehall and turned in towards the office of the under-secretary of state for Foreign Affairs. Ten minutes later he was sitting opposite a grave-faced John Hookham Frere.

'I regret it extremely, my lord, but what you ask is not possible.' The under-secretary spoke slowly and carefully, as though weighing up each word. 'His Grace, The Duke of Portland, is otherwise engaged and is likely to remain so for some considerable time.'

'Did you tell him who it was who wished to see him?' said Camperdown, his voice rising.

'Most certainly, my lord.'

'Then I shall have to see the minister.'

'My lord, if I may speak freely . . .' Hookham Frere spread his hands, his eyebrows raised. He waited for Camperdown's nod and then said, 'You are, of course, aware of the attitude of the Administration to your recent visit to France. A great deal of time was expended on the consideration of any action thought to be appropriate to your case. In the end, as you know, you were given the benefit of the doubt about the reason for your journey—'

'Where is this leading?' interrupted Camperdown.

'Allow me to continue, my lord, and I will explain. Sometime after your return, it came to our attention that a friend of yours, Sir William Bolt, had also crossed to France, and sought an audience with the *Directoire*. We believe that, following this audience, a French agent by the name of André Dubois was dispatched to this country.'

The smallest of hesitations, then, 'I still fail to see—'

Hookham Frere held up his hand. 'Dubois has since been seen, on at least two occasions, at Sir William's home. We now discover that Sir William has died following what we believe to have been a duel. You will note that I say nothing of our suspicions about the identity of his opponent or the reason for the duel.' The under-secretary tapped his desk with one finger. 'What I will say is that such help and assistance as your rank may have entitled you to expect from your peers will not, in the future, be forthcoming.'

'This is outrageous,' said Camperdown, leaping to his feet. 'I demand to see the minister.'

'You are to consider, my lord, the position in which you find yourself. I recommend you do not press your case lest it disadvantage you. According to our sources, you are under investigation by the marine police institution. To put it plainly, under the present circumstances, the minister will not see you.'

Camperdown left the interview, his confidence badly shaken. His rank, which had until this moment saved him from the consequences of his transgressions, would no longer shield him. If Hookham Frere knew about his connection with Bolt and had learned of the presence of the French agent, it could only be a matter of time before his own involvement in the matter was discovered.

He crossed Horse Guards Parade into St James's Park and turned up towards Piccadilly. He'd heard Dubois was in custody, and if what Hookham Frere had said about the police investigation was true, he was likely to be next. His heartbeat quickened.

The consequences of the duel, he could live with. Just. What worried him was Dubois. If evidence was found to suggest that the Frenchman had attempted to assassinate Wilberforce, it would not take much to drag others, including himself, into the treason net.

But what if Pascoe could find no evidence of wrongdoing against Dubois? What then? As far as he knew, the Frenchman was suspected of two murders, both connected with his attempt to assassinate Wilberforce. And in only one of those cases was there a witness. The witness was his own slave, a man who was, even now, on his way across the Atlantic, destined for oblivion.

He breathed a little easier.

CHAPTER 41

'I think you've got a case.' Harriot tapped the document lying on the desk in front of him and regarded Tom with a quizzical stare. 'Certainly it's enough to send before the Grand Jury. What troubles me, though, is what to do about the fellow once he's given his evidence. He won't last five minutes with Camperdown's thugs looking for him.'

'So far as I'm aware,' said Tom, 'Camperdown is under the impression that Ebenezer is well on his way back to Barbados.'

'Are you prepared to take that risk, Mr Pascoe?'

'I suppose not,' said Tom. 'We could always send him somewhere where he'll be safe.'

'Where d'you suggest?'

'I was thinking of Sierra Leone. That's where he originally comes from.'

'Have you any idea how much that would cost? Who would pay his passage? And once he got there, what guarantee would he have that he wouldn't again be captured? No, we need a better solution than—'

A knock on the door interrupted him and a moment later Dr Patrick Colquhoun came into the room.

'Harriot, my dear fellow, I'm so sorry to have intruded. I'll come back when you're free.'

'Not at all. As a matter of fact, Mr Pascoe and I were discussing an interesting dilemma connected with slavery. We'd like to hear what you have to say, particularly since you have an interest in the subject.'

'Be happy to help, if I can,' said Colquhoun, beaming at his colleague and seating himself in a spare chair, next to Tom. 'What's the dilemma?'

'Mr Pascoe has a murder case coming up for committal. You'll recall you have agreed to deal with it. The problem is what to do with the principal witness after we've finished with him. He's a black runaway slave who is being sought by his master. He's agreed to help us and I think we are morally obliged to help him, in return. The problem is that the Lord Chief Justice has already ruled in the master's favour and, if the slave is caught, he will certainly be sold back into slavery.'

'Tricky.' Colquhoun got to his feet and strolled over to the sideboard where he helped himself to a cup of coffee. Returning to his chair, he looked from Harriot to Tom. 'The first thing to note is that there's no obligation in cases of this kind for us to seek to return a runaway slave to his master. What is less clear is how far we can go in assisting his escape. But assuming we have done nothing in this regard, the question of his continued freedom is easily dealt with.'

'Really? How so?' asked Harriot.

'Are you familiar with the case of *Knight* v *Wedderburn*?' said Colquhoun.

'Can't say I am,' said Harriot.

'No, it's hardly surprising. It's a Scottish case that came before the Court of Sessions in Edinburgh some years ago, involving an

African fellow named Joseph Knight. Knight was captured and shipped to Jamaica as a slave, where he was bought by a man named John Wedderburn. Sometime later, Wedderburn took Knight back to his native Scotland, and there employed him as a domestic servant, albeit without pay. It was at this stage that Knight became aware of the Somersett ruling in England, which was popularly supposed to have outlawed slavery in this country. With that case in mind, Knight brought a claim against his employer demanding wages. The case eventually made its way to the Court of Sessions where, unlike the case of Somersett, it was ruled that slavery was incompatible with Scottish law.'

'Then there is our answer,' said Harriot, turning to look at Tom. 'Tell your witness to go north where he'll be safe. By the way, are you sure he will stick to what he's said in his statement?'

'I see no reason why not,' said Tom.

'You told me he's a frightened man,' said the magistrate, looking at Tom over his steel-framed spectacles. 'In my experience, frightened people do not make reliable witnesses. And then there's the question of his competency in the witness box.'

'I don't follow,' said Tom.

'The court will need to be satisfied that your witness understands the nature of the oath he will take. If he's a Christian, there won't be a problem. But if he's not, the court may take some convincing before accepting his testimony. Is he a Christian?'

'I doubt it,' interjected Colquhoun. 'Converting negro slaves to Christianity caused more problems than it solved. Many of them believed that becoming a Christian meant they were free.'

'Then we'll just have to wait and see.' Harriot paused and looked at Colquhoun. 'If it's all right with you, I suggest adjourning the committal proceedings for Dubois until ten o'clock in the morning the day after tomorrow. By the way, what of Ebenezer? We can't keep him locked up in the cells until the trial.'

Tom smiled. 'Everything, sir, is in hand. We've got him a bed at the Devil's Tavern with instructions not to move until we come for him. He'll be taken there later today.'

The following two days passed without incident. At exactly ten o'clock on Thursday morning, the courtroom at the Wapping police office rose as Dr Patrick Colquhoun, superintending magistrate for the police offices at Queen's Square and Wapping, entered the room to take his seat on the bench. At once, the noisy hum of conversation that had reverberated around the room fell silent.

A moment or so later, the door to the gaoler's room opened and André Dubois was led in and directed to toe the line in front of the magistrate.

'André Dubois.' The magistrate's clerk was on his feet and reading from a large sheet of paper. 'You are charged that on divers dates between the sixteenth and the twenty-second of September 1799, within the jurisdiction of the Sessions House of the Old Bailey, you did murder John Dean, against the Peace. How do you plead? Guilty or not guilty?'

Dubois remained silent, his face turned to the ceiling.

'Enter a plea of not guilty,' said Colquhoun, flicking an irritated finger at his clerk. 'Read the second charge.'

When that, too, brought no response, Colquhoun dealt with it as for the first, and the committal proceedings got under way. William Watson, the serjeant-at-arms for the House of Commons, was the first to be called, followed by Tom and then the physician.

'You are the physician who certified death in the case of Mr John Dean?'

'I am, sir.'

'And I think you also attended on the coach driver whose body was found in Great Dover Street on the nineteenth of this month?'

'That is correct.'

'And the cause of death in both cases was, what?'

'Strangulation.'

'Tell me, doctor, in your opinion, were the injuries to both men caused by the same implement?'

'Yes, they were. The marks left on the necks of both the deceased were identical in pattern and strongly suggested the use of the same implement in both cases.'

Last into the witness box was Ebenezer, giving his deposition in a halting, nervous whisper, his eyes darting from the magistrate, to his clerk, to the public gallery, and back again. It was a slow process.

'You were brought to this country as a slave and have since run away from your master. Is that correct?'

'Yes, master.'

'While on the run, you saw something happen involving the passenger of a coach. Can you tell the court what you saw?'

'I sees the man point his gun at a man in the coach.'

'What happened then?'

'The man got out of the coach and he was told to get on the horse. Then they done ride off.'

'Do you see either of those men in the court today?'

'Yes, master. It is him,' said Ebenezer, pointing at Dubois. 'He were the man with the gun.'

'Are you quite sure about that? It was dark at the time.'

'Yes, master. Ebenezer sure.'

'And while you were there, did you see another man?'

'Yes, master. But he were dead. He were on the top of the coach.'

'In the driver's seat?'

'Yes, master.'

'Did you see the man with the gun again?'

'Down by de river. I see him carrying a man on his shoulder.'

'Are you certain it was the same man you previously saw by the coach?'

'Yes, master. Ebenezer sure.'

'How can you be sure?'

The questions and answers droned on until, finally, Colquhoun appeared to be satisfied. The committal, when it came, seemed almost an afterthought.

'Andre Dubois, you are committed, in custody, to stand your trial at the current session of the Old Bailey, on a charge of murder, contrary to the Peace,' said Colquhoun. And that was that.

By mid-afternoon, the bill of indictment, together with Tom, Ebenezer and the other witnesses, was before the Grand Jury, at Hick's Hall in Camberwell. An hour after that and the indictment had been marked as 'True', the trial set for the following day – Friday – at the Old Bailey.

Dubois did not sleep that night, pacing the small cell on the second floor of Newgate Prison, his thoughts on the forthcoming trial. The evidence was damning, the outcome, inevitable. He was an enemy spy, caught in the enemy's camp. Worse, he was charged with murder. Not one, but two. No court would think twice about the appropriate sentence. He sat down on the edge of his cot, his head in his hands, self-pity sweeping through him.

He blamed Pascoe. Had it not been for him, none of this would have happened. Self-pity gave way to loathing. If the chance came to settle his score with the Englishman he would seize it, whatever the cost. He glanced up as a pigeon flapped its wings outside the cell window and flew off. Beyond the prison walls a silence had spread over London. Nothing, it seemed, was moving, the city asleep.

He shivered. The dark, sombre hours, lit only by a silver beam of moonlight streaming through the bars at his window, seemed to accentuate the shadows of the night, stirring his deepest fears of the abyss awaiting him. He tried to think of something else. But nothing could dispel the blackness of his mood. He got to his feet and shuffled the few paces to the window, gazing up at the moon, trying to gauge the hour. It was around four o'clock. He rested his forehead against the cell wall, his hands gripping the window bars high above him. Five hours, maybe six, before his trial. He returned to his cot and lay down, sleep overtaking him in spite of his fears.

The harsh scrape of a key turning in the lock woke him. For a heartbeat he stared at the ceiling, wondering where he was. The cold, grey light of early morning filtered through the window. He lifted his head off the mattress and looked at the cell door as it opened.

'Good morning, Dubois.' Tom Pascoe's tall frame filled the doorway.

'What do you want of me, *monsieur*?' said Dubois, letting his head fall back on the mattress. 'Have you not done enough?'

'By eight o'clock on Monday, it will be all over for you, Dubois,' said Tom. 'You will have gone to meet your maker. You might want to clear your conscience and tell me about the people you killed.'

'There are too many for me to remember, *monsieur*,' said Dubois, a look of sadistic satisfaction playing about his lips. 'They mean nothing to me, especially the woman.'

Tom took a step forward, his jaw muscles tightening, his fists clenched. Then he seemed to relax.

'Let me take you through what's going to happen this morning, Dubois. I think you might find it of interest. It might even remind you of a few details you seem to have forgotten.'

Tom closed the cell door and, leaning against it, faced the Frenchman.

'At about nine o'clock you will be taken from this cell, through an underground passage that takes you directly into the dock of the Old Bailey. As you walk along that passage, you might like to reflect on the fact that, beneath your feet, lie the bodies of men who travelled that same route before you.'

Tom sauntered over to the window and looked up at the overcast sky. When he turned back, he said, 'It's called Dead Man's Walk.'

'You are wasting your time, *monsieur*.' Dubois laced his fingers behind his head and closed his eyes. 'I will tell you nothing.'

'What a pity.' Tom stifled a yawn and resumed his place by the door. 'If you had decided to help me, I might have been able to help you. I might even have been able to save your life. Did you know it can take up to twenty minutes to die at the end of a rope? It's the reason they call it the Newgate Dance – the death throes of a man being choked to his mortal end. Very unpleasant.'

'Why are you telling me this, Pascoe?' Dubois looked up at the man in whose death he would have delighted.

'Let me be clear about this, Dubois,' said Tom. 'Few things would give me greater pleasure than to see you hang, but I want something from you, and for that I will try to save your life.'

Dubois felt his heart jump. A glimmer of hope fanned into life. He hid it, determined to show nothing that might convey the impression of weakness.

'You want to know about the woman,' he said. 'I will take all I know to my grave, *monsieur*, and may the devil himself take you for the scoundrel you are. I will tell you nothing.'

'Very well, I'll see you in court.' Tom turned on his heel. At the door, he looked back. 'Let me know if you change your mind. Hanging is such an unpleasant way to die.'

CHAPTER 42

Tom could just hear the distant clang of the bell of St Catherine's tolling eight o'clock as he mounted the steps to the police office. He was disappointed, but hardly surprised that he'd been unable to get anything from his interview with Dubois. He'd recognised the thin veneer of bravado that so often cloaked a man in the face of imminent death. He'd seen it time out of number in the speech and counterfeit laughter of men in the hour before battle, when, robbed of activity, they had been forced to wait for the terror that was war. Dubois was no different in that respect.

Tom knew the Frenchman would receive no sight of the evidence against him. Nor, unless the judge were to so direct, would he have any expectation of a counsel to advise him, examine the witnesses, or speak in his defence. Even the judge, ignorant of Dubois's circumstances, would be powerless to help him. Dubois would know he was a man facing almost certain death.

Tom moved down the passageway and had almost reached the main entrance of the police office when he heard John Kemp's voice behind him.

'Why, Kemp, good morning . . .' Tom stopped a look of sudden concern in his face. 'Where's Ebenezer? Were you not to bring him here? We've to leave for the Old Bailey in an hour.'

'I regret it extremely, sir, but he can't be found.'

'What!' Tom stared in disbelief.

'I went round to Ebenezer's room at the Devil's Tavern, like what you said, your honour, and he were gone. Landlord said he saw him leave the house on his own, at about seven this morning, and he ain't been back since.'

'Doesn't give us much time to find him,' said Tom, removing a watch from his waistcoat pocket and checking the hour.

'Just one thing, sir,' said Kemp.

'What's that?'

'Might be nothing, but the landlord told me he saw three men standing on the other side of Wapping Wall, about the time Ebenezer left. He'd seen them before. Reckons they drink at the Queen's Head . . .'

'Boylin's old place? In Griffin Street?'

'Aye, that's the one. Anygate, when he next looked, they'd gone.'

'Come with me,' said Tom, running back down the passage and into Wapping Street. 'If it's what I think it is, we've not a moment to lose.'

'It were like I told Master Kemp, here,' said Thomas Gillings, the portly landlord of the Devil's Tavern, wiping his hands on an old blue apron he was wearing. 'First thing this morning, I were standing by the window, over there, looking out on the street. That were when I saw them three cullies I told Master Kemp about.'

'What were they doing?' asked Tom.

'Nothing as I could see, your honour,' said Gillings. 'Except they kept looking over this way. It were as if they were expecting someone.'

'I believe you told Master Kemp that you saw the black man, Ebenezer Samson, walk out through the front door. Is that right?'

'Aye.'

'Was this before or after you saw the three men in the street?'

'It were after,' said Gillings. 'I remember it, clear as day on account you said to me he should stay put. I did ask him where he were going but I don't think he could've heard me. He were staring at them cullies. Seemed to me like he were afeared of them and were trying to get away from them. Anygate, I didn't think no more about it. When I next looked out the window, I sees the three cullies is gone, and so had the nigger.'

'But I think you said you've seen them before?'

'Aye. Irish lumpers, they are. Drink in the Queen's Head.'

'Can you tell me what they looked like?'

'Tall one looked to be a bruiser. Big lad, he were. Wearing red and white striped slops. Other two were shorter, maybe five foot six, but looked like they might like a fight come Saturday night if you know what I mean?'

'Thank you, Master Landlord. If Ebenezer returns, please tell him to come to the Wapping police office immediately.'

'Where to now, sir?' asked Kemp as the two of them emerged from the tavern, onto Wapping Wall.

'The Queen's Head. With any luck the landlord there will be able to tell us who those three cullies were.'

'You think they took Ebenezer, sir?'

'Wouldn't surprise me none,' said Tom. 'If Camperdown had anything to do with bringing Dubois to this country, he'll want to make sure he don't go down for anything at court for fear he'll talk. And if there's one sure way of making sure he's found not guilty, it's getting rid of the only witness.'

The Queen's Head hadn't changed much since Tom had last seen it, back in the days when Joseph Boylin had been the land-lord, ruling the criminal gangs in the port with an iron fist. The green paint on the woodwork was a little more faded than Tom remembered; the grimy mark that ran at shoulder height along the length of the buildings was more pronounced. But that was all. He pushed open the door and walked in, the conversation amongst the dozen or so customers faltering as he made his appearance. Soon it picked up again.

'Top of the mornin' to you, Mr Pascoe.'

'Is it a drink you'll be wanting, your honour?'

One way or another, they all knew Tom, had felt the lash of his tongue or the thick end of his stick. Some had paid a higher price. But none had ever doubted his honesty and tough brand of fairness.

'Why, it's Captain Pascoe, ain't it?' The speaker was a bull-necked man of medium height, his sloping shoulders bulging beneath a thin cotton shirt.

'Hello, Davies,' said Tom, recognising a former shipmate from his days in the Navy. 'Haven't seen you since ninety-four. The *Amphion*, wasn't it? What brings you here?'

'Discharged, sir. Crushed foot, sir. Ain't no good to man or beast.'

'Kemp,' said Tom, turning to his crewman, 'speak to the land-lord. Ask him if he knows those three cullies we're interested in.

I want to know who's been talking to them and where they are now.'

'Very good, sir.' Kemp knuckled his forehead and moved over to the bar.

'Trouble, Captain?' Davies raised an eyebrow.

'Could be. We think a friend of ours was caught by some bully boys from here. We need him back, pretty damn quick.'

'You say they came from here, Captain?' said Davies. 'What do they look like?'

Tom gave him a description of the three.

'Aye, I knows them,' said Davies. 'Not to talk to, like, but I sees them most days in here. They was in here last night, talking to a big cully what looked like he were a gentleman. He were asking questions about a nigger what he knew. Seemed mighty anxious to find him. Reckoned he were a slave what had run.'

'Where would I find the men he was talking to?'

'On the *Sally Anne*, as like as not,' said Davies. 'They's been unlading her close on a week now. She lies off the south bank, opposite Cole Stairs.'

'Thankee most kindly, Davies,' said Tom, taking his leave. He called Kemp and the two of them left.

'Anything from the landlord?' Tom asked as soon as they had reached the street.

'Aye, he knows the men. Bully boys, he reckons. Do anything for the price of a drink. Said he didn't know where they were, though I think he were lying.'

'It doesn't matter. I just found out they're likely to be on the *Sally Anne*, off the Rotherhithe shore. Did you get their names?'

'No, he never knew what they were called.'

'Pity.' Tom took out his watch and snapping open the lid, looked at the time. 'Cut along to the police office and tell Mr Harriot what's happened. We need someone to ask the court for a short adjournment; give us time to find Ebenezer and get him into the witness box. When you've done that, meet me at the *Sally Anne* with the rest of the crew.'

The *Sally Anne* lay at her moorings, close to Roger's Timber Yard, a few yards downstream of Randall's Causeway on the Rotherhithe shore. Tom hailed a passing wherry and had himself rowed over. His initial impression of the barquentine as a tired and untidy vessel was confirmed as he drew closer. With her scuffed paintwork, her yards askew and her patched and dirty sails loosely brailed, her appearance did nothing to endear him to those who had charge of her. Several lighters were fetched alongside into which a constant queue of men shuffled, their shoulders bent under the weight of the heavy sacks they carried. Coming alongside, Tom paid off the wherryman and made his way to the barquentine's upper deck.

'And who might you be, boy?' drawled a truculent American accent.

Tom swung round and found himself facing a man of about his own age. He was carrying a spliced length of rope, about eighteen inches in length.

'Tom Pascoe, Thames Marine Police.' Tom gave the man a glacial stare as he flashed his tipstaff. 'And you are?'

'Mr Boscombe, mate of this here vessel.' The tone was still belligerent. 'What's your business, Pascoe?'

'I'm looking for three men I believe to be unlading the *Sally Anne*,' said Tom, his eyes scanning the line of lumpers streaming past. 'They may be able to help me trace someone I need to find quickly.'

'Aye, well you'll not do it on my ship, mister. These men have work to do and my captain ain't going to wait around just for you.'

'Mr Boscombe,' roared a voice from the quarter deck. 'I'll thank you, sir, were you to come here.'

Boscombe scowled and trotted over to a tall, dishevelled-looking man, his long, black hair hanging down below the rim of an exceptionally dirty tricorn hat. In a moment Boscombe was back.

'Captain says you can look for your men, but you's to be quick about it.'

'Where might I find the master lumper?' Tom was growing impatient.

'Over there,' said Boscombe, nodding at a skeletal figure standing close to the larboard main chains.

It was the work of a minute to describe the men he was looking for and have their names given to him. The master lumper was not one for a confrontation, and the sight of Tom had been enough to convince him of the need for co-operation.

'All three of them is in the hold,' said the man. 'Ain't seen them this past half-hour. Don't want to, neither. Nothing but trouble, they are. Watch out for Will Haynes. The other two take their line from him.'

Tom thanked him and crossed the deck to the main hatch where he joined the line of men descending to the hold. Reaching the orlop, he stepped away from the ladder and looked round.

The gloomy half-light of the hold made it difficult to see clearly, the shifting outlines of men coming and going amidst drifting clouds of dust. It was, therefore, some seconds before he saw the three men sitting together on an upturned barrel, drinking what appeared to be beer.

'Which one of you is Will Haynes?' said Tom.

'What's it to you, cock?' said a tall, well-built man, sporting a broken nose and the look of a pugilist.

'It's a simple question,' said Tom. 'I'd be obliged should you answer it.'

'Fuck off, cully,' said the same man, turning to look at his two companions. 'Can't you see we're busy?'

'On your feet when you speak to me, mister,' said Tom.

The man sprang to his feet, his balled fist travelling fast. Tom swayed out of the way, pulled the man towards him and brought a knee up into his groin. The man doubled up and sank to his knees, a long, low groan of pain escaping his lips as his forehead hit the deck.

'I'll ask you once more, cully. Which of you idle, good-for-nothing villains is Will Haynes?'

The man's two companions stared, open-mouthed, and said nothing. Another groan came from the man on the deck.

'I can't hear you,' said Tom, bending down. 'You'll have to speak up.'

'It's me, damn your eyes. I'm Will Haynes.'

'You, and your friends here, were seen outside the Devil's Tavern at first light this morning. What were you doing there?'

'Where?'

'You heard me, mister. What were the three of you doing outside the Devil's Tavern this morning?'

'We been 'ere since first light,' mumbled Haynes, levering

himself off the deck and attempting to stand.

'Stay where you are, Haynes,' said Tom. 'Where did you take the negro?'

Silence. Haynes glanced helplessly at his companions. They turned away, and stared into the gloom.

'I asked you a question, mister.' Tom prodded Haynes with the toe of his boot.

'We was told to do it.' Haynes was having difficulty breathing.

'Who told you?'

'We ain't seen him before. We'll not be after knowing his name. We was in the Queen's Head. He came and talked to us. Told us he'd pay handsomely if we got this nigger from the Devil's Tavern and took him to Cole Stairs at first light.'

'What happened after you delivered him?'

'Don't know, your honour. We was given a shilling apiece and told to keep our mouths shut. The nigger got put onto a skiff and taken afloat.'

'What ship was he taken to?'

'Didn't see where they went. Sure, it was none of me business.'

'Sir?' Tom turned to see Sam Hart clattering down the companion ladder, shortly followed by John Kemp and Jim Higgins. 'Everything all right . . .? Well, I'll be buggered if it ain't Will Haynes.'

'You know this scrub, Sam?' said Tom.

'Aye. Old Will and me go back a while. We was both in the fighting game, once.' Sam paused and looked at Haynes. 'Still doing Camperdown's dirty work, are you, Will?'

'He works for Camperdown?' said Tom, surprised.

'In a manner of speaking, sir,' said Sam. 'His lordship enjoys a bit of scrapping now and then. As often as not he can be found in the company of men like Will Haynes here. Why, I've heard he sometimes entertains a few of them at his home. Of course, it comes at a price and he'll sometimes ask for the favour to be returned. There's plenty what'll do his bidding for a shilling or two.'

'Still reckon you don't know the gentleman you were talking to in the Queen's Head last night?' said Tom, turning to look at Haynes. There was no answer. He looked at the other two. They, too, remained silent.

'Take these men to the galley, will you, Sam? They're having a little difficulty remembering anything. A bit of thinking time in the cells should do them the world of good.'

'We ain't got time to wait for them to change their minds, sir,' said Sam. 'Tide turned two hours since. I reckon half the bleedin' ships in the port has weighed their anchors and gone. Won't be long before the rest of them follow. If your Ebenezer is on one of them, I reckon you'll have lost him for good.'

'What d'you suggests we do?' barked Tom. 'You think I don't know time's running out?'

Tom bit his lip, instantly regretting his outburst. Sam and the others were just as tired as he was, just as worried about the disappearance of their witness. They deserved better from him. It hadn't helped that Sam was right. If a ship was ready to sail, she'd choose the first hint of an ebb tide, and have a full five or six hours of a following stream to help her on her way. If Ebenezer was on board, as now seemed almost certain, he would shortly be beyond reach. Even if Tom did find him, he didn't have the legal authority to compel his return to give evidence.

'Take them up, Sam,' he said, wearily.

'It were the *Jamaica Belle*, your honour.'

Tom and the others looked in the direction from which the voice had come. It belonged to one of the two men who had, until then, remained silent.

'What did you say?' said Tom, releasing his hold on Haynes and stepping closer to the man who'd spoken.

'The nigger, your honour. He were taken to the *Jamaica Belle*. Leastways, that's what one of the men in the skiff told the waterman. But she's gone, sir. Sailed as soon as the tide turned. I saw her go.'

CHAPTER 43

'The judge has agreed to a short adjournment,' said Harriot. 'He was not best pleased, but he's agreed. We are due back in court at two o'clock this afternoon. Now, Mr Pascoe, perhaps you'd be good enough to tell me exactly what's going on.'

'We believe Ebenezer was captured on the orders of his master, Lord Camperdown, and placed on board a West India brig, the *Jamaica Belle*, for transportation back to the West Indies . . .'

'As he is perfectly entitled to do,' said Harriot.

'Yes, sir, he is, but Ebenezer is a crucial witness in a murder trial. Without his testimony, Dubois will go free.'

'I'm well aware of that, Mr Pascoe, but there appears to be little we can do to remedy the situation. If I understand you correctly, the *Jamaica Belle* sailed several hours ago.'

'We could still overtake her, in a fast ketch.'

'Yes, you could.' Harriot fell silent, his fingertips rubbing his forehead. 'We could try and persuade the judge to issue . . . No, he'd never do it.'

'What wouldn't he do, sir?' said Tom.

'There's something called *habeas corpus ad testificandum*. It's a writ which requires the production of a prisoner at court in order that he might give evidence.'

'Then why don't we apply for it?'

'The problem is that Ebenezer is not, strictly, a prisoner at all. In the eyes of the law he is an indentured servant bound to his master, which means the judge would be most unlikely to issue the writ.'

'What happens if he does?'

'We serve the writ and take possession of your witness until he can be produced before the court.'

'And if we don't get the writ?'

'Then I'm afraid that would be the end of the matter. We certainly would not be permitted to remove Ebenezer by force.'

'We have to apply. We can't just give up,' said Tom.

At shortly after eleven o'clock that morning, Lord Camperdown knocked on the door of an address in Baker Street and handed his visiting card to the maid. Several minutes later, he was shown into the light-filled, airy, first-floor drawing room.

'Good morning to you, my lord,' said Lady Annabel, casting a surprised glance at Lord Camperdown's tired and crumpled appearance. Suddenly her hand flew to her mouth. 'Is it done? Are you hurt?'

'My dear Annabel, I regret this intrusion. No, I am not hurt but alas Sir William is dead. As you know, I called him to the field of honour. I could do no other. You know the reason. I told you all when I came to see you. We fought and he was mortally wounded. I've not slept nor rested since. The constables watch my house in London and the estate in Surrey, impatient to lay their hands on me.'

'What is it you want of me?' said Lady Annabel, her hand still at her mouth, her face drained of colour. 'You must know you cannot stay here. I am alone. It would not be right.'

'For the sake of what we once were, the friendship that was ours. The servants' quarters. Anywhere. I beg you, Annabel. Two, perhaps three, days and then I shall take my leave of you. You shall not see me again in this life.'

Lady Annabel hesitated. They had once been intimate, in the years before her marriage. But that had ended in acrimony a long time ago, the events still fresh in her memory. She had been eighteen, he barely two years older and a lieutenant in the Navy. She had thought they would one day be married. And they would have done so but for a single night of unbridled gambling which had cost her brother, Henry, the promise of a commission in the 1st King's Dragoon Guards.

While the details of what exactly had gone on that night were shrouded in mystery, the outcome was not. Camperdown – then plain Alexander Thorngood – had persuaded Henry to guarantee the stake, and any losses, in an all-night game of Hazard. By morning Camperdown had lost the twenty thousand pounds and, with it, Henry's commission. The family had tried to get the money back. But to no avail. Within days, Camperdown had rejoined his ship and left on a cruise that was to last for the following eighteen months. He and Annabel had not exchanged a word since, although, in spite of it all, he had retained Henry's friendship.

Annabel glanced at her visitor. He was watching her, waiting for a reply. In spite of what had happened all those years ago, there was a part of her that wished that events between them had happened otherwise. She looked away, banishing the thought.

'Very well,' she said, quickly. 'You may stay in the servants' quarters. I will tell the coachman to expect you. There is a spare bed in his room.'

At two o'clock that afternoon, the Session House at the Old Bailey rose to greet the common serjeant of London attired in a red robe, black sash and powdered, full-bottomed wig. Tom watched as the judge bowed to the row of barristers, and received their bows in return. Then he sat down, the stone Sword of Justice seeming to hover over his head.

'We have, I believe, an adjourned case before the court, have we not, Mr Clerk?'

'Yes, my lord.' The clerk twisted round in his chair and looked up at the robed figure sitting several feet above him. 'There is an application for you to hear in relation to the case, before the prisoner is brought up.'

'Very well, please proceed.' The judge's eyes searched the well of the court as he waited to hear the application. From amongst the black-clad figures below the bench, a man stood up.

'Yes, Mr Hornby. You wish to make an application?'

'I'm grateful, my lord. You will, of course, recall that a case due to be heard by your lordship this morning was adjourned in order for the necessary inquiries to be made as to the present whereabouts of the principal witness.'

'Yes, Mr Hornby,' said the common serjeant. 'I am well aware of the circumstances. Do you now wish to address me further on the matter?'

'I do, my lord,' said the barrister, glancing behind him to where Tom was sitting. 'It is our belief that the witness, Mr Ebenezer

Samson, has been taken, against his will, onto a ship within the Port of London. We believe this vessel is, at this moment, on her way down the Thames to the open sea. Clearly, my lord, there is no intention on the part of Mr Samson's captors to permit him to attend this court to give evidence.'

'And you are suggesting . . . what?' said the judge.

'My lord, we seek a writ of *habeas corpus ad testificandum* to be served on the captain of the relevant ship. Your lordship is, of course, already aware of the circumstances relating to Mr Samson's captivity and his status as an indentured servant. We suggest, however, that the actions of Mr Samson's master, in removing him from the jurisdiction of this court, are merely a device to prevent the witness from giving evidence. There is, furthermore, some suggestion that Mr Samson's master may, himself, be involved in the case before this court, and has, therefore, a singular motive for removing the witness from these shores.'

'I sympathise with your difficulty, Mr Hornby,' said the common serjeant, peering over the rim of his spectacles. 'But I regret the application must fail. A writ of *habeas corpus ad testificandum* has, as you are doubtless aware, a narrow and well-defined application and can only be issued in cases where the person sought is in prison. Clearly, this is not the case here. Mr Samson is in the lawful care of his master who has chosen, for whatever reason, to require the witness to leave these shores.'

'I am grateful for your clarification of the law, my lord. But perhaps I might be permitted to suggest that the case in which the missing witness was due to give evidence involves not one, but two indictments for murder. Indeed, one of the two victims was a Member of Parliament. The defendant himself is a French national who, we allege, came to this country on the orders of his government for the express purpose of killing a leading member of the Administration. In the circumstances, my lord, you may wish to reconsider the basis of your argument with a view to allowing the application.'

'I regret, Mr Hornby, I cannot agree with you. The law is not to be blown this way and that by the vagaries of circumstance. And though the consequences of my decision will doubtless be grave, I must have regard to the letter of the law rather than that of expediency. The application is therefore refused.'

'Thank you, my lord.' The barrister turned and bent down to where Tom was sitting. 'I regret, Mr Pascoe,' he whispered, 'that unless there is something you have not told me, there is no longer sufficient grounds on which to proceed with this case.'

'I agree,' said Tom, feeling suddenly exhausted. 'Ebenezer was the only witness whose evidence could have convicted Dubois.'

'My lord,' said the barrister, 'in the circumstances, the prosecution offers no evidence in this case.'

Minutes later, Tom glanced over his shoulder as a grinning Dubois climbed the stairs below the court and stood in the dock facing the judge. He didn't wait to hear the formal judgement. There was little point. Dubois was not to be prosecuted. Bowing to the judge, Tom turned and walked out.

The sun had barely cleared the rooftops of Limehouse when the driver eased his coach through the heavy press of lumpers, gangsmen, cart drivers and the rest who'd been at work on the

Custom House quays since before dawn. Unusually, the window blinds of the coach were drawn and nothing could be seen of its interior. The driver got down from his seat and made his way to a door in the Custom House. He walked in and climbed the stairs to the first-floor landing where he made his way along a corridor. He stopped outside the second of a row of doors and knocked.

'Come in,' said a voice from inside.

The driver was greeted by a slim, smartly dressed man seated behind a desk. Standing next to him was another man, his nut-brown face suggestive of a life spent at sea.

'Do you have the passenger?' enquired the seated man.

'I do. He's in the coach, presently at the quayside.'

'Any difficulties?'

'None.'

'Very well. Go with Captain Smythe here. All the necessary arrangements have been completed and the passage to Barbados paid for, in the name of Jones.' The man paused and looked at the captain. 'You are, I think, ready to depart?'

'Aye, sir. High water in just over an hour. We'll be on our way shortly after that.'

Five minutes later, a heavily muffled man alighted from the coach and, accompanied by Captain Smythe, got into a waterman's skiff, to be rowed out to the West India brig *Argos*, presently at anchor in the Battle Bridge tier of the Upper Pool.

An hour and a half later, the ebb tide flowing, the *Argos* weighed her anchor and began her journey to the sea. Alexander Thorngood, the Second Baron Camperdown, did not look back.

CHAPTER 44

Tom let the police galley drift down through one of the central arches of London Bridge, past the legal quays and the fish market at Billingsgate, and on towards the sombre outline of the Tower.

Dubois had been released, the court having accepted the submission of King's Counsel to offer no evidence on the two counts of murder for which the Frenchman had been arraigned. And since no one from the office of the secretary of state for the Home Department was in court with an application for the prisoner's further detention, he was released with immediate effect. Tom shook his head in disbelief. Common sense had no place in a court of law, let alone justice.

He was suddenly aware of a commotion on the Middlesex side of the river, angry shouts from the deck of a ship. He glanced over his shoulder and prepared to investigate. A brig was clubbing down on the tide, its fore topsail filling in the light breeze. He waited for her to pass, raising his hand in salute to the captain on his quarterdeck. He felt the familiar catch in his throat, a sense of longing for the open sea and the feel of a heaving deck below his feet. He pulled down on the larboard guy and took the galley below the brig's stern, reading her name, painted in gold letters below the stern lights: *Argos*. The commotion he'd heard had died down by the time the police galley got there. A trivial argument over the remnants of a pot of beer. He left the warring factions and continued on his way. It was time to hand over to the next crew. He was looking forward to a rest after a long and uneventful night.

He promised himself he'd not think about Dubois. What had happened, had happened. There was no sense in dwelling on what might have been. The villain was probably back across the Channel by now. A surge of anger rose up inside him. He checked it with difficulty.

Nothing seemed to have gone right in the last few months. Only now was he beginning to escape the constant yearning for a drink, the downward spiral that had plagued his life since Peggy's death. But there had been little else, save perhaps his meeting with Lady Annabel, for him to cheer about. He'd never really got to the bottom of Sir Henry's shooting, and perhaps might never do so. For a while he'd suspected Camperdown, a man with a reputation for duelling, who was known to have argued with Sir Henry. But the point of the bullet's entry had seemed to rule him out and pointed instead to Bolt's involvement. Tom shook his head. His only hope of finding the truth lay with Camperdown. No one else had come forward. It was the same with Sir William Bolt. Tom knew Bolt's opponent on the field of honour had been Camperdown. He suspected there were any number of people who could testify to that fact, but none had chosen to come forward.

'Stand by to come about,' he called. A moment later, the galley had begun her turn up into the tide and was crabbing across to the police pontoon. 'Rest on your oars.' A pause, then, 'Toss oars, make fast fore and aft.'

Tom climbed onto the floating stage, stretched the stiffness from his limbs and waited while the crew removed the arms' box and cleaned the boat.

'Feel like some breakfast after we've finished here, Sam?' said Tom, as the two of them walked up the stairs to the police office. 'If so, I'll meet you at the usual place in St Catherine's Street.'

He should have taken the first ship back to France. God knows there were enough of them making the crossing, even in time of war. He should have accepted the fact that he'd failed. His acquittal at the Old Bailey had offered him a second chance of life. Dubois ran his tongue round the inside of his mouth. Going home would certainly have been the sensible thing to do.

Yet returning to France empty-handed was not an option he cared to think about. He'd failed in the primary task for which he'd been sent and, perhaps even harder to bear he'd failed to even the score with Pascoe. He leaned against the wall of the alley and looked at the Wapping Police office on the other side of the street.

It was Pascoe's head that he saw first, mounting the stairs from the river. Beside him was Sam Hart. They were deep in conversation and for a moment stood talking at the front door of the police office. Then they parted, Pascoe turning in, while his friend continued into Wapping Street.

Dubois settled down to wait. It would have been difficult killing both of them, particularly given the number of people moving up and down the main street. He retreated further back into the alley.

He did not have long to wait. Ten minutes after he had entered the building, Pascoe again stepped out onto the passageway and walked down the two steps into Wapping Street. Dubois waited a moment and then fell in behind him, as his enemy walked west towards Hermitage Bridge.

A cart pulled out from the brew house, forcing Dubois to stop. By the time it had cleared, there was no sign of Pascoe. He'd been swallowed up by the crowd. The Frenchman pushed his way through, his eyes flicking from person to person. He got as far as the bridge over Hermitage Dock and stopped on the brow. Still no sign of Pascoe. He looked behind him, convinced he must have overtaken him. About to give up, Dubois saw him, fifty yards ahead, coming out of a shop of some kind. Dubois ran towards him, dodging in and out of people's way, his knife now tucked into the sleeve of his jacket.

He was close now. No more than ten yards behind Pascoe and on the opposite side of the street. He saw him turn off to the right and begin to walk up Burr Street. It was the chance Dubois had been waiting for. He ran across St Catherine's Street, knocking over an elderly woman. She screamed abuse at him as he regained his balance and started to move away.

A man grabbed his arm and spun him round.

'Where d'you think you's going, cock?'

Dubois let his knife slip down his sleeve and into the palm of his hand. But he wasn't quick enough. Rough hands knocked him to the ground and a boot was placed on his throat.

'I asked you a question, cully. It ain't polite to go barging into folk and not apologise.'

Dubois dropped his knife and held up his hands. He knew when he was beaten.

'I'm sorry, *monsieur*. I was trying to catch my friend. I did not mean to cause you offence.'

'Is that so? With a blade, were you?' said the man, removing his foot from the Frenchman's neck. 'But that ain't no business of mine. Best you be on your way, lad, before I change me mind and call the watch.'

Dubois sprang to his feet, picked up his knife and, without a word, sprinted to the corner of Burr Street. There was no sign of Pascoe and the street was all but deserted. He ran to the corner of Nightingale Lane. It was equally deserted. He'd lost him. Yet he had to be somewhere. He remembered overhearing the brief conversation between Pascoe and Sam Hart as they talked outside the door of the police office. He'd not heard what Pascoe had said; only the reply.

. . . *the usual place in St Catherine's Street.*

He thought for a moment. St Catherine's Street was where he'd just come from. Why would Pascoe have come into Burr Street? It made no sense, unless it was to visit someone who lived here. He retraced his steps, searching the windows of each house as he passed before turning right at the bottom.

He smelt cooking and felt suddenly hungry. A few yards away he could see a stall, smoke rising from its chimney, a few people gathered round it, eating. He decided to stop for a minute or two. Get some food inside him. He ordered bread, a slice of beef, and a mug of strong black coffee.

'Mr Pascoe, sir . . .'

Dubois swung round at the sound of the name, his eyes searching the small crowd. There was no one he recognised.

'There you are, sir,' said the same voice. It had come from the river side of the street, perhaps fifteen or twenty yards away.

It was Sam he saw first, standing by the narrow passage that led down to St Catherine's Stairs, a mug of tea or coffee in his hand. Then he saw Pascoe, walking towards his friend from the direction of Burr Street and wondered how he'd managed to miss him. For a minute or so he watched the two men talking to one another. They'd not seen him. Then he slipped across the street and inched his way towards them. He'd made his mind up. He would shoot Pascoe and, in the chaos that followed, drive the blade of his knife into Sam. He'd be away before anyone knew what had happened.

He was less than five yards from them when Sam spotted him.

'Behind you, sir,' shouted Sam, leaping towards Dubois.

The crack of the pistol was followed by a plume of white smoke rising into the air. Tom ducked, his pistol already in his hand, its hammer cocked. On the other side of the street, people were running for cover. Soon the three of them were alone. He could see Sam, hand clutching his chest, a shocked expression on his face. Beyond him, through the drifting curtain of smoke, was Dubois, the Frenchman's eye seemingly focused on the barrel of Tom's gun.

'You all right, Sam?' Tom's eyes never left Dubois. The Frenchman dropped to a crouch, the blade of a knife visible in his hand.

'It's nothing, your honour,' said Sam, forcing a smile. 'Only a flesh wound.'

Tom felt a cold hand clutch at his heart. He didn't like the sound of his friend's voice. He risked a glance at the expanding red patch on Sam's chest. It didn't look good.

He swung back. Dubois had sprung to his feet and was moving towards him, his knife pointing at Tom's stomach. In an instant Tom had levelled his pistol and was pointing it at the Frenchman.

'Stay where you are, mister.'

Dubois stopped, a mocking smile playing about his lips. He let his hand fall to his side and release the knife.

'What now, *monsieur*? You cannot have forgotten that I am a free man. Your own judges have said so.'

For the second time that afternoon, the air around the early breakfast stall in St Catherine's Street reverberated to the sound of an explosion.

Tom didn't see the Frenchman's lifeless body pitch forward onto his face, his view obstructed by the billowing cloud of gunpowder rising from the muzzle of his gun.

POSTSCRIPT

Four weeks later.

At sea.

Rain had fallen during the night and the upper deck of the *Jamaica Belle* was still slippery underfoot as she made her way through the Atlantic swell, the sun already hot in a cloudless sky.

In the cable tier, below the upper deck, Ebenezer Samson lay in his own filth, the air foul with the stench of vomit and excrement. He could barely breathe in the heat of the confined space, his lips cracked from lack of water. What light there was filtered down from the upper deck, and was scarce enough for him to see more than a few feet.

He'd hardly eaten in the weeks since they'd rounded the North Foreland, his once muscular frame shrunk to the point where his skin hung on his bones. Such food as he'd been offered he'd refused, his appetite gone.

Not once since he had been brought to this place had he been permitted to see the light of day, or breathe the fresh sea air. His previous escapes had seen to that. Now he was confined with a chain passing through the iron hoops locked about his ankles, the rough edges of the metal cutting into his skin, turning it into a pulp of bluish black. In the delirium of his mind he neither knew nor cared for the passing of the days, nor even of life itself.

A voice drifted down from the upper deck. 'Reckon we should be in Bridgetown in seven days if we keep this wind, Mr Northey.'

'Aye, it's about what I thought, Captain.'

Ebenezer closed his eyes.

Through the fog of his fading consciousness, he knew what awaited him.

They came for him that night, summoned by the crewman who had brought him his evening food. Ebenezer had died as he had lived, unknown and unloved. His lifeless body was taken up on deck and thrown to the waves.

HISTORICAL NOTE

This has been the story of a nation of its time, faced by the threat of invasion from across the English Channel while continuing to expand its commercial interests, aided by the hugely profitable trade in African slaves. It is, of course, a work of fiction but I have tried, as far as my limited capabilities would allow, to set the fictional story against a background of historical detail. Ebenezer Samson did not exist, but his character did. Much of what happened to him really happened. In 1799, a man named John Hamlet, an illiterate negro slave, was brought to England. He ran from his master, was caught and bundled aboard a ship for return to the West Indies. His case was taken up by the abolitionists who brought a case against his master. The magistrate, Mr George Storey, sitting at Shadwell police office, confessed himself unable to deal with the case and suggested a writ of *Habeas Corpus* would enable the matter to be better examined before a higher court. The Court of King's Bench subsequently threw out the application for a writ in the full knowledge that Hamlet would be sold back into slavery. And he was.

A feature of the Hamlet case was an earlier ruling. In *R v Knowles, ex parte Somersett (1772)*, Lord Chief Justice Mansfield, sitting in the Court of King's Bench, ruled that it was unlawful forcibly to remove a citizen or resident of England from these shores – including those brought here as slaves. As a direct result, many plantation owners compelled their illiterate slaves to sign forms of indenture, effectively circumventing *Somersett* and allow -ing owners to send their 'servants' back to the West Indies.

The situation in Scotland was different – at least from 1778 – when the Court of Session in Edinburgh got the chance to rule on a similar case to *Somersett*. Unlike the English court decision, the Scots made it clear, in *Knight* v *Wedderburn (1778)*, that slavery had no part in Scots law.

The trade in slaves using British ships did not become illegal until March 1807. Slavery itself continued to be lawful in the British West Indies until 1834. Even then, former slaves were compelled to work for nothing for a further six years.

Ebenezer's memories of Barbados are accurate, although not necessarily in the time span of this story. The tale of the two slave women crushed to death by the rotating mill wheels is true, the incident occurring on Barbados in 1779. So, too, is the story concerning a benefit performance designed to compensate a slave owner for the loss of his slave. It involved a young black boy killed in July 1813, again on Barbados, while moving theatre props. The benefit performance was for the female theatre owner to compensate her for the loss of her slave.

References to the Impress Service (through whose actions men were forced to serve in the army and Royal Navy) are, I hope, reasonably accurate. Many of the men pressed into the Navy were already sailors and showed a remarkable reluctance to escape once they had been pressed. Their style of dress and mannerisms marked them out as sailors and there was, in that sense, nowhere for them to hide once they were ashore. This, and the need to be amongst their own, might explain the refusal of many to take the opportunity of escape when it was offered.

The story of Camperdown crossing to France is a little more tricky. The Second Baron Camelford – on whom Camperdown is loosely based – is certainly known to have made the crossing in October 1801. Travelling with a letter of introduction to the French revolutionary *Directoire*, he was later to claim his motives were to assassinate Napoleon. He was captured by the French, to whom he stated that he admired all things French. He was sent back to England where he was lucky to escape a capital charge of treason, probably because he was a first cousin to William Pitt and brother-in-law to Lord Grenville, the future prime minister. In the absence of a court hearing, we will never know what his real motives were in seeking a meeting with the enemy. He was certainly not on good terms with his cousin and was later to end his life in a duel with his closest friend, over a manufactured argument about a woman.

Joshua Van Oven (1766–1838) was a Jewish surgeon and communal worker who trained under Mr (later, Sir) William Blizard, principle surgeon at the London (now the Royal London) Hospital, in Whitechapel. A tireless advocate on behalf of the Jewish community, he had frequent meetings with Patrick Colquhoun, the co-founder (with John Harriot) of the Thames Marine Police. Later, Van Oven moved to Liverpool, where he remained until his death.

The prize fight between Jack Bartholomew, then the reigning champion, and Jem Belcher actually took place fourteen months later than in my story, on 5 May 1800. It ended Bartholomew's championship reign and was the beginning of Belcher's. A highly skilled boxer, Belcher died prematurely at the age of thirty, in July 1811.

Sir William Bolt's old regiment, the 17th Light Dragoons, were sent to the West Indies in 1789 to fight against the French in what became known as the Maroon Wars. In the course of this they deployed to a number of islands, including Jamaica, where it is more than likely Sir William was introduced to the profits of the slave trade. The regiment returned to England in 1797. The regiment later changed its name to the 17th Lancers and, fifty-seven years later, took part in what was to become known as the charge of the Light Brigade during the war in Crimea.

As regards the attempt on the life of Wilberforce, he is known to have been the subject of several threats and, while none of them can be said to have involved Napoleonic forces, there is nothing that definitely rules it out.

GLOSSARY

Bakra   a West African term *m'bakara* . . . he who governs. In later usage it tended to have pejorative connotations. e.g., in Barbados, poor whites are, even to this day, scornfully referred to as Bakra Johnnies.

Common Serjeant of London   the second most senior judge at the Old Bailey. His formal title is Serjeant-at-Law in the Common Hall, usually shortened to the Common Serjeant.

Court of King's Bench   now defunct, but for nearly five hundred years one of the two principal courts of Common Law in the English legal system, dealing mainly, but not exclusively, with criminal cases. It was chaired by the Lord Chief Justice of England.

Habeas Corpus   literally 'produce the body', an ancient device in law requiring a person holding a prisoner to present that person before the court, for the legality of his detention to be established. From it are derived several ancillary writs including *habeas corpus ad testificandum*.

Legal Quays/Custom House Quay   I have used these names interchangeably. The legal quays were, historically, the only place where goods could be brought ashore for the London

355

market. It was here that customs officers used the King's Beam to determine the duty payable. The Custom House occupied part of the length of the quay.

Nose   eighteenth-century cant for an informant.

Old Bailey   actually a street within the City of London but for several hundreds of years the name has been synonymous with the criminal court for the Middlesex area of London. The court is now known either as the Old Bailey or, more formally, the Central Criminal Court, Old Bailey.

Press, The   the means by which the armed services ensured a sufficiency of men to fight wars. Its formal title was the Impressment Service. Press gangs – usually around a dozen men in the charge of a lieutenant or midshipman – would round up men they thought suitable for service and 'press' them into the Navy (or army). It was always recognised as a deeply unpleasant but necessary aspect of national policy.

Protection   the letter of exemption issued (usually) by the Admiralty to persons in certain occupations, protecting them from the press gangs. In times of emergency, these protections were invalid. The order 'press from all protections' – known as the 'hot press' – meant that no person was exempt from impressment.

Roads   those areas on the Thames given over to barge moorings. See also Tiers.

Sand box   used before the days of blotting paper. Sand was used to absorb the excess ink on the page, and was normally kept in a tin, or other metallic container known as the sand box.

Sandbox Tree among the largest trees of tropical America. Can grow to over a hundred feet and was frequently used by slaves to find their way home from the fields.

Serjeant-at-Arms the serjeant-at-arms is responsible for security and good order within the Commons part of the parliamentary estate. His counterpart in the House of Lords is Black Rod.

Somersett the celebrated case of *R* v *Knowles, ex parte Somersett* (1772), in the Court of King's Bench, believed by many to have abolished slavery in England. See Historical Notes for details.

Thole pins vertical pegs between which an oar is passed and against which it pivots.

Tiers those areas on the Thames given over to ships' moorings. See also Roads.

Westminster Hall the home (in 1799) of the Court of King's Bench. The House of Commons sat in St Stephen's Chapel (part of the same estate) until it was destroyed by fire in 1834, to be replaced by the present building.

ACKNOWLEDGEMENTS

The Rising Tide is the result of the collaborative efforts of a large number of people, many of whom will, doubtless, have forgotten the moment they picked up the telephone to find themselves answering questions about London life at the end of the eighteenth century. Among those who are unlikely to have forgotten is Dr Ruth Paley, historian, author and currently Section Editor within the House of Lords, to whom I turned for help on questions on slavery and the law of England in relation to it. Others include Karl Watson of the Barbados Historical Society who dealt with matters Barbadian, and Adrian Brown, Head of Preservation & Access at the Parliamentary Archives, who answered questions on points of detail concerning Parliament. Also in this list is Brian Lewis, master tailor of Savile Row tailors Meyer & Mortimer, who spent time taking me through points of sartorial detail. Finally, there is my permanent support team without whom not much would get done. Chief amongst these is my editor, Jane Wood, my agent Oli Munson, and my copy editor, Liz Hatherell. Liz once attempted to strangle her unsuspecting husband in order to demonstrate that one of my villains could not have been killed in the manner I had indicated. *Such* attention to detail! Finally there is Sara, my long-suffering wife, who is obliged to listen to, and (tactfully) comment on, the various stages of the writing process. To her, a grateful and heartfelt thank you.